PEOPLE of the SEA

A Novel of The Promised Land

by

JACK DEMPSEY

for the family

Dr. Jack Dempsey
jpd37@hotmail.com   AncientLights.org

COVER: Philistine vase from Ekron (Tel Miqne)
in central Palestine, c.1100 BCE

another one thanks to
the intrepid Brian Shillue, of:
DIGITAL SCANNING, INC.
344 Gannett Road, Scituate MA 02066 USA
www.Digitalscanning.com

Tradepaper ISBN: 9781582188836

Author's Note

The Western heritage is older than books, and more telling. From about 3500 to the 1400s BCE, the families of Minoan Crete and their surround of Mediterranean peoples kept on developing their web of cultures. Neither primitive nor utopian, they were centered in cycles of nature, in their ancestors, kinship, festival and trade. Because of them, the first 2000 years of that heritage progressed without entrenched kings.

So began *Ariadne's Brother: A Novel on the Fall of Bronze Age Crete* (1996), and *People of the Sea* tries to speak further from the lives and adventures of these unheard ancestors, returning to the sun in new, precise and dramatic archaeology.

Natural disasters, invasions and political change drove many small kin-groups and banded individuals to migrate and mix with their neighbors---from Troy to Gaza, from Cyprus to Sicily, from Libya and Egypt to the Near East. Ten generations after the fall of Crete's Knossos Labyrinth, some of their Iron Age peers called them Sea Peoples.

Egypt and The Old Testament inscribed them as brutish invaders. What do the sciences say of their *Pulesati* or Philistines' creation of Palestine in Canaan? Did they "sorely oppress" the inland Hebrew tribes, as The Bible says, to keep the emergent *Yisryli* (Israelites) "in their power"? In *People of the Sea*, a man who was once a Minoan priest-chief lives to see those days. His tale explores fact with fiction, and fiction with fact.

Sustaining these 20 years was a journey to the spring near the cave of Crete's Mount Ida. There, my host cleansed the ancient stone basin with scouring-pebbles and her hands, and welcomed me to drink. I was obliged by that gift, and by other springs as old and refreshing.

4

***

The rationalists had their first setback when Sir Arthur Evans uncovered Knossos, with its labyrinthine complexity....The most fantastic part of the tale having thus been linked to fact, it becomes tempting to guess where else a fairy-tale gloss may have disguised human actualities.

Mary Renault,
note to *The King Must Die*

You have to see how everything turns out, for God gives a glimpse of happiness to many people, and then tears them up by the very roots.

Herodotus,
The Histories I.32

***

PEOPLE of the SEA

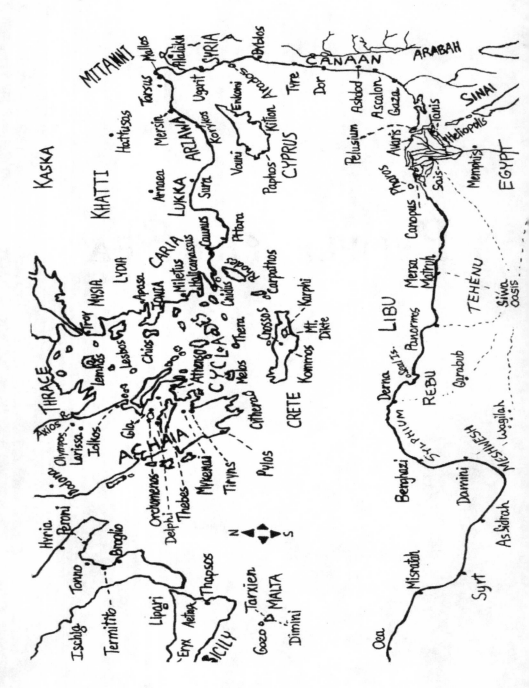

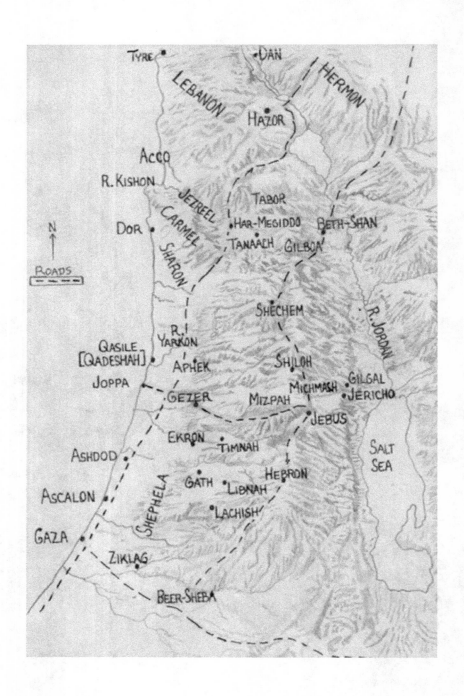

Prologue:
Out of Djahi

His skin was red-brown copper, the face sun-lined, civilized, old with a young smile. On his head, a crown of curls so raven-black it was almost alarming in a man of years, and dark eyes, island blood. Many harbors liked his boats. They took him for a trader, a planter of vine and olive. Or was that his father?

Each tribe of families, he fabled with a name: Deucalion Sweet Wine, Flood Rider, Otus, Iakos. Where a land met the waters, people welcomed his oil and wine and spirits. So they suffered no trouble to his ships, whose come and go they envied---like wild cranes, going their ways around the killing.

The mothers' eyes had long been closed who saw the island-mountain Thera fall in fire; and after that, Knossos Labyrinth. But this man lived for generations after them---a blessed curse, a cursed blessing---while the tribes of their children, confounded by their ancient dispossessions, wandered into war. Where waters met the land, they cut down every would-be king in sight of The Great Green.

Now, alone before them, stood The Nile's third Ramses. He had bled them once on the Djahi killing-grounds, but his armies were weaker than his father's. So the tribes still wanted that vast green country at his river's mouth, good for boats, fat with grain: *her seven arms wide,* they sang, *to wed new husbands from the sea.* Home-earth, bread, harbors: their tents had spoken, and voices keened from the shoreline's darkened dunes.

A fire burned in the midst of battle council: the speakers of their twelve tribes, disconsolate, and this man. Somebody, begin! Why not him, in that pilgrim's cloak of his, pouring? What news? The wine they smelled remembered homes where he had poured it out before, to turning tides. Or was that his father?

Ready now to betray them, and their enemies, he spoke with a cup in his outstretched palms.

--This be the center of the circles of the world.
From a hundred camps of exile, here
we dedicate ourselves beyond our names,
sisters, brothers,
untamed equals born of Gi, Ptgyh, Earth Mother.
Drink, and stand before the fire, woman, man,
once in truth before you die.
Look your family in the eyes, and say
why, in this fight before us,
your courage will endure your blood upon a blade---

why moon and sun shall see
an end of wandering, people of the sea.

***

As ever first to rise,
Pelasgoi, and a woman---a Turan, as we say Lady.
Pyx the name,
a daughter of Earth-Gaia's first human beings.
In every one of you, that blood
bears memory of your first mothers and fathers,
and sure as your feet know
the paths of your grandmothers' orchards
we know
Goddess
brought Herself forth
and gave Being
space and light
in parting waters from the sky.
Her senses
like a crane rising into the morning
rose to the goodness
and in joy She spoke
Her name of great dominion,
Eurynome.
The word
in its vast vibration of Her happiness
became a rhythm, and Her body
danced a gentle joy

that rose within Her senses
to the knowing of Her own infinitude.
Her spirit moved in love on the face of the waters
and Her dance raised up prodigious wind
behind Her, shimmering, quick-bright, silver,
a thing mysterious, beautiful, a monster
who came awake in love with what He saw.
Hai-ee! Snake, prodigious beast of being
following Her, became
Her Partner in this dancing of the world.
Hai-ee!
Beyond themselves, between the world's pillars, together
the dance love incarnate,
the horned new moon the cradle of infant suns,
the swaying of the sea beside the sky.
His wanting Her is the deep waters girdling the world,
the serpent in the swaying of my hips
and in our gardens, holy communions:
to Her he poured his coiled-up innards out,
and love brought forth The Egg that birthed the world.
Who remembers this world young,
full moon the mate of summer sun, the first dawn of Gi
when the green mountains sang in flowers,
rivers clapped hands
and every star of morning shouted joy?
Pelasgoi. And so with our first eyes
we see the ruin you blood-sick boys have wrought,
you kings, you walled-up thieves who made us peasants.
Six hundred spears of family come running to this fight,

black as this remembering blood between us.
Tell you why: never once surrendered, not a child of us
to that first fool of you, posted at your crotch:
Snake, prodigious Ophion, the father of your imbecilic lies.
Who saw the splendor of the world
and told His Mother and Her young, *I made you*:
She gave Him Her good heel across the head,
kicked His teeth out, too, to help him think again,
and from those teeth Pelasgians were born.
I give you this, it's why we make such troubles!
Younglings of the never-conquered sun,
we are The West, the flight from madness:
daemon of you all, ragged tribes, silent, sullen-proud,
first and thirteenth people of the world.
Flood-riders, children of the cranes, the salt in you,
raisers of gigantic stones that outlive memories of men.
Gozo, Nuraghi, seed of the Tyrrhenoi, from Thessaly
through the Cyclades and the twelve great isles of Asia,
we taught men's hands the ways of grain
and now we scrape for food in holes of mice.
Squanderers of seed! Great chiefs, dispossessed by wishes,
taste in smoke and fire what we bore first.
Do not say it, Achaians of the south and north,
Argivi, Ironheads, that your fathers did not take
our grandmothers' groves, their mysteries and children
from Argos plain to Mother Kriti's isles, Miletus, Troy.
Never speak again that we forget the great homes
roofed with rainbow tiles, shining by the sea at Lerna:
the first age of the world you turned to slavery and ash.

Your broke-tooth misery is Goddess law come down,
and we rejoice.
Hai-ee! Tomorrow, the last of our bloods marry after all.
On Ramses' jaw-hook blade? Or a spread of bottom-land?
See you at the altar.

***

O, Earthling woman, freedom to your tongue. But sharpen useful things on Ramses' doorstep. Another Djahi waits to drink our blood.

Fotya, my name, one chieftain of these ragtag Achaians. Argivi, if you please---Fotya, a son of Melas The Black, nine fathers gone. I make no apology for a sire like him, who took everything his life could reach. No man lets another set his limits. That is Achaian way, even in our southern precincts on the sea. We are all kings' sons, even our fathers who cut their first boats with Cretan axes.

The woman speaks ill of our fathers. It is Mother Ma-Ka we do not remember well, and from the first. In days before we Achaians had a word for The Great Green, the land that birthed us was far north. A land that was an ocean of green grass. She, was it Asia? Drove us from our perfect place, alone. Turned on us, in a mountain of Her fire and ash. Selah, her daughters' second place is balm for that, and just.

Woman, we brought good horse south to Pelasgoi country and the sun's little black-haired folk. But we were men, born to run the house. Your emmer wheat made Argos a place worth making ours. Your daughters we gave proud husbands, Godfather King-Horse and His sons; Poseidon Earthshaker, Enyalios of War, Paiawon The Maker. So, masters we became of another paradise; and then there was a world across the sea.

Cretans followed dolphins to their home: no better, sure, than stallions we to ours. Cretans---shaven men, and strutting like the world was bowing at their boots. *So what*, a thousand years before our country. There was more to envy and to fight in our blood-brothers' houses, and lions we became on the land's strong places. War, we said, shakes the best from men's days. So it was mother's milk, my grandsire's tale of taking Crete---a world of gold and women to be had, when the ash of Thera mountain brought her low. For that, look at me! Crackle with a laugh, like your daemon-brothers in our fire.

For that was our beginning, and where our end began. We plundered our teachers. Into The Great Green we pushed, and took where none could stop us. From your cities, islanders, and Cretans; from your people, Carians, and Shekelesh, and Trojans, home is waste. Laugh, at victory's wretched robe! My father's land was by the great house Pylos, till his wars came home to burn it. Make me a ploughman. Enough of our dead haunt the sunshine.

Earthlings, take us back into the fold. For the woolly beaten brothers here I say, our slashers and our spears are at your sides. There come times to turn with the wind. It is to be sick of ourselves, sick of blood and smoke. Tomorrow bring us one good sleep or another. I have not slept since war made me a man.

***

Unashamed I tell Tehenu's words. Some people say sister, brother, only when they are afraid. You, Pelasgians, Pulesati, masters of beasts you call ships, you said it to us from the first. You followed the winds of your birds and flocked south to us; and now we flock together, like your cranes. With Doku, this man, come a thousand Tehenu of Libya. Around us camp people of The Great Green northlands; and I, who saw Pharaoh's men kill six thousand in a day, never have I stood among so many. Wealth of trade you brought our Olive Land; wives to make us cousins, and ways to bring our men into the world. Look at you now, kin of Minos, Achaians, Alashiya's Cyprians, Danaans!

I am here that my little girl Atana will not starve. Your paths meet ours in the basket of Pharaoh's bread. You will see we fear nothing of the front line's knives: like birds we Libu fall and fill the sky again. No shields before our bodies, with sticking-spears and clubs we go in, naked. We are the hand-to-hand men, sons of The Nine Bows, who fight Kemeti people of The Nile to standstill. Pharaoh's men fight in gangs of four---each to keep the others from running away!---with heavy rods to break your arms and skulls. Last moon, they bled us many friends. Not this one.

Our Lady's name is Dripping Rain: Ngame, Neith, Athena, the mother of our cattle, Who taught us homes we love to build down in the Earth. She came forth from Herself and birthed all living: my girl wears the pointed goatskin cap of Her devotion. We remember our sons at oar and sail with Labrys at the prow. We belong to each other, cranes, whose wanderings and secrets no men see, but they allow it.

Waste your lands must be to bring you here. How, great sisters and brothers? You burned the ports and trade of Ugarit, and took from Hittite mouths the southern grain, and Hatti fell. Now Pharaoh trembles before you, who broke his great enemy. If we take his good Kemeti country for our farms, will you share the bread better?

What made our people bloodsport? Who took our young for slaves to move their stones? We push back, and Nile calls us animals. In Libu, the weak men steal. Who fetches home a wagonload of hands, and penises cut from battle dead? What gods desire these things, in halls of gold? Is it to comfort them, to tell them we are dead, although we live? Pharaohs. Men afraid to love the flesh and bride they so desire.

Our children starve, and smell Nile barley burned to spite us. Last time, by the blood of grandfather Merire, twelve thousand Libu broke at the edge of Memphis. In us at least, he fights fresh. Our Meshwesh cousins, here, made peace---putting spears to Pharaoh's service. Are you sick now, kinsmen, of the crusts his table throws?

Raids make wives and cousins. But we had no cause to war, till he made his. Neith gave birth to Ra the very sun, and still Libu fight to be men in his blind eye. Tomorrow, close and open it again! My girl lives hungry in an ox-cart.

***

Equals, the Qaraqisa say me Neos. Kari my kin, sons and daughters of Car, Who is the heart. Tomorrow, cousins, trust your flank to the horns on these helmets with moon and sun between. They come of days like Doku's, with Mother Kriti on the island seas. Those days our harpers sing; of Leleges, the Twelve Isles and the Cyclades' sailing-sons of law. Great Year in the sky. Still here. Before us, never more to win at once. For that, we sharpen axes.

The towns Car built along our waters bothered no one. Though Hatti, Pharaoh's enemy, was hard across our Asian backs for constant tribute. They reached to drag our sons to every war, in lands never theirs. We bought them off, and kept our heads down. And still here, like Po-ni-ki-ja, Phoenicians. Say of Kari, we lived through. When Strong One, Kriti fell, these Argivi and Ironheads got their free Achaian hand, to make us fear where they could not make war. Selah, each one of us tells the like.

The thought of fear that we accepted built us forts, and brought the rule of warriors isle by isle. We gave ourselves to war to keep them out, and we were theirs. Kin who hear me, what was right? Half our families sailed to save their young. In us, their sons, our old lands bleed; and generations-on, the pirate's reach not far enough behind. What is left, but turn and stand.

My mother Kari to the bone, my father's fathers--- By your leave, let me sing it, as our house does every year.

Whence Norax? Cretan crane, he sailed to Paphos,
and built with Car's Miletus wealth of trade.
His daughters wove anew the ancient secrets
before the bearded cutthroats came to raid

Cousin Trojans, how many Kari died to help you? Say it, Achaians, our fathers' axes taught you what your civil ones now confess. And then we were ready to help the thieves of Hatti into the dust. Good neighbors at our backs, they who swore to let us live for half our wealth. Such was the bond they chose to make with us. Them, Pharaohs worry no more.

So we come a thousand skirmishers. Orphans of the lands we broke and burned; of our own madness. It must be here! We bring good hands, that can fight and build, and solid seamen; daughters who can weave and plant and sing.

A man is more than a locust. Nothing more to say.

***

I kiss my mother Earth each dawn and dusk, that no lie pass my lips. I am Nush: eight hundred Meshwesh camped here call me mother. Let Doku say we live on Pharaoh's crusts: no longer. His work is his rule. Tomorrow, cousins, watch Meshwesh javelins and clubs along our line.

This Libu name is yours for the tribes of us, west of Nile to Atlas' shoulders. It was not we who changed, because we lived as the land taught us. Goddess made the world, pouring forth salt-blood. Three years, three moons Her nether-upsurge fountained from the deep; and every tiny thing She made, down to the mud, was Her. *Neter*, that even in the change of death makes life.

Kemeti folk of Egypt knew this. The sun fell and rose in Her arms, between the horns of their ancestors' mountains. Why, then, did priests of Ra turn up their noses? The lords who sat in Isis' lap climbed down, and turned their backs on us. Priests raised up stones that blessed their greed and royal right to plunder. Look what floods down-river now, gods Kemeti change with every king. They kiss the toes of statues till their grandsons knock them down, to put up new.

Their lords shot us like rabbits, yes, and robbed us of our days. The Nile's good common people who remembered, the priests drove out, and wiped their footprints from The Earth. But from them, our mothers learned; contrived to send big Meshwesh sons to man royal forts along the western Nile. It taught us what it is to plough wild ground. This Ramses now thinks the figs of our oases fall for him. Doku's Libu called us dung-beetles. So. Dung-beetles ride the flood.

No king made fools of Meshwesh. Generations our mothers pent up cattle, learned the olive tree. They fed Malkata palace tables good beef for Amenophis. Grandmothers round a fire sang us old Hatshepsut, mothering peace: her mother was our blood. Can you Tehenu here recall ten years before this Ramses we fight tomorrow, when Meshwesh put another kinsman on their throne? And here before your faces, we confess it: nothing changed. I have kissed The Earth. You prove right: we will always be dogs to them. Game.

Doku, your lands fail to feed your daughter. When your fathers crawled to the feet of Merneptah, he gave you grain. When it stopped, you gave him war. So we were faced with fighting you, our blood, to keep our homes.

The fathers of that war came home to make us wiser. Now we fight alike for Libu's girls. Let Meshwesh help; and all you build helps us. We are eight hundred clubs and javelins. No need to tell us who our friends are.

**

Good! Well-said, for a woman. I too have a kinsman here, if not a brother. And he, poor Fotya, told enough of gods. I speak of men before this fire. We northmen---Ironheads, you say---wear an equal's mock with pride! And we grieve, to hear him talk of sleep with his beard yet brown. We northerners are never so beaten as we look. Then, you see us no more. What a pyre I will make, that no low thief pick my bones, nor a Hag's crone-fingers! A man should fight, or serve the best; otherwise, work, or die.

I am Pagos; son of Bom the holy might of Enyalios, red star, lord of war. Bom the son of Axios River, terror of the Pindus Mountains; and I Bom's first-born, last of his eight sons, who all died hard. Our tribes are all kings' sons, peers of the north wind, eyes blue between our locks. I can row across the wind three days to pick a fight; find water by the smell, good horse and woman too. A legion of my bastards carry comforts of my tents. My sword, the best of secret forges in the west, you see twined round the hilt with gold. Try us. Or, if your wits can murder, insults: you might live to drink me dry this cup, my kylix. The golden rim gives wine savor of ambrosia. All won with these arms, town by island, my ten toes to death.

Gold in battle fetches men who strut their own: so, every fight, I die or strip a prince, and I never wash the gut-blood from my arms. The little brown slaves of Kemet will scare, before our hacking-swords and heavy spears. We bring no horse or chariot now, but this you need not worry. Our harpers said it every song of those to whom we sailed to conquer: *Their days are dust.*

Our sires burned the last ports of Minoa. Wanderers we came to the ocean, wandering we love. Our grandfathers bodyguards, no less, to a Pharaoh gone mad looking at the sun. And still no home we really want. What is home, a farm where you graze, staring at a grave? My father helped Mykenai's Agamemnon break the gate of Troy. Killed for pay in Libu's battle to the west. Understand? Merire fetched us in with forty ships. Not ten came out. So tested there, likewise we will sail, when this storm of yours rains gold.

There is no quarter. And do not stumble in our sight. Curse us for Thapsos, Miletus, Cyprus or your Alashiya too, and Ugarit our share. We do not say, gods rape likewise: gods are jokes, and goddesses the more. Thank the men of us, that we tear the world from games that hide the weak. Tomorrow, thank our swords that sharpened yours.

Live, devour, shake the world. We come for spoil: it is enough for the men of us. The world's only edge is our best blade. My name, my name, my name is Pagos, son of Bom---holy might of Enyalios, red star, lord of war.

***

This place is wild to me: the fire of our speaking feels like home. I am Veda, headwoman honored to speak for Pulesati of Alashiya. Do you see these arms that I lift and cross before my face? They X and answer the sign on your pots and painted flesh: the sign of our old koine, the web of every one of us. See then, these rites and meals, our talk and fights and festivals still hammer out our will. Our damos lives, old, new, the same, and different; and many headbands feathered like our own, with quills of crane.

It speaks the bond. Nothing now will stop the jaw-hook swords and axes of our men. Cousins, I am ninth daughter of Pyrrha, old family of Paphos, where Aphrodite rises from the waves. Our children were Her Graces, and they bathed their Old Mother every spring, and life was young again.

We have fought to fill our bellies day by day. Tomorrow? Where are the seeds of the garden? Alashiya was rich like any crossroads. In our cities gods and peoples met: they did more than meet in Aphrodite's gardens, the houses of our mothers. Bonds, from blood to business, must go on: we bring more than weapons. Our motherlands are red Phoenicia's cousins, Byblos, Tyre, Arados: they shipped us Canaan's grain, these years of none. And now, though you Ironheads itched to take them, they will be there for us through our first hard plantings. If we hold together.

We call them men who sheathed their swords in The Lebanon. Him we call a man who just admitted, Crete was squandered. Your Achaian fathers changed old ways not understood. No more herbs by which women manage birthing; and soon, too many sons, war their only bond.

Freedom without kinship? A delicate creature, Achaian way: one late snow, one early frost, and off they marched to raid their brothers to the husk. Their ways were failing when they took down Thapsos, in the west, where Pulesati towns had planted potters, artisans. In kind we burned their pirate-outposts on the coasts. So, so.

Their Lion of Mykenai learned enough to build a lion-gate and walls. But not enough to change his dreams. Then, Agamemnon. Resolute as fire to force his fathers' folly on the world. He burned it like summer sun, and fell the same. Pagos, when Troy broke your fathers, you came to us armed refugees, stealing, raising forts to guard your business on our land. From the isles, our sons sacked Pylos among many. Rains died, war, nobody planting; and here we are. Achaia's Lion builds more wall, as if a wall is what he needs.

My sons and daughters hated you; just like our mothers, who gave us your blue eyes. Such is Alashiya: such is Aphrodite, and Asherah the Lady who walks in the sea. Waves roll over us. We rise; and me surrounded now by ironheaded Graces. You laugh well! In this fire, men come out into the world. So, hold together. Time will not change a day behind us. The garden is remembering we are in it. We are Goddess' fingers, sisters-in-law to the nations. None but She rule what we make of this.

***

I am not so refined. Tolema, woman of the Shekelesh; for sons whose swords buy power. Shekelesh way before battle is silence, till their death-name harrows through the foe. Friends, my two sons shout it with a thousand men: it panics ponies, stands the hair up on my neck. These are men will give life's day, if their dying decide it. Their fathers fought both sides in Pharaoh wars.

The learning of it cost. Too many sons of Sicily made livings out of wars, and that before the rape of Thapsos. They will not let you see them trembling; but I know many with dead limbs uninjured, who cannot speak, or sleep, beat little ones, drink poppy till they die. And so, on eve of battle, I give you my back. Before The Dead here among us round this fire, I am ashamed, for the lives we waste. And now we will pay more for our mistakes.

As Pyx said, I remember; and that is the hope I have. Shall I tell of vine and olive Kriti planted us, when Shekelesh went naked, picking figs? More like, you remember our Kokalos, who cut his way to kingship on that first wealth---Kokalos the Achaian shill. Who led our sons into pirating Mother Kriti's trade.

When Labyrinth ships and law came hunting Kokalos, he broke their strength by treachery and luck. What Sicily got for taking sides with lions, you may guess. Gracious sister of the gardens of Alashiya: our mothers knew your reasons when you helped us. You sent us ships with potters' wheels and artisans; and we cut pretty things in Libu ivory for your trades. I stand here shocked to learn we have kin with these Danaans---one of those Alashiya builders was Podargos, Aktor's brother! And a second time, I turn my back, to beg our Dead forgiveness. Why were we not content with wealthy peace?

No mother can make a farm or shop shine brighter than gold. In travels with their trades, our sons caught the drunkenness of wealth in the cities of the east---fools' gold, got by war. Swallowed this they did, like a bass some shiny lure. And once the hook was set, was there a war they did not fight, one side, the other? They were not going to learn until life broke them, like kingdoms of the east. And those are dust.

We all fight feuds, and every house its fools. There were Shekelesh never did forgive the Cretans that first war, and left our island. Quiet, Shardana, till your say! Hear me! Ninety years we fought you, our own blood, if just to spite you in the Khatti wars with Pharaoh. Was it ten years after Kadesh that our mothers' Thapsos burned, and your homes too, Sardinia?

And now I turn to you in every eye. Comes our turn to perish or lay both hands on one wise thing. Djahi, give us back our healthy sons.

***

Viri, to speak for Danaans encamped below. Our names, let them vanish like dew on the grasses of these dunes. Tomorrow we die with our teeth in the neck of your enemies. See, from this pouch, this feather of a crane. It is nine generations old, and four hundred of us wear the like: men who choose their tribe for reasons, over blood. Weighs nothing. Keeps our hearts alive. Let it go, the breeze takes it into the fire. We never have, we never will.

A tribe is the people you belong with: a tribe of heart or spirit, as of birth. Do you see the buskin-boots we wear, our women's robes, the kohl about our eyes? Goddess is the last thing foe-men see. Down come Snake and Griffin in the markings of our arms. She is our armor. The craftsmen with us make fine metal things, but White One is our shield. We laugh to hear our Achaian cousins' hulking corselets: is it fear of Mother Night you drag all clatter to the line?

In the first days, Danaans were a small tribe camped among Pelasgians. Marrying in, they learned. Their name meant White One, snake-mother of the rains. But Ironheads were coming south: thunder-gods, and strength of spears to plunder. Like Cretans, we let the winds bear us clear of harm. Set adrift like husbands of Danae with common foes. And Alashiya, with her reasons, made them cranes to the last refugee. Including Aktor, whom we call medicine father.

The world seemed broken-open to those tribes. Aktor's father sacked a city that had helped them; a black crime against what feathers mean. To answer that, Aktor took arms: he gave up home and learned the sea, to fight the tide of men making choices like his sire's. It was family and rage that dressed Aktor this way, in honor of The Lady, to spite and terrify. Women joined him, enchanters, Telkines: their young raised three good towns in Rhodes. Yet, the more we fought back, Achaia grew.

Mother Night, come down! No man can know what killing men will make him. Our sins have summoned Her as much as weariness and prayer. Blood tomorrow, wash them from hearts and hands. It is well, for tonight we see the Great Year way go on. Bad blood every side who eat together, work as one. The snakes along our arms bear the chevrons of White One, deeper than blood, closer than skin. We are you, kinsmen. This fierce thing in my fingers is our bond.

Mothers, no fool hurts you and sits back to listen to the lay. The ashes of Achaia say so. White One, weigh our souls against this nothing in my hand!

**

Worotu. Chieftain of Shardana battle-line. The tales you tell of sufferings conquered---and still so many, weary of life?

Giants built the stone Nuraghi towers of our island. At twenty with my father, I Worotu shipped to feed the flames of Pylos. Not in hate: Achaians taught Shardana fathers war, and helped the rising of our kings. They used the well-paid swords of strangers like ourselves, because we had no qualms for hurting local people in their way. Pylos faltered in the rules of its own game; and our homes, their survivors crippled to the crops.

Selah! Forty years, three hundred swords the kind men envy, and I Worotu wake up across a boat's plank with my mate; the sky red over us, raid or trade our way to hunting-game, or island water. Shardana children in the hold call every beach home. Djahi, the sea has fish. Be warned, brothers, we have cousins on the enemy line coming at us with the sun. Let them come. Our thirst is not for water anymore.

Our fathers who abandoned Sicily were no shop-folk, living lives of clay spinning knock-offs of fine cups. War, Shardana's fathers said, is one hazard of a will to live no limit. Drunk, my eye! We choose the hardest honoring of seed-divine in us. Till now, I never said good and Shekelesh in one breath. But Tolema, and Veda too---under these dented plates sewn in my leather, in you I feel long strength. A home that can last.

Chieftains, you face the strongest army in the world. Stick close. Better close your grip around good reasons. Ask our only fighting-peers, of Libu. Win, lose, nothing wears away the stone called Pharaoh.

For an age before Kadesh, Shardana earned The Nile's gold, fighting sand-farer Sutu on a river of the east, called Jordan. For long-lived Ramses, too, we guarded Great House from his own. Talk, talk---Another Ramses will be master when our dead feed birds. No more gold. We have learned what is stone, what is sand and water.

Our mothers' looms wove robes for Libu princes. In western reaches of The Green we built trade in amber, and slashing-swords. Farm figs, feed them your tears! We like that Canaan country the Sharon, and mean to plant in the rot of its dead kings. Teach Ramses war, and Canaan's Dor can berth our shipping south of Byblos.

Three grandmothers before Kadesh, cranes were weaving nests there. Teach him his equals---and our trades grow wide as The Green. If this is the way, Shardana come: we sleep like earth, on graves of men or in them. Tomorrow, brothers, will be more than gold.

***

Wilios, a priest of The Great Year: Wilios, named for Troy-town in your tongue. A Cretan name: my mother and my father, Troy's last keepers of the dance of space and time. Look at me, old, bent. Why do four hundred javelins and swords send me?

You victors drink and stare and tremble: I talk for sons of warriors too, who wait the dawn. From the memory of defeat, we bring---contempt for victory. Fotya, our Achaian brother lives it. Better life his sons.

The Great Year dance of moon and sun, of light and shadow, is the harmony of circles. If those very powers of life follow laws, what is our excuse? Men who toss their anchors grow confused, and then afraid. Troy grieved Kriti like a mother; yet, six generations we prospered by her lights. Our last queen's headdress hung down drops of silver thicker than her hair. Black Sea river-gold. For trim, blue lapis out of Asia, and every water-cup a little spiraled vessel for an altar. When Achaians smelled our wealth, we built our strength; but see how we failed.

We closed the north to them, and used our straits for our advantage. And so Troy feared resentment, needed walls; certain, sure that we could handle what destroyed us. When councils let our kings rule more than a Great Year's counted moons, our people's ways broke off from that real world. Was one king, Priam, any better in the end? Our fathers bled ten years to save a wall. I buried that last headdress in it, when the measure of our greed smashed through the gate. We milked the Asian trade and liked the butter. King! An office built to fetch disaster.

Our families slaves, made nothings by a sword: no sweat of labor gave them back their souls. Achaians, we will never forget, nor forgive. But look at us. Tomorrow we all win, or lose. The way is in our hands.

Oblige us in the ancient way, then. Remember the abandoned things that made us orphans here. Before our eyes, The Great Year turns in moon and sun, our anchor in this world. Return, return! A web of cousins equal. Fools leave now who lust for more.

***

Nobody walks away. I see no beaten people here. Maybe, you flea-bit pharaohs, a seed to plant.

Padi; as you see, a gray Wanassa of the Lukka, the Turan of our chieftain, Chimaros Night Flame. He sleeps now, poppy-drunk. Just between us? His life is one whole cloth of nerve and larceny. His name too has a Cretan touch: great ones, does that ring with your own pardon-tales? Tell it to a pirate.

Before this fire, truth for truth. You bring us Lukka here to build your numbers. Now you seem to have knives to help the poorest isle-folk. So then, know why our skills red The Nile again this year. Good children of Goddess law, a long nose blocks your eyes. Your sea-law made the Lukka hated, in the midst of your own crimes across The Green. Now you know what it is to do things you hate for the sake of your children.

Lukka laugh at big words, like the pennants men fly on their war-wagons: they flap more wind than the ponies. Our camp sent this bent old lady, I confess it, as a mock. But we too loved our lands along the sea. Cousin Neos, we remember Khatti people as cousins, in times-back when Hatti was their Mother of the Sun. Then, you know the story. Their fathers threw down Goddess and her daughters, put up stone-beard statues of themselves---and marched on us, for our last sheep and son. We Lukka too learned blades in Hatti's front lines against Pharaohs. So! Out of that, our elders' new choice: keep bleeding for Hatussas, starve in hidden places; or, bury regret, and take for ourselves as others take.

Now you understand this intolerable camp of children's eyes. Yonder! a slow fat ship riding low with grain, and wine, and metals---Great ones, you were nobler in your pain? Chimaros drinks to kill the spirits of his kills. Dress your idols as you like.

The Hatti fought old Pharaoh to a standstill at Kadesh. And then what surprise, that such a slaughter turned their minds to what had made things work in the first place, marrying up? But the fight wore out Hatti's arm, and we turned on them, with relish. That was our mistake, you men have said it! Sweet righteous poison, blood-justice, and our very own right to steal---Puh! Brought us where? Homes of flame, our mouths big words, our bodies criminals.

Before I sit, mothers and fathers, what will you lay upon the mountain's bleeding-stone, that your ancestors bring you back to life? In each of us, the fool must die. And no offering we make can match what must be won.

I know the wrinkle in my boy's smile when he hurts. The color of my girl's hair is an oak-leaf in the seventh waning moon. See, then: those with nothing yet can give most dear. To Gi, Pytogayah, a little one. My littlest one. She went like sleep. And this night, she climbs into the lap of Shapshu, the living sun.

Our sisters hide their faces in their palms. They know what is torn from us, in hope of one heard prayer. Tribes they come from, men will weep, and have no tears tomorrow.

Eh? You muttering lords of standing water, pull out your own best offering to sunrise. Go on then, brother pirates, cat-call, clang your cups, howl the holy curses! How many children wasted on your altars to yourselves?

***

I

A wind of the sea ...

1

--Are you gone mad? Burn Knossos Labyrinth? Your own family's house!

--Criminal, said another. --Talking slaughter, like some king. Then what?

--Oh, Sweet Wine didn't mean those things, said the gray goat-bearded priest who was kneeling over me, flat on my back like an X in a pile of bed-skins, my head a mountain coming out of mist. It was Makris, gazing down with a new-moon smile

--Please, you two, he said. --The man was struck by lightning, and good as dead three days. Let a brother get his breath!

Makris pulled the old hides off my bones and worked his hands like a midwife's up and down. Revived out of nowhere, mountain air ran along my flesh a breath of wings. And that first full drink of it, cold as black water from a spring, swirled through me. It was an ecstasy of waking up, and underneath all being, an undulating sorrow that time would not change

--Go on now, men, cry the town that Deucalion lives. We dance, and festival, while the new year sun stands still. Find the women, and his sons!

The two incensed cousin-townsmen grunted, and turned for the dolmen door. One thumped his boot on the threshold, and spoke without looking back

--Hey, priest. Ask this unconquered son why as soon as he swore blood, a Griffin's tongue of lightning blew him off the sanctuary. Not with our sons!

--Out!

Where? Karfi: a colossal gray crag-faced spike of granite rising straight up from the shoulders of a mountain, hammered like a nail in the heart of our island Mother Kriti. Whoever sailed the sea miles below, or stole up into this country, Karfi saw them first. Old times of our mothers and fathers, Karfi was a high place of dance, of feast and healing, between the stars and the horned mountain caves of our families' sleep. Now in a world torn off its wheel, The Nail was a refuge that only self-exiles would choose. A hostile crag, as far as possible from homes we could not let go

The air was medicine, sage, thyme, artemisia, and my body felt the mountain hold me up to the circles of the sky. But the snug cypress-beams over our two heads roofed a house that was one room and one window more than a boulder goat-pen. Every wall a common wall in this honeycomb of lanes and shelters, huddled down out of wind and sight behind The Nail's northern cliffs

There was sting-fire up and down my arms out of deep red slashes I had cut, for blood alone awakened family sleeping in the mountain, that they speak. But the wounds were clean and crusted, with a smell of Makris' diktamos poultice. Now he raised me up to ladle water, icy and mineral-sweet

--Come to your house, Sweet Wine, Dionysos, true of speech, he chanted gently out of funerary song. --What do you remember, Deucalion?

I remembered that remembering made me want to die. Near thirty years ago, out of the ruins of my own and my family's mistakes, turning my back on the figurehead throne of conquered Knossos and dragging my first son up this break-neck mountain, to keep him from the mainland's Achaian squanderers at arms. An island, you see, a whole exquisite island one day's sail from our north shore, had blown itself into the sky, and they were making the most of our wrecked land. Too late we had found ourselves only prey in mainland eyes. Our every answer played into their hands, and the woman who walked the world as the soul of us lost her life by our confoundment

The wind and cold we found up here, the work for every morsel of comfort---and the harvest, for a sand-blasted wine god, a king of things other than war? An outlaw inheritance for two sons and a girl. Futility, while a violent handful of red-beards and blue-eyes kept on bleeding the ancient household

Outside a rebel yell broke the morning twilight: *Hai-ee! Hai-ee!* And women's voices trilled up out of the town, *O-lo-lo-lo-lo-lo*

In my left hand, the hem of Makris' deerskin wrap, with a tiny stitched-in row of running spirals. The back of my skull still felt a clout of thunder, and limbs and looks moved slow, as if enormous. Things buzzed, like a mountain alive with summer bees. And here we were again, through annihilating fire

    –Better say what *you* remember, brother

    --Ho! Makris laughed with a wag of his chin-bristles. –Why, it was everything to look for in a Moon Bull, a Minotavros---and so say all three camps of cousins up here, who love you. May I? Son of Pasiphae Who Shines For All, and of the Minos, Keepers of Days in The House of the Double Axe, Labrys. Blood and rightful husband of Ariadne, Lady of Knossos Labyrinth, heiress of the ancient queens, and no man and woman ever will be closer. But now---argh. The last son of Labrys Clan. The last to hold the Great Year throne in family honor. And he left it so

    --Makris, what happened?

    –It was you, grown so black and quiet everywhere, down with the men guarding trail, or pruning trees, or ripping out wood for somebody's broken loom. I saw you, listening, looking, that restless rolling shoulder. And then, talking straight out with people, here at a table, there at the spring, or a grave. Saying plain what I see, too, in their faces---that it's no life to hand on to children. We are dying on the vine up here, the goodness of our seed. We, a pack of highland outlaws---there's a backwards bone to choke on. Well, *I* knew, Makris laughed, --that you were the fellow to turn things, Knossos Labyrinth spectacle man. You, to pull the nail out of people's smiles

    --Yes, yes. Five days ago. It was the dying of the moon just ahead of winter solstice. You climbed up onto

the sanctuary roof. From there on the edge of this world
you called out the mountain. People came in from hunting,
climbed their ways over rocks from the other houses---we
crammed the lanes and roofs to see you up there on The
Nail's last point. I remember, you began to move, and I
was thinking you were like old Keret, from the songs
sailors fetched out of Ugarit. A well-born man, a loving
man, homesick for his house, for his family, his mate. Not
a straggler up here who couldn't feel that, with elders'
graves and a burned-out farm behind them

   --Remember what you said? I felt the breath go
through my body, Makris sighed, --and every other body
in the press. You said you climbed up there to die with the
sun and moon. You were going into the dark with them,
and coming out alive, or you were going to jump---but for
you, The Nail was finished. You slashed your arms till I
winced, and the altar-stone took your blood and word.
Keeper of Days, that was a Minos speaking

   --Then, wonders, that's all! I know you saw your
sons, and daughter, and how many people kept vigil for
you up there. Prayers, torches, pipes came out, a systrum,
a daouli-drum, the githa-bag wailing to make your nape
stand up. On you went, and no moon in the morning sky.
Rippling off old skin like winter Snake, ramping along that
edge a spring-crazy Bull. You belly-roared like summer's
Lioness, with young to feed

   --But oh Sweet Wine, you made us wait for the
shiver of death that Griffin brings. Second night with no
moon, and still the arms up and out at stretch, all runs of

blood. Then, you'd done it. Down over Dikte mountain came a thunderhead, so big and louring-black that it made people hide bunched together in their houses, and the dogs in too. When the rain cracked open out of that with thunder, you were still up there, turning and howling like the world. Well, you climbed down inside the sanctuary, and came back out with Labrys---the last big bronze double axe we had, with the doubled blades and spirals

    --Ho! said Makris. --Lightning snapping and booming around us in the rain. Back you climbed up onto the sanctuary roof. The last altar of the world, it looked, because it is. And you turned in place and doubled back to face us. You lifted the monster both hands high, and your face, Deucalion, the eyes---I don't want to see that again, till Griffin take me home to Snake. The waters pouring off you. You bellowed out, *Knossos Labyrinth will burn!* And, *Crack!* That bolt was so close and blinding-blue I see it now. *Crack!* Down you went a dead man, right through your knees, and Labrys in blasted pieces. Mercy! I never will know why you didn't pitch back off the mountain

    Makris breathed out, and rested, brooding still over answers to the offering. I saw the last sign of our family's understandings, Labrys, broken by the hand of light and shadow that had forged it. How had I not understood the grief and clamor of our elders' graves? It was criminal to leave a thing once holy unbroken, unburned, unburied. So then---the end, and our way out, lay where we were born. House of the Double Axe in funeral flames. A night of the Griffin, lit by the last Minotavros

Suns and moons had endings. We had been clinging to a corpse. Now, the baffled man inside was finished. Watch new metal flowing from a forge, you see the slag drop off, and feel the hot pure incandescent blood of Earth. It cools, and hardens: that was what I found inside. Morning. Ferocious, loving---real again

--Well, your good sons helped us carry you in, Makris smiled. --And here we are. Back from the other world, and come to your house. Home, Deucalion

--Home. Be careful, man who just called the dead back, *true of speech*

--Oh, you don't want to kill anybody! Makris cajoled, grooming back my father's thick black hair as I managed to stand up. With no answer, he loosed his highland whistle toward the door, and ducking in under the lintel came a troop of smiling cousins, kinsmen who had kept his vigil for an end or a beginning

A good eight or nine mountain-people of the town arrayed themselves to stand gazing in a group, some with a flute, a drum or censer in their hands. All together they lifted their palms up and out to me in a sunny welcome's blessing, little ones in black and white wool wraps, hard prime men and women in caps of goat, and the haggard buckskin elders. I doubled this, grateful, but their faces were fear behind Karfi smiles. Now, three of the women with bright eyes piously lifted their wraps to show their breasts, singing out sweetly: *Seam, undo yourself!* Mollifying voices, luring men back into the world of hope and shipwreck

--See? Makris said. --Home, and this is your family. Some of them. Come now Deucalion, you know every face. Here's Pereko, and Cissia the potter, and Donos and Arge. Look, young Oinops brought us a rabbit

--Otus, I told them. --Otus climbed out of those skins. *He Pushes Back.* Family, are we finished weeping on this stone? See this cup I make with my hand. The Sweet Wine is turned. I pour it out. Earth Mother, turn it again

They knew me not a man to call for war. To live on The Nail was to know our enemies' hope, that we should live according to it, for a weakling's benefit

--Say no more, Makris cautioned. --We know, thirty years and your family's house still bleeds in the mainland paw. I mean, why make cousins nervous. You like it here. We see you happy at the chores. Festival is medicine

Deft fellow, Makris: stall, deflect, show the crazy man normal things

--You saw me taken, soul and body. Family, what we grieve is gone the same. And we cannot leave the great house of our families, the core of our memory as she is. Come spring, I am going to burn Knossos Labyrinth. Or, die where I was born. I will kill every cheese-counting Achaian squatter with a knife in the way of that pyre, and take the sunrise after

--Now, this is true: good ships are sleeping winter in the sheds along Amnisos shore. Five moons from now, we can make them ours and sail The Great Green. The wind can tell us where to go, but no more this. I will push back, against squanderers who imagine that what they have done here *works*

    --Stop! said Makris with a stamp. --There are families up here mainland blood. They won't kill their kind! Why, Melas is your brother-in-law

    --Yes he is. Melas is Achaian family. But say it, this once: our end was their beginning. They had no word for ocean, coming here. The best of our houses rent themselves making them at home, and we lost ours

    --Say it! What made Melas family? He turned his back on kinsmen still at pillage. But we cannot just walk away. You do not hear *war* from me. But where stealing begins, family ends. Griffin tells me, Karfi is not enough

    In the silence a thump of mountain wind touched the house, and people started to ease themselves back outside, some with the half-smiling wink of any morning, and some with nervous formal hails of old time, fist-to-brow. Bluntly cordial, scared: Cissia, with the black-haired almond-eyes touch of Egypt, Oinops my rugged nephew with the north islands' twinkling smile. In each and all, the gardens of Crete had mixed proud Aegean shoulders, the locks and olive-bronze skins of Canaan, Libya and Asia. Off they went to put it off, in little joys of morning

    --I ask not a man of you along. But where to, cousins? Hovels, not home. Are we not sick of how an island blew into the sky, and it rained white bulls?

    --That's alright! See you at celebrations! Makris called after them. --Same old fellow, don't worry. He loves us all three houses! The women are coming!

But Makris stopped short, with an uncertain clutch of his amber-bead necklace. Makris, our dear gray he-goat out of Malia, grieving his home since it burned: pretending we did not see him bent and wasting, too, before our eyes

Anybody, I tried after them. *A way to start again, with any honor*. The one answer was a young girl's voice

--Keeper of Days, keep us in the circles of the sun!

I might have said, *No more, no less*---but running in past them through the door came my girl-child, Little Zoe. She vaulted up into my arms

--Papou! --Sweet girl! --There, that's the medicine!

Zoe, eight, happy, gangly and lithe, with strong hair and eyes dark brown as ripe carob. The monkey clung to me laughing and the sound and feel of her drove deep a sword of gratitude. We spun, kissed, and bumped the table: the ache of life came back

The greased-skin window, the portal-stone were glowing new-moon orange. New sun and moon, bearing days and crimes unpurged back into the world. A man can understand that joy alone kills the killers, and yet go on

For you see, Knossos fell, and Ariadne died, and then the first order of Achaian business was to murder Crete's elders in their houses of the mountain horns. Me they spared as a useful effeminate idol of old blood, and things in reach I twisted back Crete's way, while they took down the land. In five years or so, my son Prax was born. Four years more and I, twenty-nine, walked out with him, his mother of her own will keeping to the house; and Prax was ten on the mountain when Podargos came into the world, Bright Foot my second son. Then, last spring, Little Zoe straggled up these trails like the rest of us. People called her my daughter because one day, I chanced to see her first. She was singing out alone to Earth and sky, moving one foot at a time toward a sure-death fall. When I showed myself, she turned to me a seven-year-old face with the nose cut off. In its place was a grisly blue-black failure of healing, an open crime

Achaians had ruled the house fifteen years when Zoe was born. Since the end of easy plunder, they had little to show except land that needed toil. But the spider who replaced me on the throne---an old baron of Mykenai's, styled *Koreter*, the man---had bribes of loyalty to pay. He sent his clanking bronze Companions out into villages, where orchards and fields and kine still showed the shocks of our catastrophe. As part of their new-style ceremonies to engender fruitfulness, they snatched up the two-year-old Zoe and cut her nose off. So that her life, each day, would rub her town-fellows' long Cretan noses in the dirt. *You can make this place produce for us, or watch it burn*

Zoe was going to jump, the day I chanced on her. She had come alive as pain in the faces of most home-people. Her blink of years convinced her it was best she be forgotten. I tried what I had, some foolish drinking-rail clowning along my end of the precipice, holding her eyes. With a startling honk, she said *That was stupid*, backed up, and asked what I had to eat

In Little Zoe's shadow we learned to want the sun again. It was she pulling out the nail: if we could make her love her life again, we could love ours. We were mistaken to oblige our guests and disappear. So, there in the house and more times, I should have heeded her. Zoe snatched up my tiny silver Labrys hung with rawhide

--Look, Papou! she cried with a sprig of ivy up to see: between its jagged leaves, one twice-born shoot sharp green. Tongue in her teeth, her fingers fixed it on. --I have a *dance* today. The *sun* is back. Come see, Papou?

She said rain had washed snow off the mountain, and since my sleep, more Little Summer on the land. I craved bright air, but knew what was coming with five days' new year duties. So I asked Makris for a shave and dressage, and he took out the few best things which, good, would conjure another man. Zoe dangled her feet on a creaky chair, but then ran out to look for the mothers who called me house-bond

Trews of the mountain's red deerskin, tall boots of double hide: a mainland-style leather corselet lined with fleece thanks to Melas' house, and this inside a short wool cape with a sash to the knee, vermilion. Last, a green sariki-headband. Gone the days of spotted trouser-skirts, silk codpieces, thigh-high kilts with snakeskin weaves of colors: my sword of rare iron, gift of a good man gone, one left sleeping for these days. But Labrys and Great Year walked round my neck, and its nub of winter green

Outside, wreaths of ivy and pine-cone hung in wheeled X's here and there, and you felt people like mice in the walls waking up and getting ready. The little cobble-lane that dog-legged up through the houses was bright, wet, warm and still. My door was round a corner from where the way widened into half a courtyard, and right away Donos, a cousin from the vigil happened to stray down from men who were talking up there

He whooped with black eyes happy to the others, and here they came with this and that touch of festival to their leathers---a pack of growls and laughs for this moon's best cheat of sudden death. Norax and Melas were the oldest two, with Donos and Kinuwa, Pereko, Winato

--Clever fellah! --You're late, priest-chief! --Hai-ee!

We kissed around except for Melas, who never did such, and hands put a skin of moonshine in mine. Mountain-milk! First, a poured-out thanks, and then the raki burned down in, from head to boots. White lightning! Every swallow was a lick of Griffin's tongue, and Snake's blood of resurrection in

While the skin doubled round, the four young fellows kept an eye on the second-story roofs, for this was pushing festival propers. *Bunch of nurses*, Norax laughed at them, and he, the mountain-man of us, stepped up eye to eye, clapping solemn hands on my shoulders

--Steady me, I said, my forehead to his chest

--There is nothing to worry in answering what we owe, Norax said in his low slow voice. He doubled his kisses both cheeks, and it bent my knees, dropping half my fear and solitude

Norax's clan came of Phaestos. There was a priest-chief in him, tall with the south's touch of Libya, his hazel eyes a lion's in a tangled mane of fierce-red furze. We were house-bonds and brothers-in-law through Honeybee, we bled together pushing thieves back down these trails--- always trading straight-shaves and boasts of wounds or pedigree. Norax! Born to the dance, he could banquet on a prickly-pear, and who troubled his household, he opened like a fish. Now, Melas jostled in

--Let me view the body. Praise Poseidon Lord of Seas and Mountains! Here, another drink. One is good, two is medicine!

Hello, Melas---stocky, stolid, and strangest of my fates, married in with his big blue Achaian eyes through Ninna, mother of Podargos. Marriage, Melas called the Cretan tangle around men's will---although like Norax and myself, Melas did not mind knowing who was the son of whose blood

Where the hill behind Karfi was Honeybee's household, Ninna's stood a mile eastward, facing Dikte. Norax and Melas were each *damokouros*, their people's man. Not a council over figs but Melas wore his heavy-bone face like a solemn mask. So he stroked the red and fair hair of his jaw-line beard, as I drank

–One more now. Up, down, Melas said

--Easy, Norax warned with a rogue's smile. --Three is festival, four is trouble

--And five, you say, is blood, said Melas. –Good brother, are you well now? I only want to say. Or, that is--- ask, he began. But then, Melas halted

--He wants to know if his kinsmen get it, Norax said with a stabbing hand

--No joke! Our own sons will front the line

--Stop! said Donos. --It's mad. We don't council blood in the street

Seemed that Donos was feeling a bigger man's swallows, youngest and shortest of the four: a squinty mason out of Zakros with a touch of Alashiya blood, now of Honeybee's house. His was the voice I heard on waking, and now that he spoke, the others burst out too with worries worse than Melas'

I needed to hear this cross-talk, because you weren't sailing far without craftsmen and folk of metals, weavers and planters, potters, masons, any skill. They had wives, apprentice sons and daughters, they had wrested Karfi life from broken stone---and I was not going to ask one man to pull knife or oar. I knew that turning their backs on home had not worked for them either. Blood of Snake inside me listened

What about it, Pereko? Master hunter he was, a bowman with a sharky jaw, and chameleon swivel-eyes: tough island mothers had planted his town Praisos, now of Ninna's and Melas' house, a would-have-been Cretan marine like his father. For himself, Pereko was in---but he X'd across his mouth to say no more for these five days. It was bad luck, with the door between the worlds wide-open under this sun

Kinuwa drank, smacking his long shaven jaw, a keen gentle face like a red deer's: Carian stock, with eyes and arts for metals. Kinuwa too lived in Melas' house, but no young family: a grudge-bent smith from a works at

Myrtos, he had already killed his way out of mainland servitude. He cribbed an extra swallow and used it to say that he, for now at least, stood with Pereko

Well then, Winato? *No*---and there was plenty more *No* going round the mountain, he declared, with a roll of his shoulder for the lot of us. A likeable lout of Honeybee's table, Winato's head looked misshapen whatever the cap, his farmer's face out of Messara pocked and weathered. The Nail's man, he, for vine and bee and olive; but, Winato said, his jewel was his wife, and the girls she taught as mistress of the looms. Winato knew what he had in his tumble of a house, and he meant to keep it

Back around to Donos, listening and flexing his stonecutter hands. Donos' woman was Norax's own niece, Arge, fetched up here to safety. Donos a man of obligations, a wound on each arm, but his hands loved Arge and his hammers. –I can fight, Donos said. --But this is a good green mountain

--Boys who want to live, murder that, or go home!

This laughing taunt rang round the corner of the houses close at our backs, and we turned. It was Abas, dressed sharp, but out of festival place, with all four of his blades on show: a wiry man of that many winters here, fierce and restless. The group's eyes looked off this four-hilt twist of custom, and I felt the echoes of his manly mock. Like waves returning to the center of a pool, coming back in shapes of fear

--Only to protect you, Abas shrugged as he strode up and planted himself, then paced and rocked in place.

Older than Donos and younger than me, Abas stood half a head short in the group, including the old-time scavenged boarstooth helmet that he strapped to his head every day. Sharp face with a jawline-beard like Melas', quick black eyes: when he walked his hard boyish torso jutted forward strangely off his hips. Already The Nail's best blade, Abas took the raki, and his gulps dropped through his gullet. Cold, cold I felt at his lizard swallows. Unease slipped a look between Norax and Melas

Abas too had wandered up here, but no more a man, people said, than a knife and a mouth; blaming women for what was nothing but pirates' luck. *You women made them at home*, he told Honeybee at table. *You thought ceremony and feasts and gardens of love were going to tame swords. Tame Theseus!* Charming himself right out of the game. Honeybee dug it up that Abas' mother had run quite a house in the wool trade, Mount Ida country. That was why one of the names behind his back was Little Zeus; for an uppity Cretan imp of mountain-springs, whom Achaians had made a thunder-hurler

Abas was a talker, but never of his home. We figured his family went down hard, yet Abas took no comfort but a bowl and a pallet in Pereko's house. Creature, woman, child and garden he pushed away. It gave him worlds of time to appoint himself inspector of every man's worth and ways of weapons

Abas' show was to drink raki like water. Aiming at his metal manhood I grabbed up Melas and kissed both his cheeks. Offended, Melas still winked

--Well and good! Abas said, tossing Kinuwa the skin. --But I say, we make everybody drink from each other's hands on this. Old-Libyan style, right Norax? So our bite is poison to a snake. There is always some traitor in the house

--And you, Norax inquired, --to keep us honest?

--Sir, Abas smiled back, --I only volunteer, to protect our advantage. What are we, five hundred people? Otus---good name. It's a man who makes himself. Now, we'll be lucky to arm up sixty-five men worth the walk down to Knossos. Let Koreter catch wind we're coming, and *zzzzzt!* Abas hissed, with a pull of his finger ear to ear

--Otus, said Abas taking further command, --your son Prax says that his mother still lives inside the Labyrinth. Good woman? Any whispers our way? How many armed Companions around old Koreter these days?

My son. My son. This meant, put our sons up front, or nothing. What was I doing! I went a bit sick. Abas took it for the lightning: *You'll look better tomorrow, like the sun*, he said. It was nausea worse than a boat's, and stranger, as if the horizon every side were tearing away from my senses. My belly was a boat pitching down a wave, cut loose from any anchor. Could the man not shut up?

Day of days---Our eldest woman's voice obliged, from the last big rooftop up the lane. Wheeling around, we saw Mother Zoe come rising forward to the roof's edge between Ninna and Honeybee, the pillared smokes of the houses and the sanctuary horns behind them. They had left off morning rites to listen, eyes bearing down

--Shut that skin while the sun comes to, or you won't like the spirits who come out, Mother Zoe said

Little and lean in her wraps, her head crowned in long white locks: Mother Zoe made this all but a showing-forth array, and it drew our best hailing fist-to-brow. True of speech, the men of us were grateful

Her hands were holding some black thing. The mountain had called Zoe young, and she had drunk from every spring of the damos of our women, birth-stone, death-shroud, green fields between. She made highland generations fruitful in dry years. When pilgrims came to learn, to heal or make their peace, Zoe led them into the mountain. She was the voice of the cave where we began, where Ariadne, lost one, sang to wake the stones. There, a whisper was a shout, and Dikte's silence walked with her

We were looking at a Keeper of Days never lost, who kept her head when moon and sun themselves strayed off the wheel. She knew the long changes in their dances and she knew when shadow would consume them. The difference was, losing track of when to plant or jump a pasture. Those two hands tugged lambs gently from the ewe, fed them kindly, and slaughtered them for table the same way. Where Karfi people ate together, Zoe's name was in the thanks

--New year morning, mothers! Abas boldly hailed. If Zoe's eyes by turns were kind or fit to freeze a dog, she only looked down at the heavy black-wrapped thing in her two hands. So I had seen her bear away luckless births, and tumors out of healings

--You might want some news, she said

--News? said Abas. --What news? From whom, which trail?

--Pharaoh is dead

--Who? joked Winato, his noggin half-sideways

Tutmoses, third of his line: a boy who soured waiting for his throne, and as soon as he came to it, chiseled his mother's name Hatshepsut from their stones. To make her pay, our grandmothers said, for years of humiliating trade and peace. Seventeen years his armies took heads, grain, gold and slaves from Syria to Nubia, palmed them out to priests who tendered blessings; and still a boy, he stuck a knife in my father's back to hand our trade the mainland's way. A man to chop off old relation and pretend that no one saw his cheap advantage. When Achaians holding Knossos died, Pharaoh's name went into the hole with their choice swords, his threats and thanks carved in alabaster jars. His bloviating cartouched words to feed their wishes, and the worms

We still had medicine-kinsmen on The Nile, at Pharos, Abydos. But even there Achaians now, Mykenai's eye gazing from the prows of their black ships, hulling up the river: their roving sons casing cities tacked with gold

--Dung-beetles, greet the great man. Anything of interest, Mother?

This seemed to please, but after the laugh, Mother Zoe closed another door behind my life

--For you, perhaps. Theseus of Athens, too, is dead

--Who? Norax mocked this time: I looked away.

The hero of our masters' lion-pride, who marveled and sneered over water-pipes and bathtubs: the bumpkin born to save us all. The lout whose treason lost us Ariadne

Mothers' boys, who dance, not wield
the long ash spear and heavy shield,
I cast in a thrice on your marrow-bones
to call me king and lord

--Surely, Labyrinth house-bond, something to say, Honeybee invited

I might have sighed, dry as grass when the sun goes under, except for her eyes: the festival touches of her dress were enough to green dead wood. --You look so beautiful, Fourogata

--Well! she smiled. –A pleasant funeral-speech

Karfi people liked their nicknames: young Arge, Donos' partner, was Kri-Kri for her curves and garden charms. Honeybee was Fourogata, for the highlands' big fierce ring-tailed cat. When you heard those warning-yowls, you backed away. Today her black curls were on the wind, bangles, silver-sickle earrings, and scarred muscled arms with two fists akimbo at her tight-cinched waist. In Honeybee's eyes, her black lashes, between her naked heavy tear-drop breasts, a man looked for a place to lay his life down. Norax was the only man she named a son, his Oinops

Old times, when The Great Year turned, Bull chose out priests and priestesses: Honeybee at seven saw

Palaikastro devour itself, around a boy-god there turning king and away from sun and moon. The more this Honeybee bloomed, the more she lived out of sight, and keeping off the beaches robbed her of the sea. Born to ride the world, she married these cliffs, black-eyed blood of old Europa's Byblos: her kin had been in silver, she made herself to the bronze pins, and nobody drove her bargains. Kourai like Honeybee were born to grace our queens, and she blamed herself she never would serve one. Here, at least, she had stopped cutting cruel futile slashes down her arms and hands. Honeybee still had ways to cut herself, to say she was no Ariadne. But she was

--Halloo? Ninna called. --Do you hear? Theseus is dead. Let a little thing make you grateful, for the sun on your face

--Go on, give a shout then, Melas nudged and smiled. --He was nobody I call kinsman. You won! Come to think, why *is* everything so weird about you, even for Cretans? You know what I mean. You won, in a way, without trying

--Melas, you are rattling, Ninna chided

Even Abas went quiet, wanting words about the Shepherd. I wondered where my sons might be, Prax, Podargos. They and Aktor, Ninna's battle-age son by Melas, were some of the young she favored

I liked the dust-brown locks Ninna wore combed out to her little shoulders, round like a sparrow's, and the high lift of her chin. Ninna's middle years could have made her Zoe's child and Honeybee's mother. But true of speech, she walked her sadness more than anyone; had changed not a thing for new days, but stood next to Zoe in the same sun-orange saffron shawl in which she had climbed this stronghold

Ninna never left it off, in her daughter's memory. And even picking her way over rocks as sharp as wind, Ninna's hands bore along a little round house of painted clay. Inside it, behind the door between doubled pairs of horns, Earth Mother showed herself, arms up and wide as the world. That was for Ninna's great house gone. She said the little face pinched and painted into Goddess looked, by luck, just like her girl

Theseus! Ninna had known his like. A mainland baron whom she called Botcher came storming up into the olive hills of Vathypetrou, with the Achaian vanguard. He killed or shipped off anybody seeming to dislike him, and then went looking for help to make the wrecked olive presses flow again. It took work, botching a trade for which the world had no substitute: he made the potters of his jars build thicker feet, as if The Great Green might not notice weight of oil. At hand, he wore out every chance with nickname-insults, Slope and Dingus. Drowning in his boredom with the land, Botcher watched as Ninna gifted her daughter with that shawl in the year of her moon-blood. And, he figured, marriage to a Cretan child would bring this place to heel

Instead, Ninna's daughter shed her gift for a walk to the sea, and jumped a cliff. Ninna staggered into the mountains, and Botcher flamed out after her with chariot and spear. Luckily, he ran into farmers, who beat him to death with olive poles. They ate his horse, scrapped his bronze, and dumped him chariot and all down some ravine. That was the end of Melas' older brother

Melas that day, to his honor, had followed Ninna. But she, never broken, had begun to bend. Here from below I saw poppy-shadows in her eyes, the finger-stains it left when people took it for more than pain of body, or a medicine dream. She was falling in with artisans pushing custom: they called these poppy-stupors helpful to their crafts. Well, their pots' crude stick-people never pleased my Knossos eye

So there we were on The Nail, each letting go of a world going dark, and no answers

--Ninna, I said. –This day, many things are dead

From the black cloth in Mother Zoe's hands the two blasted lobes of Labrys' head tumbled down, and they clanged and sparked the cobbles

--Watch out, Zoe said. –Come spring, young Bull, south wind carries desert over the sea. The Breath of the Ass, with claws of sand and flies that make men mad. Watch what pushes and follows your back! What will you husband---garden, or a rage to make it desert?

--Mother, I said. –If mainlanders wondered, we would not be hanging on this hook in the sky. Tell me how to make us heard

Loving, cold as well-water, Zoe warned: --*She licks up heroes like dust*

--Oh, these impossible foggy sayings! Abas

exclaimed. As I stood there, Melas gave Abas a smirk of fellowship, and it spread into grins on Pereko and Kinuwa. Under the rose, they were medicine-sons of Poseidon, another old imp of springs proclaimed omnipotent. Such were the tides to keep pulling, if we made it to the ships

Ninna missed no looks from Melas. Indignation took her a step to the edge of the roof. Whether in care with her foot, her words, or both, when she opened her mouth the little clay house fell through her hands. It dropped and shattered where Labrys lay. Ninna's face went wide like a man's run-through. Honeybee, quick to Ninna's elbow, kept her standing till the three of them turned away from us, and helped each other out of sight. Honeybee looked back, and hissed through open fangs

--That cat, Abas said, --pulls my stick like a wand to water

Norax's back-hand struck across his teeth. What froze that scuffle was Fourogata, storming back into sight with her sizeable knife in hand

--Now Ninna wants to burn her shawl, you bloody fools! Well, heroes, look at *this*, she snarled. --Convince us. Is it worth one boy? Convince us. Till then, if you move, taste *this!* And Fourogata vanished. Into the void, Norax:

--New year, all. Whatever you do, you're going to be sorry

--Wonder how they got outside news. Argh! Melas grunted. --Bet your bones, they'll play us with it. So, friends. It seems we resolve not to resolve

--Wait. Theseus, Abas said, but nobody else cared

to hear, and we dispersed. He gave a little chin-strap pout, then slapped his sides and, resigned, drank green morning air off the mountain

Snake came first in the first day's rise, turning new time's wheel. Still no sign of my sons, and once I had a basket to collect the broken things, I found that Makris had gone ahead from the house with our best old painted vase of offering and pouring. I was angry, running rocks and fat cushions of spiny-spurge, till I pitied the sight of him trying to climb and lift the vase up where it first belonged. Age up here meant more than birth or names, but late years, Makris had grown too feeble for the part

There were beings in three stones standing near our houses, shaped only by rain and wind: the head of a mountain-man, long-nosed and bearded, his hair in a bunched top-knot; a woman in a crested diadem, round and smiling, singing out; and between, the shape of a round-headed child, with one high-hailing arm. When you climbed their crag, and held that vase to that child's hand, you placed it in the horns of a mountain far off to the west, shining white these winter days. It was to tell the whole world of our families, we remembered. This made it fit to hold water of memory from our spring

I got under Makris' butt and pushed to help him do it, and he went happy the long climb down, rock by thicket along Karfi's western fall. People gathering quietly were smudging with diktamos, near well-kept graves and tombs along the mountain. A fine full Little Summer was opening wraps and everything green was bright. Makris smiled and passed the vase: *Here boy, draw the water, take the poison.* A pleasure to hold this thing, slender with a birdy neck and five-bough palms. Clambering down, I took the folk-medicine, as people of every age and grudge dogged me to the spring

--Yah mule! --Yah! --Don't drop it, stupid! --Get my boy hurt, Keeper man, I chop your legs off! --Some year-king, slower than last winter! --*Op-op-op*, he's coming! --So is Bull, and his sons are dragging him!

I scoured the spring's old basin with grit, then laid in the vessel, and it drank. At the tombs, each person to the child was anointed, and set to work with kinsmen clearing brush and moss away. Scarcely a sound in the mountains' good silence, till drums and clatter stirred our dogs. My sons came up near the head of that hundred

Whooom, whooom, whoo-oom! It was Bull-roarer, thunder and love-call: Podargos, stronger than I thought, swinging a rope and oaken board that wrought the sound. As usual fierce and happy, showing the cold his bony chest, he snapped the roarer back once neat to his hand and grinned my way. Then came Prax, walking between Bull's horns in his best buckskins, tall as a sunflower. Indeed he tranced right past his father-alive---a hurt that turned me proud. Girls like Zoe, and crones with willow who had beaten the slopes all around The Nail, were singing now to daouli-drums, rattling things, swinging hips, their brown and gray heads tossing in wild unison

Melas was shining on his fair-headed Aktor at the head of the young men jostling and jumping. The day asked: was Prax, with his curls and his Knossos-speech, their better anymore? Prax meant to make a poet. He sang out now full-throated, and with all but the lost one's voice I had craved these thirty years. I heard her, in him:

--Leap, leap at the head of your daemons,
Kouros of things newborn, gleaming,
and all mankind be held about
by wealthy peace! And leap for us, too, leap
for full jars and fleecy flocks,
leap to bless every tree, and make hives drip honey

Aktor's face was twenty years of Karfi granite, hair stronger than Honeybee's: a hunter cool at arms, that boy. Blast, to see my sons was mad medicine! They gave me life, and now their lives hung from what had to happen

This moon's Bull wanted flowers, but his thanks were strong. The woolly githa-bag came out and its high crazy pipes made people writhe. I coaxed out the shiver and the nod of his horns: this year, Arge had honor of the mace. She struck a good stun, then gripped his mane and knifed in under. Bull heaved, and went down. His steaming spring of blood we mixed with waters, and Arge marked an X in red on every grave, and brow. Mothers taught girls to chop and portion, men shouldered up Bull's head; and gathering now, around the undying painted palm that I hefted high, this spattered holy ruckus of hands and feet helped each other up the mountain, sanctuary-bound

–Dapuritojo, way to the light! --She waits in the door! –Guide of all souls, bring us round the wheel!

The northern cliff's long fall kept people from crowding up too near. They pressed in on the cobbles and roofs and across the whole saddle of The Nail to wait, to see. My last this day until the moon was to climb up there and pour; and this, when the sun cast no shadow, to open the little niche-in-the-mountain door with its double horns and doubled spirals

The waiting became the people's pouring to each other: one sat in place of family-gone, the other poured and spoke their mind. Some said nothing, wept, or nestled like a child. This was another way not for Melas, with his bone-deep dread of playing gods. He never could say where else he hoped to meet them

Midday! The spirals swung in, people breathed and wept and hailed, and out walked Mother Zoe, Honeybee, and Ninna bare to the waists, their loving solemn faces meeting every other. Zoe held high a little clay horned Earth Mother, arms up and outward to bless; and all of us, now without a Labrys, lifted our palms high in answer. The last bird on the mountain went still, and a breath passed through the world

Now came drink and out with stores of food like summer feasting, and double-spiral dances, waiting night's moon: the high-sun hours of Lioness, devourer, whom we loved for the young she nourished. I ate with my sons and Mother Zoe, but seeing their joy with the day in hand brought back the worst of a nausea. I left, and walked, and walked as if chasing the horizon. And there, *tock! tock!* down in an oak grove by a pool, was Abas, teaching knife to some young boys. I heard him call a good throw a Griffin, sudden death out of the air. --You boys belong at feast, I said

     --Not really, Abas shrugged. Then, aside, he pricked me

     --Mistakes, you say you've made your share. But why burn Knossos? Shame to waste a house so useful---old king of the hill! he nudged

     And who would be the new one---you, Little Zeus? Look out. This lion with no young to feed would feed the young to lions: all to gain, little to lose. This mountain, this Theseus, I was not going to wait for harm. I sickened, murder in my hands---but he might talk me into it. The same wounded cunning. The blather, leagues out in front of his secret wants: a walking reckless appetite, endowed with skill to poison and mislead

     I stilled my heart with stars that night, at the windy open niche beside Bull's head: the million eyes of our ancestors looked down, and not unkindly. If I were wrong, it would not be from lack of listening. New moon climbed up out of Earth, a little girl's cup, a yellow talon

     --Father of my body! Crown of law! Moon King who stepped forward, whom no weapon saved, what is the way! Let them use me like a shield!

     Festival laughter, crashes, reels and whoops. *Come to your house*, Makris sang. Well, we were coming

     I stayed and prayed and listened till night itself lay

down under paling stars. Fighting just to get born. Heading down for the house, I turned the wrong cobbled way, as clumsy as a calf

A woman at the full of life was standing by my door, dark eyes, high-cheeked slender face: a kindness not quite smiling in her lips, as red as fig off the tree. An evergreen cloak of many folds held her shapely body, a great white-beaded headdress crowned her hair, and round her charming chin, a lowered veil with spiral-chase. In the bend of her arm a red jar nestled, and I saw its painted bird, a crane of skill and grace

--Deucalion?

--Oh, lost one

--I am not lost, she smiled. –Don't be afraid. My name is Pyrrha.

2

A dozen daemons forgot me to look for strangers with outside news. So, to this woman, I wondered why Karfi had delayed her welcome. More than chance had likely placed her here

--Sir, this Pyrrha smiled, --your rites of sun and moon. Before that, you were indisposed. You know me, sir. And I bring good things to explain

I had not seen such wealth of trade and travel since merchants had mingled on The Labyrinth's west court. She showed no disdain for The Nail's hive of hovels, although from her headdress to her rings and her purple curled shoes, her style was Alashiya, of Cyprus not Crete; but this woman was living what families here remembered. The scents from her were palm and ocean

--First, she answered my eyes, --I was going to the tombs with offering of home wine. Alright then, a clue. See what this remembers you, she began

–Once, there was an unthinkable red-black Bull. He lived on a mountain with lovely groves of trees, above a tiny town. Bull was crazy, flick a whisker and Earth shook: he liked his fun, though it never made him cruel. He loved the tiny town below, the sweet noises it made; how the people, afraid when he moved, sang songs to soothe his blood. He would have been glad to kill anybody who troubled them, but he was too big and crazy to live there.

So, the more he loved his groves of trees. If Bull could not come into the town, he let nobody walk his mountain; and all the girls and boys were told never to stray up there

--But, in the town, there lived a certain girl; and somehow, only she knew it was alright. There's always a girl born wise, to fear no thunder. And, if this one too was told never to stray up that mountain, she was a bit of mischief. She slipped off, and found herself climbing through glorious groves of oranges, fat figs and olive trees

--Old Bull, he heard somebody, and he mosied down to see who was so foolish or so brave. And there on the mountainside, he saw the girl, sauntering along, singing, her hair tied up in back with little stray strands of it on the breeze: she had a gay summer-shawl across her breasts and shoulders, and he liked how her tiny bare feet kicked out the hems of her sunny skirt. The girl was only half-looking for him, really: she met his eye, and went right by him. What! Bull couldn't think how annoyed he was. He galloped out ahead of this girl, who didn't spook even when he turned and lowered his shoulder

--Boom! He rammed into a fig tree, just to teach this one a lesson. Poor Bull! He must have hit his head too hard. He knocked a lot of figs down, and the girl picked one up. Now all he did was watch her sit, and eat, and the crazy in him melted. How the girl marveled at the taste. She ate that fig like her first one, or her last, with bright eyes, and smiled with teeth white as lily, as if it were naughty to enjoy a fig so much. She swung her pearly thighs, munching, and sucked her fingers

--Well, good thing nobody else came up that mountain. Bull tossed his horns, to say he'd be twice-glad now to kill them, any or all. Zoop! And the girl hopped up, grabbed his horns, and nestled her bottom in the wooly curls between. Bull laughed, his greatest-ever thunder--- and that won't hurt a fly. He said, *Sweet Thing, I was born for you!* So, since that day then, yonder, love? He curls himself the world around her sleeps

--My mother's mothers' tale, I said

--You told that to me, Pyrrha smiled. --And a little girl forgot to thank you

--What? When? Pyrrha, I said, hoping for years to say her name. --Let me fetch food. We have a sitting-place

--Good, Pyrrha said, with a pat to her painted bird: it was a long-necked crane-hen, totem of her clan, and wine inside to pour for Mother Kriti

So we parted on the cobbles. I watched her go stately down. Woman, traveler for family, trained, trusted: how many house-bonds, how many kids?

--There's a man hit by lightning, Honeybee teased: her house fed me most days, and that was all she let on, busy toward the rites. Little Zoe and Podargos gnawing mutton, Oinops: after kisses and gathering things, Prax I took outside

--I am coming with you, he began. --I don't forget, you told me of so many men who rushed to fight for things, and got poison for it. But, father, I want to bring my mother out of Knossos. Where do you think we'll go? he finished

This in the spell of morning twilight on the mountain: it was Little Summer warm, but southern clouds were climbing. Look at my son! Pride and worry circled through my chest: no sleep, but I felt eager again, ahead of the game

--Mother Zoe swears to see me through, Prax told me. --She wants me to stay. She worries things lost, if I take her learning with me. But Zoe won't hold me, if the house leaves. Why can't I have both mothers?

--That is Zoe's pain, Prax. Things coming apart, and no way to teach enough. But listen, I said with a palm to his shoulder. --In training, you stick close to Norax, and men of his tribe like Donos. Let Abas teach you the close-in, but put wax in your ears. And more, Prax. We count on you with Bright Foot. He is not of age for this. We'll be short of hunters soon. So, tell Podargos that no man can fight without his rabbits. Put him in charge of boys cutting arrow-branch, but keep him out of this

--Thank you for your faith in me, Prax replied, and I let him go with praise of yesterday: my son, another in our line of priests with different lives forced on. Aktor, watch his back!

Down the mountain with a skin of raki, raisins, rare cakes of honeyed wheat from fields that we managed off The Nail. Pyrrha finished at the tombs, and I took her to a bench-stone near our spring. She filled her jar, then sat with legs tucked under her, hands in her lap. Her slender back and bosom reared up from folds of her cushion, the green cloak: she'd dropped the under-veil from her white headdress too, a different flower now, the wind rippling a full-length cotton robe of lightest lavender. Canaan-colors: one ounce of that dye cost her weight in bronze. I yearned for the world in her. We ate and watched the hawks circling level with our eyes. One had a murder of crows nipping at his tail, and he gyred up and up as blithe as life till they fell away. The whole land answering the sun. With a rock I cracked almonds like a cave-man, and Pyrrha's lips relished their fresh oil. I could not remember her

--It was only thirty years ago, Pyrrha laughed. –I was born far down there, in the valley behind old Amnisos, she pointed across the plain, where clouds cast green and silver shadows. --We saw you sometimes at your mother's ceremonies. Then, one morning, after the mountain of fire, people put me a little girl on one of seven boats. They were Crete's last boats, that you and Ariadne found. This was after the waves. One, your men had pulled down from a tree. People called this just a visit-ride, but we knew. The mainlanders were coming

--Excuse me, sir, that I spoke the name you buried. But you were a sweet wine, we were all in tears that day for leaving; or at least, because our elders were. You and Ariadne looked torn open, and you told that story to our boat of spoiled children. So, today, I have this circle's honor. We made it to Alashiya, because of Ariadne's house. My grandmother five-back was Alashiya, and Paphos made us family. So, sir, your pardon; but this once, I may say it. Look at me now, Pyrrha beamed

Glorious, and something was coming. She

straightened up, waist, spine and shoulders, raised one palm and lifted her chin to speak as embassy. Achaians said a woman made good hostage in affairs, but from Labyrinth days, such daughters had borne things of moment. Trained and seasoned queens of their kind, they understood each other, and midwived standards for a fractious Great Green

--Minos, Double Axe Man of mountain, moon, sun, shadow, and the pole-star door: Deucalion Minotavros, Otus who Pushes Back. We come back for you. We want you and yours to come to Alashiya. Our home is a garden

Pyrrha was looking out with peace of heart on country her own mother. These years of days had burned my eyes on the shape of Dia Island sleeping off the coast, where nothing needful had killed Ariadne. Overwhelmed, I wondered could I grow a soul her size. Could I really let go, leave, and keep her grace

--Home out east, Pyrrha said, --the mainland ships with eyes dare only trade. We let them think we do not know the crimes behind them. You understand, then, sir, I am our family's message. I don't dress this way every day, Pyrrha smiled, palm returning to its mate

So this was how a mountain felt when it sloughed off a slide of stones! I couldn't be true-mad, feeling only grateful Mother Zoe's way for this. But I blurted back, asking Pyrrha how many house-bonds lived with her

--Well, she answered with a slow-music tilt of her chin, --none of them ever sat enthroned as a Keeper of Great Year Days

Beginning, that, to say what we might do for them: bring Labrys Clan's good name in trade with Ugarit and Canaan, and skills that built the suns and moons into public binding-rites. I had sailed my father's fleet for war with three thousand different creatures, and wondered the mix of them in Alashiya. Her mothers sorting seed, weaving up the fragments of our web---busy creatures, when the lions were at bay

--We never forgot Ariadne, Pyrrha said, --and you beside her, standing on those hills with your arms up, a doubled pair of palms out high to bless. We cried, and our mothers looked Ariadne in the eye till the sea took our sight of her. In time, at Paphos, when we heard what happened, we built a house in her honor. Traders can tell you that. But those same years, they said you still lived at Knossos; and then, not. We got a new Achaian story. You were killed when they broke The Labyrinth's doors. It told us something, to pray for you, because they were devouring even yesterday

--Now, I have a sister, named Kai, a midwife, and keen as mortals get with dreams. At harvest-last, Kai dreamed Ariadne dying in childbirth. We realized what we owed. What we, the saved, might save. But her dream said, *Quickly*. So, when Little Summer came this year, we trusted that: we chose lots, and off I sailed, to see if Dikte knew your fate. And now, if I know clouds, Little Summer is closing, till The Sisters take Double Axe down the sky, and it calms the sea

--A daring ship is welcome home, I managed. Now,

clear as a dream I saw that morning and her boat, the waves rising and falling in fire and honey of the mountain-blasted sky. Queen of my spirit's hand in my hand. Seaborne children taking to waters that had borne our first clans here. Now returned, to sail again, falling and rising

A woman's dream oceans away, a blink of weather; and here was help to save us worlds of trouble. Help unlooked-for on the air, if I could just keep waking up. Palm, and ocean: Pyrrha basked, and lifted both arms to settle her necklace of white cowrie, her breasts full-round as ostrich-eggs. How to say what still demanded doing?

--So, they killed me at the door. Poor work, Koreter! I laughed down the mountain. --Poor man, he can never sleep. Words, reasons, rules and knives, because life lives wild around the lies. Our governor's dry canals fed them into our ears: *You Cretans lie. Zeus is no boy, no moonstruck man who dies for mother's green. He is king of gods, of thunder, and of men: he rules, and lives forever in the sky. Take fear of Zeus' pelekus, Cretans: you are all liars.* Labrys, now the battle-axe of fraud! Well, Pyrrha, this changes our councils. Who can stew any longer, burn his life talking back to the breath of an ass

Then came Pyrrha's first touch. Soothing my brow like a plough-weary brother's, a fragrant palm along my jaw, she gathered my hands then in hers. I trembled, but with fresh strength cutting loose

--Three feasts we owe already, yours, your crews' and sister's, I told her

--As your house considers, Pyrrha said, --I boast

not Alashiya copper. But, with the right smiths, we begin to work iron. For myself, *ar-yan* is dark. It pulls warmth out of bodies any way you touch it. But some things need to change. Out there, Otus, iron gives a house two edges: breaking bronze, if we have to fight, and careful trade of it with influential partners. Some Noisy Boy grafted us good vines, so now we trade the wine I carried here; fiery-red, like my name. And island-veil, like this: many Cyclades mothers home with us, not waiting for heroes. Not two sets of loom-weights the same, and daughters of Canaan's kings fight over shipments for their gowns

--If I may, the best for last. You were born a priest-chief. Torn from that, like your father. I see pain in most of Karfi's eyes. See ahead then. I speak of our gardens of love. The Mysteries, and more. In Alashiya, Pyrrha said, lighting up in the sun, --our gardens are queen of life. Out of festival, holy communion, and healers. Out of funerals, marriage beds. She is more than natural ceremony. The listening on her damos benches tills the soil for wisest council. She finds good ties for trade. She answers pain with simples, comforts death. Many people came to Alashiya hurt by the mountain of fire, and see the world return before their eyes. What can you not grow there, seed of Dikte?

--My brothers and I will need a place like that. Because in doing what I tell you now, Pyrrha, we may go mad for awhile. What, why are you laughing?

--No, no, Pyrrha answered settling down. –I feel light inside. Like a girl glad to find fire in the mountains. I promise to listen, she said, --not forgetting you are crazy, to most Cretans

I did not want to lose Pyrrha's hands, so I waited. But that echo from lands below stung: we, crazy, while the lowlands worked their way out of ash paying Koreter's protection with their best. Good as it was to hear them mending, she did not withdraw at the rise in my blood

--Idiot Koreter, I finished. –Spider, he only looks a harmless little old man. His priests salt our memory, tell us that if we had a way, it was doomed as childish rot; and first and last, that we as Earthling-dirt owe kings our lives. Protection---from themselves! They march up here all weapons to count the last sheep. Houri, we cannot leave The Labyrinth his. Of course, I won't always be poison-mad, I tried to laugh. --I know how much is finished. Lady, help a stranded sailor

–Otus, she answered, --Alashiya will understand

Pyrrha's face was still, her eyelids down: her fine hands moved in feeling mine. --You know, Kia is right more times than wrong. But for me at least, sometimes she looks too far. She said once: *All things of substance pass away---gone where? Into dream. So dream is the last real thing: the only substance.* Now, I ask you!

Quick as water Pyrrha laughed, one eyebrow askew. We sat together, but not too long. She asked me to cloak her shoulders, and it breathed up something more wondrous than jasmine from her hair. --Shall we? she adjourned. --First the babe is born to hand. No cutting till we lay him on the Earth and look him over

This second day of moon and sun saw blessings of the trees and herds, and sanctuary offerings of little beasts in clay, pinched out in prayers for plenty. Karfi gave Pyrrha and her people fine welcome, but I wasn't much good to the rites from there. At once, the four full moons before we moved felt short, and a duty of a day now seemed interminable. I fought that, for the pull of poison that it was. But Makris, and Abas, pulling opposite ways, demanded a muster that night. Honeybee, too: *Convince us.* This fear already I had launched: people wanted to know things, now and plain. So there we were in open talk of killing, in the face of festival

--You know me, I began when the sun touched the mountains: with Pyrrha at my side, I was facing ten times the people who saw me dance, spread out in the twilight down and up the back-saddle of The Nail. --I ask no war. One night, one fight: a funeral-fire that will take us through the door to a new life. This day's feast and pouring, you met this great lady. Alashiya remembers, and reaches out with help. Ask Pyrrha and the people of her ships about tomorrow. Bottom-land and pasture, peace, trade---and, interesting evenings, I said to the men's light lusty laugh. --This one way out is true, and worth pushing back for. Stand up now, sisters, brothers. Speak!

--Get to the bones of it! called young Donos: weighing his chances still

--Alright, I said. --The worst thing first. This comes from Prax's mother, inside The Labyrinth, I began. --She stayed because, there, her hands help Crete the most:

Klawiphoros, they style her, Key-Bearer. She counts fifty red-beard men at arms around Koreter, his Companions. And, she says, the blue stallions stitched to their tunics look like brood-mares, fat with feed. A second troop, about forty Libu, hoof their sentry-work for pay. Long spears, for the fearsome show. But let one man or two step forward for a family, and sixty will do

--In we go, with Key-Bearer's help, and burn our way out to the ships. Understand, we will be coming from *inside* them. I know those turning halls. Abas knows that long spears lose, in close. Behind all this, our families slip down-country, and meet the boats. In Pyrrha, you see the good place waiting

--Sir! It was Abas standing up. --We don't have the weapons, or the metal

Yes, we did; and we had Kinuwa's skills to work them. There was a country house burned thirty years ago, burned in such frothing Achaian rage that it collapsed before they sacked it. Inside was a lion's share of ingots, a trading-hoard of ready-mixed bronze in Labrys-shape. I told about their chieftain raging at the hasty fire, set by the fools he had nursed on rage; and so, with a plan to double back and dig those ingots out, they had raged on forward to the next big house with horns. There, they found a quicker troop of kinsmen raging. Easy as ice, they all fell into fighting for that prize, and the red-beards who remembered anything happened to get killed

--The end, I finished with a thud, and the mountain laughed away the question. This had come thanks to a

very old woman of the Messara who, dying, let me hold
her hand, and asked my help to plough her hatred under.
The ingots, I told Abas, were his mission, if he'd take it. He
sat down more important, and men touched his shoulder

    --Are there kings in Alashiya? asked the wary
young Arge

    --No, Pyrrha answered her. --Are we missing
something?

    Pereko was restless in the laugh, but he kept his
vow through festival and did not speak. Up stood Winato,
with slow folding arms

    --Otus, this hangs on a whim of the wind. Poseidon
will not help Cretans to steal mainland boats. What if we
come bleeding through the house, and the sea is wild?
Their chariots will run us down

    Dark was falling, dread moving through the bodies
    --This fight, I said, --is in The Labyrinth. Bleed
them, Winato, and bows like Pereko's will serve until we
sail. I only say again, I shrugged, --that I am going

    --Well then, Winato answered, and he took a
redoubtable pause. It looked sure that his *No* from
yesterday was final, and might carry. Most people here
were like him, wild enough to live isolate and cold, but
keeping their heads down out of lightning. I failed to count
on Pyrrha feasting people's eyes

    --Well then, Winato finished. --You good men of
arms, and you, brother Abas, will teach us more. Teach us
till we know we will come through

    --Teach that to me! Norax joked; and Karfi went on

talking, through the starlight. At the first pale of sky, people turned home for the central day, and nothing was resolved. Except Abas, who was at my door before the sun

--Why, Otus, they're lining up to go. What I can't wait is to get back and start blade practice. We'll do with wooden weapons first, he said. --You, while I'm gone, have Kinuwa carve his pouring-moulds, and build the forge we should have raised already. We'll want a good hot furnace roaring for those talents

Their going made me glad, until we were twenty men short for that third day's double-spiral dances. More, the men young and old who danced wore their mountain-knives on show. Blast! Mother Zoe understood what they were saying. Ninna, who had shed her shawl, raised fists instead of palms in our weaving lines. This was my doing. I had opened the door. Solstice festival was light and shadow, and now nobody could look for spring without fear of unnatural blood

With the last two days we danced new movings of the sun against our mountains. Icy wind and blind gray walls of mist took turns again around Karfi. Pyrrha's people shivered, till even she broke down and pitied us aloud. We talked and talked when I wasn't chopping wood or helping Kinuwa hunt good stone. Nights, I envied the Alashiya men who piled with her for warmth

Abas came back in the last of that moon. They had the bronze, and by then, he had Pereko and Donos seeing to his orders with the others. *Bright and early on the barrens!* they kept on, while Abas pushed his lamb away and drank

--More men will show, once practice builds a few, he told me; and blast again, Norax, Melas and I needed fresh looks at Knossos

–What about your Prax, and Aktor, are they in?

--Drink up, Abas, rest. Ask them, I answered

--I will. By the way, Otus. Just to be proper, with a business you dislike. I respect your mind about the burning. But we just dug a king's treasure missed by fools

--You want pillage of the house, before we burn it

--No, no! Not pillage, Abas said, with the first hurt look he'd ever shown. –Do you think me less Cretan than you? Look at it this way. Knossos will have more than rusty bronze. Bind these men together, take that gold, and gold brings a man more men. Then, more gold. Do you follow? This is good for everybody

--Try to keep your head, was all I told him

The three of us slipped down off Karfi at twilight, goat-trail over path, woods over road. We slept the day in maquis thicket, and made Knossos valley the second night. It was crucial to stay clear until the last house-lamps along the slopes went dark. But when I saw our house again--- the knoll of her alabaster wings and stories, the red-pillar colonnades decked with smashed-down horns, her closed-up doors and overgrown walks---well, manly Melas be damned. I hid my face in both palms and took my heart's purge: done, it would be Karfi iron coming back. *Otus, look!* laughed Norax on point. Their dogs, the imbeciles had short-chained outside porches: they felt us off in the darkness, too, and barked, but nobody answered

We watched the hours from three hills under olive trees, picked out guard posts. With the blue stars of winter Labrys falling from the sky, we crept down to wade the stream under Labyrinth's southern foot and gardens. The cat-tail reeds both sides made cover. Then, deep-in under pilings of her causeway, we found my door to the water-tunnels. Our masters had blocked all these they found. To them, indoor toilets were womanish, so the house smelled like one. Our door was a narrow downspout fed off the tunnels, well in under Labyrinth's hill

We pulled back a tangled bank of dry creeper, and then took down the rocks and mud stuffed in by my younger hand. I stepped forward in alone, to see the way clear to Key-Bearer's part; and then slipped sideways between wet walls, in under the southwest wing. The great slab-stones had slanted, silt sucked my boots, but I knew those floors above to the corners. Hall by hall, I felt along cobwebby joists, and found overhead the slab intended. I pressed my upraised palms against it, trying to feel Key-Bearer. Behind my eyes, her shade gave way to spider Koreter's. *Go on snoring, king,* I had to whisper

We went in scared, came out relieved, and covered every sign. Now, the ships. We could run this road in half a morning, but we hid up instead, and took another night slipping field by hill down to Amnisos. Melas thought I was crying again, but it was joy of the sea, the night-black pounding pulses of her waves, the strong salt air. *She wants us to live, the ocean,* sang a voice out of memory here. Norax picked up a white chunk of pumice for his Fourogata

Three new stone-built quays, we saw: the fishing pinks slept high, the big Achaian vessels in long low sheds near the shingle. Inside was exemplary order, masts and spars, the sails dry-wrapped and oars in bundles, stacks of rolling-logs: six beasts, six oarloops to a side, and a Lion's eye each prow. Crews, guards? We followed late-hour skirls of music, and found some eating and splashing wine on the terrace of a house lit up near the water. Doubtless, more of them who might fight for their boats had charmed ways into other houses near. *Fast, and ferocious,* Norax mused, *or we will not win.* The smoke of those braziers made our mountain-bellies weep. Roasted mullet, sea-bass, octopus, and roe of urchin fresh in the spiny shell

--I like The Green, but not at my back, Melas worried in our hide. –Say that we do raise sixty men. How many get this far? Wind wrong, we won't have the oarsmen. Otus, who listens to the dead! Blast you, keep them where they are, hungry, jealous, vicious. I will not have Aktor down here dodging Libu javelins. Poseidon help my brain, but I want this! Talk, Norax! You have the Libu blackguard's blood

--Lower your voice, and calm down, Norax told him. –Brothers, look. Family used to say that if Libu have a house, it's dug into Libu ground. Their life is circles, oasis to pasture, with their animals and rains. So, these Knossos Libu will go far, to live like townsmen. Otus, said Norax lifting up a closing fist. –Griffin first take Koreter's Companions, man and mother's son. A stranded Libu, then, might come to terms

--Terms! What terms? Melas scoffed

--Pulling oars for a stake in Alashiya. Would you bleed for a boat, and then answer a hungry Lion? And, no more honey of the wagtails of Amnisos

--Well! What can go wrong, Melas ended

So it went as we talked the way home---every part of this a clutch of fear, work and problems. Half-way back, before we faced Karfi, we hid up another day to do nothing but talk. What night, Keeper of Days, would be The Labyrinth's last? Key-Bearer chose it: the fourth month's second night with no moon, before the fifth one's new little horns showed in the sky. The dead were said to walk those hours, and wise Achaians kept indoors. Till then, we had three moons. Melas, the gnat, had to know how Prax's mother talked with her mountain-man. I asked him how many highland ya-yas muled their tribute down to Koreter. *Women! Dreamers who never sleep*, he grumbled

--Watch now, Norax told us. He picked a pine-cone for each ship and one green needle for a man. If we had to row six boats, every two Karfi men would need a third. More, sixty men could take only two family each, plus a dozen-odd spaces---because it was fifteen riders to a ship, and a Great Green full of corpses who pushed their luck

So, to our shock, it was two out of five on The Nail going anywhere come spring. Better that pain, than leaving people to the Lion. In time, we could pluck more off Crete's wild southern beaches. But not until the first of us opened the door

--Mountain, lift me up! Norax shouted when we

sighted Karfi home. He'd used to say The Nail on her ridge was a beaten man's last tooth. Now I felt the granite of his son alive in him, and shouted likewise: I saw the prow of a great stone ship abreast a wave. Melas sang *Oh, peace, and rest!* We got almost none from the first climb back

The women who built ovens had plastered Kinuwa's forge, and its stack as tall as a man was roaring. Kinuwa's old father oversaw the work, and he who had grudged every day up here was strutting his young days' rooster. We saw the moulds of wicked blades and points those two had cut, and the forge's bronze poured in: below The Nail's back hills, a spreading barren of cut trees kept feeding charcoal to the beast

The clouds about us hid the smokes like help. And there, good Abas ran blade practice. Makris said the twenty men who fetched that bronze were turning out, and some few more. Others wanted in, except for Fourogata's knife and Mother Zoe's words

What words? He said that Zoe had walked into their first dawn practice. *So!* she said with fists on hips. *This is on? You break our way of council, to protect it?* Zoe would have done more, said Makris. Now it was Ninna who had turned to the dark moon, and she was pulling Mother to let be, to let Abas run

--Speak of the man, Makris told me before he let me sleep. –You need to know when you see your son Prax. Abas beat him to a pulp. Yes, I mean Prax was first man on the barren, that first morning. Abas used Prax to show the stakes of any weakness. Well, Prax just kept on getting up, be proud, till Abas finished him. Otus, blast the truth! I'd see Little Zeus bleed Prax again, if it helps a poet stay alive

I listened. From that night together, we helped Prax to understand, and my iron slept beside me that I wake each day more like Norax: hard, and none more loving with his house. As it turned out, this time Norax told The Nail everything we learned. Melas laid his damokouros face across his worries: Norax made the mountain feel it could and should be done. Families argued in and out. By the dark of that first moon, men were bringing more men to the barren

One evening, with a crowd of us keeping warm with wine and music in Honeybee's house, the young head-man of Pyrrha's fifteen came to find her. His style was Squiddy, long and gangly with merry bug-eyes either side of a raw tuber nose: Podargos was showing his men good hunting. Squiddy knocked and ducked inside to us, and took off his cropped-feather headband. He looked so grave that we asked him who had died

--Friends, he answered. --The lot of us here talked this well. I speak for ten of Pyrrha's crew like me, who are for this fight. Excuse the other five of us: in Ya, our home, we never shame the choice. So, understand, Squiddy went on. –The world is circles. Someday, you Cretans will help Ya. Take us on, ten Squiddies, yes? Good, good! he reveled with a clumsy hug around the table

–More! Squiddy put in. –Pyrrha's three good ships with thirty crew sleep south of here, at Myrtos. This moon, I will make the trek myself, and spring, they can bring our boats around to Malia. See? They beach and wait for us, hiding in plain sight, just season's visitors, he laughed

--Squiddy, Pyrrha said, --let me show your crown. See? A wheel of crane-feathers, red, white, black. Cranes taught Crete her farmers' season-times. They fly higher than eagles, far: they never lose their way, and they carry counsel from the dead. Here, then, I pour for you, brothers of our family

The wheel of days kept turning, dark and light, light and shadow. When Squiddy announced for the ten Alashiya, that was the day we raised our sixty from Karfi: more, we had to choose the last few out. No mountain-milk doubled our strength as fast as Squiddy's ten, with their jaw-hook blades and axes and big bows. All in, with half the mountain watching, we were tossing stones like medicine-balls when Winato asked Squiddy who, back home, was worth a fight. Good man, good man

--We feud. Men will, Squiddy shrugged. --The worst are men who cross the sea for kings. Times---not too often, when they feel big---their sons, in boats, pay Ya some visits worth revenge. So we understand yours

No more talking! If every man had a trick to teach, Abas worked us for our lives. Blade-practice day by night, no matter how cold or preposterous it was to be out there in windy snow, wrestling, sparring, scrambling up and down the stony mountainsides. Abas' pair-off drills for blocks and close work turned arms black and blue. Weeks along, he said we should practice clearing lanes and houses on The Nail as if they were Labyrinth halls: it frightened every household, but even Norax found himself in favor. So was Abas building his standing as we learned to hack and push and master a corridor, or turn a spear with your back against a wall

    --The way we're going, Norax warned me, --we had better bring him in somehow. Help Abas belong with some household. Without that, I feel him the kind of man who starts to think they all belong to him

    --Suggestion?

    --Don't know. Your house? I found my place when I told from my belly what made me climb The Nail, and hearing others. Maybe, start with what Abas wanted to hear. About Theseus

    Norax worked it a few nights later, inviting Abas to drink and counsel *with just the head men*, as Norax said it. We drank more than we talked the plan so far, and then by design, Melas pretended to need help home from Norax. I fed the fire, and the drink and the dreaming red embers eased Abas down into rare long silence

    --I knew Theseus. And the secrets of power that Theseus thought he wanted. Do you know, Abas, why the damos of family women here keep a washed-up priest-chief like me in their circles and confidence? Because we live at Ariadne's altar. Not the particular girl with the lovely crown of hair, who liked wild venison and dance and mountain music. Whose voice in song could turn men inside-out. We mean the woman who rose to that office, because her learning and her gifts from nature showed us what we were. Young, she was what Mother Zoe is. Our memory of what we are and have been, for as long as the damos remembered

--Theseus? said Abas, but without much the usual impatience

--On his way. Just understand what was waiting for Theseus here, back when all of us were young. The Labyrinth was no palace for a princess, let alone a king. Our first families built it in their own midst, for all the clans' different ways of ceremony. Our family, then, Ariadne's family, were Keepers of Days for the island, sun by moon by shadow on them both. The towns of Crete, born to be rivals, built places like Knossos, and took their turns at who could raise the bigger wilder festival. Strange now, to think how the annual fist-fights worked to keep the main peace fresh

--I chanced to be born Ariadne's younger brother, and watched her become the walking inheritance of all of this. The damos lifted her to the Throne of Days. It was Theseus and his days driving her courage, and no one did more to keep our pride in a marriage forced on her, to hold the peace between Crete and mainland. Her altar is memory and courage in the women on this Nail

--Hear-tell, Abas opined, --that at my age Theseus cleared the mainland roads of robbers. Not bad, doing for the land what Crete did for the sea

--Not quite. He was one of many things changing. And when Knossos sent our older brother to say that we noticed, Athens gave him a spear in his back. He came home ashes in a jar. My father pulled every thread of our web, and massed a war-fleet. I sailed with him, and Athens took the choice that we gave. We bluffed them down, and took thirteen youths to Crete, to learn the web of the world and bring it home

--Theseus was covered with wild red hair, brawny, loud, cunning. He was our great hope, from the first day I bristled at him. What choked me was our family's gamble that somehow, this bull from the sea might prove himself, and wed Ariadne. My intended queen

--So, years this fellow lived with us. His charge of men and women, one by one, could bear to learn. For Theseus this was rank captivity, his next great trial from his gods to bear toward glory. Or something like that. It meant nothing we had spared him and Athens. He thought he was on to something when he found Ariadne what he called, only a girl. Back of all his best moments, a broken world was coming. He detested obligation, there could be no edge or limits but his own

--Theseus guessed our thoughts for him, and made them twisted-true. In the Great Year of my father's willing sacrifice, Theseus killed him, with his fists. It was perfect. Execute him, and take on war with both sides of the mainland. If Ariadne married him, we blessed his sacrilege. Our house was torn apart, and the island staggered to see these things unfold from Knossos

--Theseus respected Ariadne where it suited him. But he was bred to some mission beyond his own brain, no man for the damos' every view. Ariadne almost broke between him and Crete's indignation. Out of seeming nowhere, our mother was killed by a boy gone as crazy as the world. Matricide, here. Then it got worse. The island Thera's mountain woke up in fire

--Under the smoke and ash, the best of Crete's young women came to Ariadne's side. One of them, Phaedra, knew she had Theseus' eye, and tried to grow things Ariadne planted. She got less than our queen for it. When the mountain exploded, and the great waves crushed our coasts, Theseus disappeared. The mainland, from Mykenai to Athens, had built a fleet for war. And it was coming

--Our ships were stretched then, Rhodes to Sicily. I did my admiralty-duty, gathered our brothers in off the sea to come home and guard our waters. And this was what put them in front of the waves, that sucked them up and smashed them to a wall of bloody kindling. Ships miles inland. Ships in trees. Ariadne and I found each other in our people. Some we sent abroad with boats to hand. Then we waited. When Theseus came out to join his brothers pouring onto our beaches, he showed the whooping warriors whom to kill enroute to Knossos. I threw my sword and life at what he meant for her

--He had the fearful sense not to rape Ariadne. He raped me. His soldiers killed whom they feared, or shipped who pleased them home for slaves. Theseus basked some weeks of feast and looting. Good sport mopping up resistance, snapping his fellows back to hand. He dabbled as he pleased in religion and government, and then he got bored

--But what to do with Ariadne. He couldn't take her home, and let mainland sheep see what she was. Nor leave her here with all that honor. He worked it out by taking her hostage for my servitude, and then because she kept talking, he dumped her off his farewell ship. Trying to take her back, I killed a man, and that was what killed Ariadne. Our war to possess her. She saw me spear an Achaian guard, cried out as the world went through her, and there was nothing since to cut me so. Her life was prayer that peace prevail in the face of blood. I was her Sweet Wine, her champion, and even that our blind white bulls had turned

--Theseus sailed not home, but to Athens, where a throne and a citadel waited: he only had to help his father off them. He proclaimed himself a new force of mainland law, a cry not pleasing to The Lion of Mykenai. Where he tried to plant his Cretan seed, he found no field but walled-up warlords, and gods of the topsoil dreamed up by priests. His peace needed walls for his cities and loot from the islands

--Bored again, he sent for another Cretan woman to amuse him, the young wood-pigeon Phaedra. Her grief for Ariadne turned her sharp and stealthy as your knife. In Phaedra, Theseus' crimes tore his house out by the roots. It cost her life, but it shattered his. So, what great surprise at his end we heard from Zoe. Banished by his own, he jumped a cliff. Well then, Abas? Even here you find women with happiness to give, because we know who won. We *are* who really won, as we remember

Silence. I had told not a Theseus he wanted. Nor did our captain of attack even touch the floating question: *She lived to keep the peace, and you honor her with blood?* It was all I knew that the voices of our graves said there could be no walking away. There with Abas gazing into flame and embers, I knew afresh how much he desired what was coming

–What about you, Abas? Mount Ida, wasn't it?

--It ended, he answered like a wall. And he took up drinking more. A kind of blind raw hate of everything set his jaw and took his eyes, till he said he had to go and sleep. *Why go?* I wanted to say. *You're sleeping now*

So it went. Each sun, first strength went into strength, with speed and evil tricks aimed for the nose. We had big men to beat, and boats to row. With the hook of the third new moon, Abas talked his worry about Amnisos. That turned into drills very queer on a mountain. Teams of us relayed rolling-logs back to front for an invisible ship. Men on stump-seats six to a side rowed grooves into the snow: as one, and under fire of rocks and sticks

More trees cut off the mountain made us practice-masts and yards, and full moon watched us hoist and brail up patched-together skins. Taking turns, doubling, alternating, each man was learning every part. Donos, and Winato too, began to like our chances

The day of equal dark and light fed hope. The crown of this, men said, came with the going of third moon. Mother Zoe, with Ninna and Honeybee, walked out toward us across the night-black field of stumps. We saw their shapes coming against the sky's great Labrys. And out came three faces white as corpses with the blood gone. We had to call the bolting men back. Abas was one. And Mother Zoe laughed, with us

--These, my sons, are the faces *you* will show, come Griffin down from Dikte! she promised, and the man of us loosed her a shrieking roaring sound

We knew ourselves the fear around us, and loved our women's medicines. Winter jars were hollowing out, but Ninna made a point of feasting men at arms: her house we liked for wild goat melting in your mouth, hot soothing teas, and music of her friends. We were there with the final fourth moon swelling in the sky, and Melas the jovial lord of court. I was troubled that Prax had stopped his singing, and a little thing broke worse between Abas and Norax. It never came to knives, except the words a drunken Abas cast behind him, storming out

--What man tells a man his limits? I make men weapons, I keep you safe. I want first claim! he told the house. --Wake up, Otus, what do you think made lords of Melas' brothers. Blast old blood, I want what I deserve!

Men were leaving, sour, and then it was Melas's turn. He took me outside the house in moonlight, facing snowy Dikte

--Weather is going to break, he said. --I wonder when Abas will. First time we talked this, I said there is your traitor. A man with the will to shill for Lions. Now I think him maybe mad, gone poison-sick. Otus, this is good we talk. You know me for nothing like that. But what are we going to do---I mean

--With the Companions' women and children, I finished for him: I had drunk a surly share myself. –You mean, with Koreter's people not under arms. I don't know. But a dread in me grieves for them, as if I do know

--Well, Melas broke in, --I think I have a right to some, for this house. You know the sweat begins in Alashiya. I don't like it, Otus, but we will need slaves

I stilled my feet and only looked away. Ugly jokes were going round about the men we meant to kill. *Why is Koreter a spider? Because Achaians only build where they can suck good traffic on the fly.* When they talked Poseidon, they had no word to say was he a *lord*, or a *husband*? Cretans knew what was hiding in that hole. And the man I thought I knew was quite in earnest

--Melas. Ninna would say, make them cousins

--Fine, cousins. That is not what Koreter's disappointed nobles will call us, when we chop up their men. Better they go to my house, than Abas'

--Really! Have you cut shares?

--He has nothing, exactly! Melas said. --You or I, or Norax can make something from this. Abas is---dust

I wished for more raki, and having none, wanted to slap him. –You know, I said, --we have no sailing-space for such. Melas, of all preposterous things

--Nonsense! he said with a half-turn away. --Norax counts a dozen in after each man brings his pair. Otus, you know why there will be room

--This builds in blood

--Well! Hail brother! Melas breezed. –Who, they say, goes harder than Crete's crazy Boy on people who reject him? Fine. We will see what happens, he said with a waggle of his beard. --At least we spoke to this. Good night then, Melas said; and he left me looking at the monstrous mountain in the moonlight

I refuged in our ways. With the pourings at the center of our rites came offering-meals that fed our sleeping families, and the fourth moon's fullness crowded people in for the high two nights of them. Raw goat and bull of sacrifice we passed in bowls across our benches, our facing pairs of Karfi stones, with bloody lips and fingers. Some ate full-silent: others tore aloud into grief long-sleeping in this place, and both worlds listened

Final things were passing every way: Donos and his son Butes leaving Arge, all hoping for Malia; Kinuwa choosing his two fierce parents for his pair, and they had eyes for metals under earth. Pereko, taking Cissia the potter who could row, and his son at arms Oka smashing down our straw-men targets, sick with the leaving of their girl-child Eos. The more it meant when Mother Zoe called me out one last day: a gift was here on behalf of the mountain. It was Little Zoe's coming with my sons

--Because this is all your fault, Mother Zoe cracked. –You listen now. The girl is luck for everyone. So, we give her your thirteenth place. Zoe, ride and guide the monster! Say your nickname, girl. You are my Europa doubling backwards, if you can!

The weather warmed the mountain. Our legs and grips had doubled, bodies felt quicker with half our clothes, and surer feet. Everybody bound their hair for luck of wind and sea, and when the crimson poppies opened to the sun, we were leaving. We brought up one last bull from the meadows of Lasithi. The last and first rite was going to be a night walk, westward to the feet of Dikte, and the cave

Once more, days before our going, our gardens of love in the houses of Karfi. Winter made my hands two hammers, and they marveled the softness and the curves, the tenderness and heat. So small, women felt in my arms, that only in them did I worry death; them without the bull that feared no dying, that they live. My treasure-jewels, my figs, I poured out roaring and heard the bellows of my brothers, house and mountain: women trilled and danced upon our tongues, fingers spiraling their nipples. And Pyrrha, door between worlds, opened to me. Her first touch had come with words from a dream, and her love was another. Bull-leaper, sweet rider, eyes of thirteen daemons, glorious grove delicious. In the half-light of beeswax candles in my house we rocked and ploughed, I carried off her women-folk and she rode the rocking sea at mast. Eyes dark within black tresses of her hair, the locks down over her bird-soft breasts and the serpent-sway of her back arching as she rode. She liked to lay me out and crouch beside me on my fingers, moaning serpent in her mouth. We laughed, because from the first, even our feet made love, like a double pair of long-lost mates

She fed me a Syrian story of a temple in the deep, the house of Ea. A god of sweet waters, Pyrrha winked, who loved mankind. Not so all the gods of Syrians. Some, annoyed with the noise men made, sent a flood to wipe them out. So, Ea found a man, Utnapishtim, the son of a king, first priest of a city before this flood: a maker of peace, a trickster not always kind, a man named to see life and to find it. *Tear down your house*, Ea warned this man, *and build of it a boat*. Then, seven days and nights poured down a killing-flood. Alone, Utnapishtim found land, and life unlooked-for

--Otus, trust your guides! I am here to put real things of hope into your hands. Makris calls you Keret. Only, Keret was bluffing, when he swore to burn the city that made captive his beloved, lost in darkness. Still I think of you in his tale's end: *He shall live at the mouths of rivers*

Pyrrha, Pyrrha, so much arising since I fell down, and you climbed up: bright answer to the blackest thing inside me

Sunset of our going, spur of the green, Makris drummed us down to the tombs. We offered Bull there, sang, slashed our arms and shook them hard to leave our thanks, and raise men's wrath. *Oh-lo-lo-lo, Oh-lo-lo-lo-lo-lo* the women trilled us from above, and the din of cries filled every lane, the homes we built, the tombs our bones had longed for

Had we not all died, and risen? Then, down the mountain's western trail: Mother Zoe raised and waved one torch beneath the sky, lit from our Nail's last fire

I was walking toward the sun setting into the mountains, people gathering to follow as wrens and goldcrests sang the twilight. Mother Zoe, cowled in black below, herald of a dream watched to see what gesture. I turned to The Nail and laid my brow to stone and dust. Then, eye to eye she gave me a torch, and lit it from her own: each person coming on took one the same. So we walked, Little Zoe's hand in mine: ahead no light but ours and the vast red sky. The trail descended between dark hills, and into the plateau

Before us swung the great open circle of Lasithi, ringed with mountains, as level as liquid in a cup, and Dikte watched in her white spring crown. Pyrrha too had dreaming in her face as she took Mother Zoe out into the grass: they stood a parting-point, and left by right Zoe cast a circle of us, five hundred torches bright. For a long time we stood there breathing, drums gone silent, waiting the eyes of the stars

Makris looked warm in the fleece I gave: it seemed beyond belief to never meet again. I never said goodbye at Ariadne's grave. She was with me tonight between the worlds, in the voices singing on this raw blind edge of things, in hope. Such a sight, this burning circle ringed with mountains and the stars, that my spirit eased beyond itself. Alive was pain and joy with equal peace

Prax had come through, his hard ease said it, the grace of his hand to his blade-hilt, torch high. He had a song near-finished

Gold is the home of Sun's reflection
Silver the Moon cries
Family is resurrection

--Need the last line, Prax said, and I smiled, but warned him to let it rest until we were oarsmen

--Finish, and begin! Mother Zoe cried, with her torch high at the center of us, her free hand beckoning closer. --Yonder our mother, sisters and brothers. Take her with you, kourai and kouri. Want to tell you something, though. Do you see this garden, in our midst? Always, you are in it. Act like it. Now I'm going to give you, plain, the way we did old times, your mothers' secrets to help find a way. Sisters and brothers, whatever becomes of you, remember this place where our one soul was born. Come times you want to die: All-Giver is a monster, too. But Dikte is touchstone. The core of our ways to the light

--One way is, to love someone, Zoe said. --To love until your dead skin drops like Snake's. You can be grateful, over all you lose. And, you can consent: consent to know this dream your own. To love, be grateful, consent: remember! Alright, that's all I have to say, goodbye, Zoe finished with a flippant cast of one hand, turning her back. --Farewell

She broke the circle and disappeared away through the combing grass, going up to the cave. Never her old shoulders back so far and straight, as if she had resolved on and arranged her own abandonment, to scatter living seed abroad. Nobody moved, at first. I saw not even Ninna quite in tears, for the plateau's air ran upon our skin, every stone and star and peep of creature perfect and in place, like jewels in the veil of things

The waning moon came up yellow, like a magic boat's curved yard. My place was first with Zoe in the cave, and I climbed the twisted trail to the torch-lit precinct, unchanged to the stone since my father taught me here. Overhead, a mossy shear of limestone bigger than a ship hung dripping down, hairy with lichen and nests of fork-tail swifts: under this, a mouth into the Earth, green and wet as you worked down in along the boulders

Down, and torchlight showed the ceilings growing fangs every color, livid like the things inside a body. Down, and in the first grotto, pillars big as oaks, man-shapes, pregnant crones oozing water, mock-faced hunchbacks, guardians to pass: the deeper underground, your own sounds loud and louder. I went past some monstrous thing growing off the wall like liquid rock, with a thousand labial grooves across its jaw; and tucked in almost every groove, some rusting prayer, a tiny Labrys of green bronze, little animals in votive clay or people's limbs that needed healing. Sealstones cut with signs of their visions. I turned and found a being at my side

The thing was to breathe as the caverns took you down, and closed dark silence round your crackling torch. There was icy water to wade now, but dittany-incense rising past me. The walls turned, and beyond was a massive crevice leaking light

She was seated at the cross-legged feet of a shape

five times her size coming out of the wall: wings outspread but ragged, older than time, and a face of molten rock half-crone, half-insect like a mantis. I froze like prey. When I managed to move before her, fist-to-brow, she kissed Labrys at my neck and hung a leather pouch: white gypsum powder. She had the same for each man's face before the Labyrinth's door of life

In this place, care and question melted in your hands. I wet my palms on icy stone, pressed them to my face, and turned without farewell. Sorrowing to lose her, I began to climb away. Down were come Podargos with his roarer, his last gift; Prax with our best vase to pour. Little Zoe cupped three corn-poppies: Ninna held the saffron shawl we thought she burned, and Honeybee's hair was a big strong knot behind her neck. The flow of men down in with torches flickered overhead the cave-roof's spikey hollows: Norax and Oinops, Squiddy's men, Winato and Phitios, Donos and his son Butes. Aktor steadying Melas down the turns, his father in a cold sweat worse than the undulating walls

I came out into night air balmed with diktamos and artemisia, and music in the soft-sway rhythms of our camp below. Halfway down the cave's doubling path, Abas stepped out of the brush and stood there, facing me ten steps off, his smirking face death-white already. No cave nonsense for the man. Well? Was this to see if I would spook, or draw? A hollow depth inside me smiled, and I asked him how he got ready to die

--I get ready to win, Abas smiled right back

--Enjoy, I said

I walked down past him, wanting nothing but a pair of feet moving with this medicine night, and the keening bodies' sway beneath blue stars. Pyrrha waited with her hands out, like a bull-leap catcher in a fresco

--You may feel a sharp pain, she said.

3

At our descent the wind turned out of the south, gusting relentless down the mountains hot and dry, and shoving at our backs as we reached Knossos. Spring night had the sea's salt cool there, gardenia and jasmine along the valley's riverbanks. But this was heat off a desert, squalls of sand that rattled trees and drove waves backward from the shore. We laughed to call ourselves the first Cretans to revel in its curse, because it was perfect to push our boats out. Cicadas hatched too this year, and the valley's cypress and tamarisks rang the loud grindings of their wings

We moved like weapons in the dark, slipping to the west before Knossos valley, away from the town and up behind the long dark hill overlooking it. These were burial-grounds, with Labrys-shapes sunk in Earth, and round tombs of overgrown stone. We lay there hours to make the best watch drowse, and I stole up and down our squads, hammering plans

Somebody showed me a tomb torn open, its portal a scatter of shards, rags and bones. I did my best, then filled my fists with soil. --Thirty years we let this pass, I finished. --Not tonight

When the last Cretan servant had gone home and the lights of their houses guttered out, we came downhill and into the ravine where the stream's west leg ran spring-

high over rocks. For all we knew, they ate their dogs,
because we heard none. We crossed the waist-high icy
water, moved in under the southwest wing and gardens,
then crowded ourselves into shadows of the causeway
pilings. Most of us wore little more than kilts and boots
and small round shields on our arms, our way to turn the
naked body's terror on our foes. But in the dark we had
layers of cover, the wind and grinding trees: we saw no
guard at post or corner. Not even Libu liked these nights,
and most Labyrinth porches wore their shutters. What
lights we saw were drowsy flickers. *The contempt!* Norax
said. I had always known Achaians men to leave the boat
unmoored, for all their pride and glee at the steering-oar

At our entrance we softly pulled back creeper, and
cleared stones. All began to white their faces. I saw Prax
tremble at my own. I turned him and pointed Kephala and
the house. Still luminous, her white facades three levels up
the hill, the clusters of her shrines and shops, her crypts
and living-quarters. Far side of her central court up there,
the whole upper east wing was the same great slide of
rubble made by Earthbull, under patches of unfixed roof
askew with broken horns. Still, from here we saw one
inside-wall of a portico over the causeway, with painted
proud young men of our inland houses bearing vessels
and first-fruits up a colonnaded stair

--Every pillar remembers that life, Prax whispered.
–And, betrayal of your queen

--Look at me. Do not think, and do not drop your
guard, until we sail

My son and I breathed deep, and I turned for the open black door. Nothing waited but fulfillment of a part, and sooner or later, sleep

--Mountain, Mother Darkness, be pleased!

I squeezed in again side-on between wet walls, Norax behind me, then Melas. The tunnel's dark was absolute. One scrape of metal on stone behind me, a curse or a whimper, and I stopped to make them sweat till silent. First turn; then deeper-in, my eyes reaching up to find and finger-count the joists, where solid blocks became the halls above. Having given, being taken up: second turn, full in under the west wing now. Blind, counting, remembering feet and faces at a thousand walks up there, pouring blood around great pillars in the offering-crypts: communion-meals with family on the benches. I groped one more turn of walls, and we had made it

There was now no slab of floor to hand above: Key Bearer had pulled it. I took hold on the edges of the portal, got my head up through, and found myself inside a big round-belly storage jar for grain, the bottom tapped out, its foot just big enough around to hide our door. It was tall as a man, the lid was on, but under the jar she had tucked one shim for a crack of light. I eased back down, and listened. Then, to my nod, Norax squinted and made a brutal pout, and he looped his hands

I drew my iron, put my foot in his stirrup and Norax launched me---twice-hard as expected. It drove my blade upward too, and it struck away the lid. Bouncing down on edge it ran off a crazy wheel, then tipped and smashed on the floor-slabs. I had to clamber up and hop free off the whole egg's wobbling rim

Three things hit with my feet. The great jar needed wrestling off the hole. Then, where we were---in a square ceremonial audience-hall with pairs of pillars to each side, now shocking blue to the painted posts. And, the old man's instant scream. A priest alone at the hall's far end had startled from his napping-bench, his robe pale-blue from silver locks to sandals. He jumped up, saw my face and sword, and in this half-light of four little lamps his look flashed---disbelief, then rage, and then a kind of wide-eyed swoon. He wilted, turned and ran without knees for the corridor rightward: the central court was fifty feet too far. Norax had Melas on his feet as I caught the club of silver hair. I was no more. I dragged him back and he screamed not curses, not for mercy, gods or guards, but to himself. *It cannot be! It cannot be!*

For his life he could have been Makris: I had nothing to say and his blue eyes watched a death-white daemon from someplace called the world drive sword through his plexus. He sucked air, his face blanched, he withered, and went down. Foot to his chest, I pulled, and blood bubbled through the white stallion on his robe. Karfi men were pouring up into the hall and I left him there, a mask of disbelief

Norax, Abas, Melas kept the men in order of their parts, and I prowled up that mouth of corridor leading out to the central court. The house felt so quiet that I heard swoops of wind: not a houseboy had answered the crash.

Thirty-six, thirty-seven men and more with white faces of nightmare up from the underworld, the highland underground, afraid, swords out, nocking arrows. Melas was turning in place, the blue walls a dazzling surround of country hills, and pairs of stallions rampant, roaming

My blooded blade pointed the inside corridor: Norax, Melas, Kinuwa and Donos took twenty swords that way. *Brothers, nothing stop us but our families' eyes!* Their part, to take the whole west wing's long hall of storage, and then reverse direction, turning right round that corridor's end. That led through the northwest precinct's tightest turn, where the Libu guards had quarters in old storerooms. Kill as they would, Norax meant to trap and talk the Libu out of fight---or drive them out the corridor's far door, and onto the central court. By then, I'd have my dozen swarming out from this end, and the Libu's backs in front of us, with bows like Pereko's

Prax at my back. Now came Abas up beside me at the central court threshold. Twenty-six men cat-crouched behind him, poised to cross and strike straight into what remained of The Labyrinth's east wing. Down off the great turning stairway descending that side, Koreter's Companions and their families had fixed up our home, Ariadne's rooms, her breezy birdy lightwells, her dog-leg stair to mother's halls facing gardens, the river and morning sun. We meant to make the house jam them up and now we heard the first screams and blades and smashing-sounds out of Norax's corridor. Abas sprang out into the open and his twenty-six crossed court after him.

No sound but a blast of wind: they dropped in pairs down into the great stairwell, and Squiddy last looked back our way with some foolish gangly gesture of excitement

Out of Norax's corridor a sound like snapping metal trees, a melee of murder: we thirteen fought our feet to wait, but it was not long till bloody clatter came bursting backwards out that far door. As hoped: Norax and Melas were driving the Libu. They came out to regroup more than twenty-strong, set their wounded down behind them on the stones and shouldered tall man-covering shields, to get a foothold

We let them deploy their backs to us: another ten backed their way out, to a man large and burly, sleek legs like horses' under blue gold-belted kilts, and many in round bronze helmets we had never seen, with little horns flanking a disc. Cold well-drilled professionals like their fathers on ships of the line; and all at once these men made a sound like lions with empty bellies. I let Prax go and screamed our battle-name. Arrows, javelins loosed and sang and struck like Griffin-wings. *--Meee-nohhh-taaa-vvvrohhh!* We charged them as three of their men fell down screaming, hurling ourselves up-court with our left the west wing's porticoes, crypts and the great pillar-shrine

In fear my eye never left those we were charging, and still it saw the lines along west wing stones where mainland claws had scratched gold pittance off the walls. That was where my howl like a running animal's began, because right here too that ignorant prick had rammed his member of the sun into me, torn and pounded my intestines as the gift of his will triumphant. Now that pain remembered became mine. Kill! Kill! The Libu folded smoothly back into the northwest corner as their shields took second volley. Our faces made some of them cry aloud, but nowhere to go: they had barred their masters' fortified north gate on their own backs. Chop them up!

There the four doorways down into the crimson chamber of the throne. I knew he was in there, spider Koreter. Its sunken anteroom threw light of lamps across the Libu, thrust-and-shoving hard to hold back Norax. Just as we closed, the one sure Libu officer spilled out from the inside slaughter. He was tallest though he had lost his helm, a sword-sling of zebra down his side, blood-splashed: in a thrice the man dodged two arrows, his eyes took in the house, and when he shouted, half his men again moved back to brace for us, long spearpoints waiting and behind them hook-blade knives

Hot wind raked the courtyard night. We gave ourselves to death to see them face more than hungry mobs. Shields and bodies smashed together

I lost everything except the Libu head high over me who took my blow and shoved my shield-arm back with his wall of zebra. Caught as he was without spear or helmet, I was overmatched, and his feathered fighting-arm with the hook looked thick as an oarsman's coming down. Instead of shield, I parried, and iron broke his bronze. He howled and tried to bull me over. I hooked my sword down over the top of his shield and felt it stab. He went down shrieking clutching the spraying hole where his broad nose met his eye: I turned low and swung to clear about me, and turned again

Men hacked and grappled, stabbed and fell. Whoever killed turned to stab another man hacking at a brother. Pereko's bows shot for necks or knees, but all was savage tangle between the last Libu still backing out of the corridor and our second push hard into them. I killed another man who took his eye off me when an arrow came through his shield: we knew only them from us and I lost track of Prax. They were too many men for my dozen to finish, but they started making sounds as if they saw the right weapons in wrong hands. We heard the beast coming, Norax fighting his way out, but Melas I saw first of those men. Our eyes met like closing Griffin-jaws and his face of murderous abandon shrieked to see us. I whipped my head around for the east wing at our backs

Kinuwa lay closer, screaming through the red coming out his mouth. The horn-headed Libu over him jerked out his spear with eyes for me: an arrow sang right past my ear and through his neck. Other side that instant, a Libu stabbed Donos full-through. Him I opened sideways through the liver because his blade was stuck in Donos, and when he fell I managed to drag Donos back with his plexus pumping blood. A tall broad-nosed man came over corpses and flung me down his shield: an arrow burst through his arm. Shocked, he staggered, grimaced and tore it through, still wanting me for his friend. A second arrow to his heart rolled up his eyes

There was Norax, his shoulder stabbed but driving

his last men out into this fight. I twisted the flesh of my arm to keep my senses. The Libu officer at their core raised his spear high and level, and began to sing. His voice came rich to resurrect their best, and I signaled Norax

--Sons of Libu! Norax shouted as he pulled a man back from landing blows. --In the name of your Mountain of the Horns of the Earth! Fight no more, we are your brothers *Keftiu*! *Keftiu*! Norax said, pounding his palm to his chest. --See this man? Minos, Minos! *Keftiu*, in the speech of a dog called Pharaoh! May his tiny root drop off!

The packed-together Libu heard, saw their captain stop to listen; and Norax's last made him grin with all his yellow teeth. His cool in such a corner helped to snap our brothers from their rage, and I knew I needed this man, house and heart. But that moment in the falling-off brought savage noises to our backs from inside the east wing: screams, blows and blade-clatter were coming up the stairs this way. It had to be that Achaian Companions were beating back Abas' men. If so, we had no hold on the eastern doors, and somebody sure got out to rouse the valley. We might get trapped

--Hold! Back off! Let them choose! I screamed, pulling men back all I could: Melas helped Norax's Oinops to break off, with sounds for soothing horses. --Pereko! I cried: he brought his men up sharp into half a ring, bows at stretch. Next volley, their captain looked to lose a third of his brothers standing

--Your fathers good sailors, in Moon King ships! *There* our enemies, not you!

--*Na-bacchh*! the captain shouted, and before our eyes, these Libu pulled back in kind, though brothers lay bleeding with our own. The word again: this time they snapped their spears point-up, and thumped once the bottoms of their shields. Mouths hard, their captain gazed *What now* through my eyes. Hot night-wind swooped around us and I was sick with how fast this had to be decided. Their captain lifted his chin

--You, he said, with a voice deep but curious. --The last, they tell killed? What is your name

--Otus. Yesterday, I was *De-u-ka-ri-jo*. A man of Labrys. Minos of Ariadne, Wanassa of this house

--Deucalion. This is---a good place no more

--Tell me your name, I said, glad for the news

--Merire: meh-*ree*-ray. So, you come for your house

--To burn the house, Merire, I said: he understood faster than some on Karfi. I also saw his shame, as we had caught them dodging duty for a bit of wind and wine

--If we do not die, we must disappear

--Come with us, I answered

--What? demanded Melas coming up. --The wind is with us! You know the space is better-spent

--Stop it, if you can. The east wing, man, do you hear that?

--Now, Merire! Norax shouted; and Merire, though he took his own moment to weigh things, told his men to sit. With shakes of head and eyes calming down into shame, his young men did so, Merire last. He moved again only to start tending wounds. Pereko's six best bows we stood around them, and an order for nobody in or out of that lamp-lit chamber of the throne, till I came back

That instant we turned to gather, we saw a kind of human whirlwind rising out of the east stairwell, and out onto the court: a shoving chopping tangle of death-faced Karfi men, Alashiya and white-robed Companions rage against rage, the Achaians thrusting and boxing with spears and Cretans hacking back across the shafts, grappling to get inside their swings of long sharp sword. Out here, the stairway walls no longer helped us

Surely Abas caught most Achaians in bed, and here they came up turning stairs right into us. I saw no Squiddy or Abas, it looked that they had cut their prey in half, and yet these big-built charioteers, some of them were even laughing to each other as they swung with wild despairing joy for little Earthlings. One of them screamed for Merire, and Pereko's bows bore down. I screamed our battle-name again, and forty of us slammed into them

We hit them just short of the great stair's broken portico. Melee tore me off against a big blond beard with no shield who had managed to get a bronze helmet on, no corselet nor greaves round his legs, but his arms were bigger than my thighs. He was bloody, not wounded: we circled in hot blasts of wind, his spear jabbed my sword and shield-arm and he put an arrogant this-is-play bobbing to his head, so the white plume on his helmet danced to spoil my eye. I wanted to end him, that cursed Achaian grinning down. I thrust hard-in below my shield. He was good point and butt alike because his blunt end slammed my shield down on my sword. If training had not snapped me back he had put his spear through my face, but the head deflected up to rake my temple. I cried out and he pulled back to stab. When it came I stole his trick, whacked it down and drew back through his front knee. When it folded, I stabbed through his left lung. He went down disbelieving, like his priest

About me swarms were wrestling down Companions one by one, hacking, cursing. I needed all the pure luck of battle to drop one more alone with a duck and swing back upward through his groin. That one's head I had time to lift by the plume and cut his throat. For every person who had danced these stones and harmed him not, I poured his blood. The gouts of it steamed like his disappearing soul

The night's mad din was dying, though our men were running back down into the east wing now, and up came screams of women and children. Norax caught up to my side taking ferocious breaths and cursing me to let his shoulder be. He pointed Melas over there helping to guard the Libu, rather than fight his own at last: he did not know if Abas lived, but had seen Prax and Aktor head down that stair in the northeast corner for the artisans' shops. The decent quarters where Key-Bearer had a room

We had to get out of here before any serious muster. I told Norax to start for the ships, but he refused till we were together. --Otus, watch your back. Now, go and finish. Quick, and no talk. That hall must have ten ships' store of oil. I'll put men to the fires

I walked through blood and weapons, corpses, writhing forms: Donos dead on his back, with Butes lowering a young son's locks down over him, Kinuwa dead, his old folks orphans. They helped me to eat my heart at the four doors of the throne's sunken anteroom. Down four steps inside, the alabaster benches sat empty around a floor of black ironstone, set in pink schist: naked wall where, once, a turquoise tapestry of isles

My arm let go the shield. Four doors behind me became two in front: in old days, this play the more to see nothing but The One beyond enthroned. Now this magic doubled iron in my blood. For Koreter sat there, still as an idol in the chamber's crimson flicker. Here, where seated elders of our clans had faced down every would-be Cretan king, nobody faced him

Waiting his turn; but the great palm-painted jar at his feet, the bowls on the inner-chamber benches at his sides said he had prayed. He gave me nothing as I came in, his gray hands fixed to the knees of his white gold-belted gown, the silver-pointed chin and brow high, eyes straight across the chamber. Gold his wristbands, a yoke of eight gold necklaces; goldfoil holding white locks from his brow with two winged horses, lapis-blue

He was trying to master me, and flinched not an eye when I kicked over the great jar and it smashed, pooling chrism and horsemint. Same instant, I read the wall at his back: gone the great green palm that had shaded our throne's white alabaster, gone our green hills, waters, lively quietude. Either side of Koreter's blank face, a sharp-beaked Griffin, hunters and devourers once the reach of our law. Tonight, they were monsters come for him, their hooked beaks high with necks craned up to swallow. And wingless, too! A joke laced in by our old-blood painters: no wings to carry this fellow up the sky. Too fat, Mother Griffin, with a belly full of Great Year monsters waiting to be born

I put the tip of my iron to his plexus: Koreter's breath came big, but his eyes stayed fixed looking past me. What he saw was the chamber's sunken pit, the grave of summer's sun-crown, grave of the miserable self

--Minotavros is come. The son of your own lying hand, I said. And then, louder: --You sit like a Pharaoh. Too bad you're Achaian, and in Crete. I thought you people held it blasphemy, impersonating gods. You know me for your own, don't you, Koreter

He blinked once, and then deigned to look at me

--You cursed clown-faced animal, jabbering Libu. Those guards are Meshwesh, he snarled. --Smarter dogs come in out of the rain. Oh, to see their knife in your back!

Outside, Norax was shouting. Here, I reached to rip Koreter off the throne, and *Dog's Day*, he cursed: *You will never be free of us*

My hand threw him across the chamber: he hit the facing stone bench hard and his body cried out, but not his will. He clambered half-up, and clutched the arm worst-hurt. In the throne's shapely seat I saw our moon, our sun and star above the mountain: I the first and last to do a thing like this in front of them

--Does it hurt, when somebody hurts you? Welcome to the world. Too bad you can't stay, spider

Koreter was still bent, half-up where he fell: a nice clean little old man-sire. I thought of his Lion and their sons' deeds sanctified. Hard-built towns in ash. Burly browbeaten yokels whose hope in life was slaves and jewelry, who shipped our mouthy women to their flax-farms. Zoe's nose. Flame, I no longer knew who spoke

--A thousand names built this house. For them, Koreter, I give you something. A living chance. I swear it, by our family. *Look at me!* Answer one question. An easy one you should know. Answer, and solemnly, you live

--Get it over with! What is it then! he sneered, holding hard to the bench

--Just tell us about one good thing you have done, for Crete, in coming here. There must be one good thing. Tell us about it

He tried. --Ohh, gods, *gods!* I fetched him, jerked his head back and drove iron down the root of his neck till the hilt struck collarbone. His eyes were boiling and the throat in his open mouth. I twisted hard-around, then ripped out and his lungs' blood fountained purple from the hole. When the spray of it failed, I threw him on his face at the dais, and shrieked his death delivered soaked with blood before the throne. Everything fused and married: sun-disc, star-center, navel, new moon cradling new sun: crowns of the horned mountain, and fresh blood red across their niche. *Let go. See*

Between the polished sea and mountain curves of

the throne's back alabaster stone, my shade moved in the other world, iridescent, bloody. Where the ninth curve had crowned the face of the woman of my soul, a splash of blood let two drops fall. The throne was broken, dead and killed---not Great Year way. Dead, alive and in-between, I raised the palms I had to the people who had raised it, and defended it

At the door a man of Alashiya offered to drag out Koreter. I woke to stink of iron in the pooling blood, mad noise outside beyond the doubled doors. Rocks and arrows coming down: there might be a dozen Achaians outside, men caught bunking in the town and now hoping to hold us without coming in, until they scared up who knew what, and horses

Smoke of our burning-begun flowed in gray plumes out of doors and stairways, and blasts of south wind dragged it over the court. There was Melas, his back to a huddle of women and children, all fair, sobbing in their night-clothes. Why not kill them, right there where Achaians killed ours. I found Koreter's corpse dragging from my hand, out between Merire's Meshwesh and the captives. In front of all, I chopped the head off, and held it up on high a draining diadem. The women and children hid their eyes, poor innocent locusts. Here came Melas through smoke and bouncing stones. --Where in blazes Aktor, and Abas! It's time to settle and get out!

But now we saw the blood that draped Winato, stumbling into us: Melas swung and brother-slapped him halfway back from his look of full dazed shock

--What? Winato gaped. --Abas must be dead, the way he fought below. Squiddy is. Oh, Goddess, my stomach! We caught them flat in bed down there. To come in on a family like that, swarming in---they killed us back with table-knives and fingers through the eye. I think we stabbed down twenty by their beds. Abas---He doesn't want to burn the house, Winato finished with a crook-headed laugh. –Who's that in your hand? he queried, and looking round, Winato turned aghast again. Bodies, battle-wrack, smokes, bright spreading flames

--Melas, our sons went after Key-Bearer. I'll bring them. Let captives lie till you see us. Get the men ready to fight us out the north gate. Burn, burn! We go!

Nearest way down was the great eastern stairway. In the smoke I took a shield from a man of The Nail named Idas, tangled hard with stuck-through Achaian corpses. Stair by stair, dead bodies I had danced with. I touched Squiddy and the first few, till fear of the stairwell going down took over

Where the lower level turned, there was a court among the pillars where no water ran anymore, and doors to many corridors. Shields hung crooked on the walls: the great wells for light and air were moving smoke this way with the wind, and darkness thickened with an acrid oily cloud. Now? I worked down another flight and turn: not one body still alive, and smoke on the landing

I knew he was here and I moved left, into a near-black corridor for the shops' wing. Along in front of my right hand was a series of recessed, high-roofed storage bays, walled up each with darkness thick as a cave's. They were too good, and I meant to run by them fast and low, screaming to startle anybody out and, maybe, gain a fighting chance. I took a moment, and crouched below the smoke for better breath. The instant I bent down, I heard a man land his lead-foot, and a *whoosh* right over my back

I shot straight for the darkness, wheeled around and there was Abas twenty paces back with a spear sure-Griffin coming over his shoulder. But Prax rushed screaming out of the first black recess facing Abas. I heard the spear hit meat. Prax fell back into my grasp. His legs fought to get up. Then he stretched back and died

It was all one moment, Aktor charging out as I caught Prax, and Abas' arms bursting wide as half a spear came out his stomach. He fell and curled up hard with one long breath between his teeth. Norax ripped the spear, and kept stabbing. I was down with my son's weight, mouth open. Aktor tore his skull

--He lived to watch your back! No, no

--Otus, Norax said

--Are these my hands? All these, dead. Draw the water, take the poison

--Otus, Norax said beside me on a knee. –Let me carry him. Find your wife now, fast. People count on us. Do that. Come on. He wants you to

--Fine life I gave him, I muttered, and then we heard the first thunder and collapse from the southeast wing, and smoky heat breathing desert through. Norax broke my hold. It was only remembering that fetched me

back, on the way to the small neat room where I last saw
Key-Bearer. Her name when our love made Prax had been
Tallay, Girl of Rain. She was hanging from a spiderwebbed
rafter, her arms out like a priestess soothing Earth. My
brain was molten, searing in its juices, but it saw the
upright stool she might have stepped from

She weighed no more than Ariadne. Bird's bones,
partridge eyes, never see them again in Prax: a delicate jaw
grown sharp where only a woman could hold on. In her I
saw old Diamat, too, the last of Ariadne's priestesses, who
died the only friend I had but two years after her queen.
Tallay, last of the line. I set my teeth to break my skull and
prayed their strength between the worlds, and carried her
up turning flights of bodies. Her dunned-wool gown as
rough as frog-skin, a little Cretan's rag to point the clothes
of ladies new and proper. *Make them see*

The Meshwesh watched our men weigh Achaian
weapons, strip away gold. Flames every side threw slants
of cinders up into black wind. Now an even worse
caterwaul went up from the women and children under
guard as men pointed my coming, and I showed them my
eyes. I let them quake and vomit. Tallay's body I wrapped
for journey, as Norax and Aktor did my son

--We see your hate, sweet ladies, I said. --Do you
see ours? Whose home is this? Looks-away won't do the
trick anymore

--You killed Abas? said Melas running over to the
lot of us, stones and a few arrows still falling out of the
night. --Blood of Poseidon! he gaped over Prax. --I'm sorry.

Oh, no. Oh, no. But we have to go, Otus. Pereko says we took nine dead, and---yours is ten. Plus Squiddy and Alashiya. Well, now there are only nineteen Libu left to come along. So, room for worthy freight, said Melas, this with a cast of his eyes the ladies' way

--Dog! My son's eyes on you! I cried: I saw Aktor agape at his father's words. I could have killed him, and it showed. Then Pereko was next to me, his sharky white face bright, blood-exhilarated; and his bow was at half-stretch with a nocked arrow, looking right at Melas once lord of his house

--Sir? Pereko asked me. This the man who would not talk war in festival? Why now at my side, with all my digs at Poseidon? Aktor turned his back, and it threw Melas my way

--Go ahead! Melas roared. --This is your night to murder and steal

--Pereko, lower that bow, you blood-drunk. Take them, Melas! My revenge on them is you! Cheers at last, Achaians slaves of Achaians

--You give nothing, Melas scoffed. --Minos is finished this night. I take. And more, back with family, I and mine make our own way. Without you either, Pereko

--Good riddance! I told him. --Now, see if you can do what you trained for, and go put the rear guard together. Ask somebody the way to the ocean!

Melas weighed it for a moment, the hilt near his hand. Pereko relaxed his bow. And the man who had turned his back on blood turned again

We gathered up for going in smoke, flame and cinder, rain of stone and arrow, the wind's hot blasts bending smoke northward over the court. Spring night, the end of things, the end of my mothers and fathers and my son: my inheritance

I wiped blood from my eyes, and clung to one shard of mind, our others. Aktor I began to notice helping every way. Some of our brothers came out of the stair, and from Norax's corridor, with bodies of friends across their backs: the Meshwesh had wounded of their own to carry, but Merire saw them earn their sail. *I found this sack*, Aktor said. *Show me the heads you want*

Merire swung back the great oaken door to The Labyrinth's north entranceway, and poured ten men down the ramp with their shields, under the colonnades and out into seaward precincts. We swarmed out behind them and the last thing I saw in my house was above my shield-arm, the great red ramping Bull with his shoulder down, ramming himself against a green tree, the muscles and the leaves aflicker like his tongue, flames behind us a windy roar. Something boomed, and I heard again the mountain that had said our world was over: one of the big jars catching, and a racket of toppling pillar-wood and stone

Sure enough a dozen Companions, some with bows lay waiting round the customs-house, but the Meshwesh shields took the arrows and we were on them. The same, just not so much without their chariots and armor. Out here was a huge white-gypsum pair of mountain horns and I hacked a man backward till he stumbled against them. Achaians had knocked them over on their side, a trophy thirty years of our slaughtered elders, and he died splayed over them. I'd have left him so, but in the north bastion of home I caught Poseidon's trident scratched in, the work like some savage child's. I threw his body down the north town's well

We were running black road now under tall spreading cypress, the trees rattling and grinding in the wind. Merire kept with Melas' rear guard, and his men strung hemp across the road high and low, for hooves and heads. We passed Cretan houses three-stories dark, brothers' voices mocking: *Slaves, go back to bed! Minotavros will eat you*

It took more than an hour for men who could run. Night turned from black to blue, and The Great Green smell was strength. For all we heard, the Companions left around Knossos thought us sure to hold the house or head for the mountains, and played their strength that way: others stood gaping through the night as Labyrinth flames lit up the valley of their dreams

The ships were ours because dread had gone ahead of us. Only two mainland sailors showed their faces, and they came running out of a house with more fear behind than in front of them. Cretans around Amnisos hid themselves, for their good nights roasting master's fish. The south wind and cicadas were so maddening now that I tasted the first real wine of getting out of here, but every thought came back to stone: my son. Rolling the black beasts from their sheds went fast, and putting up the masts: for ballast with the stones we packed the hulls with eleven Achaian women and young. Melas who had driven them soiled not a hand except to point rowing-benches. Nineteen Meshwesh Libu piling in

Dawn twilight lit the isle of Dia three miles off, Earth Mother sleeping on Her side. Men's eyes drank their last. Crete was Dikte snow beyond green hills, mouths of rivers, and Ida's broad white slopes high westward, rosy in first light: between them, Juktas the mountain with our sleeping fathers' face, and a black tree of smoke. There was moon's first crescent, silver-sharp. My skull still bled, and I dreaded duties done

Ships near-ready. Little waves ran backward in hot gusts. I took the sack from Aktor, and bade him wash, not to wait me. He waited. Melas saw, and Aktor let him see

I climbed a half-mile back up the sea-road, then traversed a hill of old survivor tamarisks. Their roots clung like death where the waves had gouged the hillside, with green younglings crowding for the sun where it speared their shade. Up there it was not hard to find three dead branches fit for stakes. Dewy grass, crimson poppies, ice-daisies purple as wine. Swifts and swallows overhead, and helices of butterflies

In sight of the sea, a writhing olive marked the grotto of a cave where, deep in, mothering women touched their bellies to a pair of gravid pillars. A different beast piked Koreter's head there, goldfoil, lapis horses and all, between his priest and a Companion. All gazing out on Dia Isle. Last, from my back beneath my shirts, I pulled and posted one thing more: a flat of Karfi-oak incised with signs. So. An idol of words and violence

She licks up heroes like dust

And then Knossos Road no longer led home. Ships below in the blue-green shallows, wailing for Squiddy, cries of all kinds on the air

It was time to lift my foot. It would not, as heavy as my corpse that waking morning. Then, a little old woman's cry

--Mountain mother, what is this!

She was a white-haired tiny dame of the harbor's fishermen, half-stooped and warding off evil with long bare breasts. Next to her by the olive tree, her grown daughter stood likewise, aghast, a baby on her hip

--Morning, I said. --We burned a house no longer serves. Saw you here for ceremonies, Ya-Ya, in my mother's time. You won't disturb the man?

--They'll kill us for it, she replied

--Then come, cram in. But right now. Alashiya

--Pasiphae's youngest? grandmother gaped. --You look dead, if you're not. Alright, but let me fetch a bag. This my daughter wants to go. She has a good house-bond, too, around somewhere. Can't spare good ones anymore

--Mother! the young one said. --Mother, I never *meant* it

--Come on, child, believe me, it's better this way! I'd have hanged myself if I knew I had to leave

Off they ran. All went still. The mountains had no more to say. Alone, I would have lain down in the soil. Aktor found me, and wiped some blood. He brought Merire's thanks for his men's lives; and Merire was beating them now, for drinking Key-Bearer's unmixed wine. Aktor said they called us *Sons of Lightning*

Before us down along the dark-blue shore, a long sinuous ribbon of milky white-green waters in the sun. I needed Aktor's help to get washed a little there on the shingle, to climb aboard a big-eyed vessel, and nestle awhile, exhausted

> *Gold is the home of Sun's reflection*
> *Silver the Moon cries*
> *Family is resurrection*
> *Earth the grave of lies*

We pushed out. I gave my son's words poor finish, letting go his body and his mother's as the waters deepened under us. Better The Great Green soothe them, than a land no longer home

All we had done, to watch Mother Kriti slip away; and here was the sea.

II

4

Out on the waters, most people turned green for awhile, and it took the night's rage down. We had Squiddy's men to master sail and oar, but their skills were not with mainland warships, and the wind's hot gusts made us clumsy fleet getting out behind Dia Isle. From the black battered cliffs of the isle's north shore, the ocean opened without limits, blue and blinding where the morning sun threw white fire, and the oars left rows of spirals in our wakes

We hulled our way east for Malia. We took turns wiping and washing more of the night away, but it was only my body that pulled and pushed at my bench, and my senses had to work to make sense of anything

Prax. My Girl of Rain. And I had made this happen, for twelve other families too. My head throbbed. There was screaming out of every midships where the wounded lay, the holes of spears and arrows stuffed with bread or wrapped in torn-up clothes. Sea rolled as silent as the mountains. Space on every side felt torn wide-open

The waves thirty years ago had swept the great house at Malia off its floors. We had sworn our people waiting there to keep in hiding till they saw our persons, but we found them reveling in the sea near Pyrrha's three Alashiya ships, little ones chasing blennies and gobies in the tide-pools, and a camp and cookfire under a stand of willows. *What if we had been slavers!* I threatened to bleed the next one who did the like. When people's mouths fell open, it was no good blaming wind or wound. I laid my palms to Earth and prayed to heal

Things went hard as kinsmen failed to find their brothers, fathers, sons. Lucky ones restrained themselves, others on their knees pounded fists in sand: Donos' son Butes held Arge screaming, and Kinuwa's father and mother held each other. All we had was to make our great circle again, and half of what we sang was an animal wail. With strangers looking on, I wondered how long we would seem deranged to the world beyond Karfi

When I told about Prax, Podargos ran off to board any boat not mine: Zoe gave me her back and kept buried in Honeybee's side, clear out to sea next morning. Pyrrha's eyes were neither blame nor pity. We were nine crowded ships now, almost two hundred seventy-five people including the Alashiya. Aktor's face was still a tomb, and there was no high talk about anything at Knossos

All day Crete went by, the ruins of houses in high grass, with a living smoke at the mouth of a river or a cove. We were hunting a hide when Zoe pointed cranes flying, nine of them coming out of the east. Cranes you were lucky to sight between their stops to feed and rest: Zoe tried their clanging-calls, and a few seemed to answer

--That way! Zoe cried to the tiller. --Turn, that way, they want us to follow! Papou, tell the man! And Zoe kept on, till the cranes faded in the sun astern. Thwarted, she sat down, and scowled on her ship of fools. For all we thought of her, there could be no turn away from our best help. Still, something was warning me to listen

Last light found us a white swerve of sand on the last tip of Crete, in the old days' nomos of Zakros. None of the mainlanders disdained food: three of our Karfi wounded died, and two Meshwesh. For them we dug a grave shaped like Labrys, poured and danced in thanks and honor. From that day Ninna forgot no name of those whose lives freed ours. Podargos kept away among Ninna's and Melas' household people, and Zoe likewise with Honeybee's

Next dawn waiting the tide I slipped away, to walk along an inlet with young grass and white dunes. Terns, rails and pipers sang in a quiet cattail marsh. Zoe tailed me, and then wandered her way to my side, keeping at the length of her little arm

--Zoe, you can be angry. But you and I will take care of Bright Foot. Come, sit. Won't Alashiya be good, with cousins there to help us? Tell me now, with all our different people on the beach. What is our name, when Alashiya asks?

--Zakkala, Zoe shrugged

--Zakkala! That's salty, what does it mean? What, you won't tell?

Zoe swore that the cranes had been pointing us a good place, a better place, and all to ourselves. I answered that we had lived that way on Karfi

--*I want my big brother!* Stricken beyond tears, she flailed away every touch. Well done, Otus prince of indigents, crack-headed crane. Then, Melas found us. He came unarmed, but his walk was stronger: he stopped at a distance and let his eyes ask to speak. Zoe tore away and ran past Melas for the beach

--You're not Zakkala, she told him

--What? No, I'm uncle Melas, he trifled. Then he asked about my head

--Is this goodbye before you go your way?

--Otus, we were out of our minds, Melas said. --I come to say, I am ashamed. My heart is sick for what you lost. Look, my hands shake

--Norax taking the ocean in his shoulder?

--What? Yes, he is. Otus. We need to patch this up. I like Bright Foot. The sea and the ships scared him, but he didn't cry. He rowed beside a Meshwesh, then he monkeyed up the mast. May we take so well to the new day, brother!

I might have been sitting still in a deep hole: I felt nothing, said nothing

--To me you'll always be a priest, Melas sighed. –To talk like one is hard for me. But, Otus, after last night, I see as much as when I landed here. Death---it closes one man's eyes, and opens others. You Cretans had something. We called it darkness, weakness. I was pure afraid down in Mother Zoe's cave, and then I never fought with such a calm inside. For all that---you have the words. I was not myself last night! Melas exclaimed into silence

–Otus, it has to be something in Achaian bone, that makes us push every edge. If I do not push the world, I feel myself a stall-fed ox. Some nothing of nature. You see a garden, and it's well: to me it's all confusion, and waste beyond my hands. What I worry is tomorrow. I feel--- confined by custom somehow. I think we are cut out for some new way, and I worry how to handle it

--What is it you want?

--Argh, he growled back. --I knew the Knossos captives would curse us for their men. It's worse. Ninna found out they are northern stock. North Achaians, families of the Ironheads that Theseus and The Lion of Mykenai paid to keep Crete down. There are tribes of us, Argivi, Nemeans, Messenians, all proud of our unmixed blood; but Ironheads are prouder than their mountains

--Last night gained me nothing in their eyes. I have learned from Crete. But they need to start obeying me. What do I do about this, kill a few more to make the point?

--Would that break you?

--Of course not

--Brother! I said

--But I don't have your Cretan charms

--Ninna likes your own. What does she say?

Melas scowled at his feet, as if he were trying to forget his way toward something better for no one but Melas. --What are your plans, Otus, he shifted

--To follow what worked. Did you see the woman with boy-and-girl twins, with yellow hair? They are Shekelesh, from Sicily. They were Koreter's share of some house-hero's raid. Them, I promised to find a way home, because we can build on their gratitude. Likewise the

Meshwesh. What do I know, Melas? Except we'll make them a good house to hide in from the Lion. Look---Ninna is first mother now, that matters. Give them standing, gain your home. You, in their place

--Argh! I am not in their place, Melas said. --What do I do, mount festivals, and wait three Great Years till they chop my wood? They respect one thing, that they belong to me, by war. I care nothing what they think. There's work to do

I ground my teeth. At Knossos he fought no kinsman in our cause: now, in his own, Melas worried he might hurt them. Karfi and Dikte had strengthened his battle-hand, and I growled to wonder if anything more of yesterday had come through. Tide was rising. I stood up, stepped forward and then had to try to say something

--Maybe my brain is bent. You sound troubled with abusing people, but your heart is somewhere else. Let the troubling tell us at least what not to do. We cannot turn Alashiya into Crete. And you cannot make it Achaia

--Always the tangle. Always the limits. There's my rock, Melas chuffed and ended with a laugh. –By Blue Hair's beard, you are a crank, but you make things clearer. We'll see what happens, he repeated

None of us had Karfi to hide in any longer. I was beginning to know a man who palmed his choices this way, making his wishes look like destiny

--*We are here!* Melas suddenly stood up to cry his lion-might. –That sea is a bath of ichor. Salt air wakes up your blood! Come and eat now

So, he took up my hands; but only half the gaze met mine. Always a bad omen. But how far these things might lead him, I thought we could handle

-- Somebody told me water is the solid way to build a house, I said as we walked. --Next year, we can start with a voyage to Libu, and Sicily

--Build, we will --and honor our sons. Poseidon, I feel bold!

At the mouth of the inlet Bright Foot was waiting, Aktor's hand behind his neck. --Help your father! said Aktor. --Listen to Norax! Go on, Podargos

My son's eyes looked almost crazy: swimming and fighting back hating and needing me, shock that he had loved a monster, defiant, confused

--And you, Melas told Aktor. --Come. Much to talk

--But I, Otus and I---Alright, Aktor consented. --See you next island-camp

Podargos had a ram's skull with a triple turn of horn. He fixed my eyes with his, took it manfully over to a boulder in the sand, and smashed it. Then he wrapped his arms around the rock. Anything to keep from killing me

--This year, you and I took our first turns making Bull roar. Podargos, we have to help each other. What would your brother do, for you and Zoe?

--Kill! he said. --You did. Uncle Melas said you did

--Yes. But your brother, you and I knew better

--I don't care! Podargos cried: he dropped his head against the rock, and hurt himself. When his rage broke, he stood up, and then wanted my arms. We cried, not to see his brother's graces any more this life. I set him on my shoulders down to the water, and when we got there, he was asleep

--A better father open his eyes, I told Ninna laying him in her arms. She gave me only a high-chin glance of *Glad you're alive*, her mouth a black scowl. From my belt, I gave her the tiny face of Earth Mother salvaged from her shrine she lost, and something like the sun came out of her face. With so much out of Melas, I thanked whatever had made me keep that for her

The Alashiya pushed us past Kasos that day, and we camped on a broader shore of Carpathos. Where the town had survived the waves and Achaian burning, the people lived around a red-pillared shrine in a courtyard, crowned by a cracked pair of horns. They ran from our ships, and then were gracious

They fished, had trees and planted, but little more. *This is a place to come back to*, I nudged Melas. He was more eager to see Rhodes: Ialysos was the reach of what his brethren were building on Cretan ruins. Pyrrha's men, though, hid us up on wild beach there: we were sailing mainland ships, and it was lucky they weren't yet abroad with the season. Melas was still cursing as Rhodes fell astern. We worked and camped our way east, crossing river-mouths, and coastal waters with a strange new northern mainland looming at our left

Pyrrha said that was Lykia, its little bays and valleys notorious for lawlessness and pirates: the sailors spotting its jagged white mountains raised home songs.

Ya, Ya, Ya they call-and-answered their land's names, *Alashiya, Kypros*

Then came the worst of our voyage. Kinuwa's father and mother rode their bench almost silent day by day. On the morning we struck south for Paphos, they stood up holding hands, jumped into the sea, and that was the end of another family. *Help your father*, I asked my shaken children. Podargos and Zoe both hid their faces in my sides, and any sense behind the world felt as thin as our arms around each other

When Pyrrha stood up in full formal dress again, and came down the ship's center walk to take my hand, a breath of gratitude swallowed my fear as her mountains rose out of the sea. Two great white ranges of them, north and east, and a beautiful plain up there between, Pyrrha said, with many farms

Her face was shining with home. She named every headland, each wink of a village, pointed the high Troodos and the best of their copper mines. The taste of the air turned green with trees, spring flowers and grass in well-watered tilth. Here came Alashiya's highest mountain, twice anyplace in Crete for size---and then, as swiftly as ever I saw our home-fleet work, a solid dozen sail flanked all nine of us every side. These were mostly fish-tail merchant boats but their decks packed spears and bows. The moment they saw Pyrrha's headdress and upraised arms, their will to meet us turned to jubilation. Pyrrha sang out, and a swarm of arrows shot the sun

Paphos was a curving cove of white beach with

two great rocks near shore in the middle of her bay, and the first thing we marked was how many different kinds of vessels lay in her sand or tied up along stone quays: fat merchanters, island needle-boats, elegant ships of embassy from Caria to Byblos. There were derricks and works of wood swinging bales and great jars up, or down: they even had a modest sea-wall and right there the multicolored houses began to climb the hills above port, stone streets fanning out to each bright-painted door, a home, a workshop, a villa for sailors with ships on its facades, each with a plume of smoke out the roof-hole

And people, people pouring down to shore for their sons, and climbing out on terraces to see. Pyrrha pointed the town's great house and, on the highest roof, the person of their first mother Moira under a white sun-shade. Podargos and Zoe loved the drums and laughed to see they had trained little monkeys to play them. *She's coming down for welcome; and now, look yonder*, Pyrrha smiled. And there, up among the harbor's plainer homes, the house in Ariadne's honor. It looked lifted from old Knossos, with three white stories and windows on the sea: a green palm shaded its door, the posts and lintel graced with running spirals, and on the roof, crimson Bull's horns with a Labrys of bronze between, facing Crete. Pyrrha said sunsets flamed it like a torch

--Cretans who built it have farms up-country. Some, their children work other islands for us. See the vines trained over? Late-summer leaves and grapes make it lovely, Otus. Your arms around her sleeps

I bowed my head and burned back tears. The two hundred of us looked so hapless, grouped out over the sand with blonde captives and Merire's darkest-olive Meshwesh in the mix. Then we saw their queen striding down the center-street with her retinue, and the women every rooftop trilled *Oh-lo-lo-lo-lo-lo*

Moira---She could have been Pyrrha's mother or my own an age ago, eyes and thick black tresses dark and glossy as obsidian. Barefoot, near fifty, she stood taller than any of us, a silver crescent-diadem at her brow, proud-shouldered in a red open-breasted jacket, her lean waist belted with a rainbow sash and her three-layered bellskirt a weave of seashells and chevrons, magnificent to see. Her ladies and their children crowded after her, and at each side walked her barechested house-bonds, six to a hand, men from their twenties to fifties with every color and style of hair, kilt or tunic: dressed as I had been taught priests and palace-men should, bright-stone necklaces and rings of trade and travel on show, their sly glances taking our measure. Their faces spoke a seasoned crowd who took no disrespect: they pointed this and that about our ships, and one or two creased his brow with how to feed two hundred people on their beach

Moira kissed and embraced Pyrrha thrice, her three ships' captains took a knee for their blessings, and then Pyrrha's sister Kia squeaked through the people to kiss her likewise. Midwife Kia was a small woman black-curled and stylish as any in sight, her cries and pecks quick as a bird's, and sparkling mischief in her wide-open eyes. She was younger, brisk, less stately than Pyrrha and unconcerned about it: she took my gratitude cordially, too, the bird whose dream had brought us here

--And not a man in the front row, Melas whispered

--Hush, Ninna told him. –Think what it is to breathe now, safe, and free

--I beg your pardon, said Norax with a smile; and beside him in Honeybee's eyes shone the elegance of this queen and her people, the things of the spirit-world that crowned their days' endeavors. Honeybee fidgeted, as though her feet were roots already digging in. And into the pause, just as Pyrrha began her offices:

--Zakkala! came Zoe's shout in that raw honk of hers like no one else's. None could see her behind us, it might have been a gull's cry: the hundreds about us laughed a little. We were going to find that somehow after all, it was the name that took

I asked my mothers and fathers what to do. My two arms lifted palms-out and, smiling somewhat, I met every eye I could: they took Crete's blessing with light bows of their heads, smiled back. And as if my parents nudged me to it I thanked these people for something not forgotten thirty years: for their sending six ships of their sons at Minos' call, and for the victory this brought us all at Athens. As it turned out, some of those sailors, my age now, were here and they whistled and clapped. I took up Pyrrha's hand and lifted it high, and thanked them for welcoming our children

--Good! Good! Pyrrha whispered, though I had

made her blush, and the people made pleasant murmur as their queen approached me, took up my two hands, and felt them with her eyes closed. When they opened, she looked as though her mind took a moment to come back to us. She reached out gently and touched the Labrys at my neck, and asked me for names all around. That led straight to Little Zoe. Honeybee gripped Norax

Zoe stepped out and met the eyes, from queen to people. Something had turned in her, for a girl once so sure she should be seen no more. Zoe smiled and waved the way a little bird tipped a wing. She saw the breaths drawn, the hands covering faces and the half-turns away, and she simply waited

Pyrrha said this had been done by Mother Kriti's enemies. This was the only time outside of a death that I saw Moira's mouth tremble. And somebody in the crowd, a young man, began to sing a low, slow rhythm of a soothing-song, the kind a healer might use to calm the mind before painful work. In the same slow-rising voices, more and more people began to hum for her, and sing, and we knew they had seen hurt worse than Zoe's. I held my girl close in front of me, and then Pyrrha, and Moira, and Kia the midwife one by one embraced her. The sound faded: Honeybee lifted her palm out high, and Moira, lifting and lowering her own, moved to other matters

Her eye picked out Merire's Meshwesh, the hostile Achaian faces, and she said pleasant camp waited everyone while we made new arrangements. She greeted all the little cranes with us, who needed a good place to hide till they learned to fly; and when she said at last *Be welcome, Come, unload your ships,* she meant *your* ships. She knew that we brought things to build on. It eased our minds of shame in so much need, and we leaped every way to work with her

Indeed they had done this before. We gave up counting the mules and help that got us ready that day to move from port to the hills outside of Paphos. On the way there was more, because Moira led us first through Ariadne's house. I came off the sea black as iron to let go the world for tomorrow, and here was a place like home as fresh as sunny day. Inside, midwife Kia kept three chambers, and in the first she and her sisters stretched me out in a spiraled clay tub, in earnest of rites for everyone. As our people filed through and left little stones or seashells with their prayers, Kia had me oiled and dressed again in the chamber of their birthing-stone, a strong gray boulder with a shape to help comfortable labor

In the middle chamber I saw what made many people weep: a chest-high altar horned in stone, and the horns looked cut by hands that built Knossos. More, along the dais where the room's low running benches joined together, a crowd of nineteen little standing Earth Mothers, every one of them different, with birds' or women's heads or standing on a talent of good copper. In the midst of their Great Year dance, another big stone the perfect shape of a seashell. Honeybee and Zoe tried to blink this dream away, an oracle and house of birth where even She Who Walks On The Sea found new life

The sun was going down on our first day. Camp was a wide spread of level-topped hills, dry with thick grass and the shade of old willows and tamarisks, a loud stream running seaward. It was work to unload so many loaves and cheeses, jars of wine and oil, baskets of dried almonds and old-store wheat, and a score of sheep came after the mules. Beneath those burdens the town had folded up half a village of sailors' tents

So camp was touched with hope: the sea breathed softly under these hills, and through the trees we gazed on our ships and wide-open world. We could have been plundered that night and heard nothing: on The Nail we had forgotten how to sleep

Through the next half-moon Moira's people all but left us alone. I raged and ached, missing Prax. This was cruder than Karfi life, but there was a safe sunny beach where we taught our young to float and swim. Norax's Oinops and Arge's son Butes took straight to it. Those days we always saw Winato, the man hurt worst inside by what we had done, sitting alone by the waters: now it was the turn of his son Phitios and the queen of our weavers, Euryale, to make him want to plant and build again

He could not let go, he told Honeybee, of things he had done to people in our fight: the more because on Karfi, he asked to learn how. *Who was that man!* Winato tore into himself. To me this likeable lout was the opposite of Melas

Alashiya night was full of owls, jasmine growing wild: we began to dance again, and shouted back to Mother Zoe. There were few chores but wood and water, so things went well enough for Melas and his surly blondes. As for his household, Pereko made up for the threat that night at Knossos. Behind that was Pereko's Cissia the potter and their son Oka. They pushed Pereko back close to Melas because he was going to lead new uses of our ships, and they wanted their little girl Eos off The Nail. Still, Melas was waiting for Moira's other foot to fall

--Ahh, he said beside me some days later, when an invitation came: the town's latest crop of kourai and kouroi were returned from their year of separation, and now came feasts and ceremonies of their welcome as adults. We wanted our young to learn belonging where we were. Podargos and I led a hunt so we'd have at least rabbit and partridge to bring: our women picked flowers and wove up garlands for us to wear and throw. Melas thought he was on to something, but our whole camp went down to do them honor, even those bickering mainland sailors, the Meshwesh and Merire

Paphos turned out twice-again as rich and proud, the women with strands of carnelian and lapis in their curly coifs, their best flounced skirts lifting with the turns of their welcome-dances and the men wild and fierce to rival them. When the sun was high, priests and priestesses from the upland places of their learning marched into town at the head of pipers and drums, chanting a birth-song and swaying great palm-leaves as they led their new adults back into town. These girls and boys had left almost naked with shorn heads, and now they too wore young curls, the women in fine flounced skirts and open-breasted jackets, the men in pointed little sailors' caps of leather and a sword of hooked bronze

A host of fifty youths marched singing past us toward Moira's precincts. The women were bearing baskets of saffron-flowers picked that morning, and their bare feet were torn and bloody from the hillsides. The men carried nothing, but any wound their bodies had suffered this past year of learning blades and hunting, they had laid open, and these bled likewise down their chests and legs and arms. Not a face went by without the eyes wide-open, tranced with their own strength coming home

They filed up into separate houses in the town, for secret things and taking of a name. And then in the great open crescent of space between the town and the sea, where we had stood, the new ones rejoined each other. Before us the men gently washed the women's feet, and they the men's wounds. Merire, beside me, made a sound as if he swallowed the world's best fig. And that was the end of formalities but one, as the young men and women formed up now, their walking-groups as friendships made them, to stand before first mother

We followed up the hill among houses bigger and finer as we climbed, and the painted and gilded and flower-bathed white stories of Moira's pillared halls stood the greatest, with terraces over us full of well-dressed people and the ground-floor gardens open for the feast. It really was a hive, brisk with business and easy with its aims. We followed the Alashiya, left our sandals with theirs, then walked along a bright wide hallway of tapered

red pillars, whose floors were crazy-paved slabs of pink schist. It brought us past two smooth stairways, then in under a lintel of spirals in red, white and black. We had entered the great hall, and before us high at the far end was Moira: enthroned at the top of a three-leveled dais, the wood of her comfortable three-legged chair like the dais white as ivory, flanked by palms in red-spiraled planters

Fom her earrings and necklaces to the weavings of her garments, she was Earth Mother, silver and gold, all crescents of the moon, smokes rising from censers burning cedar, dittany and other sweet unknowns. She was receiving the last few men and women, who climbed the dais toward her with eyes averted and, reaching her, held out their palm; and in each she placed the feather of a crane, which they kissed and slipped in a pouch or tied to necklaces. Each bowed with hands covering their faces, lifted their arms and held them out and open: a gesture like a bird's at stretch to fly, a courtly thing of gratitude. With that, one by one they backed down the triple-dais for the doorway, then turned and ran out under the spiraled lintel with a whoop for the gardens and their friends

Their wounds left smears of blood on the floor, and their faces shone. They had earned the totem of their clan, and full belonging; and with a touch of Egypt that our women understood, the token spoke of the Earth Mother too who waited to weigh each person's soul against a feather. Alashiya married that to their sign of family in this world, made harmony the path to afterlife---this breath of a thing with weight for their living. It told us the strength in their happiness, their confidence to suffer with and for each other. We all moved to venerate her likewise, and Moira gave us each a feather too

--Ahh, said Melas holding his own up to the sun as we were heading out, into the gardens for the offerings and the feast

--By Zeus! I said. --She's got us by the quills!

--I tell you, Melas vowed smiling all around, --the other slipper will fall

--My slipper your backside, said Norax. --Is it so much, what we owe? These people have what it takes. Otus, give me the big word. Substance

--Seduction is substance? Melas laughed. --Maybe to you

--Look! Norax pointed at him for our tribe. --It's Melas, alone with a thousand fools of us. Melas! Norax laughed. --Go on then, tell us you won't crawl back up this street if she winks your way. A man can die in those arms

--More than once, Merire grinned; and Melas grinned along with us, but then, with a cordial *Gentlemen!* he slipped away, off into the courtyard's gathering crowd

--When you and I talk, it tries to get somewhere, Aktor said to me, folding his arms: he looked flush and strapping with his usual fair-brown club combed by Ninna into swept-back curls. But he was wincing watching Melas ply the loud sunny swirl of families. --He shrugs things off. He jumps all around. He doesn't listen, uncle Otus

--He tries. Come, let's together in our cups, and see who gets carried home

I had said the word, about a tent in a strange meadow; and as Alashiya's drums and the wild chant-music took us up, I kept him close, this youth, who helped the pain awakened by his black-eyed beauty. *Here we were*, and my heart leaped into the half-dancing circles with Aktor and Podargos and Merire's men

The rites were majestic, with Moira's house-bonds offering big-shouldered bulls between the garden's two tallest palms, and then meals along the benches of their common-houses. Their fiery red wine they sipped at first in brooding silences. Slowly the hours and wine flowed on: Norax for one met a man and woman of his old nomos Phaestos, now of Miletus. For him, they took pains regretting their family's leaving Crete back in the hard time, and then they insisted that Norax come and see what they had built. Pereko and Winato picked up offers too. A woman of Troy on business liked Pereko's sharky look and archer's eye, and Winato in spite of himself hooked an old Carian man out of Caunus with chatter of his looms. It was as Pyrrha said, you never knew whom you'd meet. The worst thing to do was let anybody see your empty cup

Our women were already thick with Moira's: the people flowed from common-houses into gardens, back to friends' houses, where they pleased to talk and drink and play and eat. They said nobody grew any older while they sat at table. There was more ceremony honoring Pyrrha's voyage, and Moira gave her no less than planting-land. *See? See?* Ninna tugged at Melas

Drunk by dusk, we lost Merire somewhere. The

hours turned soft yellow, red, then blue with a breeze like balm. Moira's dozen house-bonds and other men began to disappear into the torch-lit town. The new young women were offering themselves, their houses Goddess' house now, bringing love among the people, gaining gifts to start their lives. From youth I knew the calm a man took home from those customs. But Aktor turned nervous. I told him to turn in place eyes shut, and point; but just before he knocked on his chosen door he looked back and said, *My father thinks this her shame*

    --Prove him wrong! I drunk-whispered, and Aktor went inside. Along came Merire, weaving, wobbling, singing downwards to his codpiece: he walked as big as Norax with the mantle of black matted locks, dark-olive skin and wolf-shiny eyes. Now that he wore nothing but a belted kilt and boots, his chest and back showed scar-tattoos that half-covered him in webs of woven X's. Cranes' nests, among other things

    --You look destroyed, what happened?

    --Moira, the man sang out, his muscles limp with wine and ecstasy. --Oh, my tasty tuber drops off!

    Jealous, I bucked him up along the camp road

    --She makes strong war. Spirit-war, Merire explained with a drunk sly grin. --For the young ones. Did we not see power today, to bind them? Kings, tricksters--- traps they weave around you, things you cannot get out of

    --Well-ended, I laughed as Merire threw up

    In the morning we were seated at Moira's sunny table, and broke fast with her and Pyrrha. I dared not be cordial as before, because on the road we heard about one of Moira's house-bonds starting trouble over the Meshwesh in her bed. *And you*, Moira glowered on the man, *intend to do what about it? Well then! Go live elsewhere as you please, and take your nose along.* The woman was a mountain or a moon, something almost too much to be seen across a table, the animal beauty, her solemnity and hidden skills. I hardly spoke. She and Pyrrha talked Alashiya's sister-cities, Amathus, Kition, Enkomi: older and bigger, but built with more bricks of Canaan

Before I knew it we were walking home again, and our steps were strides. Moira had asked me to travel a year with Pyrrha: port by port around The Great Green, our work to seed the world with gifts, and draw more trade. It was fundamental custom, full of future. Scarcely beached, my being leaped to it; to see the lands and cities that had sent my father ships. Merire's men would see home that winter of the voyage, and right away he said half of them agreed to guard us all the way back. Sicily was a port of call to keep my word in Shekelesh. To that, Nyasha the mother of the little blonde twins offered work as Pyrrha's lady. The hazards I feared, and Alashiya hands I trusted

We built a good fire for talk. It haunted me that I had ignored Zoe's cranes, and I wanted this right with her: she cried without asking to come, and promised to help start our home, for we had land to plant through Pyrrha. Ninna had seen it, a long level valley half-a-day's travel up the river feeding Paphos, the soil black and the green slopes fine for vineyard, fig and olive

Honeybee saw good in my going, the sooner to wean ourselves. We had partners to hand, like that grandmother and her family from Amnisos: there was even a quarry of limestone one day off by oxcart. And Honeybee, in seeking out the families of Squiddy and his lost mate, had already crossed a mason in their midst with one of Karfi's best weavers, a gazelle we called Brimo

Podargos won his fight to come along, because his other choice was a young man's year in the mountains, too much like The Nail just now. He was turning out no boy for priestly things, and this could help him every way. Norax meant to stay and work, that was all, as he liked the balmy flat open spaces. And he made sure Melas knew that people needed him here---although Melas' hope was now to refit the ships and make the most of them. Aktor's face longed to come but he claimed next voyage. I was glad for him at Melas' side, Norax and Ninna on the other

It took half a moon to make ready while our hundreds moved. As usual, second camp built better, and home was all the hills, woods and water one could ask, with gulls and ducks and cool air coming up the river-mouth, the sun each day dying in the sea. The place we called Zakkala too. The name had stuck with Alashiya, we liked its salt and music; and nobody now wanted Zoe to say what it meant

Moira mounted a feast for Pyrrha's going. Our lead-ship's captain was there, a stick-thin leathery gray-stubbled cuss called Ramose with black Syrian eyes: Pyrrha he worshipped, and me he cut like chub for hooks.

The mission is yours, he said. *The ships are mine: there's a reason, prince, I'm fifty and not fish-food.* So we had yet to drop sail and I felt like a water-fly; but Moira's instructions made me want to rise. *Show your Cretan. Remember, each place you visit, to honor their officials even more than their gods. Where your hosts are familiar, be judicious with gifts: be generous where people are building. Keep both eyes open for things of house concern---and whatever happens, respect old Ramose.* I could scarce-believe I was going, let alone try to tinker with ships of their wealth

I remembered loving Pyrrha since I saw her on Karfi. Her house-bonds were like Moira's, working hard their range of skills, living well and grateful for her rain. Their gambling and meals were all excited talk that this was Pyrrha's last trip for awhile, and they teased over whom she might make a father. In hand I had a year of days alone beside her, but they stood to win when she came back. When I fumbled around these things with Pyrrha, she said that we knew much, we were going to find out more; and she laid her arms around my neck. *Cranes mate for life---unless it's not working*, she smiled

There was one last day that made me proud and sorry to be going. Two of the mothers out of Honeybee's household---Arge, who lost Donos, and Winato's worried woman Euryale---launched a plot that startled me out of my tent, surrounded with a four-deep circle of every young man and woman of our camp. Their own sons Butes and Phitios, Norax's Oinops and Pereko's Oka pushed Aktor out in front as their hundred young voices boomed out a good-voyage song. This was thanks, said Aktor with a laugh, for pushing everybody off The Nail. Best of all, they gifted me with the only thing they had, each other: he meant their oaths, as cranes and Zakkala, to astonish my eyes and Moira's too when I came back and saw their year. So, I left this home with a treasure inside that no misfortune of The Green could take. It brought on likewise the last thing Melas ever said to me. *It is just not fair!* he teased as we were drinking. *The things that come your way and you're not even trying!*

Pyrrha, Podargos and I rode Ramose's lead ship, and hers the best aft cabin-space out of the sun, because the way she looked was half our mission. Merire sailed with us while his Meshwesh plied a second at our side, and I began to divine some secret with him and Pyrrha. In a day we rounded the great cape south of Paphos, bypassed Amathus and followed Alashiya's southern shores: the mountains turned their shoulders, stretching out of sight along her spine, and then Kition's white curve of houses and their smokes, a city nestled in a bay between wild marshlands. But we did not put in, only took in convoy two treasure-ships, and two more with Alashiya guards. From here on we were six vessels sliding in and out of the wind as it helped us, bound for Enkomi, where we took on crowning touches of our gifts

Ramose was strange, a man happy only when bored because it meant things in order. But that was his home's way, Enkomi's. From her stone-built ports to the upper city's ramparts, through their gates and then the doors of great houses, some official like Ramose or his mother moved us place to place, experts of protocol bored and glad to hand us on. What was *that*, some bloody thing on the beach the gulls were at? A rapist, we were told: a sailor from Tyre. They had pulled his eyes out, cut off his genitals and staked him for the crabs. Anything he owned was now his victim's

This, and the shore's heaped ramparts, ugly and inconvenient, were new-drawn lines. Canaan was changing, pounded by waves of Hittite and Egyptian arms, both come to plunder. Alashiya saw its share of brain-crazed refugees. The third Tutmoses had beached here in our grandmother's days, killed and kidnapped for tributes of copper a fool could get by trade. Now that he ruled a house of worms, these people let his praises slide, remembered his mother and mocked the walls his monument. Better get ready, Pyrrha warned, to see what men were doing in his wake

I had glimpsed two sisters of Paphos, her thriving elders and, in each, a coequal court like Moira's. The garments, the jewelry gleaming at the tables laid to feed a tribe of princes---all this and people actually hailed fist-to-brow when they saw Labrys round my neck, praising Moira's hands. But I knew myself outside their high councils, not even peer to Cretans long mixed-in, and curled to my sleep a child

Next day on ship, most eyes were on *Ya's* last mountains: mine kept measuring the wealth in our holds. Bales of cloth to make spoiled princesses gasp, rank on row of copper talents, bundled logs of rare wood from the islands; Canaan's tin and ivory coming home in fine swords, carvings, plaques and ornaments. Potted seedlings picked for people overseas, rolled rugs and tapestries years on the loom: fat-bellied jars of olive oil and wine, fish-sauces, pickled things, and more holding straw-cushioned pitchers and pyxes of aromatic resins, tiny statues, cups and goblets gold and silver, clay wares. By the time I thought myself something again, we sighted far mountains of Asia red in the sun, and steered south of the great one called Zephon, toward a river's channel. The coastline pinked, and sweetened: the sailors called it White Harbor, the cliffs and hills behind them gathering us in with fields of fennel-flower, bright as clouds. Ugarit

They gave her temple fires old cheers: three smokes of evening prayer were climbing her skies, two from the white roofs of town-sized buildings on the north slopes of the city's gentle hill, with smaller shops and houses bunched around them. The third rose out of a palace rooted in the hill's south side, the house of their royal ones with main wings and courtyards bigger than both temples, and another little town of kinsmen's residence behind. From the shore to the brown inland hills a rampart of earth and giant stones embraced it all, with towers in its flanks--- a place as big as two country farms, a thousand houses sure with green open commons, gardens, spider-paths that followed the hill's lay, orchards. I walked forward mouth open as we neared the warehouse-warrens. There were *four* harbors, and strong smells on the air: mud-sour marshes flanked the bay for miles where river-horses swam, and out of Ugarit's dyeworks, perpetual decay from sun-cooked fetid mounds of crushed-up shells

--Good berth the quay to port, I pointed for Ramose

--Been here before?

–No, I answered

--Then go sit down, he shrugged. Back I went between grinning banks of oars. Pyrrha told out reasons why a new man would be gaping---how Ugarit ruled a hundred towns, that Thebes and Hatti claimed her, and more. But this little thing commenced a year that taught me my inconsequence. Green Man now was mostly green. From there I swore to shut my mouth and watch the people who could swim

Tying up, we lost sight of everything under the rampart, but the entrance gate at the top of stone stairs was a mouse-hole in a giant's wall, no wider than a one-ox cart, and low: inside it turned us quick to the left into a court that made defense like target practice. Coming through, the city's hill climbed away all yellow lamps, the shadows of her breezing trees in rhythm with the shore, and meat and music on the fennel air

We stood in the dusk and only felt the guards, then saw long-robed people striding down our way, each head a rival hairdo, some piled tall as a Hittite's helmet. The portly bright old man in front was Arkhalba, factotum of the king: he knew Pyrrha, and so did wife Naka who instantly gave her a necklace of blue stones. Officials, gods, leading families, craftsmen, people---our visits aimed to sweeten things and leave them eager for ships of trade behind us. So she had gifts for each high priest at both their temples, and for the women's houses in-between. Their high god was El, a spirit-son of Earth and Sky: he was all power and strength, although they never saw or pictured him. Baal his son was the substance of their king, and him we gave our best. Even Naka caught her breath when our crew unrolled a rug made for this Baal's house, a magnificent white dove soaring azure-blue

Arkhalba rubbed his hands together, every barefoot citizen seeing afresh their king's international weight. Their other temple, to El's brother Dagon, I liked for its open sides and the skylight over its dug-down sanctum. Dagon was their wheat, the strength of their gardens: Dew of the Land they called him, or Zeus the Plowman. Fine; but I wasn't going to ask why their kings were Baals if Dagon was somehow El's brother. I did hear one of the public prayers call Baal a son of Dagon, and in that I smelled old-home: a farmer's god was turning king of storm and war. Their rites were thick with Goddess-wives and sisters, but we saw no separate houses in their honor: Earth Mother here was Astarte, and Asherah, with a third besides they called Dione, The Lady of Byblos. Pyrrha shrugged: it was only what you got where clans from all directions mixed, and men had pushed their own importance longer. She was generous, where I saw men losing track of their inventions

We had one day and evening with king and queen, and they used Pyrrha's golden goblets pouring wine in furrows of their fields. He was a black-bearded bear with one eyebrow and a leopard-skin robe off one hard shoulder, front teeth gone from battles, gold and silver shocking in the gaps. I fumbled his long deep-Asian name, but he was full of regard for The Minos, and told many nights of music in the city's Cretan quarter. The queen might have been island-born, her bellskirt's flounces hung with silver pendants, her hair a peaked-up wonder, and cat's eyes to rival Honeybee's. But her fashionable jacket was cut to hide her breasts, or rather, to hide most of them

To the rites of day and feast of night they called every craftsman and person of standing at hand: it seemed they made war with their styles, their halls a clash of Egypt cotton, breastplates and bangles, Hittite wigs with island-kilts thigh-high, a jaw-line beard of Babylon. For that, their servants, *people of the king*, got on as family with full *sons and daughters* of the place: they bickered, danced together, ate from sharing-dishes, mocked the slobs who left the mess. Slaves there were, but few from war: most had either committed some crime or turned themselves for awhile into wealth they could build on. They courted skills because that was how you climbed their web. And connoisseurs-all, they loved the trees we left them in planters, banana, and a plane-tree with big five-finger leaves: a strawberry tree that bore red winter fruit for a soothing drink, and a Cretan palm, for the city's high center looking seaward

The bad news here was Egypt. Tutmoses was dead, and his son, a second Amenophis, had already marched so far north that he crossed the Orontes River in Ugarit's back-country, crushed any tribe with nerve to test old tributes, and sailed home with seven princes hanged head-downward on his prow. He was another one to keep the wives at heel, and carried on the gouging of Hatshepsut's name from their afterlife. I had thought us deranged by The Nail. And yet, in a slipshod little travelers' house with barley-beer and fish-soup, I watched an Egyptian and a Hittite break bread at one table, sharing their finger-dishes and arguing accusations as they ate, for both had families here no matter whose king claimed the city. Against the tavern's inner wall, a black-bearded Hurrian livestock-trader nursed his mug, grinning like a potted gladiolus

Ramose never forgot ships' business: he rotated men to keep the ships' guard fresh, oversaw every store, and then lounged in taverns and in houses like our gardens. There were men-entertainers in women's wraps who gave knife-throwing shows, women for holy communion in the temples who never bore children, musicians and grain-grinders and mobs of sheep and cattle driven through the streets: any given hour half the city rang off the rampart with an uproar of work and reveling at once. As we cast off, Ramose was singing catches picked up from the *kosharot*, the city's guild of songstresses, and best he liked the ones about misfortune

On ship, Podargos and the little yellow-haired Shekelesh, Kopi were taking a shine. It was otherwise with Pyrrha as she cast her first luck-stone in the sea. Miles out, she began to talk in hopes of putting age behind my eyes

--Where I see women covering up, she said, --I see
men who can't control themselves, and women settling for
boys. Where are their teachers? Fool me: the rites sing
pretty Goddess, but the young girls love The One behind,
Anath, because She's fierce and lusty. What tames them
down and spoils them? City things? They learn to want
husbands who cower for place. He beats her where her
powers temper his. And she would rather wear gold than
show her teeth. Life gets easy: all it costs is the light inside.
It is not good omen, Pyrrha finished

Ahead the coast kept shifting shape, its river-bays
and one-ship yards like buds of ports, and The Lebanon's
green-gray hills with mountains blue as thunderheads. I
prayed to be useful to her one dawn to the next, *shachar-
shalim* as they said behind us, and practiced tongues she
taught me. Next day there was still darkness on us after
pleasant things, as if the light of the world were going
down. Then we saw Byblos

She was a city like a white crown for the two strong
hills beneath her. There was a valley between the seaward
slopes' great terraced houses and the humbler, many-
colored town, and over the walls Pyrrha pointed green
heads of palm-trees in a circle round that place. They
shaded a freshwater-spring and courtyard, where women
of The Lady held rites with the people round a sacred
pool. The slope of the beach was so crowded that Ramose
had to work at space for six: fishing-skiffs, fat coasters,
barges set for sail with men lounging on stacked trees,
even a Nile reed-ship

We climbed smooth-cobble streets past one-room homes, then bigger ones, with polished plaster walls and some with running benches where the families sat and idled; and scarce a person without some amulet or carnelian jewel in the nose, The Nile's good linen and touches of gold for Byblos fish and timber. It was a city that stood its ground through siege with deep water cisterns, and here and there a courtyard with some lonesome obelisk, gilded-grand with Pharaoh's unintelligible glory. The place had an open seaside lightness, the presence and the taste of its Lady and her court. Even Egyptian soldiers walked unarmed

She was Astarte, Anat, and Asherah as everywhere this land, but Byblos called her Ba'alat-Gebal, and hailed her mate Adonis. The Lady's diadem above green eyes was pure bright silver, a crescent pair of horns that spoke laws as well as mysteries, and even in her mate with his young curls and bicep-bands of gold, we felt a lively peace---a confidence in long-productive kindness with a good salt of cunning. It was like meeting Moira's elders. Their Akkadian and honey-beer ran like a stream and so did rites and trade we chanced to see: like Ugarit, they played Egypt more than bowed that way

More wonder to my eyes, their feasting-hall was glorious with work by old-home painters: lilies, lotus, papyrus-reed swaying alive with butterflies and ducks, tandemed dolphins in a blue that shimmered yellow, and no less than a big-eyed bull with leapers near my chair. I drank their wine, to keep my soul in Byblos where I sat

We bypassed Sidon with its stone-works and trade brisk as Byblos', for others of our ships called there. Our task was Tyre beyond the headland, two cities, the old one the main and the younger jam-built on an island one mile out. Fetid reek of dyeworks and decay: both throve the like on trade of olive oil, oranges and lemons. But our work was with a rising family of the island-town, as Alashiya copper needed eastern tin. As visits went, we gained fair ground: it was getting in and out. Ramose also knew the edge of his captain's rule here. He would not leave the ships for the press of bodies jammed into those streets; nor give me, in a port like this, more than twenty guard for taking Pyrrha through

First try and we wound up stuck, our gifts and spearmen, in a sweltering fire-trap of an alley called a street between two walls of timber-thin houses: the passage was single-file one-way with exceptions for the brutes walking over you, and spearmen hardly fazed these blanked-out faces of the world. Word came back that two or three lords off the land were finishing a fistfight up ahead, and every window a different human tangle, families just watching, an ale-house loud with cups and screams and music. Right over us both sides, men with less than princely faces stared down, sizing us up

Patience we tried. I blanked my face and browsed a hawker's stall, where black meat hung on hooks. When I asked the keeper what meat it was, he tapped it, and a thousand flies flew off it into the pack of people's faces. They dodged and bumped and started fighting too. *Troop!*

Turn! Present! I shouted: my panic was Pyrrha hurt, or Ramose's tongue if we got robbed. Our men clacked their spear-butts and gripped them for business: we shoved our way back out and found the ships. *And what would you have done?* I asked Ramose the smirking cuss: really enjoying his little kingdom of the sea, and I hated him his mastery of it. Tyre: house of Earth Mother of the families and Her Baal named Melkart, the ceremonies ancient, business shrewd. If that was the home of old Europa, it was good for her jumping the first bull out of town

Ashdod, Ascalon, more and more the walls and boats of Egypt's garrisons guarding royal road, though Ascalon faced no wall to the sea. Our competition was not so welcome there and we sailed them by, liking the miles of trees and untilled country where their little rivers fell. Within a moon we bore down the coast for Gaza where routes for spice and incense met the sea

Old Crete was gone, and everywhere: small as Gaza was, and full-occupied by Pharaoh's soldiers with horse and chariot, the strong house on the hill beside the river boasted paintings and more people from old home. Come caravan and Pharaoh, people still called it Minoa; and as some had married Ugarit and others in their trades, they gave their thanks for crops Dagon

The road of Egypt's power ran through Gaza's north-south gates, and ships and beasts of burden shared the travelers' houses. Podargos loved his ride on a monstrous long-necked horse with one hump. It spat at Ramose, and he spat back

Gaza's men of the desert burned their fragrant wares in Pyrrha's honor, and never let us see their wives in tents outside the walls or watching herds. It seemed that kings and occupations had worn away a place for queens: our gifts for the Egyptian lord were bribes to let us treat with caravans. The desert-men rejoiced in every courtesy, thought most of our sailors were women, and nights they loved dancing with each other or, if drunk, with girls of Cretan blood. Under infinite stars their music wailed out of skins and pipes every kind, with a clatter of little bronze discs above the drums

The more we traveled, Podargos grew happier doing things with Kopi. He liked each place, he felt my eyes on him to learn, and missing his sister, he taught Kopi games from the mountain. Sometimes he let his homesick father in. Both of us trying to find our feet, and so many strong different ways all about us

We sailed on south past the river of Egypt, and again the land changed. Losing its garments of good soil and green to show another world's bony barrens, rock and sand-dunes, dusty highway, salt-lakes where reefs had trapped the sea. *A metal land*, Podargos said. The Sinai; and southward in those sun-cracked mountains, mines where people dug out Pharaoh's gold

--Point the Pole Star, Ramose challenged one night where we beached: he laughed when I showed him Head of the Dragon

--Got news for you holy Keepers of The Door. The star that never moves has moved. Follow Dragon north now, you land four days off. We follow Kochab, yonder. So much for your verities!

The land turned our ships toward the sun, and now we drew near Pharaoh's port Pelusium, her red-brown water channels strong about her fort with the last of Nile-flood. Our gifting stop hardly touched the river's Ways of Horus and the south. There was no end to the wetlands, marshes and reed-circled lakes, lagoons and canals that dead-ended in crocodile-swamp or brought you a town with gold-peaked buildings. And this was only To-Mehu, the land of the river's mouths

Yet, as we passed inspections and were led up toward official houses, we seemed to---lose the land. More and more from the moment their bare-chested priests surrounded us with purifying smokes and half-heart song and gesture, every wall inside and out of these brick-built houses fit for kings was covered in their carved and painted picture-words, their gods and totem-animals rivaling their colors in your eye. I followed Pyrrha but I must have been dazed. Even a window looking at a one-tree marsh felt like relief, and there were none in the great hall for business

We washed our feet before enormous doors of brass cut with giant priests praising Ra, their sun. Those opened to a cold hall, then another pair of doors the same; and these swung back into a hall with red-stone lamps like towers, one at each corner of a polished floor with pictures in it, a duck-hunt on the marsh where the big man's arrow took a score of birds. Inside, it pleased a man alone in a great cedar chair to receive us, like a bald brown child in white and gold

They gave us quarters painted Cretan, cows among rushes with their bulls, fresh enough to ask about the artisans. A priest said they were wanderers living on their skills: their styles improper for grand places, they slept where they painted and moved on. There was nothing on those walls for his eyes, except perhaps relief from the swarming symbols on his walls. Proud as I still was, those people were all that I wanted, so far, out of Egypt

Westwards we hit the worst squall of the voyage, and I was too afraid to smirk that Ramose had misread wind and clouds. There was no place to beach in time and he cursed himself reefing sail and running up and down, even tying Bright Foot and Nyasha's crying blonde twins in place between benches. The ship began to pitch, yaw, roll and sway, heave and surge down waves as big as country hills: sometimes the whole prow went under, and once it was only his arm that kept a midships-oarsman in the boat. He took us through, then looked ashamed: we had nothing but smiles. Yet Ramose took no food or wine that day, and there was plenty

The boats near Pharos looked poorer, clans of fishermen and families working skiffs, and needleboats of sodden reed riding low with the west's rare woods, pistachios and oranges. Passing, they politely hailed, admiring not too much our ships: the mouth of Nile lived a steady state of things in rhythms of the tides. After Pharos, the land west of the river began to shed its green again: marsh dried out to a desert-edge scrub, with steep north-faced plateaus in the African distance. Tamarind trees, acacia, mastic, junipers clung to their soils and waited rains: we saw cranes again, for they liked winter here. We camped at Merire's call, and there were worlds to learn from him, little places of water with figs, dates and oranges, green Meshwesh farmlands facing the sea road

Each day of sail there was an outpost walled in around a well, two or three mud-brick stories high with rooftop battlements: the olives and cow and pig pastures spread away feeding the families of settled-in Libu, who manned these westward forts. There we looked to lose our best guards, but only a few left the ships. Mersah Matruh was like rowing a boat through liquid light inside a sheltered bay. Six days on, their towns were stone-built camps for tribes who roamed the seasons of their land: the houses at Ngame were three-fourths underground, with stores off every living-space. No people wiser with their water, the houses cool through summer and warm in their windy rains

Merire's kinsmen thought him a shade, and all his brothers: then they covered their eyes and wailed, fell back fainting, danced like trees, and feast was on. Every body more than twelve years old showed Merire's same webbed X's in their scar-tattoos. Three days and this was only getting started. His mothers sent off news to other camps and, over and over, we watched families running in to explode in grief and joy around their sons. Some had already named sweet black-eyed children for these dead, and solemn rules fell by. When the year's circle turned at midwinter, Ngame mounted ceremonies that meant our full adoption: it was their best thanks

Good winter there. For the burdens of our hosting there were traders' goods to come. We ate couscous-wheat with mutton, sipped warm teas and spicy sherba-soup. Merire took us hunting gazelle, and when I bested Ramose that way I could have slept smiling in the rain. Most of all I was marveling at Pyrrha, how equally at home she was in a formal court or a camp under trees, changing and always herself. The one loathing in her world was funny to me, with the way our feet made love in bed: she abhorred a dirty floor and anything to do with other people's shoes. Nyasha the Shekelesh had one carp the whole way, saying Pyrrha did not seem to need her much

Come early spring, she went away for awhile with Merire: she called it their mission from Moira, and when Pyrrha came back sure of what she knew, she opened their secret. A plant called sylphium grew only here along these shores, a big stalky aromatic like giant fennel, sweet for sheep or to flavor up a fish, but its bulbous root a surer thing against childbirth than wild carrot, or a pessary, or wool soaked in lemon and oil. Merire had told Moira about it, that night of their garden moons ago. So it was Moira, wondering what sylphium might become. And the two of them said I was welcome to partner if I pleased

Merire made a point to walk his ship-fellows home, and soaked up gifts and obligations, we his ornaments for once. In each little town they had a spirit-house like

Ngame's, where their girls and boys learned strengths of
Libya's Lady, Dripping Rain. She was fierce and lusty as
Anat, old with magic to save, or kill; and they learned
battle and the ways of love in goatskin garments till their
day. When the Seven Sisters set, they extinguished all their
fires and made love three days all comers. To spring's crop
of youth, their mothers gave them leather from their cows;
and as everywhere, the daughters gave their flowers to the
mysteries. Young men brought them necklaces, hard-
earned cowrie-shells twined with shoots of Green One. A
hard flash-flooded country, her gardens underground, to
be missed, and curried

Launching out north and west for Sicily, for the
first time we lost all land. Seven frightening nights we
rocked out there against the wind, tiny creaking toys: the
moon was waning-weak and if the sailors were nervous,
so was I. Ramose wasn't just sailing aslant each sun that
set ahead of us. One eye on a cloud or star, he sniffed
wind, fished out seaweed, dragged a reckoning-rope; then
he ordered turns and turns-again, as if he saw interlocking
rivers in the waves. Turns in the middle of nowhere!
Breezing up-deck past me with a riddle-tune, adept of the
world, a sea-king

No wing or oar can reach me, no colors like my own:
no sailors ever beach me, except as skull and bone

--Who am I? The sun, the sun! Podargos said
Sicily, close-in, almost dwarfed the ocean: broader

than Crete, with a vast volcano's mountain green and gray to the snow on its shoulders. We beached at Thapsos, a little bay facing sunrise between two headlands, with a river on each side: a dozen fine white stone houses clustered on a neck of land jutting from the beach, and the shore's grassy hills showed clearings with round wooden houses of their families. It might have been Paphos long ago, everything building: now it was Nyasha's turn to be the wonder among tears and feasts. Out of that, half a ship's trade of gifts, and buds of business: the families of their farms had young people eager for a craft, and we had eastern rarities and teachers. The thing most promising went hard. Podargos told me he wanted to stay, and not like a boy only sweet on little Kopi. He was living the vast spaces seen all his life from a goat's ledge called Karfi. Had I not hoped he would rise to it? I felt the healthy ache of his age to get out from under Ninna and his tribe awhile. Nyasha I trusted, whatever grew or fell out of Bright Foot's heart. So I bit down on my own, as I remembered Moira's counsel on where to be generous

True of speech, it was good to see Podargos' spell of panic a few days before we sailed. We calmed each other planning out a meeting in about two years. So there I left my living son waving as we set out toward the sunrise. I worried his wild early life, and liked more and more that idea about sylphium

The bay of Pylos was a blue curve sheltered by a long green isle, splashed with spring's red poppies from hills to seaside, and in the isle's lee a powerful row of black ships waited work. Near water's edge, a burly ash-wood statue of Poseidon-Earthshaker guarded all with lapis eyes, his arrogated trident high in hand, horse-bridle in the other. He had come far since Dagon-days as a boy of mountain-springs. Pyrrha said he had a sister here, and come high-summer they decked a marriage-bed for them; but his was the only image from here to house. I saw works of Cretan hand that brightened halls with women riding chariots, but most Pylos priests and priestesses, rich with the run of their gods' slaves, worked the land through sanctuary-places in the hills. Good stone roads for chariots led every way. Below the walls there was no place just to sit and not be thought idle

The great house was a fortress walled with enormous stones, the roofs of three buildings and a warehouse of their wines on one hill stark above the town. Houses ran from well-cut stone to wooden shanties, and the bay felt crowded, as if inlands bred sons they couldn't keep. Guards in chariots met our sails, the rigs tricked out with horn and inlay, drawn by horses twice the ponies pulling Earthling carts. Brethren of Knossos' rulers in the same white-fringed robes, they drove us each in honor up a piece of stony road, and through massive bronze-braced gates on hinges

They left us at a stair up through more doors to hall, and out of the sun, the tiled courts and corridors dazzled with romping animals, lions and great-winged griffins, hunters and marching men at song. We were marched to chambers with spiral-painted bathtubs, and

black-haired Pelasgian slaves with blank faces poured our
hot and cold where no pipes ran. Fortunate, sullen
Earthlings, they oiled and scraped us, fussed every curl

At feast the lord of Pylos, another Koreter in white
and gold, displeased his queen indulging Pyrrha like a
bird no other had upon his arm. His queen had her own
throne, but she sat the evening smoldering at his side, fine
as Moira to the jewels in her hair and speaking as spoken
to. Bearded husbands, women with gold-chased breasts
half-covered, the sires drinking mead from stone cups cut
with scenes of battle in the islands. We ate around a hearth
in the middle of a great four-pillared hall while a harper
played sad things of lusty war, and lounged as in a camp
of people wandering still. I watched my looks and studied
Melas' dreams made real

They had a woman of court, Eritha, to handle our
gifts, which house-pride would only accept as trade. We
looked to make an inside friend, and Eritha poured wine, a
hard Achaian jaw to her handsome forties, a peaked cap
that let brown locks curl down her temples to her blue
robe. She began to moan last year's crops, pointing from
her terrace mouths to feed along the bay

In short, she needed twice the usual trade-lots for
her basalt. Pyrrha calmly mentioned droughts in Alashiya,
crews and cargoes lost in storms, and we had not doubled
our demands

--This is all I can do for you. Most people don't
mind, Eritha shrugged. Pyrrha minded, but she managed
to regain old terms with a bribe of Gaza myrrh, and a

Meshwesh jug of something quite reliable. And still Eritha wore a cheated smile, as we were marched and driven out

Ramose eased us around the main's steep headlands, eastward for Kastri, Cythera: once I looked to point dolphins for Podargos, herding their fish with wings across the waves. Cythera lay days before the Cyclades, and them I had not seen since my father's ships sailed for war. But Kastri told a story echoed at Melos, and Naxos, as we threaded the islands for Miletus and home-coast. Everywhere old rich Cretan houses ashes, labyrinthine living-places never far from crude new rows of Achaian market-stalls. The Cretan blood alive in these places had long dug in among kinsmen of the isles' strong houses: our gifts were to keep ties young. Earth Mother stood as ever at the core of spring's wild venerations, and meals that made good talk on good stone benches

Yet, a tide was dragging the anchor of the islands. Thirty years since earthquake took down half these cities of The Green; as many years without laws of Dikte on the sea. From Kastri to Melos and Chora, the rich port of Naxos, the houses had stood or fallen raiders' prey by their own arms, and men gained ground in people's thanks. But what had they learned? Why were more of these peoples of the sea marrying in Achaian seed without threshing the harvest? They worried neighbors' strengths, turned farmers into guards; then saw this in each other, and kept going. By Naxos I hid Labrys under again, to help me shut up while kings on their balustrades boasted to me about boys with sticks marching after mens' parades. Pyrrha marked the same places boasting each a Goddess born to them. They might as well have claimed the sea. In Naxos no less, Dionysos born from Zeus' thigh

Not long ago the world had shattered: who was helping them take it like some judgment on their ways, a call to change? More and more beards, more places like Pylos with a throne that made no answer to moon or sun, the shops and trading rebuilt separate from ceremony: more of these marriages that filched daily powers from the damos. Earth Mother's split-off totems splitting families. Naxos was rich because their great Mount Za caught the clouds, and made them rain. It was one thing to give a Zeus gratitude. Another to point *me* a cliff above Chora, where Ariadne jumped into the sea. Conferring her upon themselves, with kings to shake the tree until fruit fell

Miletus' bay on the Maeander was half of Ugarit's, and young as she was for a Cretan-born town, had never burned yet. Carians had been allies of my fathers, and stepped forward far into the islands. Their feather-crests and boarstooth helmets were liked where their ships patrolled: the men had old-line spirit. Like Earthbull's, crazy for a fight sometimes, prouder than mean, but murder where they saw a threat

We heard of Norax well-received. I wondered if he saw Miletus' other side. The Qari and their coastal kin had Hittites at their inland backs. By turns their men fought off Hatti's reach for taxes on their sea-trade, and other times when the price was right, they trained up young hundreds to help Hatti's wars against Pharaoh. And now they had a trade in slaves, the wreckage from inland. We saw the naked bearded men strung along by rope collars, women and children sold strictly together, a rule to keep them docile and productive. Their hope lay with the house that happened to trade for them

So we coasted another moon home; saw Qari's smaller cities Cnidus and Caunus on their fingers of blue bay, and the wild shores of Lykia. Every land its flowers, secret waterfalls, and hosts of brilliant birds in circling thousands. In the wake of Pyrrha's welcome at Paphos I had to find Ramose, to say the thanks he hated every time to hear. Spotting him still on ship, first I just watched him once more, his pure attention on each little thing. It seemed I had been looking for the way of a king without kings, and that somehow he was the man best living it. There was no way to say this and it didn't matter because when I came up Ramose rushed me, seized my cheeks and kissed me on the mouth. *So long,* he said and he turned away again to coil his lines

Paphos' people made a welcome, though Moira chanced to be in the summer mountains. As no one from Zakkala knew we had beached home, I looked to surprise them, but they gave me one. It was in every face like a death no matter who kissed me. Our young, who pledged their building, had kept their word to make a father weep. At last it all came out as we drank sitting round a fire, under the moon. *Melas had raided Carpathos*. Ninna had washed him from her mouth. She would not even say where Aktor was

Melas had worked six months pulling in the skills to put those boats of ours to work. I could see the man's feet itching stuck on planting-soil. Then Melas and Pereko went to Moira, for the touches to open doors with Rhodes. But they could only raise one ship's crew out of Zakkala's Karfi men. It was Aktor who noticed that most of those, like Pereko's son Oka and Butes, were men who trained at knives and might have gone Abas' way

Aktor raised a crew with half the trouble, and Ninna's blessing was the wind behind them. Someone remembered it was strange that, for once, Melas did not want Aktor with him. From there, the rest was pieces off the wind. A ship of Qari beached, whose captain told Moira they were hunting any boats of strength to have wasted Carpathos. She told them places where raiders were like to sell the families. Two moons after that day, Melas himself had had the dumbfounding gall to come home making gifts of their spoil

--Twenty men banished, Norax said. – If ever they or Melas show again, Moira expects us to kill them. She gave them curse to white your hair

--I am a fool, Norax went on. --I thought we knew the man. Aktor never came home, nor any of his twenty. So, I hold, said Norax showing fists, --to the nothing we know. Carpathos must have killed some of ours. *Some of ours!* I want to crawl down under a mountain

First time I saw Norax at full cry. Butes who had lost his father Donos, gone with Melas: Phitios gone with Aktor, wanting something for the shattering of Winato.

Pereko gone, and Cissia doubly desperate now to bring their daughter, Eos, off The Nail

Botcher's brother, prick royal, desert dust! Everything we had for comfort scared the man. To hide that, terrify the world. *You're not Zakkala.* Zoe, a child had seen it

Come daylight, I raised a Great Year dance for Ninna's and Honeybee's glorious beginnings. My heart was an ache for many sons, but I had glimpsed a world to work with, and come safe home. Sleeping at Zakkala beneath the summer trees, *shachar-shalim* I heard the sea, and the rhythm of its rise and fall. In dreams I was striding out to meet black roaring waves, arms high like the horns of a white moon. Yet always waking up, just there; and then, not far, the real ones' scent and sound.

5

Our first house we plastered white two years later, and over its door went Moira's gift, a limestone brace of mountain horns with three spirals facing the morning. Six rooms with a ground-floor center sanctuary and benches round the walls for communions, two stories with good windows, a rooftop garden: it was more than Ninna ever hoped. The crown of it was HoneyBee's motion to anoint her first mother, with the standing of old Zoe in our midst. Ninna filled her hands arranging labor to raise other households along the valley, and in the evenings people came back to our first fine yard, with its gathering-tables under plane trees spreading forty years of of shade. To Moira, we sent every first-fruit. To Melas we lost about one in four Karfi people, but a good dozen babies like Brimo's were fat ones

Keeper of Days was going to need some years to sight the sun against our hills. The moon's days told me when and where to start, and we had our own festivals winter and summer along with Moira's. For Aktor, Ninna dug in beds of herb and flower, lily, jasmine: when the earth felt good to her hands and feet, she knew the pleasure went deep enough to find and fetch him home. HoneyBee said Ninna's breathing was prayer. We never kindled morning fire but the candles were already lit for her shrine in the house to old family and old home. Ninna sang their names and people caught pieces of their ways and stories through her. She might by the season be one of a hundred women out on the land stooping over for greens, or carding for the looms in homes nearby. Always, when people came in to a meal, the savor was from Ninna's hands. Her quiet broom swept gently neat as an altar until sunset, and then back every evening to sing her candles into darkness. She was tearing up weeds one day, and I said she should rest

    --I wonder, Otus, what I failed to do, even while I see that blackguard now, that failed man

    --Honeybee told me that you turned his beatings into marriages for the house. You, first mother, are the warrior conquering Alashiya

    --Otus, curse my mouth, I could see Aktor dead and feel better than I do

    Honeybee and Zoe kept Ninna near: *We'll make it so good here that Aktor will know he must come home.* They took Ninna gathering crane-feathers every season in the shore-lands' nesting marshes, and brought stately things to Zakkala ceremony. In the midst of our losses it was Norax's Oinops coming to the front: of old days, he was always third man with Prax and Aktor, and Norax kept him close with their pleasures in the land. We cleared for grain, orchard and olive, planted our nurseries: there were nights of love alone with Pyrrha, with others in the gardens of Paphos

    Pyrrha never named a father of the child she was showing by late autumn's moon, but when I asked what names she fancied, she said Deucalion for a boy. *Why do you cry? Is this not why I found you, and why you came, to bring sweet wine back to the world?*

And then she wished that somebody grow trade of sylphium, promised with Merire. Easy for her to line up men to work Zakkala in my stead, and Ramose to sail as far as Sicily: I could see Podargos. Moira was ready to send masons and potters out Thapsos way

Last to this push, there was Cissia the best potter out of Karfi, as ready as a sailor. No surprise, losing that son of hers Oka to Melas' dreams, besides her sharky house-bond. And if lady Pyrrha could take a year at sea, Cissia meant to have young Eos off The Nail. So, I talked this out with Ramose in her name

--Give you ten days of Crete on the home leg, and then I leave you there, he answered: a double-edged promise the pair of us enjoyed

Instantly I missed our tiny trees, Ninna's yard with its moving shadow of the horns, our river's talking stones. But again I surrendered to the sea because, if we did not vanish in it, there was gain every side of going. If we brought back Eos, there was standing of the kind I wanted with Karfi people at Zakkala

--Keep this up, you'll be walking sailor-legged, Norax joked. He had his own request: to make as bold as I could to find our good sons yet alive, perhaps, with Aktor. There in our last cups came Oinops' turn to plead his own year under sail---saying out first that he disliked the sea. Oinops had Norax's fierce-red hair and was grown as

Libu-large. When he settled for Norax's word against it, it was good to think someone had learned from our dead man Donos, who had worried his chances of coming through Knossos and bet the wrong way

Honeybee and Zoe made me feel the last of home. Ramose was less annoyed with me this time, and listened when I asked to beach near the Achaian outpost in Rhodes. We coasted past the ruins of Trianda: for Pyrrha, I never told the end of Cretans there, and our boats made into their little bright bay Ialysos. The usual bulky men at arms had a boulder-fort with a few stone houses near it for their families, and these ran a works like Pylos' little brother. Harbor-master must have heard about Melas, and was not pleased to feel some reach of Alashiya where he lived

I learned nothing for gifting their yellow-bearded chieftain; but when I saw the size of their ramshackle potters' barn, I kept the man's cup full. Hinting at business, I wondered if they had enough ships to bear so much stock eastward---and he roared back *Why!* at almost battle-pitch. Because, I said, the tables of Ugarit and Byblos began to like Achaian clay. *So you say. We will discuss it. Come back,* said yellow-hair. And I knew that, with him, I had just cut myself out of a rising game

--Cursed croc-eyes on their prows, Ramose said

On Carpathos, shells of houses where Melas burned his name. We coasted well off Crete's southern mountains, put in at Kommos the best jumping-point for Libu, and Knossos' cheese-counting grip was no more. The Messara plain's plenty was fetching back things of the world, and Kommos was growing houses, ship-sheds, style. From the beach I saw the great humps of Psiloritis wrapped in cloud beyond her harbor. I was building, working, free, with a boat and home; drinking new ways and places, the problems and indignities turning into play

I left offerings for so much help from my family, and paid a skinny boy to bring Zoe and Makris a prince's box of myrrh. I schooled it into him, *Sweet Wine comes for Eos and six more,* and he switched his donkey up trail. I felt ready to carry his water, yet I breathed a world that was enough, and lost the sorrows of The Nail in the name of a boy that might be born. The winter with Merire and his three new wives was full of hunting, sleep and plans

In the middle of The Green, while Ramose wove his secret sea-paths out to Sicily, I heard lewd skirls and thumping songs that men at oars never sang for Pyrrha

Away away we sail and row,
off we go, wild wind blow
sweet for the girls who won't say no
in the boats of Alashiya

When we put in at Ugarit
she screams my thing will never fit
we leave them happy where they sit
in the boats of Alashiya

The water-boy, the water-boy,
the master wants to boff him

he stuffs his twat with shards of pot
to keep the bugger off him

In all our mothers' lands of trade
it's every mother's son gets laid
here comes a gift will never fade
in the boats of Alashiya

--Papou! Podargos shouted for old times coming down the grassy hills at Thapsos. Look at him! Two heads taller, straight brown hair out loose to his muscled shoulders, and he still had his bright mountain eye. Podargos was thriving, and if I thought him young to be turning himself into a house-bond of Nyasha's, that was what he wanted---belonging to a town and people with equal room to run and build. His pairing up with Kopi was part of a feast that coupled many. If it smoothed the way for business, there were fist-fights too, fierce enough to tell of real resentments

--Some of the old families here remember Minos badly, Bright Foot explained: the people here were all Shekelesh, but their first king Kokalos had wasted many sons against Knossos. The families grounded in that grudge had marked themselves Shardana. Like Cretans they honored their tombs and remembered the people sleeping in them. But these Shardana scorned old-Cretan strut, scorned Thapsos' imitations, and scorned the second-hand Alashiya breed of it alike. So this was the grief behind Thapsos dance and music, that almost half of their men from families of that grudge had sailed off to the west, for another island. Not unlike our Karfi exile: their new place was far away, but not too far

At the talking tables, these Shardana cousins foxed a few of Moira's artisans to their houses, flashing amber and things worth silver in the east. In ten years, while Thapsos raised two big stone warehouses Alashiya-style, Shardana ships better than their first sardine-chasers would be sailing with knock-offs of Thapsos clay. Bless Bright Foot that he kept his Cretan head down, turning into a herdsman who loved the level lands and The Great Green air, like Norax. There were sure to be children his line in the house of Nyasha. He gave me a doubled pair of gifts for Ninna and Honeybee, but he could hardly sail right now. So my days began to stretch the heart of me, Sicily to Zakkala

The trip's dumbfoundment came when we saw Aktor. Cissia spotted him, in Pylos watching our ship come in: Aktor and, beside him, Winato's son Phitios, the pair of them in front of the fortress waving our way, their backs to Poseidon. And down our sons came running in a heavy jog, each with two blades slung over corselets and bucklers, their locks back in tight clubs and their faces all hard prime, like a pair of officers off some Kari ship. Such gear they gained somehow and I disliked it. I saw a few familiar heads around their beached boat, too, the sleek Alashiya double of Aktor's father---and hid my prayer against the fear that they were tied somehow to Pylos

There was half a stranger in Aktor's eye, as if the

shocks of our first days off The Nail had become his life. We kissed, and Cissia pulled us over to Aktor's ship where, sure enough, the full twenty young men we had known since Karfi life looked well, but in the same ways as Aktor and Phitios: most of their gear the lean things of a fighting-ship. The corselets of one or two showed the sewn-up hole of a stab through a previous owner. There was a cold bond in their midst, and Cissia felt it: right off she tried to make them know about Alashiya. That life's good wheel of The Great Year was still turning, and for them. The woman even named out babies born, and trees in Ninna's gardens; all of which made Phitios cry, and Aktor sullen

It was nightfall near my boat before I was alone with Melas' son. His granite face had thinned, sharpening his eyes and nose to the look of a falcon. Aktor showed me his right-hand sword: black iron, with three hacks in the edge. --Show yours again, he said. --No better feeling than this weight at your side

--Yes there is. Show me your feather from Moira

--Good old uncle Otus, Aktor smiled, and he dug out Mother Zoe's pouch strung round his neck. It had suffered, and Moira's black neck-feather of a crane in it, too. With both hands Aktor touched the red feather given me, and I saw his dreams of touching Ninna's face: the news of Podargos gave him a Karfi smile, in which there was memory even of Prax

--Children every port, eh Minos?

--You know, I said, --an Alashiya metal-master

warned me about iron. Bronze breaks it, unless good hands have tempered out the brittle and the soft

    --You still talk like a priest, too. Alright. He's dead. The stranger whom my mother called my father got himself killed. I heard it told for a joke where men drink. He got stabbed in some tavern north of here, in Nauplia, The Lion's port. Over a woman fetching barley-beer, Aktor said covering his eyes. --What did he think himself? No matter. What I do now matters

    --Aktor. Come home, I'll stand beside you

    --You always did, he answered. --You always listened. So please, uncle Otus, listen now. Before we left Paphos, I noticed the men he was choosing for his ship. I could feel my mother uneasy, so I made myself her eyes. We put to sea for Rhodes, and then my father and Pereko broke off south for Carpathos. When we caught up still on the sea, shouting questions, he just kept waving *Follow* from their stern---*Do what you're told, Do what we do, Follow.* So, we followed. But we hadn't hit the sand ourselves when we saw the men of his boat pouring over the sides, and charging that little town with their weapons out. My father himself came running to have us arm. And when our Alashiya ship-captain asked him was he crazy, my father killed the man. Right there. As if to force it on the lot of us, there was no going back

    --He was raping a town, uncle Otus! Was I supposed to kill my father? I got our boat out of there. And he cursed me for no son. Do you know the last words I heard from him? *This is for you!*

With a ghastly laugh Aktor covered his head in both hands. --We failed, we failed to help those people! he raged. --After that, we were adrift. I could not kill my father, nor cousins off The Nail. We tore our hair, hid up awhile. And I got us talking, like you before Knossos. We had to stand for something. So, uncle Otus, we push back. We do the hardest thing we know. We kill raiders. Now, if we find Pereko, cousin or no cousin, we will kill. We say we go home when we stop finding these fools. We do not want trade. We want the road open, for people who remember how

--You misunderstand. We broke and buried a sacred thing, and it was done. You make it war. Aktor, you make life war. Still, I know why you came here. To look your father's god in the blue eye and have done. Good, because it's enough. You have many fathers. None of them suffer the choices of one fool

--Uncle, please, Aktor said, turning his homesick smile away. --Just say we are out here, watching your backs. We cannot show our faces, until we---Arghh! Who knows! Till we help more people than we failed

Such was Aktor's answer to the islands' dragging anchor. This son had come down off The Nail a ready killer, like the others I had poisoned. In Alashiya, he grieved for Prax, and none of us healed faster in her arms. Now it seemed that his father's dumbfounding crime had twisted him twice as hard. I fought to stay calm with one likely chance to fetch them home

--Aktor, our families live. There has been enough

--And who, Aktor broke in coldly, --who gave me words from the lips of Ariadne. *When the people suffer, somebody has to be brave*

--Have I known braver? I asked, making sure his eyes met mine. –This comes of honor. But it is a mistake. Aktor, Mother Zoe said it. Earth Mother eats mistakes

--Yes. And when I showed you my best edge, Aktor said from a pause, and then a smile, --you saw her teeth. The Griffin's teeth of Lightning-sons

I snapped my mouth shut. Because I knew that I had bent the balance between Aktor's bloods, melted down his losses into a new but twisted kind of iron. He was not going to listen. I left this hanging and dug up makings of a lean meal for everybody with us. Phitios sat beside Cissia for stories and Zakkala gossip: if we could pull him home, the rest might fold and carry Aktor. I told them we were bound back to Karfi on our way home, to bring little Eos back to Cissia; how fine it would be to see the place and elders, and to feel their guard around us through the country

Only Phitios bit the hook. The pull of his hurt father and the nature of a planting-man put him on our ship. With Aktor that dark morning tide, his sleep made no difference. I seized him where the slings of his swords made an X on his chest

--Aktor, if this is what you want, you cannot do it better than from Alashiya. Both my mistakes, I put in you! At least, consider, that boat of yours belongs to Moira. At least make right with her, for your family's sake

--You tell them what happened. And we will keep on making right with her, Aktor replied: he kissed me both sides, and that was our farewell. Years along, I was still seeing his falcon look, his homesick eyes; and the Karfi-granite jaw, locked around a thing that could not prevail

By then the sun was a moon past its summer crown. Ramose rammed us down the wind, full-wide of the usual rest-isles and Kommos too. He was salty with sitting ten days at Myrtos before heading home, but at least we disappointed neither him nor Cissia. Merire's people had seen their son return unlooked-for, and so The Nail saw us. For me it was climbing a mountain wide-awake into the place where old family were sleeping, and all of it a dream: most at the grassy sleeping-place, side by side in a double-axe shape, of Makris and Mother Zoe. Apart from the peace of those graves, we never stopped talking, and this time said goodbye as if we lived on the next hill. Six more people sailed with us: five days later, home. So that voyage was the start of two trades, with Merire and Sicily, and the more it did for Paphos, the better for Zakkala

When Alashiya learned of Melas' death, people made him even more of a lesson in disgust: the kinder they were to Ninna and ourselves, the more his name was to spit. Ninna, overwhelmed between, slashed her arms for Aktor and blooded the horns above our door. For him we made rites every moon, with Honeybee's and Little Zoe's help in the house of Ariadne, where they served and learned from Pyrrha's sister

On the birth-stone of that house, Honeybee gave Norax a daughter, Aithe. I grew my trees, Ninna the household, and Zoe with a midwife's future if she pleased. All helped with little Deucalion. *You will plant, you will prosper*, Ninna sang to him: *hear now the great ones on the sea, protecting you. I sing you brothers' hearts to shame the sun*

I adored my wives their strengths and where they needed me; could suffer with our men digging ditches, learning the water-cooled saw that cut our stone, and in the evenings longed to plough, especially with Pyrrha. Phitios came home like resurrection to Winato, and they made famous husbands. Podargos came to visit, his herds turned into ships' business growing in his pouch: Norax and his Oinops plied Miletus as I did westwards, and some of our men fished mackerel and tunny with Trojan partners. Like them, more of our young scattered into the islands, eager for their own

The more I traveled, I learned to confess it: when things were good with Egypt, things were good. We were Canaan's kin and partners, but their own little status-wars cost more than Pharaoh's taxes. The second Amenhotep kept their peace with a hand much lighter than promised early-on: when he died after twenty-five years, I found myself grandfather to Podargos' son, named Prax. They were both in Alashiya because Ninna was dying. She entrusted little Prax her crane-clan's feather: she wanted to die in the garden, and she gave me my first clue that something was not normal. Now from these days onward, a life and world began to fade

--Do you think it's the sylphium shipped these years? Ninna asked

--What, I said. --Dear one, men do not drink that

--But you don't change, she said. --Your eyes are older. But your skin. Your face. Tell us. Tell me, Ninna pleaded: she was not afraid of passing through the door, only speaking from the first unwilling steps

What could I answer? Many men belied their age. When Ninna died, her mask was smiling. Though Aktor never returned to her, the last she saw was the line of our young people coming through her garden: they kissed her hands, for the strength to lose a home and build another. She slept below a pretty hill, and many times our dances turned her way with palms out high

The next Pharaoh reigned ten years and, nothing like the Tutmoses before him, he all but left the east to its affairs, a man for his dreams and monuments. I lost my Nail-hard brother Norax, who died in a good bed in the home of his son Oinops' family, out in Miletus. I sailed there with his daughter Aithe, cut my hair, my arms, and we danced his honor. She had twin daughters now. Oinops' house stood partners a long time with Zakkala. And then came a third Amenhotep, a little boy-king, whose mother's family Pyrrha had sailed to see. By the time he put on his blue war-crown and crushed the hope that Libu had breathed into Nubia, Honeybee too was passing

--You won't share it? she wept. --You can help me, and you won't?

--Share what! I answered, kissing her work-battered hands. --Oh, Fourogata, the people who walk proud here learned from you. You were the altar that you raised for Ariadne, you made it worlds more than trade. Honeybee, don't leave us

She did. And I did not die like everybody else. Like Moira, like Ramose, like Winato, more and more of them. Arge, and Cissia, Euryale and even Brimo the once-gazelle. And one by one, the people grieving change beside a grave saw me not changing. Their playful envy cured into wonder, and then became unease, resentment, fear: the thing I loved most began to turn

Sport of nature! I say what I know, that if skin and hair and strength of body speak of age, mine stopped getting older from that time forward, through the lives of many families. It was not a gift asked for, maybe a curse deserved. I never looked it in the teeth. There were tales of men burning the world for what fell into my hand. And in the place where I had landed with it, a man who hoarded blessings was in trouble

I shrugged that I had been struck by lightning. What was my diet, what did I bathe in, what root or talisman? With no answers, rancor grew, and worst where it counted, in the elders whose hard-earned status this unnerved. Alashiya's elite were shrinking in their jewelry and textiles, turning skeletal under fine wigs and melting cones of saffron, and I went about a black-haired farmer whose skin still liked the sun. Vain I was, till smirks became accusations. *He drinks the juice of monkey-stones. He*

comes to your house to lance a boil and two days later
grandfather is dead---dry as a fly when the spider is done

I stopped trying to answer. Did they expect me not to eat the whole fruit fallen to my hands? Pyrrha's sister Kia died. Next we knew, most of Paphos' traders refused to carry produce of our land. They wanted an answer; but the Lady after Moira, Arne, had not won her office on short memory. Zakkala was her elder Pyrrha's child. Arne shipped out all we had and it fetched a good year's silver. That shut people up, and the envy got worse

Merire died. I was asked to make offerings at Sais: the Libu all but ruled that town on a western branch of Nile, and the temple there of Neith was immense, full of people and learning. Inside, Merire's property by work went to all their children, his copper sword to his sister's eldest son. After, I sat outside that portico and learned the words inscribed above the door

I am all that has been, is, shall be
No mortal ever lifted up my veil
The fruit I brought forth was the Sun

Podargos had all a man could want. He and Kopi raised four children, Nyasha bore Shekelesh sons to reckon with, and they kept Bright Foot clear of Sicily's worsening feud. My son Deucalion was a man to name every bird in our orchards. Zoe grew to a woman with a gift like Kia's, and all but lived at Paphos' seashell-oracle. She played with people till their own sense served them, and it grew the oracle's name. *Should I sail this year?* a trader would ask her. *Will you feel more lucky next?* Zoe also bore a girl, Kaliopi, with her dancing-feet. I watched their lives ripen through fine evenings under the great trees of our yard. Grandfather now, I did begin to dote in the sun. Old Crete, even The Nail, grew sweeter: this should have been an old man's nap. Instead, I was still fit for voyages

Travel kept me some from Pyrrha, but none of the trouble touched her. In Pyrrha we lived past measure: Zakkala was home, music, dawns and evenings jasmine-scented, strong harvests, children, swimming with them in waters like liquid sky. She and I never got enough of holding each other, naked, kissing: our feet still rubbed together, making their own love every time the first

And then I was kneeling beside her last bed. Pyrrha told everybody else to leave the room: they went out smirking-sure that, now, for her, daemon-man would work his gift, and it would out. I had nothing: words

> *You made my heart big as the mountains*
> *not even mountains could love you more*

I watched Pyrrha traveling, returning from visions that soothed her pain. This the woman who forged two trades with Sicily and Libu, now crosslegged upright in her bed, like some tiny ancient seed a child of herself. She lifted her hands toward the room's light, and her fingers were a clumsy girl's: she was in her mother's Cretan kitchen, tongue at her mouth's corner, one eye shut, learning thread and needle. Her hands rose up together again and again, threading the eyelet like a gesture of solemn praise: it tore down my bitterness till I was left only shattered, and in awe. The other world had opened in the room. The thread in her hands was real and infinitely long, and the line of grandmothers teaching: I saw worlds vanish in her passing, and their gestures and praise untouched by it. Pyrrha slept, and then the eyes in which I lived came back, lucid, radiant

   --I dreamed, she smiled, --our first day together, on the mountain. And I wake to my beloved, and the world we made together of what we said

   --Pyrrha! Pyrrha!

   --No, no. Listen, she said. --These years of talk, I arranged to help you. Sweet Wine, Zakkala is our family's. But---you had better leave. Make yourself their agent on the sea. Don't wait till someone wants to see if you can die. Strange man, crazy man! Sweet Wine, take your name back. That is all we can hope, is it not, to bear with everything, and keep our honey?

   --Go back to Kemet. Take my name to Lady Tiye, who rules with Pharaoh. So much land, they ran the country till he grew; and Tiye wants island things. My winter snake, be brave, whatever keeps your summer rising! Husband, brush my hair, before the women come

   I gnashed my teeth not asking to die with her. If I did eat poison, or drown, would I be a walking corpse? She looked down generations: the choice was live for that, or ashes now. I swore my Pyrrha all. She closed her peaceful eyes. I kissed her mottling hands, and when her breathing ended, sat her up, and brushed her hair. When I pushed the room's shutters open, the midday trees were still as if the last bird had died. Below, Paphos faces stared up from her yard. The wine of my blood turned fiery: in that window I took my old name again. People turned their backs

--Not even for her! --Curse your man-selfish secrets! --Why don't you leave, like your kinsman that other murderer?

I went into our orchards and hills along the sea, and crushed the tears from my heart. When it tore me inside-out, I was back in the paradisal night with Mother Zoe under Dikte, and we laughed that I had found her right three ways. I refused to see Pyrrha's grave: it was a lie. And then, I never worked so cold and sure at things whose end or reason, I knew not

Zakkala had standing to fetch good crews. Ramose had taught us to turn ships over when rot crept under the rowers' benches; so by trade and silver, three new boats were mine-outright, fat-belly galleys with more ways to work the sea's whims. The captains liked what Ramose taught me about who commanded them, and the rest looked like ordinary business. So once again I was leaving a valley we had built, with horns and spirals in the sun. *I was out*? What trial was this? What stupid dreams repeating in my life! I never forgot presents-home on top of any cargo, just for spite

Pyrrha's palm tree now stood with the tallest in

Ugarit. In Tyre a new head-family was squeezing the land-locked sisters of her trades. Byblos went on as if there were no yesterday: Gaza too, with her Sutu desert-music and island flash. My eye began to like that little Ascalon, unwalled against the sea, the white cluster of its royal young buildings and the spread of the town like only the best of Ugarit. Podargos' sons took Shekelesh business there, and Shardana amber. Even shops' quarters they planted with green, as if to please the passerby

We coasted to Pelusium, and Pyrrha's name produced a pilot up the channels of The Nile. The green shores narrowed, turned, offered several turns, narrowed again, pretty village girls waving from the old shaduf: blue and earth-brown the waters, the wind at our backs combing vast fields of wheat and barley. Put aside snakes and crocodiles, I never took to these steamy flatland warrens of the river. Dead-end marsh and quicksand warning you not to lose your way

Our pilot concealed his landmarks: I began some. And as the river's inland branches joined and we started to row through city after city, I found my spirit lowering its shield. I was alone with business crew. There was nothing for it but to learn: a casual might was staggering my eyes. Walls and roofs of temples high as country hills stood above the walkways of the guard, with pennants ranked along the roofs on poles twice as tall as ships' masts: where the gates stood open we glimpsed white limestone streets straight and broad, plazas lined with obelisks and gargantuan seated kings. A double-row of seated scowling lions flanked a boulevard of stone that looked as if it walked to the horizon

Sandstone, granite block within block of painted walls, giant forests of pillars, temple-facings glowing in shadow or colors ablaze with the sun; and along their foundations, no end to multitudes streaming every way on errands of the realm, priests, farmers, herdsmen, officers, work-gangs, clutches of families, carrying-chairs. We passed five cities bigger than Ugarit before the river's channels joined to one; and for miles between such places, the fields that fed them stretched out of sight

Kemeti called everybody children, and we never had liked our island-share of it. At Giza, though, at Memphis, and every mile up that river, we saw how they could say it. Their merest travelers' rest-house would have graced an island chief. In a few days we beached at Akhmim, on the eastern bank before the great turn into Thebes: Akhmim was Tiye's family's hometown, and here the house of her mother. Tuya, by name, came out her doors between two peacock-painted columns, and stood there a kindly-smiling, spider-thin matron in a black wig and red-sashed gown, flowing like water down her bones

--Ahh, the Alashiya! Tuya said. I bowed and proffered a massive gaudy fruit bowl cranked out in Crete: her toothy frank smile made me sorry to present such mock. What gave Tuya pause was Pyrrha. --She was a flower, Tuya said. --We were brilliant together. And you must be her son? What does your name mean? Won't you come in, captains and all of you?

Deucalion, New Wine Sailor kept his mouth shut
except for sweet tilapia-fish, eaten as they did with right
thumb and two fingers. Tuya's grandsons in short red-
sashed gowns joined the table, the elder maybe twelve
with fine black eyes and a glossy mane, Tutmose: the little
one Amenophis, with sunburn peeling his shaved head,
was pudgy and interruptive. Tutmose spoke enough
island to try a joke that shook the table: Amenophis alone
didn't catch it, Tuya scolded him, and he mocked his
steady brother in reply. Both of them I gifted with obsidian
razors, and met the next Pharaohs in their eyes

Tuya regretted that trade had to wait: this was
second month of flood season, the family was due up-river
in Thebes, and she asked us to sail behind her barge. A
festival founded by Hatshepsut was on, so popular that it
ran longer every year: eleven days in honor of Opet,
another face of Isis, mother of Green One. The rites kept
Pharaoh young

--She's a big fat hippo with a lion-lady's head, and
a crocodile down her back! Amenophis laughed. --Blap!
She farts up bubbles in mud, like a priest

--Her powers helped your mother to bring you
backwards into this world, said Tuya gravely. --Mind,
because Opet likes big bites out of vulgar boys. Now,
Deucalion. Comfortable in Thebes, I shall introduce you to
Anen, my brother-in-law, chancellor of our lands to the
north at the river's mouth. He will take you to Khaemhet,
who manages grain for the throne. Then I am sure, with
your mother's charm, Tuya smiled, --you will return here,

things in hand, and we can proceed. Your cups, gentlemen, more of this wonderful wine. I taste your limestone earth and herbs. To the house of Lady Tiye. And your house? she invited

In Egypt you felt like young dust

--Zakkala. Thank you. Thank you, I said

And then, Thebes, like the mother of cities seen before; and within it on the western bank, Malkata, palace of Tiye and her Pharaoh. He had raised already a stupendous temple in the place where The Green One's mother had rested after labor: I learned he was a king to build on wisdom of his women, in the faces of his priests. Their pride lay with princes of old who had captured Thebes and made Amon-Re god of gods, forgetting the mud: this Pharaoh had himself blazoned as a vessel of Isis, shaped by Her hands on Her wheel. I stopped trying to count the people walking and singing in the main procession, behind golden well-dressed statues of Amun-Re, Goddess Mut, their strapping son Khonsu. Pharaoh himself led chariots twelve-abreast down a vast open avenue, westward toward the river; then he and his family boarded barges, and from the halls of Karnak the people's march trailed his voyage south, to Luxor sanctuary. Thousands of people that day, and each with an offering to follow their king's: baskets of lotus for the priests' hands, fat cones of joss and jasmine, wine-jugs lashed to flowery oxen, braces of duck and striped gazelle. I gave our crew little gifts to be seen, but none of us saw inside these places. No one did except for the wealthiest, and clergy. If the painted elders glowed from the strength of Pharaoh's prayer, people took rub of youth and good moods from them; that Opet had given him suck, that no one thirst nor hunger forever

Amenophis strode back out of Luxor's towering gate, and gave his golden mace a randy shaking for his multitudes. I was with Khaemhet by way of the chancellor. The man beamed bright as his hard-won breastplate enjoying the cheer, his head like a raisin with gold-drop earrings and gappy teeth

--Green One shines, Khaemhet said. --Your ships are timely to buy grain

--Dew of your land, I smiled, and at the words, somebody jostled into me: a servant-girl not twenty with a chaplet of greens in her black curls, melting cat's eyes like green stones, and her gown a diaphanous festival-dress of island weave, likely borrowed, exquisitely too small

Nofret, her name: we were wanted back for Malkata's midday feast, and she clung to little Amenophis' wrist. --You can play with Nefertiti anytime! Forgive me, sirs, he has no respect like his brother

--Piss of the land! said Amenophis skyward

Malkata's tables were spread below Tiye's and Pharaoh's in a hall of gilded stone three times the yard at Zakkala. Pillars the girth of its trees sang back music, echoed our clatter: with each course a painted man or woman brought a fresh fingerbowl of lemon-water. This palace housed three hundred lesser wives. Gangs of fellahin were digging an entire lake off the river for the house. If Kemet ever turned all its strength to war, the world had better stay home

We ranked no audience, but Lady Tiye met us in her gardens. In its great pool, hatchling-crocodiles lunged among the lotus, rippling its mirror of the sky. The country loved Tiye's round brown eyes, her skill with festival and her scowl that froze little Pharaohs. She chose me a Nubian orchid, then sat and took my hands with ready terms. Where I looked for dismissal, this great lady reached out for Labrys round my neck, regretting old-time amity with the islands. Equally vague, I mourned the loss of bonds by which bad things happened

--I always liked island diplomats, Lady Tiye smiled, pleasant memories sparkling in her eyes. --Enjoy your stay, New Wine Sailor. Your name will be welcome in my ports. Be assured, my husband makes more than grain grow. Bring us the islands, and reap ten-fold

The smile she left me with foretold the night, because Nofret climbed into my bed, a girl full of pillow-talk charmingly sure of her own great house someday. Next I knew back at Tuya's, I was hearing the virtues of a marriage. This was more than I had hoped; a small inconspicuous niche that worked with what was. Now I just had to stay ahead of my problem in people's eyes

So I left Egypt glad for the humbling this time. There and around The Green, I learned to sow reassuring intelligence, and Tiye said it helped to keep garrisons just the right strength in Canaan, and the vain bloody squabbles of its kings in Pharaoh's courts. Amenophis must have ruled forty years, and after those early killings, he scarcely bothered even Libu. The islands never saw so much barley for their wine and fuller's earth, their black obsidian and marble

By the time the third generation of my children bore the fourth, the rhythm of my ships on The Green was the rhythm of its festivals and gardens. Where a man remembered unburdening himself in his cups of good Zakkala wine; where a woman remembered the wild feel of my hands, snake and tongue, as I had learned pleasures from women in the land of Dripping Rain and other places; where I taught some family arts of vines and olives, there in time fathers and mothers told a child of Deucalion's. And down the years of Merire's family, the sylphium trade kept growing

--Wine for love, and sylphium to cull the fruit: bless a man in the middle!

In the harbor of Naxos I answered, and met Afti. She was daughter of a famous house of weavers, with black hair and eyes almost paralyzing blue, silk-clad breasts, her hips a honey-jar. Brazen for what she wanted, her spirits quick as island currents; and curiously, half her pleasure was in hiding ours from a lord of a husband. I saw her women tuck my trade away in baskets, hiding it

--You, calling any man lord? He doesn't know what sylphium is

--We want it that way, Afti answered. –Mine has a name that keeps criminals clear of Naxos. He wants sons and more sons. Thanks to your cousins' clumsy jars, I give him what Naxos can feed. Would I rather a priest in my bed? Yes, and without the man as he is, look at our neighbors. Women, children kidnapped off a beach. The weak, the ones who do not face up, they burn

--Let me guess. Your mothers chose his kind of strength for your sakes, and now they find raiders already in the house

--And what then? Afti would laugh. --Run off and live on boats? They are boys, you are a man. I want to hear more about The Great Green, the shores you know, the shapes of places where the lands fall in the sea

Her honey took, and her predicament. It was her husband's *cousins* in the islands playing their part in these games. King's trick! If she and her ladies called him *boy*, why hand him the house to stop a tantrum? *Grow up, Afti, while you can!* I'd say. It was not my views she wanted. Years over her, I took fool's chances: her lord would have spitted me. There was something in Afti like a Karfi artisan mired in poppy. She liked her dark old man of the sea, foxing the simple sun king who made her feel safe from games of death. When this had unmanned me enough, I let go. But Afti was far more than honey and surrender

When she died, a sister took over meeting me for sylphium, and slipped a rolled-up present in my goods. At sea, the world unfolded in my hands. To the stitch, there was every coast and shape of island I had ever scratched in sand at Afti's asking. Hold it up, and through diaphanous blue-green waves, you saw the edges of lands around The Great Green---the way a crane saw them, from the sky.

North to south my routes from Troy to Libu, the Cyclades, Byblos to Sicily: Alashiya, The Nile's mouth, Crete with my warehouse at Kommos in the midst, and towns even on the isles in silver points. Years it took her, stitching out the countries in her head: a being like that, tangled in boys' arms. I treasured that gift its help, and never showed it anyone. Not until I learned what desperation was

I knew not why my years ran on and on, and with nothing about it promising *forever*, I feared like every man an ugly death. What was there but to live? I rode the trade and gifted families. In Libu the people were the strongest around their mothers that I knew outside of Crete or Lesbos, and knowing my blood with Merire's line, Meshwesh children called me uncle like the rest. I kept moving, turning over ships and crews so that no one quite tracked my years. Each day like any man's, yet not so much as a bad tooth. What was this *for*? Each home a refuge from the others, I gave every one of them feathers of a crane. I saw my children travel and learn their cousins, and always, lonely on the seas between. They throve and died, went on, forgot, remembered: at first I grieved them as for Prax, a child passed-on before his father. But the longer I lived, the more alone. Old bull on a mountain, watching his little towns; knowing he could not live there, but loving their songs

Pharaoh's strong first son died untimely. I was at the Kommos warehouse and it pleased Lady Tiye that I sailed. My little jewel there, Nofret, had ripened to Tiye's coveted servant, and she gave me daughters and sons.

They sowed flashes of island style where they worked, and it put them among the innocuous few on the good side of second son Amenophis. At a dinner I saw the pudgy boy grown round-shouldered, long-faced, slack at his doting father's side. Nofret said his outbursts had become tirades against priests of Amun-Re. My mind had to turn like a sail and yard together, to grasp that his priests despised him because his eyes were in the spirit-world. They wanted a king for armies, for keeping Canaan's wealth away from Hatti, without the bother of trade. But Amenophis was not his brother. His father had shrunk, but he was the man who looked as though the world were already too much. He had the luxury to answer with a mild glassy gaze, punctuated by rage

I went back once in the next five years, when his father died. Amenophis made me see myself at my own father's death, rising to his flower to find old ceremony broken. His priests glared through his lackadaisical rites with no idea who had taught him the emptiness of pomp

In Tiye he confided, she understood her son, and she gave me a commission. She wanted an island-wife for him, and artisans, too, without Egypt's eyes, for some momentous thing they had in the works. *If you call it momentous*, I said, *it will terrify me*. Tiye answered, *You won't be alone*

There were Cretans to locate already painting in her lands, and from Sicily to Ugarit I spent Egyptian gold, and earned my share. For his wife, affairs looked best in Melos in the Western String of isles. The woman they chose was a kourai named Kiya. Melos her island had Achaian ships in their waters, and a wary eye born of Crete's fall. Through Kiya, then, Melos expected strength over wealth. They were disappointed

I heard only talk after Amenophis kissed Kiya's hands. She bore him six daughters, more than any other wife: he made her at home with the artists and their kin, and servants from my family of Nofret too. In turn, from their inquisitive dinners Pharaoh drew what he called new thoughts. *Yes, yes,* Nofret told me he would say: *Of course, why not, paint what you see!* He was searching for something. He began to like the island way of letting children feast, and it helped him shake his priests. The little ones laughed at painted men in gold hashing out the solemn meanings in his stool. Amenophis ecstatic just gazing at a wall now covered with crazy sprays of birds, big-headed lilies, bulls ramping after cows in green labyrinths of rushes. Amenophis called for *paint what you see* in his family's images: *You asked for it,* said a Cretan painter's eye. And there he was, a pot-bellied father, kissing Kiya's babies in his lap

His priests detested him. His loves were contented insults to their aims. For a moment Amenophis might have shown the world new kings. He did so anyway. Beleaguered, he snapped---around some hope that, becoming one with the flaming crown of the wide world, he would change the way he looked to dogs in daylight. He took a new sun-name, Akhenaten. And within ten years, he and Tiye moved their country's entire capital city days down-river, to a place no builders had touched before, because it was stony red desert

At a stroke, Akhenaten shut the country's temples down, cutting off his enemies' river of wealth. Having idled so many, he raised armies but with chisels, to hammer all gods but his own blazing sun from their stones. And for such a public enormity, he forced nobody outside court to go along. The people of the land kept more of their produce, but the sun beat them hard as ever in the fields. They liked Isis for Her thousand family-touching names, and Green One. His image went into the ground with them, a tiny man squatting in a pilgrim's cloak, like an exile bound to win the world

Akhenaten lived behind the walls, and for the signs they cut and cut again. In a handful of negligent years, Hittites were taking over town by town in Syria, creeping up on outright-rule of Ugarit. Tyre on the sea was under siege by a gang of her cheated neighbors. On both sides of that, Shekelesh and Shardana men fought each other in old-home feud. In boats like my son Bright Foot's they had come to see cities, and learned to get paid kings' gold for killing people. At Akhenaten's back, priests were encouraging trouble in towns across Canaan

Nofret aged, and steered our ship deftly like a tender of Tiye's barge. They farmed our children out to the house of Akhenaten's gruff vizier, named Ay, and to a rising general named Horemheb. Both men were Pharaoh's close in-laws, but they disliked his insults to the past. In Nofret and in them, our family there survived

Twenty years and the Hatti pushed Egypt out of Ugarit. We paid their big-hat viziers the old protection. I went my careful ways, till Tiye sent for me through Gaza

--The Great Green life agrees with you, she smiled horribly. She had shrunk beneath her plumes and polished disk to a black-toothed creature, tiny and always cold on her cedar chair. This time in Egypt, I knelt with my heart. Tiye had given me life

--My son is going to fail, she said. --The priests and the old land will win. What in the end is the point of just one god? But fear not for Nofret and your family. Others will rule before Horemheb, and his house is trusted army blood. Now, old friend. If ever we talked about what Canaan can become, do what this old woman asks

Drawn in again, I should have known what came of it. Byblos liked its tithes of trade from the small towns of northern Canaan. With Hatti marching into them, a chieftain named Abdi tried to forge his own new country from the pieces. Egypt's garrison caught and killed the man, but his son Aziru held the tribes together, and kept Byblos' shares of trade. According to practice, Byblos complained to Pharaoh's ear. He was not listening. While Tiye looked into matters and sent messages, Akhenaten's priests sent Aziru gold. To build the threat themselves, and make a man of Akhenaten. But of all this, Tiye intended something else---a kind of buffer-land in Canaan, between Egypt's and the Hatti claims. My part was to pacify the king of Byblos to it, Rib-Haddi

He knew me a son of reliable Alashiya, agent for

his cedar-wood. He crowed beside Adonis' ancient pool, a rooster between imperial example and neglect. I said, Egypt's hand went heavy where kings failed the whole: a buffer-land would keep both masters from his door. Rib-Haddi would not hear that Byblos would never be Thebes. Having bullied neighbor-towns to cut his losses, he was drunk with mutiny and meant to try the edge. In a few days, with sobering word of soldiers on the royal road, half his men left the walls, and Rib-Haddi slipped out after them. I was working to find him exile when he was murdered at my back

What had I done? What was I doing? Tiye never faced me again. For years, trade in Ugarit said that Aziru's northern buffer-land did work: he wrecked it himself, selling out in time to Hatti, which drew Egypt back into Canaan and spilled blood. Nofret passed away. I grieved on the ground. Kiya disappeared from court, and for asking, I got no more than a painter's black look

Drowning in consequences, Akhenaten broke as his children died. When his gaze fixed, his priests rifled his city, buried his name in kind, and back in Thebes raised dazzling restorations, to help everybody forget they were making it up. The artisans wanted ships out, and it was time to let a few years sow confusion round my name

From the islands to The Nile, I sailed with a belly sick of men. Sick of priests, sick of kings and chieftains, sick of tricks and walls and fables, and filling their mouths with wine and oil. I blessed the sea's salt curses, the cranes' free cries of exile as big as the world. Had my own Kemeti family any memory or pride, to bend a knee where men made gods like pots? For Nofret's children, I bit the words back. A little boy named Timo looked a promising fellow, and I watched him from afar

My buffer-lands were time, ships, the meltings of my names. There I was, estranged four generations, no land home; and what to do with this gift, or curse? I was adrift. But Horemheb was not. He built his house through fifteen years, cut the noses off officials caught with bribes in the wreckage of Ahkenaten, and when his time came, he pleased people with building his throne from their queens' line. His balanced hands made high priests of men he trusted from the army. But he knew my face, and I never went nearer than his ports

Horemheb ruled twelve years, and Timo, fourth of my line, had Nofret's eyes and hair black as ironstone. As a boy learning cipher, Timo sent me a greeting on papyrus: when he wrote again he was a well-spoken infantry corporal, hoping to meet someday. Another soldier. At least he belonged. Timo outlived Horemheb, and a year of a Pharaoh Ramses. When Seti took the throne, Timo was fed into new divisions of soldiers being raised: Seti styled himself The One Reborn. Canaan's towns read the omens of a Mighty Bull with powers not those of spring, and reinforced their walls. Adrift, I was ripe for what happened. And so was my grandson

I went back to Alashiya named Iakos. My eyes filled with the place as keen as that first day at Paphos. It was the last crest of spring, past the moons of crocus and crimson corn-poppy on the hills. The rivers high, rock doves sang in flowering thyme: the air was thick with water, the trees budded out in sweet chestnut, mastic, pistachio and plane. It was people's favorite time except for harvest, crops in, the dead well-feasted from jars of wine and seed: they swept their houses, purged themselves of grudge and sloth, and rose to the high weather days

I had not expected to breathe as if great windows had opened in moldy walls. I was a mark, mouth open, wanting in

--Been here before? Ah, Alashiya, queen of islands. Please, sit down

A black-bearded man at the fig-shaded table of a common-house: Enkomi-born by his nappy curls and jewelry, Ugarit the loom of his long gown, a black Hatti knife. One eye gone from its half-open socket, a veteran's wound. Ugarit these days forced men to Hatti arms, and Hatti used them to practice up for Egypt, butchering Hurrians in Syrian river-towns. Smiling the man poured barley-beer with ritual pleasure, and I longed for old Norax, for brothers to make the most of what was left

--Like it here? the man said in keen Akkadian clipped his way. --A land of weaving dreams. Health, sir. My name is Mopsos. Ah, good barley, he sipped as he read my trim, my old cropped-feather headdress and Labrys too. --Alashiya knows ferment. She *is* ferment, he laughed. --Hard old Cretans too. You appear to be of means

What was I doing? Circling Zakkala's garden of

our seed, horns and spirals; afraid to see it, and afraid to be driven out again

--Ah, Iakos, this stranger rang on. --Now come the new birds, birds of prey to feed on fat. Achaians: some pay for trading-camps, some build outright and dare complaint. They plan to steal, you see, so they build their high points first. I wonder, what will come of Alashiya patience and generosity? Achaia breeds too many sons. I have seen Mykenai, the house of Achaia's Lion, the walls they build and the circle of their fathers' graves. Their chieftains' eyes look inward, but they never stop pushing their reach. What will happen, Iakos, when Achaians are at home here?

--These islanders know, they feel it, like cranes the wind. They will fly, taking even their mothers: they sail before they slaughter over land. So, their Mother will step down from her copper stand. Now, think you, Iakos--- where will they go? Where they always go: where trade is and no Achaians. Here, then, good man, drink me a profitable secret. Partners, you and I, we can be waiting on the hill. No cost to you, Iakos---an interesting journey, to a place where Cretans live already. Do you understand? When Achaians take the copper, the hill to wait upon has tin! Go east, old man

--Will I do well? I asked, my judgment as blunt as my beery fingers

--You should, Mopsos lilted

I had to believe. Every horizon made me homesick. I tracked down people who knew this man: there was no end to trade in the east, and anything with promise of a place, I reached for

I took my ships across to Ugarit, and on the high ground of the great bay's southern rim was another Achaian camp: my good old spiders, right in the face of the city trying to pluck their passing trade. We coasted south, the mountains descending to Syria's inland plain, then higher and greener north of Byblos; and this time at Tyre, we bore up her river, into a great valley flanked by spines of mountains. Every travelers' house was an easy find with the painted papyrus Mopsos made

When I was satisfied berthing my ships at the caravan-town, we followed road and trail out of there for days toward sunrise, south and east, up and down the half-desert country into Hazor. Beyond where the trees gave way to sage and stone, that was a city with thick walls equal in power to the rocky steeps on which men had raised it, a place with no match for commanding the roads into mountains east and west. There was so much traffic of trade and the force to protect it that they left the gates open till each sundown. In the house of their divinities, Egypt's statues stood both sides of a simple standing stone, cut with signs that pleased me: a pair of hands upraised toward a disc within a crescent. Here, the dust of traffic on the roads was all the Nile's overseers wanted, and Hazor was as thick with sand-farers as Tyre with her sailors. Sutu, Shasu, desert-people who moved on foot with their pack-animals: our quarry was connection to the far east flow of tin. If they could stand the heat, so could I. Days we walked the coast of a sea with salt-white shores, and westwards at our right hand, rising uplands. Good to see they kept the same traditions of rest-houses on the roads.

Beyond the lake, a broad river valley, the Jordan's running south beyond sight, and green as a little Nile between close hills. There the signs went bad. Sutu tribesmen, a few, then bands of many began to come past us day and night, running north and east: bleeding men laid open, struggling to help each other away from something very bad. The camels they had left were limping, slung with bodies, Egypt's arrows in their sides. Where the mountains fed another river down valley, we turned its way west upstream, as if trailing the vultures. Ahead, many passes crossed through these uplands under a great soft-shouldered hill. Across its high points, a brick-walled citadel flew goldfoil pennants of Thebes. Beth Shan. It was bright morning, Dagon's green dew on the air, and a drifting char-grease smell like nothing from a priest

First thing on that plain before we mounted for the city gates, my eye caught a pennant flying Timo's Division of Seth, Mighty of Bows. But no Kemeti would talk. The place to a man was still in shock with yesterday's horror on the plain, and fighting to keep control of itself with work-details on pain of more death. In the citadel shops I found the Cretans, a handful of wizened potters and masons, sons and families cowered in a clutch around a little house of Earth Mother: like a double of Ninna's, and one lazy dog on its roof. When I gave them Mopsos' name and asked their help to meet some master of their metals, the oldest woman answered, *What? Mopsos promised you would come with ships to take us out of here!* For me it was over. I wanted word of Timo

In the citadel courtyard Egypt's wounded writhed on stretchers, shrieking across the droning of priests for the arrows and heads of spears dug out of them. Their dead lay yet among Sutu desert-men out under the hill: half the able and their prisoners were gathering bodies, building the pyre, and the rest fetched baskets in. Severed Sutu heads, hands, ears, genitals, dumped in rancid heaps to console the wounded

As I waited outside their governor's sunshade, his scribe threw up on the papyrus addressed to The One Reborn. --Start over! Where was I? *Hail and greeting, Mighty Bull, who makes the chiefs of Canaan cease every contradiction of their mouths.* When I managed to intrude and inquire, he waved his golden hand saying *Oh, somewhere off the hill. Ask for yourself at the victory-fire*

I went down, and seeing the smoke at the plain's far edge, tried to get there where officers ran muster and made lists. Acres of Sutu strewn in sunken clumps of desert-black, laid open, twisted on broken backs in tracks of hooves and bladed fellie-wheels. Faces bashed to pulp by heavy fighting-rods. Camels sprawled in red sand, entrails out where swords had pulled, disarticulated pieces, vultures cursing, crowding, craning to swallow. Feed, Mother Night: she eats mistakes

The potters said that desert-men pushed in and out

of this plain. This time, their game plucking trade and women had stumbled into Pharaoh's. The One Reborn broke his water with three divisions of chariot and foot against two hundred camels. And now his blood was up to meet the Hatti

A rat came out the loose anus of a horse stretched out in golden tack. In green grass an axe's work, the ragged left piece of a face. Nearing the pyramid of Mighty Bull burning on the plain, I knew Timo was in it

Did he live to realize he too was adrift? I lived to see his death bring our family more standing on The Nile, and the comfort that Nofret's children took in their priests' labyrinth of reasons. Time, twist the knife in a sport of nature! Could I help my memory from Knossos? If this was belonging, tear out my tongue, my spit never stop

East wind rose with the sun. Human punk drifted with crackling-sounds of hair in fire. I covered my mouth with what I had, and it was Afti's folded weaving. It came to hand Sicily-up, the opposite edge of the world

The Beth Shan Cretans paid silver to get out. In fact, two brothers of theirs saw Labrys, heard where I was going, and staked me a year of service for the voyage. From there, as it was working, I sailed Iakos, and learned their names

The warehouse at Kommos made for crude winter. Like The Nail, it taught us each other, the places grieved between us. Before we sailed that spring we were pilgrims together, and climbed into the midst of all we wanted. These circles of rising stars and flowers. To speak our thanks and share our meals along benches of communion, to lift our palms, to be the circle and the center of a pouring. Cleanse the spring, weigh a feather, love, be grateful, consent; and gardens under great-grandmothers' figs in the good high places. Learning to see the great subtle breathing of the mountain in yellow gorse-flower; hearing its half-sleep murmur, under the bees

We had that between us, beaching in Sicily. Thapsos was small enough yet for our strength to tip local feud, and young enough to make that first matter in their welcome-council. Their eldest woman spoke it. Whose side were we on

--Our feathers make us family, I said. --Nyasha, a Shekelesh mother here, my fathers returned to your kin. Her daughter wed their son, Podargos

--You do not understand, replied this grandmother, in a diadem of sun-wheels stitched with gold. --Nyasha, she explained, --returned here from slavery. On that she built a house of sons to keep her daughters safe. Nyasha, though, had learned from her lords, and their end. When the best of us drove out Shardana, Nyasha lived that they never come back our masters. Her sons made sure of it, but then her grandsons were no men for the plough. They ventured off in ships, and kings with ready gold found them. Shardana curse our houses, and follow us in everything---so now, for spite, the curs tail our sons into battles, and fight for the opposite side

--Respectfully, I said, --there are more than two sides. You have Achaians camping your south coast

The Thapsos council knew it, and looked down. A crowd of the curious in doorways knew it too

--Your windows look toward Pylos, I said, --and Poseidon looks toward you. Let Sherden spin their knock-off clay. Whatever the Shardana do, their aim is not Achaian; not advantage sucked from you till you are gone. Let our farms feed the storehouse, and trim Achaian sail in your sons' steads. We will not bring war, nor let it come

--So you know these big fair fellows, came grandmother's sly reply

Enough to spoil a Lion's spring. Next season we were waiting when ships full of carpenters arrived. Council, we tried: they did not need carpenters to trade. Beyond that, they had no purpose here for which men asked permission. When it turned to fight, we killed three for two, and in a year their trading-tilts were back. Blue eyes burning with royal order to behave, fetch copper and amber for their cups. That, I trusted like their love for the king who roared it at them. We watched them, and shrugged, the way we lived with a rumbling mountain

Once more I began to find. The Cretans I came with nestled into lives, had childen, died. I sailed, played old confusion-games: news of Seti said he was home, mostly, building a vast womb-temple named for Green One. Evidently his rebirths were running out. Time made me grateful past regret for our brief good place. Its brevity meant nothing. Its goodness had roots and branches, and no king's son could kill the tree

A Thapsos sailor's widow took Iakos house-bond:

Syka, for the fat figs of her land. She was all the line of old Nyasha, thirty-three handsome with the broader-faced island look; her hope to see her young son and daughter turn a smith or a potter off the farm. I could help. At a feast, Syka first said to me, *Let me take you to see the figs*, which made every Shekelesh laugh. I understood, and our ambitions wove together

I sailed only two in five years after that. Syka's house was a great wooden oval of cedar and oak, the roof crowning Thapsos pasture in sight of the sea. Like every house she hosted cousins on the circle of sitting-benches built inside: she liked to say the stars turned round the smoke-hole, but Syka's altar was the family table outdoors under trees. Sailor's hunger I had known, but I drooled for her hearth burning Zakkala oil, onion, garlic, and eggplant a big queer vegetable that ate like meat. There were always almonds on that table; wine of Alashiya, because the local grape turned your palate into a cat's tongue; and Syka made a sardine-sauce that turned even green fish tasty, better than Troy's or Libu's. On that, she could field ships. But it was a grandmother's secret, Syka said at table. And could I not just eat, let others talk? I sat back, regal as Dagon, home

One year in the great decrepitude of Seti, we caught three Achaian ships sliding northwest, past us, into Shardana waters. Beside me was Syka's son, Namar, eighteen in his first helmet: his hand was always white around his sword. We had to speak to this. We chased them up-wind and, by chance, right into three strong

Shardana ships off their island's south coast. We forced them to beach

For the first time, Shekelesh and Shardana made Achaians listen to how we did things, gifting our ways past mistrust, talking. In their holds, no goods or presents: they were hunting. And still we might have treated, till their red-beard leader exclaimed *By Zeus! Is there no end to these jabbering, effeminate Earthlings?* We made them feel lucky to run from there alive. And then, Shekelesh faced Shardana on the beach, with equal arms

Something had changed. These men both sides were young. Their fathers' skills in war were sharp, but not the first felt grudge of feud. The sight of common enemies, near home, said more than years of fathers' tales: they feared their towns burned flat more than shame across the water. As we stared, a Shardana shouted *This looks to bleed both sides!* We answered, *And no Pharaoh gold in the bargain!* So we boldly sat, traded scout-reports, then food, and bet our cups on wrestling. But feud had meant too much for easy parting

When a match brought blood, I managed to play old custom that only our two best men should fight. *No!* said the same Shardana man. *Let our two weakest fight: then each will be weakest no more!* On our side, wrestling chose out Syka's son

From the day we laid Namar beside his father, Syka made me sleep a year outside. It was Shekelesh way. Her daughter, Alexi, came of age in her brother's loss not so sweet a flower; but offer she did, the rites here as old as the houses. Thapsos' mothers nourished their gardens around so many men of war

I had to sail next season, the north isles with sylphium, and came home to a son my blood in Syka's arms. The fifth since Ariadne walked. I remembered him that way because he lived not much longer than she did. Ariste grew up in the first years of a second Pharaoh Ramses. Thapsos might have grown its Alashiya seed into a place as strong as Pylos, but there was no end to the east's ready gold for young men. I made Ariste their match at arms: he loved his older friends, and saw how few of them came back. When he took up his mother's potter's wheel, his fellows made him suffer

--If a man lives to fight, what happens to things the fight is for! Ariste raged from his wounds at Syka's table: he was a boy as well-spoken as my Prax

--Brave men bring them through, I answered touching his chest, --here, where you hang your crane's feather and memory of blood. A bond more than any king's trick

Ariste found his way. Those years, many men at arms left Sicily and towns of Shardana too. When luck failed their dreams, this second Ramses caught some of them raiding his coastal towns. He chained them to his armies, or to building yet another first city, Avaris, at the head of his Canaan road. Happy Journey, Kemeti called that place, unlike our men who made it back

Ariste learned to make copies of Achaian prize-bowls, to paint the warriors marching round between the handles, and he traded them to men at arms who stood them up high in their houses. That fed his time at his wheel. One afternoon he brought me a finished grain-jar like a child in his arms, as graceful as Alashiya work all white with its paint in red and black. Around it flowed an ocean's waves, with a darkened isle to one side where a great tree grew. Turn it in your hands, and islands crowned with trees came round, spirals between them, running spirals

I took him sailing to see other shops and ways. Ariste talked more about fuller's earth than island girls. Ugarit by then was crowded and foul, the same one sour odor from marsh and dye-works to the streets: the higher walls kept the sea-breeze from its work, built up under Hatti rule against surprises in the harbor. Jaded to the tavern-keepers, greedy, thriving-still

Ariste learned from potters there, and traded up a better-working wheel. But we could not sit for beer without hearing of a battle to the south, inland, at Kadesh. Around us wounded soldiers' talk, laments and arguments: a battle a thousand times Beth Shan. In a wound gone carrion, I smelled it afresh

--Did you smell past lives forgotten. Do you admire it, the waste, I hammered Ariste aboard ship. –And what did our great ones discover after spilling each other's guts? That nothing between them belongs to them, that the best course is marriage of their houses, and fairer trade. Are we mad, Ariste, or why do they kill ten thousand sons to learn to behave like your great-grandmother?

I sailed him out of there, this time for Ascalon. It was still the young green city cupped by the landward crescent of its wall, with the sea-side open, and only a neutral's trade about. Still like the best of Ugarit, with houses of women where women of life-long learning at lyre and flute, sang stories of their gods. I was black inside for the graves and funerals waiting everywhere. Surely we could bring home some kind of medicine, and we heard it in the songs of one named Ahlaran. Thick dark hair maturing gray, with Sutu eyes, her voice the desert longing for the rains; fingers mistress of the strings and pipes she played of every land. Podargos' trade had earned trust here, but it took Ahlaran half a moon to name her price. And that, she stipulated, paid twelve moons. So, she sang us home. I listened for the lays most soothing, for when Thapsos' families grieved along their benches

Derceto, queen of oceans, queen of the pool of Ascalon,
entwine your silver tail with Dagon's in the stars,
and sing me old Diktynna of dear mountains,
who leaped into the sea and found Your name

In the great hall of Thapsos the Shekelesh men drank to Kadesh, cups thumping marching-songs, comparing injuries and healing proud-flesh. *Hear Hear!* what they did to Shardana on a field no man's eye had seen for blood. How Pharaoh had believed two Hatti spies, and camped himself in front of their thousands one hill away. How they burned his tents, till Ramses' rage and

Shardana blood turned the day. Why, men said, their dead brothers' faces would live a god's age. *On Ramses' lying walls!* they laughed. *Hear Hear!* The Shardana's best were Ramses' slaves now. Men drank along the benches, said their brothers were not gone. When the snoring began, Ahlaran stopped, and walked out

We worked our trades and year by year played the Achaians. Ariste served too, though we never showed them more men than we needed. For all men sang of themselves, we took up Shardana's little round shields that made a clouting-weapon of your arm, their shorter blades with the weight more forward, good for hacking your way inside Achaian long ones. Had I learned? Had I made my peace with war?

Four years after Kadesh, men heard-tell that Meshwesh farms looked ripe on the western Nile. Thapsos knew that my ships knew those waters. Had I made my peace? I sailed with them, because I wanted to shame them back toward old rules. Filch fine things, but leave people food: no call to burn down houses half your own. So we coasted Libu country, and when the ships went in, I sheared off into the wind

But at Kommos in Crete, at the warehouse, came a dread that I had to get back home. Everybody fit to sail was drunk. An Achaian feast was on, to close the inaugural year of Mykenai's new Lion of the mainland: Atreus, high king of kings. *Quite a fellow*, said the sailors and stevedores under their breath. Building good roads, he was, to move his soldiers, raising flanker-walls to his Lion

Gate. *Maybe he expects company?* they laughed. People who knew better, building little kingdoms off the big one, from which they dared not disentangle; like Afti's pleasures, darker. In their corners men laughed it up that Atreus, slaughtering rivals, fed one of them the man's own children in a pie

--Well, as long as he is qualified, they joked

A Griffin's claw gripped my stomach. My ship's captain called it fool's speed to strike out across open sea, but we found enough of Ramose's turning circles. We caught a gift of weather, too---which was bad, the more I thought about it

Thapsos was gone. Syka, Alexi, Ariste, houses, shops, stores, Thapsos, gone. Gulls at bodies swollen by the tide, strewn about our child's-play walls. The strongest men curled up in surf and sand, first and last to die. A woman brained with a jar of pickled olives. A toddler-boy stuck through to cow the rest. Stone halls pulled down with prying-bars, a better job of it than Poseidon: houses rifled in rage that found no gold, their circles each a char of oak and cedar. Old Koreter was laughing in the waves, in his mad blue mountains: *You will never be free of us*

Here was the neck of a Paphos jar shaped like Knossos mountain-horns: climbing it a painted tree of life with breasts like fruit, and leafy tops for upraised arms. When I found Syka's table hacked apart for fun, then shards of our shrine, I took off my cropped-feather headdress. It fed the night's fire to a sky without a moon. The blackest thing I knew was the burning of care

Kadesh had smashed two abominations. I swore The Great Green's turn was come. If none of these lords not husbands looked any further than the day, then that was where my curse of days could serve. I swore to help them find each other, and wreck the boyish world-wrecking lie of glory in their blind collusions

Mother Night, she eats mistakes. My oath was cedar ashes to my skull, and tasted from this hand.

6

--Oh, look Papou, cranes!

Eight generations, flames from Troy to Gaza, and the same little cries: my twin Kemeti children had caught a chevron of the great birds thirteen strong, blithely crossing the blue square of sky above us. Black necks, white cheeks and crimson crests, feeding their way north for the high-summer roosting grounds; and we shut in by four stone walls of the Vizier's Heliopolis courtyard, waiting audience and war. To see them was longing. Always home, never lost, led by their bonds, and those their only limit: free wings and laughter for the fears of men, the fables of fathers and their walls. They laughed us one harsh clang, a black-lightning cry, and were gone

--Papou? We want to go with them, Papou

--Go? Dear ones, where? I said

At Thapsos I had smashed the last jar of sylphium. Three generations of The Great Green got little more. As well, I started pouring out double wine everyplace I went, and I told each peacock how his rivals drank it, deep, and unmixed with water. So, down the days of those three changings of my kin, the wine-soaked fathers on my routes produced too many boys, and made half their choices in their cups. Worse, after Thapsos, every land of The Great Green turned dry, by luck of weather. The sons who had turned their cousins into useful enemies shared no food, and the raids began till there was no food, only memory of harm. Where things were broken, people asked by whom. And at last I watched the ships of their grandsons tear down any lord-protector in their reach. Not a throne untouched, and fear The Nile's new watchword. *Stasis*: every king's taste of his own

Our savageries and sufferings were about to get worse; and then, a chance that they might turn. I polished up my double-bladed lies for the Vizier

--You both look so grown-up today, I told Pamako, my black-haired boy of seven: he was eighth son since Minos walked the world, and his name meant a troubler and a healer. Thendra his twin was my little tree of life, both of them dressed in their best Kemeti linens by their mother, of Nofret's line. What I did this day was at her back, and the children understood some dark withholding. The three of us afraid of the enormous cast-bronze doors we faced, afraid of the big little man inside

--Papou, you want to go, too, Thendra pined. --We like the islands, said Pamako with a move to take her hand

--Both of you. This is home. Your mother and I just want you to visit awhile with the nice Vizier and his family. My, look how fine and strong his house. You saw the islands. Go back? Where towns are on fire, people so angry and lost that they hurt themselves? We saw your cousins' mothers there dig sticks into holes for a mouse's bite of grain. You wished you could help them. So, we will. My darlings, somebody has to be brave

--Let somebody else, Pamakos shrugged

Wine of The Kid true of speech in his eye. What were children, by then, to a man in a salt cloak, having seen so many bloom, falter, fade? Life's power to forget; and in that, one half-free hand to try what worked

--Pamakos, my warrior, I hugged them. --Thendra, my strong little tree

The joined enormous doors of bronze boomed open, drawing day into darkness. I rose and hid my shiver like a ram unwilling at an altar. A bald brown burly priest gowned in white cotton padded out across the stones to us

--In the Name of His Omnipotence, User-maat-re Mer-y-amun. Strong Is The Justice of Re, Beloved of Amun, Great Ramses will see you now. By the Eye of His Excellency, Ta, Vizier of The Two Lands. Boots and any arms, leave here

His cautious kohl-black eyes raked me, a boat-born bastard kinsman of barbarians at his gate. *Come Come*, the priest insisted patting me, *You people always have a knife someplace!* Finding none, his back led us through a dark corridor that babbled both sides with gilded glyphs

Out we came into a hall like being outdoors in a world of stone, where everything pointed the one man fit to sit. Backed by the frieze that dwarfed him, Ta, the Vizier, sat in full pose on a golden chair upon a dais

We bowed beneath a red disc's golden rain of rays upon him. From smoky slits under the ceiling, slants of white glare cut through shadows to the floor. Out there my Great Green kinsmen wandering, burning the world they could not keep from slipping through their fingers

The priest introduced Iakos, trader-son of a house of servants back to Lady Tiye's. The Vizier inclined his metal diadem. Eyes of a falcon, his ring-knuckled hands relaxed on golden rests, Ta enjoyed my children's clothing and their bows. When I kissed Pamakos and Thendra both cheeks, a sword thrust through me, and while it twisted inside, for them I let and the priest shepherd them kindly through a door. Thendra looked back with one little fist to her brow. I ate my heart, and it was done

--A family well spoken for. Every day bring such charming testaments of truth, Ta said on high, with a casual smile that faded fast; and I saw the man who had earned his chair by crushing rebel kinsmen, where Nile met the sea. --Now, his voice darkened. --Be warned, Iakos. You speak to great Ramses. The state will not hesitate. Approach

He watched me unfold Afti's weaving. At the toe of his sandal I kept my eyes from his. --Highness, I said, --this is work of an island-woman's loom: a useful thing to look at, as if one saw The Great Green and the circle of the Earth as a falcon does

--Etana! the man yelled with loud interruptive delight, and a slap of his gold wrist-snake against his chair's arm. –I read as a child about the like! As I recall Etana, a figure some appoint as a first king, far east of the sun. Yes! Ta said with schoolboy glee. –Wonderful tale! He asked for a gift from Inanna, their savior of the wandering dead. Ahh, the days! Ta exclaimed like a man seized with sudden music, and off he launched:

--My friend, let me take you up to heaven,
you will see with eagles' eyes:
put your chest against my chest,
put your hands to my wing-feathers:
put your arms against my sides.
When Inanna's eagle bore Etana aloft one league,
it said to him:
Look, my friend, how the land is now, examine the sea

I hid my eyes and Gaza laugh. When Ta ran out of memory, the next lines fell my way, and *Yes, yes* he said with his look glazing over

--Look, my friend, how the land is now!
The sea has become a gardener's ditch

--Lovely, Ta sighed with the world at his feet. Then, the dark moon came back into his face. --And this wonder of a fabric is our gift?

--Highness, it only shows---a greater gift. As Egypt is the gardener of the world. If I may? I fumbled, angered that he should even try to take it

--Highness, Egypt is peace and safety. Few eyes notice that The Great Green went to war, and this danger on your border comes of it. Three generations gone, Achaians wiped out this city, Thapsos. After that, no place on the island was safe to build, and from here came Shekelesh, wanderers now: men hardened by your services in wars, and wounded in the place men call home.

You know how they and their old cousin-enemies, Shardana, always showed the world a face of war. But where do Libu acquire those elegant long robes and garments, Highness? The looms behind Shardana's warriors show skills, and will to work. Our families know theirs. Till they have true homes, they will make no peace

--Great Ramses crushes flies. We find Shardana swords alike in Libu paws

--Your Highness is truth, I said. --But Great One rules more than his sport. There is a way to break these peoples to your use

Ta said, with limpid indifference, *More*

--Highness. The more all sides gave in to stealing, the more their families ended; and that made danger for ships of trade, like mine. So these lands before your feet began to starve for crucial things. Kings ate their peoples' seed-corn keeping loyalties. Some turned their hungry eyes on this great city, Troy---a very estimable place for trade of Asia, and she is no more. The burning of it broke these peoples every side

--And soon, here, here, they smashed into Alashiya. Paphos, Kition, Enkomi: fruitful cities, flames. From there, old Ugarit one day's sail. White Harbor slept too long with guests-unwanted in the yard. The sea full of refugees and criminals, it was too late, even for mighty friends. But Ugarit cried to generous Merneptah. He was a Pharaoh to feed even Libu grain, a man for law on the roads of Canaan, into the hills of the Sutu and Apiru outlaws. But Ugarit burned. In revenge, the island cranes sacked the greatest Achaian house in reach: Pylos, Highness, whose fathers had burned Thapsos

--Now curse is on The Lion of Mykenai: he has devoured his own. He is finished behind his walls, and his too-many sons who know it are abroad, the cutting edge of this. The islanders who cannot flee, join. As ever, they are like to marry as to fight. But, Highness, of all these words, may the Great One hear these. At Djahi, Great One broke half their strength; and now come their families, in boats and oxcarts by the roads. Highness, they come to live or die: there is no city anymore to stop them. Ascalon and other cities of your fame had corps of chariot like the rest. But these are hordes of footman-skirmishers, perhaps five thousand men at arms, out of all their fifteen---and they grow with Canaan rabble, who will dig no more kings' ditches, but their graves. They fight to fill their bellies for the day. They will not build until their rage is satisfied

Now I gave him my eyes. --Highness, in your hands, my children, our good house. Forgive my island trades, I beg. But out of them comes to you a loving gift

From lion-headed rests Ta's hands rose slowly, and joining his fingertips, he touched them to his lips. In his eyes, the warning smoldered

--I place my hand to my testicles. I will guide them to your knives. Highness, let Great One plant the winnowed seed to prosper him. Here, I pointed northward out of Gaza. --Here, like a buffer-land, the great one's doormen, Egypt's footstool. I know the poison that drives these peoples. Use their skills to keep the highways eastward good for trade. Make their strength serve Maat, wealth and order, on so costly a frontier

--Our richest frontier, Ta said through his half-bared teeth. –Whose treachery smashed Hazor? Dared lay hands on Nile's sacred images there, and local stones alike? Fools without the skill and strength themselves to make roads flow. Who says that Nile will tolerate this long, knows not the lust of priests for the good things of Aram and Babylon. However long it takes, the blow will fall. We will smash the way open as we always have, on blood and bones. Speak to it!

--Highness, by your leave. Among themselves, these tribes brook no kings: the men who lead them act for family councils, and each with a voice in their communions, the meals along their benches. If there is a way for which cranes die and live, that is the core of it. The moons and suns between their horns are not for war. Let them be your children again. Wealth will flow, sure as their fathers the Keftiu princes on these walls. Let them build great Ramses' honor. The only problem will be, what to do with a harvest big as a mountain

--Nn, Ta mused. --I must say, this way of your people, to offer a child in extremity. Well. It cuts both ways, does it not. Nn. This might appeal, Ta said. --Great Ramses plants trees. But Canaan, a garden of snakes. Shekelesh garrison Byblos now, Shardana before them. I can name these wandering whelps, Hellenes you call Ironheads, Qari. They *are* in Canaan, man! Explain it then, Ta demanded. --Your cousins break their fathers' oaths, and raid our river. They have Alashiya, they have Mersa Matruh, and Pharos, do they not? We allow these animals homes, and they threaten us?

--Highness. Islanders are many tribes. Feuds and weddings steer their boats, and melt their names. What marches on you is, in a word, the men of them. Agamemnons resolute to prove what never worked. And years of sons entangled too, benumbed, gone mad. Where does a man go home when he leaves his garden? Highness, they say themselves, nobody wins against The Nile. They come because the fight they need is more than war. It is a thing that hurts too much to stop. A very old

--Hyksos parasites! Ta recoiled with a waggling of his chin. And as the spaces of this world reverberated with his word, his lip curled up to show one tooth, like a man half-crocodile: the eyes in the water the least you see of strength and skill and appetite

--Drunk with easy prey. The houses they burn, better they never saw. Come to root like pigs in our good black tilth. Look at us, Iakos. Look into Great One's eye. Alas for Libya, who said *We will live in Egypt*. Now. You tell a family story. We want to know what is worth the throats of a man's two lovely children

Gardens for more. To break you, and your master, big little man: to smash your desert madness into ours

--Highness, I lilted. –What life is there without Great House strong. We Byblos-boats have no interest in trouble. Last moon, I traded these people medicine for amber. They wait for Alashiya wine. With that, Highness, mix your own intentions. Djahi hurt them: now they will grab any false advantage. The men who brought me to your feet know our families' ships, and generations of our sons in the fighting-line

--And their mother, Ta said. --She approves her children mortal hostages?

--She knows her place, I said, crowning all my lies

--Intolerable mongrels. Show what you propose, Ta ordered. He promised nothing. It surprised me he did not repeat the one promise he had made. His portly priest took me to kiss the swearing-toes of statues

They wanted Canaan's cow secure; and, a man with things to lose inside the monster coming toward them, which they believed had swallowed their fathers' monster, Hatti. Ta did affirm one thing, that I knew his river's channels, where ships might well be trapped

It was for me to present Ramses sport. If he deigned to take it, I would know, my green sail and the double-axe round my neck to mark me for capture. *Keep yourself alive,* Ta said, *and in return, we shall not interfere with this Libu trade of yours, in sylphium*

We will protect you from ourselves. Would Ramses deign to listen, let alone deploy a double-edged ambush? He had priests and miles of shiny soldiers to feed, fabled fathers to outdo: he needed Canaan's roads the way The Lion needed Troy. And I was going to walk in one piece from between two armies? I set my teeth and sailed out the river, to swing the other blade

Nine generations of salt since a man called Minos.

From Dikte Cave, where I had gone to weep Thapsos, his voice and black-heart counsel in my heart. --*What are you, boy?* --A Cretan man! --*And what is that?* --A seed; and none more stubborn in a desert. A medicine, harder than men's will. --*Really?*

There was nothing to want anymore except my father's pride in the dance he taught a son. Door, edge, beyond, I was going horns-first the way he launched himself at Athens. Time melted in my love for him, the sea before the ship's prow the world's unlimited embrace, pure wild, roiling every color like a snakeskin. Our wake across the flood and wind was a path of running spirals, the vortices circling down into the black. *Deukarijo! Dapuritojo!* It was time to ground the dance, or see what happened when they chopped me in pieces

--Iakos! --Iakos ky-ee-kee!

The islanders loved a wine-boat; and there along the sloping sands of Gaza a motley of their ships, chocked-up or on their sides, but stripped for war under citadel and buildings. Around the walls in three directions a patchwork nest of poled-up tents spread out in acres of their colors, the reds and whites of women among black ones, raucous campfires under tamarisk and palm. A staging area fifteen thousand strong

--We thought you were enemy, pretty green-sail!

--Alas for Egypt! I laughed as the boat was hauled in. --You bastards know I go hard on people who reject me!

What were they doing, under the great house there, where Derceto landed in her flight from unwelcome lovers, turned, and made a marriage-peace? In the mornings with dew and mist on the red-heather grasses of the fields, men were sharpening themselves and ever-younger brothers to fight the strongest army in their ken. *Shachar-shalim* there was music in the camp, work-songs, at night the feasts of flute and drum. But weapons clanged across the days

Boys learning not to panic holding a line as their fathers hacked hard at them with their forward-weighted slashers. Scared beginners exhilarated, giving back hard and harder to survive a Kemeti with a jaw-hook blade. Skirmishes to see how long you last against an enemy gang of four, who mean to smash your bones and beat you to death with thick blunt rods. Fifty boys hurling themselves forward at a time to launch their javelins, and taking more barked commands as the long spears whooped like a bull-roarer's voice across the air

--*Draw, boys, charge, get on them! --Move, before their arrows cut you down!*

And then what, gentlemen? I threw wine at slackers wading toward the boat, and gave only greeting on the way up to Gaza. The walls had grown since Pyrrha's day, and the red-pillared terraces of the house of Derceto and Dagon stood seaward above them, the greatest Gazan building spared in occupation. Its sanctum held a horned four-corner altar, a small stately hall whose peace the sailors and sand-crossers honored alike. Good hostels here, working travelers for spice of Sutu caravans; hill-families looking for healers and dream-tellers, trading-clans at gather on communion-benches, and no Baal to botch the works

But Gaza was the barking-dog north of Kemet's front door, the Wadi Ghazzeh; and the gate that faced the Canaan road, these peoples had smashed, to throw Kemeti governors out the other

I walked into a laughing motley of the camp spread out in front of the steps of Derceto's pillared portico, enjoying a tiny woman's insults from the threshold: it was a dame of sixty named Diwia shouting at them, chief priestess of Gaza, a houri frail as a bird in saffron robes. Twelve Great Years, a hundred moons this house had helped my wines along

--Idiots! she barked. --Ruled by nothing! Get out! Get out of the precinct!

The gang of men at arms before her wanted in: they had just this morning sacked the last Kemeti outpost south of here, called Balah, and stood matted with battle-dust in sour sweat, blond manes tangled from their boarstooth helmets to the shoulders of their corselets. Ironheads, the vanguard of north Achaians with us, and the biggest a booted beast of a chieftain called Pagos

In the disarray since the first defeat on land, men had been settling old feud scores. With blood at every hand people seized on anything amusing; that Diwia, this morsel in a doorway, should be dressing down Pagos had many laughing bent over knees. Behind Pagos, brothers leaned on spears in mellow afterglow, flies at their bloody points, the wounded hanging on each other

--What did you do it for? I knew the potters at Balah. Old man artisans, boys who fetched wood for the kiln. Strong work, idiots! Leave the precinct, go!

--We want wine, and washing, Pagos answered her

--Ask for it like a man

--We did, Pagos trifled. --Behavior for a price. Tell us, goddess, as you step aside. Are you the original whore here? Calendar girl, milk-maid, nanny? Or pure hag?

--Wanassa, little prick, said Diwia: her voice made men afraid to laugh

--I am Pagos. You know what we have done, bigger towns than this. I am Pagos, son of Bom. Death is afraid of me. I live! he bellowed. --Now, aside

--Nothing doing, drunk, said Diwia, and she lifted her left hand outward on Pagos, her crooked middle finger trembling. It was a poison gesture old and feared in common through the crowd: even some of Pagos' brothers had lived to see it work, and they averted their eyes

--Step up, son of Bom, and never again lie sweet in any garden. Come in, and be cut from every cousin: world wreck your sleep with worry and revenge. Nothing but yourself---Step up, and be buried with the dogs!

Pagos handed his blades to kinsmen and cracked his knuckles. When his boot touched the third stair, Diwia said *Have you met Dagarat?* And one enormous human being stepped from the dark inside, an Annakim. A brother of old Canaan's warrior-guild, that chose out only giant men to train: I saw twenty in my father's day, and this was the biggest

He wore the guild's green-plumed helmet that showed them from a mile, and his eyes were black, big and solemn as a bull's. Black beard hung like a wolf's coat down his chest, under there was a man's weight of plate; and that was between the hilts of two heavy swords, whose blades reached down to his calves, in guards of bronze. The eyes athwart his massive nose were black and looked like slits in the sides of a building: Dagarat filled the doorway over Diwia

--Amateur, Haunebu sea-scum, Dagarat said to Pagos, who halted. --You keep this lady from her day. Leave. Or show me the weapon you will eat

--Quite a familiar, for a lady with no power! answered Pagos. --Well, Dagarat, all of us tomorrow fight Kemeti. Pharaoh's armies, as big as you. Better you should die against them

--Confused little blondie, said Dagarat's solemn face. --Our guild dislikes your odds tomorrow. Annakim come here to wash. To pray, and eat, and trade, and dance the girls of Gaza---while you die. The Canaan towns you burned, Pharaoh's spiders ran from, carrying couches. So, spider, if you live, show this door your face again. Skin you for a sunshade. Puh! Then you never grow up

Pagos, flummoxed by the match, chafed there, a little tired now, but the mocker's face he turned to his followers found them smiling into his. And then the sudden noise of voices from behind turned the crowd from Pagos: they were what-news shouts from more of our chieftains coming in from camp through Gaza's southern gate. Viri the Danaan priest-chief came up beside Neos of the Kari; Doku of the Libu's Tehenu, and more with Fotya the weary south Achaian. Pagos dropped his shoulders, turned his back on Dagarat, and laughed his way back down to take charge of the next distraction. Diwia and Dagarat turned their backs as well and slammed the door

--What word, Pagos?

--Gentlemen, the King's Highway is cleared

--The road is *warned*, now, the whole Wall of the Prince! Fotya objected

--Blast, Pagos! said Neos; and for a Kari, even to speak Pagos' raider-name was anger. --Do you know what Ramses' armies are? A lame horse still twice our kick. Do you like your house a sand-dune under sails?

--Such good, wise kings all, Pagos complained

--Only the wine-man is good, Doku put in, with a long Tehenu smile

--Is that Iakos? Pagos said, turning round to look down at me. --Grand, let the bards sing. You're the one they say breeds the balls out of bulls. What news then, you sorcering blackguard?

When he was finished, I said hello carefully all the way around; and then, that I had just left wine on the table of The First Vizier, rebel-breaker. Out with that came Afti's weaving, and I hung it in the sun between my hands

--I ask that no one touch or try to take this. This is where we are. Tonight it can show the council where Ramses waits to finish you

--Talk, now, Pagos ordered: a flash in his eyes saw

Afti's weaving in his tent, but he settled into his booted stance as great judge. –When I smell a lie, I eat your tongue

--Eat children in your fathers' pie too, I answered, despising his blue guts

--Hide this now, tonight, tonight! Doku demanded through a deferential smile; and that, with wine, landed me near their circle round the fire. No one expected the prayer with the bowl in my hands

Bad blood and good came out. The woman Padi of the Lukka was last to speak. A child had been offered. A shiver ran through us, and the men's holy curses faded. Then their silence again, and the sound of the sea. Waves breaking, fish running, birds, the world, untouched for all their smashing down of things. This time what they smashed would be there still when blood was done. I asked permission to give them my ships' eyes and ears

--Lie, and you will, came a promise as I stood and opened out Afti's weaving

--Kemet stands this way, westward. His army is two forces. Here, he waits you with chariots and skirmishers: here, where an arm of the shore swings out into the great sea-lake, Sirbonis. March yourselves beyond his hide on that neck of land, he sees your marching-dust, and out he springs behind you

--You know what Pharaoh calls a division, four thousand men and a thousand chariots. But men say now that one division, these days, is almost half his strength. They do not love the sea. His ships are few and a weak river escort. Pharaoh's seconds, then, wait for you on land beyond the great lake's western arm. He aims himself to drive you into the teeth of that five thousand. Cousins, years my eyes know these places. Hold Ramses himself to that neck of land. And hurl the ships where his strength is not: at this city, here, Pelusium

--The fort is middling strong, but no one trapped inside it controls the harbor, or the works worth having. Most years, after flood, the river's miles of salt mud protect it. This year, the waters run high, and two arms of Nile make the place an island. So---cut off the fort. From there, you can rule half the river, half his trade. In time, marry this with all our Libu kin. Before he knows it, Ramses will have to deal---in grain, or farms, or what you ask

--Blood decide this, you will still be here, like him

--Not at all like him. Growing grapes on his grave

--And this, I will eat your tongue, is truth?

--Did I say, do this and conquer? You can throw yourselves under his golden wheels. Or you can fight for once as if you know what for

So I sat down, drank, and hoped to see the light of my last day. Nobody told me to leave, or not to leave. Nor spoke to me again till they were done

It was not that they believed me. They had come of age fighting from ships, kicking over rotten things, taking only to abandon; had suffered enough to be looking for a place to rest and live. The words, and Afti's circle of the world, simply kept haunting the talk every side. This and that plan they liked better; but what if the little wine-man were true of speech?

The river was a sea people's way into the land. The warriors on foot had to hit Ramses hardest, for their thousands of women, children, and elders of their families were going to be strung out behind them on the wide-open dust of Sinai. The beating they had taken made it sure they were going to face at least four thousand men with a thousand chariots. Why should Ramses not be waiting there? The bait best for tempting him was their families back of the fighting-line. On land all they needed was a standoff, to keep one fist pounding on his door while their other took Pelusium. Worotu, Shardana's man, stood up: then Neos of the Kari, and Fotya beside him

--We come, said old Wilios the priest. --You will be trailing Trojan boats

When they started to ask whose ranks were for Ramses himself a second time, it was done. Veda the woman of Alashiya drew a flint knife that all of them used to cut their palms, and the blood-oath Pyx and Padi made had everyone press their palms to each other's, both hands, with eyes conjoined like people consenting to a dream. The women caught the drippings in their cups; and to Viri the Danaan went the the honor of pouring. Because, even counting wooly Pagos and his Ironheads, the Danaans were the craziest of all---to his twigs and berries this Viri went to council naked as the moon, as all of them did till dressed like women screaming into battle. The blood went mixed with dregs of wine into the fire, and this time, all the cups. It meant that tomorrow, they would have new cups, or never again need one

The word spread through the dawn. Diwia, on the citadel with Dagarat, watched the great surround of encampments shaking out their scaly folds. To the man and woman, people understood that the fighters on land would be paying for Pelusium. That was what brought them, in the midst of breaking camp, to the making of the largest circle, three ranks deep, that any had seen before. *We want to sing our thanks before the deed*, Veda said; and so they sang, and the men took off their headgear, and looked at the dust

The circle gave one ferocious shout thousands strong, and then dispersed to morning's work in the rising light. But you could hear the sea and the people's breathing with it, the clank of a weapon, the creak of a cart. And if I kept my blood cold, I was not sorry, because I also saw and felt again the exquisite pleasure that they relished at war's edge, the flame of forever in their senses. What monster had stunted us? The one thing more insane was getting in its way

The men and the people on land had a ten-day march to the looked-for battle point, and filled their bags and bellies at the wells. To us on the ships it was an easy two days to Pelusium; so the men and people marched to be seen, and we hauled up our sails for disappearing. When the sun broke, the best ship-borne warriors had fanned out on the sea, Trojan, Alashiya, Pelasgian vessels and Qari, Shekelesh, Shardana, Lukka; mine like a tender to their host, and Diwia's citadel behind against the sun

I tell what I learned of the battle on land from

broken pieces. The Ironheads led that march toward Ramses, they were men with nerve against horses, and Pagos would not have it any other way. Behind them flanking the great road, Tehenu and Meshwesh, sand-crossers who knew the wild fights that swirled across the open: at rear guard, then, Fotya's south Achaians and Danaans, and the rags of what this had become, a motley of picked-up arms in hands of men coming from the torn-up farms and towns of Canaan. At first the oxen-carts were at their heels, and the walking wounded, and people old and young with half the company of Danaans fallen back to keep them moving

A few miles over stones and prickly scrub, and the long unruly line of them separated back along the road, the elders this time keeping their distance at the edge of the warriors' dust, and glad to have no Shekelesh feuding in their midst. The killings since their last defeat had ended, or so it seemed. Their weapons streamed through Balah the second day, and found almost nothing of The Wall of the Prince but his wrecked doorstep. Looters they let flee to cry their coming. That day, the last of the land-men's two thousand warriors were making their way across and through the broad deep wadi of Ghazzeh. Fotya's south Achaians were descending into it to cross. A garden of a place with fig trees, date-palms, even willows nursed by trickling water and the half-shade of the wadi. Crossing through, nobody noticed that the Danaan rear guard had quietly become one force again, behind and now above Fotya's Achaians. And there the four hundred

Danaan men with Viri stabbed into their backs without a cry of hate or warning. They cut the south Achaian ranks in half with a first push down the slopes, spearing and beating men to death as if finishing prey long-hunted

The Meshwesh closest to this uproar of murder only watched: some of the forward warriors heard and ran back screaming curses. By then Fotya was down under two spears in the middle of the stream. It was more than a fight born of insult, because Viri made sure that his men kept on stabbing every man they could reach: even when Fotya's Achaians broke away forward into the Libu's hundreds, beside themselves with rage. Pagos, his guard come back from point, and Doku with his men, began to stone the Danaans: the elders and the women as they came put their children to it. It stopped Viri's men without killing them and wasting strength. But in an hour the Danaans had killed three in four of Fotya's men

The blood drew vultures. Pagos and Doku told Viri, march or die. There would be no talk now on a feud as old as sons and fathers in the islands. Nothing was forgotten, nothing would be. But this day, once the word got through ranks, the Danaans' attack became a crime in common to the others. To a man they wanted Viri's fighters moved up front, where all could see them turn their madness on Pharaoh

And the force deployed again across the wadi, out onto the great plain along the sea in sharper ranks, Achaians together now at front, Danaans between them and the Libyans fanning out thirty men across, spears down out of the sun. Hunting Ramses, waiting Ramses, the shimmering gleam of his gold mirage. Waiting to see what they would see at the end of war's road

They camped without one fire and kept pushing westward. Each day the people with their oxcarts kept a better distance. On the tenth morning, The King's Highway brought them in sight of a wide reach of land stretching into the sea at their right arm

They wanted to smell him on the air, his horses' dung. They spread out their columns wide as could be and took that way, at the double-run. Starting to shout, to lift their spears and scream surprise as they ran on; hoping to trap Great One in his ambush-hide among this place's little hills, to catch him with a thousand chariots confined, backs to the ocean, ranks of men crying out to him

They found nothing but the land, cattails, sunny estuaries, reefs of sand that shifted with the moons. When their charge had spent itself, and the wind carried off their curses and their dust toward the ocean, they heard Ramses' chariots behind. It grew from a sound coming toward them like the metal land's mountains gathering their feet. A rumbling that rose to outright thunder, as if the ground were speaking to the sea

They saw pennants and the horses' plumed heads first on the shimmering horizon. Now in the trap, they had not thought of how to fight this place. The ranks of chariots gave no time, charging on them full-stride with warriors, spears and archers steady-upright in their rattling cars. Local princes, garrison-commanders, elite *mar-yannu* the best in Pharaoh's pay, they were the face of practiced death

There had to be fifty chariots across the front ranks of them with hand-to-hand men charging screaming at their sides. When hundreds of the first began to shear off left and right, more and more of them to cut off all escape, they saw that the chariots' ranks in the center were still more than ten ranks deep. And still unfolding, three or four men at the sides of them brandishing blunt rods, hook-blades and half-shields, javelins. In they came, screaming above their own clattering roar. It began to rain stones, hooked throwing-sticks, barbed arrows

Ramses was not there. Whoever the general was, he watched from a chariot inside five hundred men of a guard, and he halved his other seven into companies two hundred strong for finding weak points, crushing in their flanks and butchering them. None of the cranes forgot they were dying to hold this strength here, Ramses or none, and they died screaming names of family, making Kemeti men pay hand to hand for each small hill, falling back to the water. Less than a thousand reached the stony edge where, reduced to targets, they laid their arms down, and hoped to survive Kemeti rage

The general pulled back half the chariots and skirmishers still on their feet to regroup and go after the families. Hearing their roar out there on the coastal road, a sound as deep as bleeding Earth went through the Libu and Danaans. Men of war had come to the limit of their mystic bond. Life purged itself into the sea

Pagos son of Bom and all their wishes died there, at the front where he trapped himself with his smiling friends. Doku, Viri, and the Meshwesh leader named Merire like his fathers. Battered south Achaians, hundreds of Danaans and Canaan's men, dressed to be seen, permanently humbled, given over to the sword. By the distant holy hand of their own true man's man, king, god and favorite of the god, by the strong justice of the Earth's most exalted servant of priests, grain-hawkers, killers and dead statues, the sun blazed straight into wide-open eyes

For years to come it crippled his omnipotence, killing so many who fought back so hard. A thousand sons of The Nile among two thousand island corpses, three hundred horses on the sand. Bellies gaping out crimson coils of snake, heads crushed in, curled up where they bled to death without an arm. Feasting flies and vultures on the peace their choices built

And none of this our ships knew, nor the harbor of Pelusium. When they came in from the darkness, the cranes carved into the ships at prow and stern were too close to the water, so heavy the packed-in men at arms aboard. And they knew what the sea would do to most bows they had. But there was no plan without disadvantage, and it hardened them

Beneath a red crack in the sky, they opened their jaws in a great crescent fanned out in front of the fort, to show their teeth. When lookouts had counted a hundred boats, they dropped their master's ensign, and hoisted a weaving that made Worotu and the Shardana shout

The garrison's soldiers were sons of a Shardana clan following their hired-on fathers' work, who fed their children where a Pharaoh lacked men, but not gold. So it seemed, with good signals. So the more readily the ships, in earnest to have this place by noon, dropped sail and oared their ways up into the channel of approach. They saw how close-in we had come, that the port and the works worth having lay beyond the fort's real reach: the fort was for launching bold strikes when men inside it liked the odds. Ahead of the ships packed with Kari and Shekelesh and Trojans, further in, the land was the land: a narrow beach and wild thorn brambles below the fort's steep slope, and along the shoreline both sides of the built-up places, heavy waterside tangles of trees, and swaths of high grass that tumbled into river-mud and rocks

My ship, like them for now, had dropped its green sail, but stopped rowing, and we slid into the way of two Alashiya boats. They waved us off with high signs: there was even laughter ship to ship, for as usual, Shardana and Shekelesh oarsmen had started to race their ships inshore. To a man, first thought was speed of taking over, to get back to sea and return to guard the families. But there looked to be nothing to bother them cutting off the fort. And so the ships followed each other's turns and then hulled past their cousins' ships just in front, turning shoreward each, the standing men growling and jostling to get their bristling weapons free of crowding on the decks. Ships crammed with Alashiya and Kari, Pelasgians made their turns; and past them, taking along full-throat curses mixed with laughter, went the boats of Chimaros The Flame and Lukka's people. Rowing hard for the mud-brick fishing town just up the river, still asleep in the summer morning twilight

The three flamed arrows that suddenly shot from the fort's roof looked like welcome, and a shout of answer rose from the ships almost rail to rail sliding into the riverbank. But I saw from my boat at the turn in the channel's mouth that their flames had not hit the water when, at once, black swarms thick as insects shot up out of the grasses and the tangled groves facing and flanking the ships. They were arrows, light javelins with them, and then whistling stones and throwing-sticks. When the first jammed-in men went down, the boat-captains and the warriors' officers screamed crossed-purpose orders

As a few pulled their ships back, men fighting to get off the decks were landing in mud or chest-deep water: boats shoved back by oarsmen found no room to turn among the others. Another swarm came down with better aim, and ships began to rock with the tumult of death and men turning round to help their wounded. And still the Pelasgians and Cyprus' best thrust their ships in, with the shield of every man up over his head, and the one roof clattering with stones and arrows: they forced their vessels in among floundering ones and to the river-banks, and the black-haired young men of Pyx's people leaped and poured from the prows with their sticking-spears and knives. Lean Alashiya men in their crane-feathered crowns and leather corselets swung long swords about their heads, furious to drive their men's axes and fighting-spears into the land, to get them scrambling up over the crumbling mud-banks and break the rain of arrows. And they were following Shekelesh, Shardana and Kari hand-to-hand men first ashore, the horned-helmet men with the nerve to get closer and so in under the volleys: that was the roar of slaughter beginning to rise just inside the trees up-river from the fort. For where they beached, they found a fast way in upon the ranked Kemeti bowmen, and they at first were easy kills with swords. Yet, there was no landward panic as they died

For then, Kemeti warriors, a company of first-rank men they called shock troops, stood up out of the pastures beyond the works of Pelusium's dye-tanks, where they had lain upon their bellies. Ramses' hand-picked giants, to a man Pagos' size, bare-chested and quick behind their shields with short hooked hacking-blades, a handful of javelins: they came in hard on the Shekelesh, charging through the retreat of their own bowmen, and two hundred fifty of them began to push Shardana and the rest full-back to the river, leaving Neos of the Kari on the ground. It worked because five hundred other skirmishers, a full battalion had rushed out to fight on the mud edge of their land, to keep the Alashiya best confined at the shore. If they managed to climb where the river-bank faced the ships, they were dying before they found their feet

The stones and sticks and arrows weltered down. Few seemed to notice the fort hoisting Ramses' gold again, because cranes were still fighting so hard to find the edge and make this work. When the ensign climbed the sunrise over the fort, a third-wave Kemeti company of hand-to-hand men hit the river fresh and fierce. Soon there were plenty of Alashiya bodies to clamber on in the mud below the riverbank's crest. Their spears were finding marks, but not enough

The fresh Kemeti at them were not yet pressing to get at the ships along the bank: they wanted the boats on the water to keep struggling to disembark their men, the ones already stippled with arrows and trying to untangle and withdraw. Now the soldiers protected by their fight hurled heavy grapple-hooks on lines that caught quick and snapped tight. Cut the lines, and more hooks came down among more arrows: the Kemeti were dragging the jammed-up ships into the shore to make a killing ground

We saw the first crane-headed boat tip over fighting to resist, a Kari boat packed with axe-men and rowers and supplies. Seasoned men fell to thrashing to pull each other from the shallows. And still, the ones ashore picked up weapons and scrambled into fight-lines. They went up the bank enraged, defiant of despair that they fought so far from touching Kemeti's strength, pouring down at them in fifty-man platoons

It carried them, for the Kari cut their way up through farm-boys and scrap-weapon porters thrown into the line. But this was just to wear them down. They were fighting Ramses' plan, the land and the trap laid into it

Shekelesh and Shardana men regrouped their hacking-swords, took charge of the Trojan spearmen still up, and a last hundred Kari---and they struck hard again to make this push work. They had to kill enough to let their brothers take the fort behind their lines. And thirty yards hacked inland showed them that the soldiers hurling grapple-hooks and heaving on the ropes were Shardana, in disc-crowned helmets of their own, down already from the fort. And they, with plenty to prove against wild kinsmen for the somewhere-watching master of their gold, began to die because the sight of them lit such rage. What stopped the Shardana from taking the fight inland was a cry of hundreds from the struggling ships. Kemeti boats were coming, ploughing water as white as teeth before them round the turns at both ends of the channel

Three ranks of warships three-across were lunging downstream from the town double-fast with their oars, and ten more with lions bellied-out on their sails were rounding the vast westward turn of the land along the sea; fanning out to block and tighten down Pelusium's door. All sides of them, like skirmish-runners, a host of smaller river-boats, trade-galleys, skiffs, every one riding low with men, more archers, sickles, and bristling spears. A thousand roaring voices pounding their weapons and the rails of their lion-headed prows

We saw them first from where we floated and I got enough green sail down to signal, then brailed it up again, and down and up; and still we sweated, bobbing there till the sea-side half of their fleet plowed into the river's mouth, shooting us a few contemptuous arrows. Chimaros and the Lukka were nowhere even to complicate the closing trap: their heads were riding spears coming down the channel. At the sight and the cry of the closing ships it seemed every man understood, they were going to lose the sea, and the cranes began to fall back and down over bodies toward their boats. As if they could have moved their vessels, where so many oarsmen sat shot with arrows, brains torn out by stones and throwing-sticks

They kept trying, even when Kemeti ships plowed sideways into them, threw hooks and started to board them ten yards from the bank. Thunder of feet as they landed and grappled deck and hold, the weapons' hacking clatter: their screams as they still fought became astonishment, as if it were impossible that so much strength go down so easily, impossible to fail and leave their families spoil, and lose the world. Cranes tried to row and haul against the hooks that dragged them toward the mud. More boats capsized, Kemeti jumped from rails onto men thrashing chest-deep in the shallows; and arrows kept on falling, killed their own with cranes. Men began to break off now to try to swim the channel for the open waves. They got as far as wounds or battle-gear or realization allowed, and then they disappeared

--Iakos? --Sir? --The crew speak, sir. –Let's get out of here! –Help them!

Before my eyes the world a killing floor. Man and mother's son in tangled heaps along the mud, bobbing face-down meat for crocodiles. I stood there agape at the prow, appalled at the scale of what my hands had helped to happen. Before my eyes the staggering stupidity of what men, forgetting and refusing, must come to; and I, the first and worst, helper and healer, had brought forth nothing but a king's fresh heap of corpses

We dragged aboard some swimmers, then rowed for a line of ten men in crane-feathers pushing a ship's mast out to sea. Spotted. A fast half-dozen Kemeti skiffs drew round us, shot the sail full of arrows, heaved their hooks in. I broke the chain around my neck and tucked little Labrys in my cheek. Once they speared the men swimming and cut away arms that clung to our boat, they noticed our drinking-wares, and came aboard to club and beat us with their fists till we went down. No one seemed to know or care what a green sail or double-axe meant

From there, as when a person is long sick, and half-recalls the daemon-places traveled, I remember broken things. Being dragged to land. Beatings along a gauntlet line of clubs and gaming-knives and spit. The men still whole and strong dragged up from the killing-place, their elbows roped behind their heads whether or not it pulled bone from socket. Their naked torsos muscular, ripped with knives in endless lines, paraded in bondage to the sun

Shoved and shoving each other into pens, a narrowing warren of wood-staked pens like a labyrinth, pain the guide: we were sorted by our looks, and told to point the leaders, or we all went to the mines. Nobody pointed, and Kemeti's soldiers laid on skillful wounds, knowing their order that we live to work. When they separated even men holding onto each other, I lost the whole crew of my boat

A solid two thousand had come in by ship, a thousand killed or going to die. Along the handling pens the local princes, garrison commanders, the officers and mercenaries and quarry-masters too, each with his merciless Melas eye. The last of the gates between pens was a man's arms wide. Men shoved to the left became slaves of mines and temples and estates: shoved right, as I was into the greater group, there was marching yet and plenty of weapons circling our rage and uncertainty. Nobody passed through without a searing-hot iron's brand to his left breast. *Criminal, invader*, it said: *bury me in the belly of a jackal's bitch*

They marched and shoved and prodded us, south was all we knew. Garden died away from the land, the smell of water. Men crammed around me grew delirious with shock of their defeat, thought of nothing but steps forward, not to fall beneath the spears. Every mile we walked, more sorting of our peoples and the brotherhoods across them: for Pharaoh was a river to his people. I saw that Balios had come through, the chief of Pyx's Pelasgian men, and Makhi, Veda's Alashiya captain. Kuro the Shekelesh leader who tried so hard to break the archers; and Sama, Meshwesh priest who led their war, and sang as he kept walking of his Rainbow, Bride of the Sky. I did not know if I could die out here, nor how a man could more deserve it. The last Danaans, shunned even now, kept tight as weapons shepherded our columns east, into the metal land. Some men, dreading the Sinai mines, ran off till laughing chariots took them down

When they ladled us water two days on, I had drifted in with twelve young Pelasgian men who spoke an Alashiya tongue, with old Crete words: *Pulesati,* they called themselves, and Labrys tattoos on their left breasts. Zakkala? They had heard the name. There was nothing to do but wait. We kissed that water from each other's hand with oaths of help: at night we huddled all but naked shivering in sand, our skins ablaze. *Look how weak the new moon,* our men said: *we should have known.* We talked, or some men talked, the only comfort outside sleep. A Pulesati man of thirty with his arm in a bloody sling, half-dead beside me. It could have been Squiddy talking

--You had an uncle or something, in Ugarit, a kinsman of your name. Now, there was a priest like the fighting ones of Libu. I used to go there with my uncle's trade. He got the stories. The man I speak of came there an Alashiya exile, in the last bad burning time. Had a bit of gold, they say, from some old hoard tucked in his wraps. Knew his papyrus too, so the temple of Dagon there took him on. Ten years, and there he was high priest, imagine, in a city like that. Nice little building that was, with a porch and a pillar to it. Big front steps, and an altar always burning on the roof, the smokes good to see from Fennel Harbor

--Well, it was hard times in Ugarit just before she burned. Desperate people made a crooked place. And this man, this priest---had nobody, wanted none, just kept the smokes going, scratching some pile of parchments, running festivals. Now. There was this cat---you know how they hang about, for mice in the grain-jars, and scraps off sacrifice---this one cat, he called her Golden Eyes, because that was the most beautiful part of her. She took a half-tame shine to this man. Nights, she'd hop up on his table while he tried to scratch his parchments; and days, he let her lie about the precinct

--My uncle used to get angry, for how this priest talked to his Golden Eyes right through holy points of business. *Keep those mouses from my grain-jars, you! Or no dish of milk tonight!* Well, one day, the priest chanced to catch somebody kicking her out of the way coming in. He went back inside---and people thought, just to make the big man wait for entrance---and out he comes with a scimitar, my friend, to take your arm off. He could swing one, too. This crazy priest, he says *The man who troubles her will find no god to honor here!* All I can tell you is what my uncle, old, told me. That Dagon's house was the last little place of decent peace in Ugarit

--People knew he was a monster, they accepted what he was, to have the place: for all the rot they lived in by those times, they wanted something like that in their midst. Of course it ended when he peeved somebody royal that way. He slipped out before they speared him. Huh! With Ugarit ashes, I guess it came out even! Things look different when you see how they turn out

--Selah! men mocked the night of pain around us in the darkness. --How will this turn out! Cheer up the lizards and scorpions!

--Argh! The stars have shut their eyes on us. --This

is the bottom, dung and fingernails to work with. --What is anybody going to make of this!

--Dark as midwinter night. I see a grateful altar. To our limitations. I mean, to each other. From bondage to ourselves, our own deliverance

--Shut that mumbling mouth! --He talks like a priest. --Like a tomb. --Like a priest inside a tomb. --Shut up the gibbering!

The men who kept walking for three more days with only the water inside them made it back to the families. Brigades of chariots broke into squadrons of ten along the highway and shot a dozen crazed men down when they ran from our column toward the sea. Here, they salted in a thousand trussed-up prisoners, the living third of island men broken and captured in the fight on land: then they turned around the oxcarts and the old and the women and children, and marched eleven thousand of us back to the ruin of Balah, on the road toward Gaza. When we got there, no water till our rabble raised up tents, the sooner to get people working, sun to sun, rebuilding Ramses' door

The guards were hundreds, well-armed and angry, but kept their distance under orders, that we might recover near the well and be more useful. In that late summer moon Ramses showed himself, whom none of us had ever glimpsed. By that time a few of the leaders left among us had been spied out, because of scorn or honor from the families. When Ramses rounded up the last they could identify, they were hacked into disarticulated pieces before his shaded chair. Like his men, Ramses took home penises that had a knobby crown: if a penis was hooded, he took hands. The festival they made that night around our bodies was named for him, commemorated each year of his power. In the morning, the labor-chiefs came at us angry, seeing how many people in the tents knew how to die without a weapon

The Meshwesh woman Nush was still alive. All this way, she had carried a baked-clay planter hardly bigger than her head, its shape with a hint of bull's horns, running spirals round its base; and in it a tiny green fig tree. The sun pounded down on our building and at night after rations people liked to lay and pile around it, and tried to sing. And Tolema of Shekelesh was there, and Veda the grace of Alashiya, old Wilios the priest of Troy, and Padi, wicked-tongued as she was born. Padi had never shown anyone but blood the little house of Earth Mother of which she was their Keeper. She brought it out beside the tree: I peeked inside and could not help a first pure smile. *You failed! Cheer up!* she said with high exasperated arms. *Love! Be grateful! And consent!* That was all there was, and the sound of the sea many lives away

Those were days of many funerals, when women kissed the brand and wounds on any man they met. Men refused their offers to brand their own bodies likewise. *Enough*, they said, *Enough tears, even if you would not cry!* A madness had gone out of us. And still women took the brand, for the new country, especially those whose house-bonds would not see it. Girls and boys, the hardest who saw the killings on the highway, stepped forward after them. Instead, their mothers charged them to remember the circle we had made. So they did, in their games, as we did in our rites. But they went on envying the mark, and made it theirs with stitching or with paint

In the heat and the labor of that place, things got better with the moons and the buildings of Balah. First we got more bread, and rags of garments to keep warm desert nights. With the seasons came dates and figs, melons and oranges, and meat or green fish. My hope was the same that I saw in others' eyes as they learned to taste these things again. When the year's last rains brought on the moon of our release, Ramses came back, and so did some of our weapons

I did not look for my old iron. Sun-King's gesture was as dark. For Ramses' fight with us had bled his arm. He was handing us his enemies, all and ancient, in the east: the troublers of royal roads through the hills and plains of Canaan, and beyond

--Mongrel mess, your faces in the dust before me! Your seed is nothing. Your gods are wild, your bonds are water, no king, no laws, you are not normal! You will take a name, today, in the service of Great House. You will make order. You will build my monument to victory, your shame. You will keep my door. You will restore the gardens of my cities you turned desert. You will turn my roads into rivers! Dogs of you, go from my sight. *Get the wealth moving!* Or there will be no grain! And the shattering dealt you by the sun will seem a kindness

--What a boor. I'm glad he's gone, said Veda, under the rose; and when we had made our circle once more in that place, she talked with me again

--So, Iakos, what does the good wind say? We have sisters at Ascalon asking for land: I'm sure they can do better than the last two Pharaohs' visits. We should be alright, if we keep close by The Green. Earth Mother, bless the kin of us heading north for Dor, matching sons and daughters. That name, people mean to keep: in Ponikija, *Dor* means *generation, family, household*. Well, Iakos, good for you---wine they will need, sylphium they won't! Ahh, but those Danaans, those vipers on the road: some people, it takes more lives than one to renounce the wishes of their weapons. We lost our moons and suns, our circles, our way, our law. May the name *Pulesati* help us to remember!

--A better name than the ones Pharaoh gives us. I have a girl and boy to find. Then, any boat I can wrangle, to see what help old stores can bring. Selah, I tried to laugh, --I'll be lucky to be farming, like everybody else

--Well, there is work at every hand, Veda smiled in her crescent of young white teeth. --We have skills. They might let us in.

III

7

Unbelievable. Utterly. A man as old and young as his tribe's ninth generation, faced again with starting from the stones. An ignorant stranger, in a land as thick as ancient blood. And nothing for it, except to go on

--You will find your way, Radharani smiled. –Sure as El found the ocean

For as she told it, in the very beginning El, Beneficent Bull who reigned from his mighty horned mountain, looked down on the sublimity and dewy freshness of the world. Turning his gaze in every direction, El basked in what he alone had created and accomplished. Yet, among all the green and gray distances surrounding him, half of what El saw was blue, in a place and a way that was not the sky. So did El descend his mountain, to see what this different blue was

When El for the first time stood beside the ocean, he wondered at so vast a living thing, as it tossed and sighed and glimmered. Now, El saw two immaculate creatures at play in the waters and the waves, sporting and flashing and enjoying themselves. They seemed to be waiting for him. Their flashing eyes and solemn looks reached down into El's great root, and stretched his being from one horizon to the other

El cried out to them, and said they might call him father, or husband, as they pleased. They gave El one laughing answer---*Husband!*---and El knew that his being and doing had never been alone. These wonders in the waters were the handiwork of Asherah, El's one wife older than stars, the walker in the sea, who had made all things beside him. Horny old fool, how had he forgotten? El's laughter at himself shook the universe awake. And together they named these immortal younglings, Shachar the dawn, and Shalim, dusk: children of the sea, Elohim, the first divine offspring

There were more than seventy powers like these consecrated from the harbors to the inland mountains of this land, with names and temples and confused crossings-over to make your head swim---each the patron of a family or a guild or some profession. Dagon and Belatu, mother and father of nourishing dew, were raisers of the grain. Their son was Baal Hadad of thunder and storm, like his father with a wish to rule alone: his mate was Baalat. Anat, ever-virgin of a million copulations, slaughterer on battlefields, was a match for Reshef her crazy kinsman of the desert, who brought plague or skillful healing at his whim. Yam ruled the oceans and rivers, Kotharat was comfort to a woman with child. Nikal filled men's orchards with succulence, Yarikh was her husband of the moon: Kothar a craftsman, and Shapshu the living sun. Hawwah and Adham, wife and husband tending vineyards on the mountain, lived like all of the Elohim forever. And the crown of their realm was the world's great Tree of Life

Mot was the name of death in these Canaani lands

and towns. He alone, Radharani said, received no worship and no offerings. After all, every day, the hand of Mot took for itself. And why was that?

El had forgotten himself in vanity. Baal Hadad had done likewise. So had another of the Elohim, Horon---a guardian of men against the desert's wild beasts, as cunning as snakes at magic and in places underground. Horon took his chance to challenge El. With a single toss of one horn, El sent Horon head-over-backwards down the mountain. But Horon, raging, resolved on a hopeless revenge. In a flash he was a snake, and he sank his fangs into The Tree of Life. It changed into a hideous Tree of Death, and Horon cast around it a sickly fog, a mist that choked and dimmed the world

From the Elohim, El sent Adham of the vineyards to fight Horon. So, they grappled up and down the thundering mountain. But Horon coiled up his vicious spite, and struck his fangs into Adham. As Adham felt this bite, and took this poison, he knew that he lived no more among his undying sisters and brothers

This was the beginning of Mot. No greater grief could Adham suffer. Yet, to his comfort came Shapshu, the living sun, to be mistress of the dead and light the way. Adham the new creature, she called man, Adam. And because for him, there was no life without Hawwah, Shapshu gently folded her hand into Adam's

But this was not the deathless hand of his companion from their vineyards on the mountain. This mortal, woman, she called Eve, Life, The Mother of All

Living to be born. Henceforth, said Shapshu, their immortality would be their children

The Elohim together, moved by these wrongs and kindnesses, turned in wrath against Horon. The Elohim forced Horon to rip his Tree of Death up by the roots, and to restore The Tree of Life, that man and woman never want for its fruit; nor shall they want who are *mujomena*, *mystis*, or understanding

Yet, for this undoing, Mot was not to be be undone. Shapshu the sun, for her part, never shone so bright. She burned away the last of Horon's sickly fog, and the land and living things were fresh as dew again

As an islander, I sought these first Canaani things in hope of their wisdom about death, and why it had not touched me down these years. It seemed their answer was the one I had from home: no answer, only the comforts and consolations of this life. This was at least fair ground for hope that I might fit in

--Urana is what age? I asked

--All of eighteen, Radharani smiled, as we watched the first of her welcome-girls stride out, covered in flowers, toward a hundred guests across the stone-slab court. Our vantage was a slot in the door of her house where it faced the courtyard: two other young favorites of the house came out behind Urana, companions of the greeting with crown-daisies golden in their thick dark hair, and they loosed one shivering call from the white conchs lifted in their hands

These girls wore no more than their festival names,

their flowers and white loincloths, like Qadesh, Canaan's Holy One. In the crowning blaze of summer solstice sunshine their garlands of flowers flowed brightly down off their shoulders, the blooms hung carefully to cross X just below the girls' dimpled navels. Big-budded vetchlings orange as a new moon, clusters of red everlasting, rock roses white against blue Syrian cornflowers, and coastal iris, with petals so purple they looked black

Their solemn good cheer quelled the courtyard's murmuring babble, and the conches cried six more calls for the summer gathering-days. People let their eyelids fall and smudged themselves with smoking cedar-twigs, fingers spiraling up and down. Behold, my new teachers: farmers of the broad sea-plain Sharon, Canaani merchants of the trade-towns, island sailors, feather-crowned Serens of the Pulesati cities, and herdsmen off the hills and pasture-heights that faced The Green. Radharani was giving them a place to make offerings to powers, that powers embrace their lives in arms of care and comfort

--Good girls, thunder! she whispered with pleasure. –Yes! Confront them, stand, arms high now, like suns between horns of mountains. Sway, lift up their hearts---and lo! she laughed. --The manly mystics crane their necks for more. They'd give their souls, to see those flowers fall! Music now, music!

Her guild of players commenced as the young girls moved in serpent sways of hips and shoulders in a line. A deep and heavy drone rose into the air with the nebel's twelve lusty-fingered strings, and a shimmering ring of little cymbals danced in and out of time between pulses of a ram's hide drum. As people answered, shaking tiny bells sewn in along their garments' fringes, two double-reed flutes began to flutter like twining birds. Softly between them climbed the ugab's long sweet hollow-sounding pipe. It seemed to cry above the droning and the drums' dark beats. If their sound had a name, it was longing, and longing swayed the young girls' hips

This was all by old custom of *marzeah*, a gathering-of-riches festival for the summer countryside around the hill Qadeshah. A generation gone since our catastrophe, I had watched this place grow from low squat hovels to a travelers' house, and then a town over the sea, with a few rolling acres of two-story homes, garden patches, and date-palms shading well-laid paths of stone. The knee-high wall encircling everything marked a sanctuary rather than a stronghold, and below the hill's steep flanks of red sandstone, a good little harbor spread out along the riverbank, with houses for stores and a fair road inland

Of all the hands that had raised Qadeshah, people called Radharani its crown: she wore her rich black locks in two big spiral curls and between them her pixilated almond eyes were bright, her thirty years' red-brown skin even darker under her long white diaphanous gown, of island-weave. She wore red everlastings everywhere and I could scarce believe another circle in my fortune, to stand beside her here

--Look at my dear fool out there! Radharani

laughed now, giving me her view. –He wants to be our baal, my king? *His head is wonderful*, the songs say---kindly, since between his ears are smoke and clouds! Make me laugh, like Asherah at El!

This was Halak, the big portly fellow now dancing by himself across the front of the crowd, the full spread of his tasseled garments swaying bright colors and shapes of Nile cotton and Canaani purple. Halak these people sometimes called head man of Qadeshah, but that was as far as it went: he had not fled north into The Lebanon with so many other Canaani, but held fast to family orchards and proffered himself for the job of kissing up to overseers from The Nile. Halak's mouth as he danced alone was open in a kind of feigned possession by the music, his beard dark and thick as fur but curled up into ringlets Hatti-style, and a tall hat rode his bobbing head. His eyes had not rolled back, but peeked through his painted lids to see which people took up his pretense, and who might laugh or sneer. Behind his back, Halak was the walking reason why Qadeshah brooked no king: he amounted to the nickname whispered in the country where his family held good orchards, Lord Of Pistachios

--Forgive me, Radharani said. –In truth, Halak does for us the things that must be done, stroking Egypt, where our hope is only to be left alone

Her hope and mine: Qadeshah was the seed of a way cracking open in the good soil that followed our nightmare. The man who left his brand in our flesh had been murdered by his captive wives. And still, the peoples in reach of his house paid their prices. To Nile we owed our place here, and the price was Pharaoh's charge: keep these lands and roads of trade in order, or lose everything. Halak was the butter we spread on his officials

Another life ago, where I thought my rage had made me a helper, I had brought forth dead bodies. Here, in the ordinary well-laid streets of Qadeshah, in the fine stone buildings raised by these people in the midst of humble houses, the seed of the way was life trying to be life again. What stood now was Pulesati and Canaani, with island touches, and Achaian hearths, and things from Tyre and Byblos: a sanctuary garden of Qadesh, white evening star, whose presence tamed the wild

--And, tonight, Radharani relished, as her hips rocked gently with the music, --a shadow takes full moon. The moon, Sweet Wine. Are you sure?

--By all my years a Keeper, this is the night, I answered her. --The worry, I told you: we can wait eighteen years and no shadow comes, and then wait eighteen more to the hour of the night, and it will show. But you know what this does to people. They think the dead walk, that daemons climb up out of holes. Every blessing and power of the moon fails, and dark things rise that can devour the last hope. Be kind, Radharani! It will come this night, because it is your desire

She wanted help to prove her house a sister of the sun and moon. She wanted Qadeshah to stand a peer in secrets of the real moon's lights and shadows, and so like other women of good houses, be a conscience of Pulesati strength. And she hoped as much that it might do something for the troubling night-time voices coming off the land: long ululating anguished calls, that she said had begun a few years ago. Their sounds, to her, were northern highland: floating voices circling strings of words, at once a deep of longing, accusation, and a warning

Our bride is in many hands

At sunrise hours ago, a hundred close-by families stood gathered at the ocean: their procession circled around the entire hill, and then wound up through Qadeshah with music to the high place trees and stones. Farmers with their barley and wheat in ranked the front of the company, Dagon's sons: behind them two feather-crowned ponies pulled a chariot with one of the house-guard's Annakim giants riding grand marshal, and behind him, Labrys walked high on a flower-spiraled shaft. And now, gates closed, more solemn things: the sun was nearing noon, the fierce peak of his powers and the beginning of his fall. Radharani and I took turns at the slot of vantage in her door, and the courtyard was packed to the pillared entranceway, the faces of her guests as many colors as their garments

The droning din of music ceased, and Urana and her sisters burst out into shares of the wild harangue schooled into them

--*To Qadeshah be welcome, all, where sun stands still and shines straight down!*

--Welcome, you wholly ungovernables!

--Today we choose today!

--Now, get out of here, clodhoppers, scribes in crooked clay, plotting rotting good-for-nothing greed-bags! Fuck your feuds, and women, go, who kiss their horny feet! Go, you broken ones who bow to weaklings and their fists---and go you rat-faced keepers of the hoard!

--Great Year wheel and blackened moons and suns, break your greasy grip!

--Snake, Bull, Lioness take you down! And Griffin grab you by the balls!

Sudden wilder music then, with claps of the crowd's hands catching on quick, and outraged raucous roars of laughter. No one departed

--Let them serve out the honeycakes, Radharani said, --and sharing-cups of your wine. Are you ready, Flood Rider, New Wine Sailor, for the day you have wanted so long? Breathe, from this lotus I hold for you

I bowed my head, and breathed her proffered queen of flowers. The house was all Lebanon cedar of its beams and burnt barley out of the bread-ovens. She seemed to know my need to keep my head, and she drew me to another look outside. A crowd to overwhelm the eyes, every pair of them so different, from head-gear and hair and beard to the blends of colors down their striped and patch-pattern robes. Rings and bracelets, clan-tattoos, earrings and necklaces, each one a work of worlds I never saw. The only common things were the lack of visible weapons and the ranks of bare washed feet. But still alive the lot of us, three hundred years of salt since Knossos. Radharani breathed herself a long deep savor of her flower

--Your little ones in Egypt, she said, one palm to my heart. --Murdered by the grief of people there, in battle's wake: they are here with you. Today, in the children you husband for this house, meet them again. Sweet Wine, before this double door, let go. Men drown beyond their depth. Qadesh spreads her wings, and breathes them life

I looked up from the flower to the graces of her eyes. --I will do as you ask, to be a house-bond, I answered. --I will speak a Keeper's secrets where you ask. But, I want to know---what *you* most desire, Radharani

--I will tell a man who lost and brings so much. Let people refresh themselves, they see me soon enough. This be the touchstone of our day, Radharani began

--When I was three, your fathers the islanders scourged many kings out of Canaan. When Nile broke the last waves of you, you came back to this land where the temples and great houses already knew your arts. But you, Deucalion, were dead to everything. Pharaoh wanted lucre for his priests. His ministers gave you choice of the peoples' captured ships. So you were wealthy again by the time I first saw you, and a prisoner to ghosts. Living in one wretched room in Gaza, on a mattress like a stone

--And how did I find you, born worlds away? You know what Yumm said, the man I called father; that I was born of the rising sun. So they say of mystery-children east of Babylon. Young, I thought me born in the saddlebag of one of his asses. Yumm called me bright as hammered tin, sweeter than the myrrh he traded west. I loved the travelers' houses and the roads and hills with him, the Sutu tents and Bedouin camps in lands of stone beneath the sky. We had night-sings, and music by the wells

--One spring, there was sickness in Yumm's tents, and it left him old: he knew his body had strength for one more journey. Yumm was like his fathers, no man to forget a debt. To pay it took him all of the western road to Gaza. I made him bring me along, as little girls get their way. So I thought, until I found he had left his wealth at home, but not his treasure. Yumm owed a Cretan of Gaza for stock of oil and aromatics. And what to do when he found he had outlived those partners---another whole company of people swallowed by The Green? He asked help from the little old priestess there in Gaza, Diwia

--She found us another Cretan. You. I remember, Yumm was too much man to cry for losing me, scrawny as a monkey then. But he cried when you, in turn, put me in the care of Diwia's house. That was what he wanted for me all along. *Why?* I cried then, because I loved him; and he said, *The lives of these great ladies will be yours: in you, the eastern lands return the gifts of the western sea. Do this for me, Shiny One, and for yourself: goodbye.* It helped me through that time to tell myself his stories. Yumm said that gods might be the sun, but Radharani is what shines; that nothing moves a god, and still her ceremonies move him. In the core of my name, I found the thing to which I meant my life to rise

--Those years, I swept Derceto's halls in Gaza, learning arts of ceremony; and when my flower came, I gave it to the god come through my door. The first I heard your name was when I drank with ladies there the drink that closes wombs. And each man gave back something to the house: the wealth that made ten fingers' worth of good things happen in the towns around those places. I laugh because I like so much a man who understands: good things happen where a woman feels safe!

--I know the men of tribes outside who twist the names of sanctuary women, houri of the hours, and call us whores for that. Men who either drop their robes or pick up a stone if a woman says hello, and give back as little as they can. But I was as Urana is becoming. I paid honor to that house, as women give to see a good thing prosper; so that loving ways go on in this our life. So I came to know and learn from the daughters of the isles who fought old Ramses. I should be---like them, finding fields with promise, if I could fetch men to it. They knew what it was to need and help each other

--The land was broken kingdoms, except where your people of the boats were sharing seed and staking farms, and building to the south. Not many Canaani, sons of the old disorder, stood in the way of people who put roads and fields and markets back to work. Women said it was like old Alashiya, every town its kinds of worship, and Great Year festivals between. I had skills to rise in that. The time came when it grew safe to travel old roads inland. In the Shephelah country that looks up the hills toward Hebron, there is an old Canaani town, Lachish, where your tribes were digging in grapes and olives. I went there with priestesses, to ask the daemons of the land a planters' blessing

 --And who was camped as well along their brook but a band of Annakim, the giants who keep our walls here, brothers now: the first men swayed to the thing born in my mind. They fight for any side, but in-between they live for drink and girls. That day, they were down from their guild-house in Hebron for both, all blades and muscle. I thought there might be some with better hopes. What are their lives, Deucalion, that music and a woman's subtle foot should mean so much? Was I not to build where they saw Asherah, Baalat Qadeshah, Hawwah?

 --I gave my learning, and they gave back gifts, and service. I asked if they had ever dreamed a garden, in the midst of pains of war and work. Well, if I knew a place like this, our red mountain of the dead, with good harbor and a road, could they move men and stones? If I brought such men of skill, would Qadeshah not stand? It was these people, all so different, wanting one place set apart. I did what Gaza mothers did, and every other house not waiting for a king

 --Oh! Shall we not have fine music today, Radharani said breathing out a sudden brightness, --and carry our prayers up to the high place, and take good meals and talk along the benches? How I have wanted to thank you, she smiled, looking us both up and down as if we had appeared full-born before the doors

--Yumm is always near me: sometimes I smell his leather travel-bags. I felt like a child when I saw you come beaching back into my days. You were the door for me to a new life, Radharani smiled. –Now, I will be yours

I still held Pyrrha in my soul, sitting pretty on a mountain. This was all such woman, with worlds more ambition for this place in the Pulesati web

--What do I want, Radharani said, searching it out: her almond eyes narrowed round the sun's dance of lights in her irises. --The trade of predictable old boats: to learn The Great Year moons and suns, and make them double crowns of Qadeshah. To that, you will speak for me this day, and put before our Serens what this evening offers. Ahh, tonight! May the shadow come to light!

Radharani laughed at herself, a trill like a spring among stones. --Sweet Wine, my life is ceremony. But it is not the regard. Not The Green's easy wealth. Nor even your Libu mystery, that keeps time for children in our hands. What I crave is beyond myself; to let go, offer, and extinguish into life, such as I knew in my first flower. To marry this my flesh to the world's flesh, and stand beyond my name and the last thought. Pouring forth, like a wound and all my joy together. A wind of the sea

Her eyes animal-alive, all shapes at once: I felt her dark-skinned body breathe, sheathed in the gown no more than a white translucence. With a sweep of her lifted hand Radharani reached for the double cedar doors, which opened into sunshine and her multitude of lives

--Selah, Sweet Wine!

Urana and the girls sang out from prayers already old to these families, and the courtyard took them up. Radharani lifted a new husband's right hand

--Across a thousand courts, a thousand houses,
men find their joy reborn in Qadesh, Holy One.
Speak, Goddess young in our eyes, in-law of the peoples,
speak the word of our father, Bull, El, Beneficent One.
Take war from the face of The Earth, he says:
Weave love into the very dust.
Let peace possess the world, tranquility the fields

Soft waves of their voices pleasured her, their bride in many hands; and Radharani answered

--For I have a word that I shall tell you,
a matter that I shall declare to you:
the word of the tree, the whisper of the stone,
the murmur of the heavens to the earth,
of the deep to the stars,
a word that men do not know
nor the multitudes of the earth understand.
Come, and I shall show it
in the midst of the mountain

--Now, let the young ones step forward! she declared. To my surprise, it was the sight of the children coming out that tore me down, letting go a father's hand or mother's robe: two boys and two girls ten years old holding onto each other as they neared the strange man off The Green. My share of Qadeshah younglings to foster

Ahh. Here we went again, this lot with dark moppy heads and pudgy faces, smooth brown skins: fine new children I could only live to lose and bury like the rest. At first, enormous words *I am so sorry* ran through my body, as if the latest of my lost ones might have heard. But these open faces, their utter helplessness told me I would die or live to protect them. Behind them was a crowd of factions each with sucking-fangs behind their smiles, eager to entrap these young to themselves

--This man, this day, is born to us as he becomes your xenos: this day, this man, Deucalion Flood Rider, is sworn to be your life-long friend and helper. From this day, you are family: from this day, you have a friend in the world, a friend who holds you first, and close, even if hard adventures hold you apart

The girls were Anab and Yamani: the boys, Woko and Bohan. *I make you my xenos*, said each one taking my hand; and I spoke likewise, giving each a small silver Labrys on a chain around their necks. Each of those I touched to the one I wore, and it was done between us, with a smile of hope and trepidation

It was done, except that now big burly Halak interposed himself into our midst, and laying his hands on two young shoulders without looking down at them, he brought his black eyes and beard of curls into to my face

--You people off the sea do not really belong here, Halak told me under his breath, like rotting meat. --Any more than these sneak-thieving Sutu savages off the hills. Well, come tonight, I will bring you a fine surprise, and we shall see who and what amounts to something

I could only give him half a smile and wait to see what else was coming. Now Halak turned to the crowd and raised his right palm out their way: a moment later, the palm was close up to my face, with some kind of black greasy smear of ash

--Do you know what this is? Halak asked so that everyone could hear. --This is what is left of the last man who betrayed our precious children! Do you see, my people, that Halak is for you!

--And what do you mean about tonight, Halak? asked Radharani, indignant as a few of the crowd shook their metals or clapped hands for him

--You will see. Halak never sleeps in his service to you, and Qadeshah!

--That is our worry, Radharani said; but Halak had already given her his back, and was gone among his people again

--A pompous fool who means well can't be all bad, I tried to quip for her

–Well. Husband, to our business. Be my charm tonight! Radharani said

I gave the children eyes that promised talk for pleasant hours; bowed, and took my leave back inside the pillared portico. Turning along good stone walls for the little entrance-room with its surround of communion benches, I picked up and unwrapped my house-gift, a fat fresh empty vase commissioned in Ascalon, tucked it under my arm, and then followed two more quiet turns of hallway for the doors of her central hall

I knew who was waiting inside and the import of this, but now I was going to miss the noon hour. Radharani disappearing behind the red fanged mask of summer's Lioness, presiding power of the gory squalor of animal sacrifice: her bloody blades and roasting-fires and endless chanted music bringing people out beyond their names and places, and into the realm where their cries and hungers broke them down and married them. *Do this! Do this!* she'd be urging them, cupping the crown of the sun between the heels of her open lifted palms. This was to long for, belonging to the spirit animal, this world. And back the next day in their mortal names and places, people remembered they had found it in each other

My knocks on the door made an empty sound, but I knew she had three men waiting inside, all in cropped crane-feather crowns. Serens: priest-chiefs

They called me Kresios and Kuprios, Mr Crete and Mr Alashiya: it was good to hear old-home humor, because these were formidable men. Symoon, people called the Bull of Gaza: a solid red-faced man with a loose black mane and gold-drop earrings, his arms as thick as legs. The damos of Symoon's people had lived there in days when Gaza was Minoa, and across the tribes of Pulesati, it was Symoon's household trusted with their gifts of remembrance, shipped all the way to Dikte Cave. His ways of speech said little, but when he opened his thick throat to boom it out, men cowed. Symoon was more, for the sun-brown brute he looked: the one Seren so far to serve seventeen years, two turnings of the wheel. A man with that much trust of his damos had proved himself in Radharani's eyes, and his fellows showed him deference

There was a long low sitting-bench along the inner wall, and before Symoon resumed his place, he introduced his peers. Cunning choices for the showing, Radharani: they came from places south to north, the full range of Pulesati reach

--I present you, said Symoon, --our brother Badera, Seren of Gath. His hair is fair because his fathers rowed ships of Troy, peace to their ashes. We call him Oily, because his mothers squeeze fine olives in a clever press. This other fat fellow is good Koru, Seren of Aphek. Koru is a man with two sides, both bad: Shekelesh and Shardana in the one, Symoon teased on. –His fathers, Koru will say it himself, shoved off a few hold-out Canaani clear to plant our seed

The three of them shared low mocking laughs, and I saw how small and innocuous they held me. –Gentlemen, I said. --Our lady thanks you for this hearing. If I may show this humble thing, and what will come tonight?

--Keep it simple. –Make it brief. –And no tricks, they all said; but these were men to appreciate the powers of crafted things and secret signs, and their three heads leaned forward, squinting and tilting in study of the vase

--Sirs. Forgive that I may tell you things you know, to show you more. First---the X inside these turning spiral wheels. This you know, from cups to the signs in people's skin, for old Pulesati; and such is the circle of the sun, one year around. Now, kindly, look with me, where the X has painted arms of light and shadow. Their different colors, count them with me, eight around

--This speaks eight years, the wheel of the grandest festivals we mount. Eight years of suns and moons rejoin them, part them, bring them together again: a doubled pair of each, at each old end and new beginning. No one knows this better than a priest-chief and Seren, because it is the span of your offices and honors. New moon at winter solstice put the crowns upon your heads, and full moon like this night's midsummer takes it. Without these times of sun and moon together, men lose their days and seasons, like ships their anchors

--Yes, yes! said Koru hurrying me on. --Elementary! We saw the sky the day our mothers set the feathers to our heads. We know our own terms

--I thought you were a boatman, hawking wines and herbs, said Badera

--Brothers! Let him finish, Symoon said

--Thank you, gentlemen. Now, if I may, Symoon of Gaza, you are the man to ask a question. Do you remember, in the time just before your first offices, a shadow over the face of full moon? And then, at new moon, a shadow blackening the sun?

--I don't even like the idea, said Badera. --It makes my bones feel hollow

--I do remember, Symoon said, two fingers to his

chin. –Fear. Crime. Keepers of Days took beatings. They had no answer, when this happened in the wheat-harvest dance. Very bad position

--And that, I said, --is what Radharani wishes you gentlemen to know. That when the Great Year doubles, look to the six moons either side of those joining days, and see the mystery that shadows both of the greatest powers of this world. Tonight, Radharani means to show you men *mujomena*---men who understand these frightening things. When tonight's full moon goes black, people on every side will see you calm, through the mysteries she knows. It holds the world together

When I ceased, their eyebrows lifted with a pleasure, but their faces went to work. The fair-haired Badera scratched behind his lapis-studded earring

--Let me grant you, Badera said, now pointing features of the vase, –that I like to see Grandfather Snake down the middle here, and Mother Griffin's lightning-tongue. But we have problems crossing on our hands

--Worse, said the judicious brute Symoon, --if I remember how a priest-chief looks all beaten up

--So, this we will see tonight? asked Badera

--Likely, yes. No rules of men are right all the time

--Sounds like a woman of Symoon's house! laughed Koru. But Symoon darkened and Koru recovered his solemn self

--Thank you, Symoon said to me. –And now, we must speak to a way you can help us, Kuprios. You know that a Seren, he began, --speaks for the women of our damos, and people's talks along our benches. So, be privy to a problem. There are troubles and resentments in Canaani towns, north to south: troubles older than we faced before we married in with them

 --Since days before we came ashore, these shepherd-peoples of the south-country hills---Eberu, as we hear the name---have lived among Canaani well enough. This is true on lands around many great towns, if you know Shemesh for one, not far south from here, and northwards too, around Shechem. Thereabouts, you find these people like any other, herdsman, planter, trader

 --I am ignorant of those places, I answered

 --Well, Symoon said now with one hand on his knee, --things are changing up country. No longer are all Eberu content to trade their wools for tools. There have been fights over untilled lands north and south, and bloodshed where the best planting-places cross our paths. What turns herdsmen into people building houses?

 --He means, building houses in the hills along the roads, said Badera

 --Gentlemen, you confuse even me! Doku objected, lifting both his palms at them. –Let me try. Deucalion, with all respect. We need people---unobtrusive, like yourself. To ease us into ways with more people of the hills. That in turn can trim the buds off trouble's tree. These Eberu work hard, good and bad very much like Cretans, they like to trade: some even marry in. We see their standing stones and sacred poles, and in their hands the little clay Asherah. Do you follow? With those things, we can work

--But other tribes of Eberu---the Yisryli, by name---have a way also, and it brings together too many kinds of foot-walking Shasu. Their fathers were herdsmen, with a pastime in highway robbery. But it seems the Yisryli feel the strength to say their marrying days are done. No wonder. Canaani lords used to take people out of their hills for labor gangs, or handed them slaves to Pharaoh

--Whatever this is, Symoon concluded with some impatience, --we cannot have ourselves mixed up in old Canaani feuds. Especially in the eyes of Eberu and Yisryli, whose lands we cross with caravans for Aram and Babylon

--I begin to see, I answered

--I wish to speak, said Badera. --Let these Yisryli plant grain, dig terraces and silos, and cisterns to catch the rain. Families of them break their backs turning hills of rocks into farms and homes. Why not? Those are all good things we do and praise. May it shut the mouths of Canaani like our friend Halak outside, that rat-catcher, who curse these people of the hills for rootless wanderers. I think, said Badera, --that we can talk and deal with people who abominate kings as we do. The trouble may come from people joining up with Yisryli success. Some are Canaani peasants, some even cast-off nobles, who took their hate into the hills when we broke land. More, men from bands of truly lawless sand-farers, Ahlamu, Habiru. For them, the world is every man his law. When they work together, bad things happen. Pharaohs time out of mind will tell you, they lack no skill attacking towns or caravans. Now, even the oldest rest-house by the road needs guards

--So, I said, --if something blocks the rivers of Pharaoh's wealth, his armies will come back

--Curse his eyes, that is why Egypt planted us, Symoon confirmed. –My own mother told me, Nile never really would let go. And here we are, five Great Years on, still paying kings protection. Well, we laugh for the way our women sing it: *The pig you keep too fat to walk won't trample down your field*

--Gentlemen, I said. –I learn, but do not understand. I only trade along The Green. I know almost nothing of anyplace outside a harbor

--So, Radharani pointed you, Symoon smiled

--To do what? Sirs, sirs. There are scores of seasoned people hereabouts

--Yes, Doku replied, --and they tell us these things as injured parties. As like, they have hill-folk blood already on their hands. We told you, Deucalion. Things have grown from feuds to battles; and now, tonight, we may see a general pay a visit here---with part of an army, that a league of Canaani towns is raising up. They know of Qadeshah's great day. They will come to parade. To be seen. And make things worse

--Indeed, Doku answered him again. –So. Will you help us, sir. It is all arranged. Understand, it was our lady in common Radharani who pointed us your way. You are a man of the world outside, and you have a good way in

--None better than wine, Badera agreed. --Yes, he grinned out broadly now, purring on the word, as he felt the vase over once again. –Start with this thing, Deucalion.

Show them what you showed us. Pour them Alashiya wine: they should want the best. Just talk with them, and get them to talk. Raise a bit of trade, and see what you can learn. You can do that. This is nothing but old damos way. One pleasant bit of purchase, and we'll tangle them in with finery and cousins off the sea

--Sirs, what is arranged? Talk with whom?

--Be sure we will remember, and good luck, Symoon smiled---and when he stood up and slapped his heavy palm to my shoulder, I was dismissed. Doku and Badera opened the doors for him, and they left me standing there between two red cedar pillars. I felt run over; yet, I liked that they were men who listened and looked forward. It might be better to stumble along on their behalf than to face their indignation later, not having tried. Another good turn three ways in Radharani's eyes, in case the shadow failed her, come this night

So, I gathered things and wound my way to a little room of waiting at the back of Radharani's house. With a wine-service tray and the Great Year vase in the other arm, I could not knock, so I pushed inside: the brown-bearded man of the two at the table stood right up, and came around to help me lay the service

--Refreshments! he said. --Thank you, steward

--Oh! said the other with a slap to his sharp gray brow. --Excuse my sister's husband, sir, he opined. –Raz, he said, --dear bumpkin Raz, this is the gentleman we traveled here to meet

--Lavi, don't embarrass me! Who is a bumpkin?

Me, with a farm near a good strong town, or you with a four-room house by yourself in the holy clouds? We should be so lucky if you and the wife come walking down to visit once a year

--Good day, gentlemen, I smiled. --On behalf of the lady of this house, I welcome you. Deucalion my name. I sail from Alashiya, an island in The Green, and that is where these vineyards fill your cups from

--I can be foolish, I suppose, said this man called Raz: he passed a cup to kinsman Lavi with a sheepish grin. Raz' eyes were as dark brown as his beard, well-combed and forty years strong to his chest. They both wore unadorned light blue caps of wool pulled down tight, like helmets of cloth that set off their deep-set eyes and weathered faces. Raz it turned out was the southern one, an Eberu out of the Shephelah's rolling pasture. Some of his tribe, called Judah, had orchards and barley safely close to the great hill at Lachish. Raz' face was round and open, and he sat comfortably spreading out his fine cotton robe. His mantle fell in blue and crimson stripes from one shoulder to the middle of his calves

There was a wide-open energy about this Raz: he enjoyed himself and might say anything to keep life's day lively. The same edge I found right away in older Lavi, but his was for cutting to the bone each thing that crossed the table. Lavi, son of Omer, son of many sons of the tribe of Ephraim: they lived in Samaria, to the north of Raz' tribe

--Fairest of the hills, Raz himself put in; and *omer* in their tongue, he said, meant the first-cut harvest sheaf.

They had married each other's sisters, Raz breezed on, and Lavi rolled his eyes. Not yet through hospitalities, and it seemed Lavi's way with Raz was a curious affectionate scorn. Lavi's beard was gray, much shorter, his leather-belted tunic of gray wool, tasseled at the hems: he said his tribe was Yisryli, but he did some trade at times at an inland city Beth Shemesh. A sharp-browed man to get things done, and keep his way in doing them

--Health to your houses, gentlemen, I said; and then I had the pleasure to watch them taste. The Zakkala was red and light, with a woman's touch of resin just enough to help it keep, and curled your mouth round its savor. Raz had known its like and gave it a nod, but Lavi right away showed a gracious smile

--My compliments, Lavi said. --Our wines, so far at least, we medicine with honey, or juniper-berries. This I like, Deucalion. Who exactly pressed it? I must know every part of its making, because our way with every food

--Lavi, do you like it? said Raz. –Now who says too much in his first cup?

--Deucalion, are your in-laws like this? Lavi smiled

--Here, enjoy, gentlemen. Let me show you something first, I said. –You know the customs Radharani weaves at Qadeshah. Today is a day of The Great Green's summer solstice, and as much a *marzeah*, that makes a garden and a banquet of our riches. Now, if I may show you this fine piece, let me tell you secrets of a wonder you will see tonight

--Tonight? said Lavi

--Naturally, you will stay, I said cordially

–Surely, Lavi answered over me, --the lady knows we cannot stay the night. Man, we cannot show our faces to the sun here. We risked our coming, I confess, because Raz convinced me to the trade. Sir, you do not understand. There are people outside who will kill me, knowing no more than that I am Yisryli

--I tried to explain your lady's way, Raz teased with a pat of Lavi's hand

--Stop! Lavi said. --So you were right. She is not *qadesh* a male prostitute!

–What in the---Sir. Gentlemen. I live along The Green. I know nothing of old trouble on this land. But any threat like that to you is rank dishonor in Radharani's house. Stay, tonight, the both of you. She has the means to keep you safe, and I will second. To learn, a man must be here, and mix in. You never know who

--Thank you, Lavi cut in. –I do worry the way home

--Home, I smiled. –A word of happiness that aches. Now, enjoy your cups, and let me tell a secret of tonight

--But, Deucalion, excuse me, Lavi interrupted now, with sharp shakes of his head: he gazed at me after one glance at the vase. –Forgive me, in the face of this kind concern. We prefer to address more promising things

--Your in-laws like this? Raz said, his face alight with Lavi's words

Well then. Perhaps Lavi thought I meant to sing a pretty fable. So much the better for tonight. And shadow, teacher, come

They both wanted places in their houses like mine here, bringing wines to their best tables and their altars. Raz laid out their country's seven fruits, and most of them might work. Grapes, figs, olives, pomegranates: these could bring good bronze tools from Qadeshah's forge. I always had takers off my boats for wheat or barley, and their women made a date-honey tasted nowhere else, as good as Syka's fish-sauce. Those things, and their almonds, I could keep from spoiling under sail

We talked many questions, but from there no wine or business brought out anything of service to Serens. There was no gauging how many people in those hills until our matters ripened; and Lavi proved no man to fall for idle curiosity. Rebuffed about the vase, I held back the secrets of our wines. We seemed to know where to let some questions pass, this starting-day

I left them sipping to find them escort. By now, the late day outside was a running feast of the portions of animals and first-fruits, offered by Radharani's hands. In the green spaces off from the houses, families were pitched to eat under bright little poled-up awnings, the cymbals and drums and the kinnor-lyres of Alashiya making gentle music in their midst; and now it was my job to pull two giants of the off-duty Annakim guard away from the clapping circle-dance they had going. It seemed the music's gentle tones inflamed them to want more, and they raised it themselves: their skills of leap and turn with such big bodies drew more people in to watch, and there was no interrupting

The wine awakened in my knees and hips, and raised my clapping hands with theirs. I saw the hands that raised this place, and the place itself raising our hands: it seemed the trees and standing stones of memory were watching, many gods, ancestors, proud, swaying, chanting, wild-alive. And where I looked around me for the crown of it all, I saw a woman crowned herself by what she saw, possessed and dancing with her trees and sea and sky. *Do this! Do this!* she was crying with her hands again joined at their heels in front of her eyes, to cup the sun. The living world poured in and seemed to lift me out beyond. The sea will say things, but it must have been the wine. It whispered, *This is God. We want for nothing*

And when this passed, I picked out Sheshai and Kenazz. They made a child of any man: you spoke to their chests with their horse-big eyes looking down to say, *Fly, why bother me?* The two of them boomed out laughing at what I proposed

--Do you know what will happen? --We need our spears, they joked

--Just stay by them, so they enjoy, like any guest

They both turned their black-woolly heads Radharani's way. She was not far off among some people, and not truly knowing my proposal, she nodded them what looked like a wish that they indulge me, the newest man about her business. That was all it took

–No feast without a fight, Kenazz mused

Raz and Lavi seemed softened by the wine, and drawn by the music's deep droning rhythms: they startled not at all when they saw the giant gentlemen their escort. As soon as we reached Radharani's open doors, the piss-drunk Lord of Pistachios was there before us. Kenazz, from behind our guests, warned Halak to keep his distance. He did, but he shook one fist at Raz and Lavi

--Who is like you? Eh? Who is king? Who is not?

--These are Radharani's guests, I told him

--Who are you? What do you know? Cursed Shasu spies for The Lightning, Halak insisted: he turned his drunken garlic-breath my way, still pointing one first finger at Raz and Lavi

--Do you think we will live to see our sons chop wood for Yisryli, and draw their water? Eh? I dare them, speak their curse of Ham to Radharani's face! What do you know, you beardless boat-boy. Go, dare yourself a day up country, see for yourself the camps they pitch as dry as rock. Shall I show you one? Look, and see as the eagle sees!

Halak stamped his sandal in the dust, and then pointed down at the print

--That is how they shape a camp. That is how they circle in festival. Do you not see, they live to put us under their heel? This, because their fathers promised them: all land where their foot should fall, will fall to them. And now you bring them here!

--Go away, drunk! Kenazz warned, turning beastly, stepping forward

--I go! Halak replied, backing off, but with a welcome-sweep of his arm. --Well and good then. Make them at home, feast their eyes. Just make them see the

great man come tonight, is all we ask. The great man to
stop you will come! Sisera will come!

--My fault, gentlemen, I told Raz and Lavi, as
Halak stumbled off

--It's nothing, Lavi shrugged

Before long, I managed to ask Raz what was
feeding so much hatred. *And how is your family?* he
cordially replied. After that I learned worse things, out of
kindness from Kenazz. He took me aside as people sang
the last of the sun down toward the sea

--Do not be discouraged, knowing nothing. Your
guests call Canaani sons of Ham, he explained, --and say
they are born our masters. The strange thing is, we are all
blood and family. But, Yisryli, we hear, swear to a god off
a mountain in the Sinai, who makes fire and thunder. They
say they were mistreated by Pharaohs. Welcome, friends! I
do not know why such a god will have a man cut the hood
from his member. I thought it was Pharaohs who cut men
there to feed their gods. Well, that is the Yisryli sign. It
makes them as tight as the old Pulesati who wore
Pharaoh's brand

--I saw a fire-mountain, I answered. --And, in Sicily

--Not like this one, said Kenazz. -- Somehow, this
god tells Yisryli that the bride of this whole land is theirs
alone. He makes a handsome offer, where he comes. This
god, who never knew us, tells our place and destiny. We
Canaani can chop Yisryli wood, we can leave altogether,
or, we can die

Kenazz had seen those foot-shaped camps on this

side of the Jordan. He told me of a town up-country called Gibeon, where in the days of his fathers' fathers, five Canaani kings had tricked their way into a peace with Yisryli. Now they were slaves, but at least they were alive. Kenazz laughed darkly, when I asked what that meant

--Huh! Green as water under boats, Kenazz laughed. --You never heard of Hazor, because it is a dead place now a hundred years. Grandfathers of my guild knew Hazor, for the greatest crossroads-city of this country looking east. After Gibeon, the Yisryli learned, and trickled a few hard men inside a gate. They sacked and slaughtered. Tore down Pharaoh's statues, and the standing stones alike: they left not one thing alive, if they could. Guess what happened then, little husband of the sea

--Egypt? I said

--In force. My father's father watched Merneptah come and scatter the Yisryli. Kemeti hate this country---but they never, ever, fail to visit when the caravans of spice and silk choke off

--You sound as if there is a war, and no one sees it

--Little by little, said Kenazz. --Yisryli fathers bought their tombs from Hatti men, no less, living in Hebron: that should tell you how mixed things used to be. Shechem, Shiloh---no mistake, we Annakim have worked that highland road. Those were good little way-shrine places, and now they mix no more. You were not here when the Yisryli tried again. They stormed their men down the middle of the land, down the valley of the Aijalon river, right into Gezer. Selah, they failed to take it.

But after the blood, some of their men, defeated, brought their families down and made lives in the city

--Enough, enough, I said

--You are not patient. You blundered helping Radharani, so I will help you one thing more, said Kenazz. --Shiloh now is the navel of Yisryli: from this house, only climb two days of hills for the rising sun. I hear their voices too, at night along the walls. But the worst of Shiloh's curses fall on those mixed-in families at Gezer. What will come, green man, now that even the Eberu fear Yisryli anger out of Shiloh, and bury their own broken Asherahs in the ground? Halak enjoys his wine and his hate. But he has reason to give sons to Sisera. A Yisryli leader's name is in the hills: The Lightning

--My head is circles, please! I said. --I need a drink

Fire in the mountains, coming down the land, a man of lightning---I saw myself, so long ago. It told me I should understand those keening night-time voices. Such different tribes, so fiercely free: they lived for their spirit worlds and festivals, and had bled under Pharaoh's blades. The lot of us detested kings, and loved this planting in. Was it Veda who had said *We should be alright, if we keep close to The Green*? The trouble was, we had to help people cross their country in order to keep our own

Radharani's night turned solemn waiting on the full moon's rise. When the crown of it came up big and orange over the dark land southward, she lit a taper from the hearth of Qadeshah and carried it three flights of stairs to the roof of her great building. Up there beneath the sky, ringed around by Symoon and his brothers with five Annakim, she gave fire to the torches they presented. And there she stayed as her guard carried fire down and lit the torches of the families clamoring at the gate. The dawn's procession from the sea was doubling back, a throng heading down for the green sandy place beside the river, to light the summer night fire. For all I had heard this day, I hoped a purge for everyone jumping the flames. Radharani up there looked the world's own answer to the climbing heavy moon, and we saw her still as we threw our torches on the blazing pile

Now the musicians' pipes and drums were coming down because they could feel people's appetite to make all this grow wilder---and half-slamming into me hello was young Urana. From her almond eyes and subtle smile to the disarray of her hair ,and the cling of her sadhin's long fine yellow linen, she looked at once lit from within, calmly self-possessed, and joyously torn down, come rolling in wonder out of some kind of loving melee

--See the sea? I see, old man of the sea, she babbled

--More wine, then you'll make sense, I joked with her over the holy racket

--Don't be a bore! I mean, this day, all-in, I see what Radharani knows. She says she got it just from watching you sea people swim in the ocean here

--What?

--You people in the waves! You play with them, ride them, let them knock you down, they cleanse you, and out you come as clean as salt! The powers, Deucalion---

they move *through* us. And Radharani builds the ways and places that it can come---to everyone! I missed my family, and I stood among her stones, and they were with me. And then the stones became the cities in our league, and I felt small and lifted up, and brave---that is why she builds all this, that each one come to living as they will. Look at her trees, her dates and figs and pomegranates and oranges, do they not feed us? And do they not teach us how to die? Every leaf falls, and every seed, and everything feeds what keeps on growing, and we are forever part of that. And then her music, and prayer and gesture and dance, and wild talk---look at my dress! I had it off with who knows who, and half-way off with a couple of women, I was touching and was touched by I don't know how many people. Where was *I*? *I* was gone, melted, it fell off, like proud-flesh off a wound, old clothes. And everybody saw, and nobody cares---Let the smelly dried-up kings of Babylon fix people names for what we do in love. The powers, the powers, they come in waves right through us, Deucalion. Knock us down, all to the good! Do you see how I see, island-man, ocean-man? Do you want to kiss me?

--Yes, I said, and did: it was like kissing the one fruit equal to the world

--That's just how it was in Alashiya! I laughed, but Urana had moved on

Raz, I saw, sang his full-throated share and kicked his feet up in the procession: Lavi walked along beside him, reserved and solemn, eyes big with the flame of his torch. When both followed custom and tossed their torches on the fire, I caught the tail of more argument between them: *They make me at home*, Raz shrugged, and Lavi answered him, *They make you nothing*. I wondered would it help to explain that people here were not in worship of sun or moon, but in keeping with the powers of their circles. Then Symoon came down from Radharani's roof, and out of that commotion came another

    --Welcome, Shiloh and Shechem! Halak proclaimed

    --Shut up, Halak! more than one voice cried: Symoon was holding back

    --But this is the night for a marriage tale! Halak protested all around himself. --I knew a man of a town up country. A man very hot to marry Yisryli---those eyes, you know. And, *Well enough*, they told him. *But you must cut the hood off your member---every man of you! And then we can all settle down like one great family*. Do you hear? Those were their words. So, it was done, every man in the town! Chop, chop! And, Oh! Oh! There you lie, with your tender parts cut up. And lo, comes your new family's wedding-gift!

    Halak pulled a knife from the small of his back, and stabbed into the air all around himself. Canaani men jumped back, but snarled and shook their fists as if confirming Halak's tale. Into their midst Symoon sprang with all his drive. He took Halak's knife-hand first, and the other palm smashed below his chin to put him down: Sheshai and Kenazz took over, but Symoon warned them, nothing more than finding the fool his bed. Still, Halak was not alone and the Canaani people with us grumbled at his treatment. Another moment and jibes began to fly. Who made anybody law and king here? Who was fit to say what any man could say? The voice of the sea and smoky roar of the green-wood fire made each speaker louder to be heard, and angrier. And now this commotion gave way to a rumbling clatter coming down the service-road

--He comes! –Huzzah! –Seee-serr-raaah!

Not only had the great man's horses drawn his chariot of iron down into our midst, with flying torch and pennants and drums and a hundred spears in double-rank behind: at Sisera's side was our Halak, already free again. The great man stood out majestically in a heavy cuirass with metal studs, and removed his tall-plume helmet, with its guard of iron protecting his great man's nose

--You are Symoon? We will not have our Canaani brothers treated so

More murmurs from all sides as this Sisera plowed on into big words about peace. I looked at Raz and Lavi. They both looked full-afraid, and sure these meeting rivers of resentment were going to turn on them. At Raz' side, I heard what Lavi said

--Go on then, Raz. Choose for yourself. Choose this life of sleeping in the mud. Or, circumcise your heart. But choose, today

--And if not, what will happen? Raz replied. –Your family will visit?

Sisera droned on. And then Radharani, as good as from nowhere with Urana and her young ones, stepped right into our midst, in front of the great man's horses

--Have you fought enough? she asked; and now she raised the largest white conch horn that her house possessed. She filled her lungs, and sounded a wail to wake an army of the dead. Then she raised her hand up toward the moon

A veil of pallid reddish gray was falling across her face. Once people saw this and their voices failed, a first few put their foreheads to the dust and kept them there. Women followed their men, men followed their women, and the children all

Sisera looked stymied, his men wagged their heads to find the trick: mothers cried to Radharani, this was frightening the little ones. And the moon went slowly dim and sickly reddish gray. Worse, it began to go black. Halak clutched at Sisera, who ripped away his arm of comfort

The last sounds of night seemed to doubt themselves as the shore grew altogether black, and the stars grew eyes. Symoon and his fellows Doku and Badera held calm and firm in half a circle with joined hands, and lowered their eyes. Sisera's surrounding men were prostrate already when at last he climbed down from his wagon, knelt, and touched his brow to the dust. Things grew still, except for whimpering, and anger, and baffled noises pleading---but not Halak, who began to make a choking gurgling sound as he spread out his arms and trembled them. His head swung around from the neck, and his body wrestled in place, as if some voice not his were fighting to come out

--Stop it, Halak! said Radharani. –The only power

seizing you, I name Horon! Shameless trickster, these people have eyes, they know what you want!

--Trickster you, Halak replied, suddenly still and all defiance. --Shamming power over the moon. Not that *I* understand this, he added quickly to the crowd with a hapless spread of his arms. --Oh, people, you should hear her talk in bed! Halak went on. --*We shall marry this place to the circles of nature*, she says. And who knows what in blazes that means! I suppose you understand this, what is swallowing the moon?

--No, Radharani answered. --If we understood it, Halak, we would be dancing it together. The difference is, I point: you push. You will not lash our backs to this plow, she said with a slap to the rail of Sisera's chariot

--Well then! Halak challenged with his arms out wide. --If Sisera is the light of the way---let light return!

> --*Or seven years may Baal afflict thee,*
> *Eight, The Rider of Clouds!*
> *Let there be no dew, no rain,*
> *no surging of the deep,*
> *Let there be no goodness of Baal's voice!*

The man was quick. His gang let out a weak cheer, but next we knew, it came out stronger from Sisera's men at arms. For the moon's first veil of gray was coming back across its face, and people took hems of their garments in hand to wipe their brows. *See-serrr-rahhh*

--Yes, yes! Radharani hissed. --Cheer for the

weapons that will not save you! Did you see the world's light go dark? You are *warned*

She turned her back, and was gone as more and more of us saw the sharp white light coming back to the face of the moon out of darkness. Then, sighs and thanks and weak-kneed laughter, as Halak wiped the sweat from his brow, and led the jibes about who had frightened first. Rising myself, I saw that Radharani had been not alone in keeping to her feet

--It's nothing! Lavi said loudly into the night. --It's nature! It's nothing! he repeated. --Are you alright now, Deucalion? Let us help you up.

8

Eager to get rid of the agent of Thebes who washed up complaining on her shore, the lady Hatiba dropped the man in the first island vessel fit to sail him home. This fell across the circles of my boat at the harbor-town of Enkomi, Alashiya. After years of this distinguished lady's pleasure pouring her guests good exotic wines, Hatiba knew my sail and the value of her custom: her promise of handsome thanks besides was a warning about the man. He was the last thing I wanted, but I made ready, waiting him and morning tide on the quay below her kinsmen's town

By then, you see, I was already grieving Radharani and the ashes of Qadeshah. A man who lived in the shadow of Mot might imagine fifty years enough to plant one lasting thing in this world. But to me her life and all she had built had lit the world and then gone under faster than one flash of lightning. Waiting this man I was looking up at Enkomi's own range of high thick walls, still black in places from the last destruction, as its people fine and humble went about. On and on it went, over and over, the building and growing and thriving until one became a fat golden target for the next tribe of outcast madmen at arms, running from the wreckage of their own rule

--She expects *me* to arrive home in *this*? Do you people know I am WenAmon, first agent of Heri-Hor, the High Priest of Amon in Thebes?

His brown Kemeti eyes were glowering in a face just over forty, his delicate jawline stubbled and his hair black and tangled to his shoulders. No wig, no paint, no stave or satchel or entourage, wrapped in a simple off-white cloak from neck to ankle with a touch of yellow in its hems, and stains of travel and abuse. Now the man laid off his cloak and inflated his chest, still solid, and proud: no sash or beaded metal mantle to color the cotton from his neck to his sandals, but marks of the sun at his wrists from precious bands traded off for passage. Proudly this WenAmon stood there, yet a man at his weary wit's end, wanting just to go home

--Climb down, I shrugged. --Walk aft between the oarsmen, to my cabin

--I do not walk well on boats. I require you to steady me

--But, surely, I said, pulling both hands away and giving in to my share of his torment. –Surely your nation can do something without stepping on people

--What! I do not care for---What! Yes, a perfect close to this journey, WenAmon huffed and grumbled

But he relented, spread out his arms and tilted along the planks to the boat's one enclosure in the stern. Bench by bench the way was tight and it took resolve not to look at one person, nor did he grace the gray-haired woman sitting comfortably wrapped in blue at the root of the mast. This fellow peered into his shelter, grumbled again, and then racked the oilskin shut behind himself

So, we hulled our way out into late summer's

northwest wind, then hauled up sail, to sight with luck in a day or two the coast of Ponikija: from there it took about a quarter of a moon to skirt Canaan's cities for The Nile. Through the first night on the open sea the wind kept fair for pushing us east, and under the black dome of stars, we watched the sea answer them with her rolling pools of white phosphorescent glow. All night this WenAmon kept to himself. Then, at sunrise seasick over the rail, he heard that once we struck Arados, Byblos was not far, and he asked to speak with me. He was miserable enough to try the lemon and seawater mixed him by old Anab, and before long he felt better. He gave her the empty cup as if throwing it away

--If you will honor me with your name again, I want to apologize, he said

--I am not myself either, I shrugged

--Friend, said WenAmon, --I have been through a terrible time. I can show nothing now to speak for me. Still, I assure you a royal reward, for your help. I ask you, in the name of my official business, to conceal my passage as we coast. There are many in these lands with worse than disrespect for the Great House I serve. Wherever I go, they strike at him through me. But more, I fear the reckoning when I get home. What I need is a fellow like yourself just to hear my report, as I prepare it

I wanted nothing from him. His nation starved for metals was digging out tombs of their fathers for the gold. I was also a fool still imagining Nile would help our Pulesati's worsening straits. And what else was there? I had sworn to help four children of her house. One of them on board still looked me in the eye, the others already dead. Curse me, in the bottom of my being, mortality was no limit of my love and obligation

--I do not like this wish to hide. Give me your word that you will listen likewise, and add what I report to your reckoning with Ramses' sons

WenAmon consented, and it was good to have the look of his eyes in it

–But, he added, --understand, sir, that I have little say among the mighty ones. Help me, then: is there ground on which I can speak to their interests?

--There is. Years ago, your third Ramses promised land and life to the Pulesati, for his service. I set my teeth to say it, but that is who rules this world. And Great House has eyes to see the Pulesati honoring those terms, four generations to this day: the sufferings of our sons make the roads flow out of the east into his temples. Bid him to ask his richest priests. Say to him, we are trying

Here, although WenAmon was still rather kindly listening, my voice simply trailed off. Deep underneath me, life felt as weary as this man looked. My marriage days had ended. It was a bones feeling that, if I could mark it, began the day Radharani died. Ariadne, Pyrrha, all the others, just the beginning of a wish to lie down among them and be done. But sick and tired as I was, I had all of them in one voice still in my ears: *Man, are you alive? Only corpses give up on the living*

We agreed to talk after food passed around, and

WenAmon liked the little three-legged stove we lit and cooked upon. --Curious fellow! he remarked with his mouth full. --You have land for such wine, and you live like this?

I vanished awhile in the simple sight of the sea. In the unmatched goodness of her luminous blue that surrounded and was bearing us, the wind's jewel whitecaps winking bright against the blue, one horizon to the other. WenAmon, for his part like his countrymen and the peoples of Canaan's hills, disliked the sight and feel and smell of her

Like a woman, she is always hiding something. Nor did they like it when she hid nothing. Men whose indignations told only of themselves in the sight of Radharani, who sometimes walked the precincts of Qadeshah clothed only with the sun or moonlight. The ones who understood or just enjoyed the shock had used to smile, *Eve is walking in her garden.* And I longed for the flame and the grace of her whom we would never see again

No, life's flashes of that kind of lightning were not born to last. Yet, neither were kingly stones, nor the hammers in their sons' hands. The Lion of Mykenai had tumbled like his hapless walls at last, achieving the perfect expression of their god. And what was to be done? I saw no cause to coddle a shadow of a senile imperial shade

--Your crew's tongue is Zakkala, like the people in Dor, WenAmon began. --That was the first place that robbed me. Me, the god's ambassador!

--What god?

--Why, Amon Ra, who owns the world, and all the ships of the sea!

--If you say so, I replied, settling in for a good one

--Near-on to a year go, I came down The Nile with a commission from Thebes, from Pharaoh's very hand, a holy mission. It was written, his very words, on a holy scroll with pictures brighter than the sky, with a holy seal and gilded ribbons hanging down. More, the god's own likeness was hung about my neck in alabaster. All men knew who goes before me, for Amon Ra protects and makes success for his wayfaring servants

As if waiting for a cheer, WenAmon cast his eyes up and down the oarsmen lounging at their benches. Their silence curled the face that he turned away. Never had he seen a greasier gang of louts and naked wolves

--Some think my country is divided now, he resumed. –I grant for all to hear of course, great powers to the mighty ones of Tanis, where I landed in the Delta to change ships: Nesu-Ba-neb-Ded, and his handsome lady Tentamon. They, at least, received me with civility due my credentials. Rather, they did so after somebody read for them my commission from Thebes. Straightaway, as they were commanded, they endowed me with riches for the mission. And which of you poor sailors ever saw a chest full of gold and silver vessels, as big as a man can carry? Such was the fortune entrusted to me. To bring back Lebanon's finest cedar, for the building of no less than the river-barge of Amon Ra---the king of all gods, in his boat of a million days

--I think we said that

--I speak as if at home. Now, it may be wise to grant you from the start, that the first bit of trouble was my fault. Tanis sent me off me in any old boat---a boat of Ponikija, that only happened to be bound my same way. And we were three days out when I realized, I had forgotten to get my sacred writing back!

--Tanis sent you off without it? Why?

--That is for Tanis to answer. And answer they shall, WenAmon replied darkly. --So, there I was, on a boat with sea-trash mongrels at the oars. But let me tell you something. Sailing north, we put in at all the old cities and ports from Gaza to Joppa. I saw two things in your Pulesati places: hospitality, and building or rebuilding

--That said, the more I noticed Dor, that little nothing of a headland where you people have raised fine houses, and orchards: the harbor is stones of size to impress master builders at home. What I wish to say is a warning---that ports of the Ponikija northward will not be pleased by Pulesati building there, close to their own

--Too late, I answered. --You will hear. And yet, you were robbed in Dor?

--Not exactly, said WenAmon with a tilt of his head. --At first, the house of a chieftain you call Seren gave me welcome, when they heard that I had come. Such wine they sent, and a joint of beef, with bread, real bread with no sand mixed in the dough. How long, though, before a mongrel of my ship ran off with Amon's treasure?

I could not hold my hand from my forehead

--Believe me, said WenAmon, --I ran to the house of Dor's chieftain, with the big red pillars facing The Green. When I showed his women-counselors the sign of Amon hung around my neck, they told their Seren that he should see me. And I showed it to him, and told him I had been robbed in his own harbor. With Amon in my hand, I warned him, solemnly, that he would be held responsible. To his credit, your Seren replied, *Honor and Excellency!* Which, at least, was some morsel of the proper respect

Even if he meant to say, *You make a fool of yourself*

--Your Seren told me, *This is always a serious crime and a threat to trade. But we know nothing about this matter and complaint. If the thief were any man of our own household, and had boarded your ship to rob you, we would pay you restitution from our own, till he was found. Things of this nature, we always handle so. But you said that the thief was one of your own. No practice of the seas would make us pay for that. Only, wait a few days, while we search for the dog who committed this crime*

--I waited and waited. Alright. Granted. I failed to make it clear the thief from my boat was no man of mine, but one of his country, foisted on by Tanis---but I tell you, these people are all in together. Did they find the dog? No! Scum, living high someplace among the houris. Well, the wretch you see me now still did his best, for his master and for Amon Ra the god about his neck

--I am a man of Thebes. I was not born to wait. I put the ship on orders off to Byblos. There, surely, people cared about right, and justice. On we sailed. But, we stopped in Tyre---and does the god who owns the world not help his servants? Does he not put before those who fear him, all they need? Behold! For there, in Tyre, in the chaos you know yourselves of such a harbor, was a ship at berth I knew not come from where. Without a man on board, that one odd moment of the day, you understand. I crept aboard, and to my hands came a chest of riches almost equal to my mission

--Surely, it should not have been there if it were not meant to serve Amon. When I had it hidden safely, I even told that ship's captain, the garlic-spitting slob, that the chest was my lawful security, till Amon's was recovered. *Lawful?* he bellowed. *Where do you think you are?* A man of unmitigated nerve, he was. His crew I liked. They kept him from killing me

--Go on, then, laugh, WenAmon said with a sigh of surrender. --You island people laugh the same crooked way, and always at the wrong time. Argh. When we did reach Byblos, that captain's accusations seemed to be waiting for us in the harbor. Meaning, me---I, who was the party suffered wrong! The house of Byblos would not see me for the cedar. You may say I was lucky Byblos told me to go home. But I refused! I held to Amon round my neck, and kept my boat before their windows, where I prayed for nineteen days

--And lo, a man of the men about the very prince of Byblos---this man, Amon seized in all his body, and threw him rolling on the floor before the prince. *Bring him up! Bring up Amon's messenger!* he said through choking froth.

When a god turns men mad like that, you can trust what they say. I declare, you people laugh at baffling things!

Trust what they say to drop more kings' disasters in your lap. Was it not so, Halak of Qadeshah, thou monumental fool? While the old barge of Amon rotted inside a granite ship-shed, the double of their senile sire

--Now, there I was before Ponikija's prince of Byblos, with him sitting in his upper chamber, leaning his back against his window on the sea. What do you think? I go over every word each day, you see, for my report that must be written down

--It shows you doing proudly by your fathers

--It is well. So, there in Byblos I stood before their prince. His name is Zakar-Baal, do you know him? *Amon's favor upon you!* I hailed him. What he said in reply was disappointing. *How long,* he merely asked, *since you left the land of your Amon?*

--So, I told him. And he asked for my credentials in this business! Was it my fault I had none? Well, perhaps it is part my fault. He thought so. The prince could not see why a rag-tag crew were sailing a mission from a god, and under such incompetent---I! I wonder if I was reckless, saying these were Tanis' tricks, to wreck the whole affair for Thebes. *And what is your business here?* he asked me. He had a most unsettling calm. I am sure he had heard the complaint from that captain in Tyre. If Amon's laws were not on Amon's side, why did he not mention it?

--Hence, I knew this man was out to play me. And all I had, or that is, all that I thought he should see, was

Amon Ra. I brought out the god in alabaster, thus, from here, where now only my poor heart has a place for sorrows. *I come,* I told him, *for the cedar to build the sacred barge of Amon Ra, king of all gods. Your father gave the timber, as your grandfather did. And so shall you,* I told him

--He rolled his eyes and laughed your very way. Oh, is it not as they say at home, childish people every side of us! And do you know, that prince fetched out---to the face of the god, like a thing to compare with the mystic glories of the ever-living sun---the prince brought out old Byblos' written records of the counting-house. Bits of clay and moulding papyrus. *Look here, and here,* he told me, such a mouse of a man

--*Your fathers paid Byblos for the cedar,* he told me. *Thebes, if we belonged to Thebes, would not have sent gold and silver, but commands. See for yourself these transactions of our fathers. Do you read there a single word of tribute? We are not your servants,* he said, *nor the servants of those who sent you*

--*Listen,* said the prince: *I speak, and the cedars of Lebanon lie cut and ready on the shore. Where are the sails and orderly crew and cordage, what have you fit for transport of goods that come of so much husbandry? You come this hole-and-corner way, and princes jump?*

--But the god Amon Ra was with me. If he, a prince, could play the niceties of practice, so could I. When I told him of the life and health that Amon Ra would send him---some people, I find, need to be told that over and over---he rolled his eyes. I took that for surrender, for straightaway he wrote a letter to the great house of Tanis.

So again I waited, and waited, days and weeks. Yet, to my surprise, this prince had good name and credit there; and Tanis sent another chest of treasure for my mission. Eight moons, these misfortunes took. And then, at last, I stood upon the shore at Byblos, about me the great trees cut and ready to serve Amon Ra

--What happened to the chest you stole in Tyre?

--Stole! WenAmon half-sneered. --Please, let me finish. Indeed, when I answer you, then you will have compassion. The prince, because of all his delays, reaped his punishment. By this time, he was unwell: *sick and tired*, as he put it, at our parting. Still, to my honor, the man came down to the harbor to see me leave, with a sunshade held out over him. I, victorious, saw that, and I said: *Lo, the shadow of Pharaoh falls upon you!*

--I declare, whatever it is, the eyes were loose in the man's very head, he was rolling them all the time. And he said, *Now I have done for you what our fathers did, though you have not done for us what your fathers did. Here is the cedar, do what you please with it---and here are words of wisdom for your way. Forget your green-faced terror of the sea: keep in mind your terror of me! Little man,* he growled, *a Pharaoh years ago sent men here like yourself. Come, let me show you their graves*

--*Oh!* recounted WenAmon with his face in fright as the words cut through him again. *--Oh, let me not see them!* There was nothing loose now in that prince's eyes. Arch, like a panther's they were, and his grin like death. I only managed to hold onto Amon at my breast, and I said, *But those men, prince, they had no god with them! And see for* *your noble self, have my words not come true in the timber on the shore? Let Byblos, then, raise up a great polished stone, to tell all time what I accomplished here. And all men will know that for your behavior, Amon Ra sent you ten thousand years of health and life!*

--*Yes*, the prince answered. *To inspire the ages*, he said. He had learned nothing. Be not so unwise, you children of the sea!

--But, clearly, I said, --you did not reach home and honor for your toil?

--We come to the end. For just as we were leaving Byblos, with all in order to my credit, into the harbor sailed three boats from Tyre! Chasing me with ugly friends of their complaint. These water-rats asked the prince of Byblos to arrest me on the spot. *They have come to take me again!* I cried. The prince wept too. But all he said was that they were free to chase me once outside his harbor. How is that for dominion? Do you see in that why you people are such failures?

--So, I waited even longer, that the Zakkala might wander off. And so they did, like children. Now, what the prince did can show my masters that even a foreigner pitied my state. He sent a singing-girl, one from my own land in his house, to soothe my troubles. But she plucked the strings of her kinnor so tenderly, it made me more homesick. And when I told that to the prince, he washed his hands of me. *Enough! Get out of my harbor*, he said, and I made all haste to do so---if you can imagine what it took me, a foreign priest, to get the boats and barges organized

--I wish you and my masters to see that, in spite of everything, my little fleet was coming home successful. Then those dogs came over the edge of the sea. Does a thief not come with arms? They robbed me of my timber! My whole commission, wrecked! They shoved me around while they rummaged and seized their chest back. They touched and mocked the god's own sacred sign. They ripped it from my neck, and threw it in the brine! Such contempt you never saw. Not even stealing the gold neck-chain, but tossing that overboard, too

--You might have been wearing it

--Argh. I suppose, WenAmon grumbled. –I had to barter off my person's last touch of civility and rank. For that, all I got was the first tramp out of a hole called Sidon, where they dumped me. As usual by now, it was headed not home, but for your Alashiya. Oh, how in the world am I going to make my masters understand?

I was looking at the rolling sea

--You can tell them you behaved like their fathers in these lands. Tell them that no matter what your aims and crimes, you are victims, because you fashioned a vicious senile god back home in your own image, who makes all well for you. Our thanks to your masters also, I said, --for what their knives have made of Canaan. Thank them for the mountains' hate of anyone like us

It was no answer, and WenAmon turned away with his face in his hands. I spoke to stab, and imagined that he felt it. Soon, though, to my surprise, he breathed deep, turned his body back my way, and with a face now brightly gracious, WenAmon thanked me for his hearing. Maybe it was just the dry sight of little Arados island, but he said he was ready to keep his word

I meant to hold my tongue till we were coasting the mouths of his river. From Arados, through Byblos, Sidon, Tyre and on, WenAmon grew very afraid, though it was not hard to hide him where a harbor-master knew me. For the rest I said my lady passenger had a sickness best confined till she reached The Nile's healers. I did not tell him how they smiled like cats to know the misfortune's destination. In the light of our fifth dawn together, WenAmon saw the little headland of Dor, and in the place of his first hospitality, tumbled and burned empty ruins

--Who did this? he asked. --Moons ago I was talking with the household

--This is how correct you were. Ponikija, I answered. --But, if you need a name, it is Halak son of Halak. I knew---or rather, my father knew his father, a lord of Canaani pistachios, who staked his land to bribe his way up as a Baal-king. Instead, he got thrown out of the house altogether. So he joined Canaani fellows northward, turning into a warlord. As usual, his misalliances killed him, but not before he got up a son his kind. Halak the younger made his fortune in trade-silver, sacked out of Dor as a prize, for the service of Tyre's little king in making his point

--No, there will be no Pulesati harbor this far north. I'm sure the wounded walked south. What you see is the tomb of a woman who would not leave the home she built with her mixed people. The walls collapsed on her. Sir, there is more to see from the rails of this boat

    --And you, WenAmon answered with a rumble of anger in two directions, --you remember your word, to protect my person

    So, by day from Dor, we kept the coastline just over the horizon, including Qadeshah and Joppa, where began the mid-country road away into the east. I would have shown him Qadeshah but it was I who could not bear the sight. We slept wild strands of beach between the few little ports, all the way to Ashdod, and from there WenAmon's increasing relief seemed to open up his eyes. The man who admired Dor's works liked Ashdod's the more, for its breakwater under stout new double-thick walls, and beyond the long hill Goliath's Head touching the sky. The wind of this stony place at least dispersed the dye-works' fetid airs, and either side of the walls that flanked clusters of houses and tent-camps, the land spread away flat and rich in olives and grapes and citrus trees. The fields looked burned off in late summer but the chaff was from onions and broad beans, chickpeas and grain. Mule-drawn wagons, shaded by tamarisks at the heads of roads toward farms and lesser villages, waited loads of fish from local punts and needle-boats

    --A fair place, again, said WenAmon. –I mean, since you people burned it, and planted in the ashes of a Baal. Oh, yes, some of you had to do that, my family is five fathers of priests and we know about those times. Join me up-river, and I will show you, my special guest, the magnificent temple walls where the islanders' defeat is made immortal

--Season is short for home, I shrugged in the direction of his tin ear. And where was my home? An oilskin cabin still, after four hundred years? Weariness, that was the shrug in my answer

--They were killing kings, in the world, in themselves. When that flame extinguished, it was Ramses who wanted us where we had always been. His sons' dues flow again in grain and goods. Who dislikes it can appeal to the owner of the world

--Ah, said WenAmon. --You will have me ask Great House for justice over Dor. Yet, you said that it was vengeance by Canaani, with another new name

--Justice can do nothing for Dor. Why ask justice from a Great House that never helped Canaani, only walked on its peoples to reach Babylon? We have built on the broken pieces. What the Pulesati want, you see in these family fields that grow your taxes. They also grow young men. When you have been our guest in Ascalon and Gaza, then you will hear of them in the tale of a beautiful woman

He was willing. We ate roasted bream and pork in breezy Ascalon houses with garden walls painted in the way of old Crete. In the town's best shrine their clay figures of Earth Mother were small and smiling like old home's too. When I asked about the strange delicious scents that smoked in their offering-stands, they pinched out nutmeg and cinnamon in my palms. It had traveled west for two years, and come to them a tiny cut of Nile trade from the hands of Pulesati, who walked at the merchants' sides. So did WenAmon touch and smell why his fathers had planted us here

In Gaza, the daughters of Diwia carried heirloom vessels into ceremony that put double spiral-wheeled X's in their hands. Years and years I had seen none the like, but when I did, the world's great lights lit up in my chest: their festival circles of sun and moon were turning still among Pulesati towns. Such was the web of time that kept their chieftains close to home and bound by custom to the damos. At the core of public prayer here it was still Canaan's dewy Dagon, and their Asherah too with a Cretan name, Derceto: our nights in the crazy company of Gaza's Seren and women burned with music, till you felt carried off by the sea-breeze

Lines of people wove themselves and unwove again, to stray among the circles of trees planted as a holy grove, where you were expected to act as in a garden. Half the trees of fifty years were big-spread salt cedars, as evergreen as the Tree on the Elohim's mountain: the others were pomegranate, the fruit fat rubies bending the branches down

--May I say, he remarked as Gaza fell behind the steering oar, --you people almost make me forget. But I still go home empty-handed, and two treasures lost. My lord and my brothers will suffer shame, because of me. *How could this happen!*

He was looking deep into the sea, weighing out her peaceful invitation

--Keep your word. It might put something of service in your hands

--What? Oh, WenAmon replied. --Is there beverage?

At least he was eager to turn his mind another way for awhile. I mixed him wine mostly water, that he remember rather than forget. My own I did not mix, for I had nothing but a legion of ghosts to speak from, people and places he had never seen or heard of. First cup, I poured into their restless sighing grave, and asked their help to do I knew not what

If WenAmon knew old Canaan's graven images of Qadesh---of Qudushu, she whom his own temples called young rising Mistress of All the Gods, Lady of the Stars of Heaven, her arms upraised like lotus-headed snakes---then he had seen Radharani. Life-long, she wore her fine black hair done up in two great facing crescents, a Hathor's crown as lure of the living and mistress of the dead. And the woman who walked that part looked frankly back on the world that gazed at her, deliciously holy, proud shoulders and inviting breasts and her smooth supple belly curving outward, above one tiny garment at her thighs. I could not say she came to her place of power up from dirt, for that was small credit to my guest. I told instead the honor of her learning by the people of a place near Dor, called Qadeshah. That she had woven its life together from the sea and land and mountains, from birth and work through death, that the woman who knew enough to get a bakery built and a stout forge fit for smelting iron, like husbands of her mistress ceremony, this woman lost nothing when one year, the pig of sacrifice and feast broke loose, and she was the one to run it down and drag it in a headlock back to the altar. That she was the moon-wise mother of many festivals of riches. That she had raised a standing stone for every town she led into league, and by the time of her last days, ten of them graced her hill above the sea. She was the one reaching out to the peoples in the hills. Nor was she stopped by their refusal of a trade which, we knew, would herald everything to come---my own failed trade that way in sylphium

She grew the name of Qadeshah and looked for ways to build its life without an army, but there were great men of Canaan at hand, and a host of worried angry arms. So many and strong their chariots that they fumbled several years over what to do with them, short of burning out the highlands' new villages and farms. They were fumbling still when lightning struck and burned another town in the mountains of the north, Taanach. Its name meant nothing to WenAmon, though it was a place of peoples mixing, in their meals and their music and rites: its courtyards, halls and houses now were charred-out pens for highland sheep

--And the mountain passes twice as lawless. I begin to see, said WenAmon

Ah, but the great man raised on high by Canaan's fears, gaining even more from the fomentations of his underling, returned the favor by proclaiming Halak-Baal--- who immediately volunteered to captain the guard at home while his master struck out northward in all

Canaan's name. They drank each other's drafts of hammer-vengeance while Radharani told them, and told them, the season was heading into rain. And *Who but Baal is the Rider of Clouds?* replied His earthly representative

Sisera marched after The Lightning northward into Kishon River country, where women of the wells pointed toward a brigand's camp. Sisera led five thousand men of spears and bows with two hundred chariots up into the flatlands of Jezreel, and then the autumn sky opened. By the time his last horses and wheels were mired in the mud, The Lightning had drawn even more men around him at a mountain there, Tabor. Down came the strength of Yisryli, and scores of Sutu and Habiru with them who liked the numbers and the lay of the fight, pouring off the humpy hill with their arrows and fat sling-stones hammering down ahead of them like hornets in the air. When the lines turned at Sisera's cry, more of them streamed out from both flanks of Tabor and into the fight. With Sisera's bowmen soaking wet, his best arms pressed to his sides against the river, they cut to pieces man and horse. Running from the rout, Sisera found a shepherds' camp, where they obliged him food and rest. When he slept, a woman with her own obligations drove a tent-stake through his temple

From that day, where this futility was told in Canaan villages, families grudged every son and bit of wealth for war. This pulled hallowed floors out from under Halak and many others: Canaani youth bore arms and dug town defenses, but they never fought far from home. Barak The Lightning faded, we never heard his end, and for years the sea and the mountains turned their backs

--And so, inquired WenAmon, --at Thebes, I am to say that Canaan's strength is gone, and you are on your own? Friend, I can tell you what they will say. It is your place, children of the sea, to learn how savages of the hills defeat your arms and walls and towers. And why---I tell you, they will ask---why do you not do something?

--Two answers, I replied

--Look! WenAmon cried suddenly, standing up at the port-side rail. --The great bay Sirbonis opens out! How beautiful! To-Mehu, I am almost home!

--Sir, I said pulling him to his seat. --If you keep your word, you may keep your head on your shoulders

--Argh. I will need something. Please, more wine

I poured. And the unmixed cups that I drank gave me counsel to pour everything. This might be our one chance to be heard by persons with an interest

Our sailing had shown him how the tribes of Pulesati, north to south, were thick with each other by festivals and marriage and memory. These were the labors and gardens of our mothers. The woman Radharani said it was like the translucent fabrics off their looms: *Where weavers' hands work best, men of iron hardly see.* But now I hung my head for WenAmon. I was going to show him shame living also in our midst

Could he understand that in the days of our catastrophe, one of our tribes had stabbed another in the back, and that every other tribe laid curses on their children? The hatching of their treason, those Danaans, was too long and futile for his ears. But it felt fair in my heart, where Aktor himself still lived, to say that his people's pleasures in a never-ending vengeance had planted them a place of all but banishment: a swampy plain along the sea called Acco north of Dor, a fetid mire of land fit best for crocodiles, that snatched children fishing to get fed

No matter that Acco's first Danaans carried the same Pharaoh's brand in their flesh. No one wanted them, work, trade or marriage, and the people too wise to call them evil shunned them, for pure bad luck

So it was that Radharani dropped one straight into my hands: a boy named Bohan, one of four young ones with whom she swore me a bond of help. You never saw a boy so shocked and happy at small kindnesses. He worked and suffered to earn his place as each man had to on a boat, and because the sea washes useless things from sailors, his fellows of the day forgot his tribe. Life-long, this Bohan itched for his next little voyage: why? *Because you feel so clean, uncle! Your bones and body feel so clean!*

--You are losing me. This wine, said WenAmon

By the time Bohan had a son, Danaans had sailed enough to wait no more for better. It was Bohan's son they sent to Radharani. He brought her gifts of baskets woven with the Pulesati crane: empty baskets, to say they were giving what they had. Bohan's son, Oka, then asked her for an oracle, to hear what any power in the world might have to say to a Danaan

Radharani took the youth into the inmost pillared hall of Qadeshah's great building, where her knee-high altar stood against the wall facing sunrise, with scents and candles burning day and night. Plenty of men objected that a Danaan foot should cross that threshold, even Urana and the women of her house---but Radharani took him inside. And after offerings, she told Oka about Utnapishtim, the old flood-rider of the east: the only man who found and kept the flower of life-eternal, whose life each day was a banquet where he dwelt, at the mouths of rivers. She told Oka she had seen this man in a dream, a hero of tenacity fit to outdo even Gilgamesh---*And yet, if you see him, Utnapishtim lies back ever at his own good ease*, she said. *Now how can that be the secret of the gods? You, Oka, you the Danaans, are the people who will find it: a good place to live, and a living to make Pulesati need Danaans again*

Radharani sent him home with more than hope. For with every public gift that old Halak had ever laid in her hands, scent or silk, he pleased himself orating about how much it cost to bring them to her from Aram--- through a Lebanon back-country thick with robbers since the burning of Hazor. *Think*, she told Oka, *what it will mean to the Pulesati: cousins with a good strong-point to guard the northern roads. You will find it. You will build it, Oka*

So did this youth convince even Bohan his father to join the spring's trying-party, a hundred best landsmen with as many tools as arms. Ready for a fight if it should come, but try they would. They followed The Kishon's waters up into the flatlands of Jezreel, and hunted up a workable trail cutting sharper north and eastward. They found one, still well-south of any claim of Tyre's princes: it cut along the feet of The Lebanon's back mountains, a dangerous way, but the road was in fair shape. Now a broad river valley opened out before them, spreading for miles before the green-gray foothills of Hermon to the east, whose flanks were enormous and snowy as if holding up the sky. They passed through forests of Syrian ash-trees, the air sweet-alive with water, laurel and birds and green-buckthorn bright with rust-red berries in the sun. Northward, they came to a shining lake, and two strong rivers fed that lake falling out of the Aramean distances

Your Bohan wept when he came back to tell me, speaking as if from my dream, Radharani said: *he shall live at the mouths of rivers. There were people camped along those waters, shepherds and shacks where women dried little fish. And there was no trouble.* Some days beyond the lake, they found three great green hills rising off the plain ahead of them: a place with good and bad approach at once, as soldiers said. They called it Laish, for the only man who outran Oka up the highest of the hills. Within three years, the last Danaans had left the swamps of Acco

They got crops in along those rivers and begin to build the hills. They had everything they needed. A name as middle-men would come, and when the wealth began to flow, the scent would turn the longest Pulesati nose

--Feel, I told WenAmon. –Feel what those people went through in finding the place. What they felt when they found it, and while they built it. Well, my happy telling ends here. A few years later I beached at Qadeshah, and the torch-fire beacon on Radharani's roof was not alight. Her Annakim said she had been sitting in the darkened house for more than a moon: not a guest or a husband or a girl in sight. *Go in to her*, they told me. *She sits in blackness. Make her eat*

Laish was gone. People who got away from the killing and the fires carried Oka all the way to Dor. *He died there with two holes in his chest*, Radharani said, her voice a crow's, a spring gone dry among old stones. Oka's last breaths said that, three moons before the end, a single wandering man had been their guest, an Eberu as amicable as any out there wanting shelter and a meal. Said he was a Levite, a priest without a place to pray. Oka remembered him not because they got on, not because the man knew words of Gi Earth Mother's songs: many Eberu sang them. He remembered his father Bohan's growing wary of this man, who seemed to be hiding the work of his eyes while his tongue was too loud with encouragements. The man asked briskly if their treaties with Ponikija were proving out good things to have, or better with Aram, perhaps. Oka blamed himself because it tricked his pride into saying they had no treaties either way. Most, he remembered that day a gentle quaking of the ground, it did their wood houses no harm, rolled boulders down the hills. The Levite, there a quarter-moon, was gone before the dust. People laughed, but Bohan took Oka aside and boxed his ears

At the harvest-end of summer, out of a lazy

morning mist around Laish, six hundred wild-looking strangers came up into open camp with a motley of spears and jaw-hook swords. Dani, they were called in the highlands, looking for planting-ground themselves. They had already robbed some Eberu houses. The priest, their guide, had found his place. *They killed every Danaan in reach. Even their animals, to make slaves of anybody left,* Radharani wept. *And I sent them there*

--Terrible, said WenAmon who, to his credit, was still listening, with the coasts of Sinai sliding through his gaze, and green home country a few points off the prow. For myself, I thought I might start losing real control because of my wine, but what came out cared nothing for my hopes or wishes

--I have killed that way myself. By cunning, with no warning, killed whole families half-in their beds in dead of night. I killed that way in a fullness of revenge for people I had known plain eye to eye, before they were murdered because they were wealthy and alive. I can show you their graves in a land as old as Thebes, stolen out from under us. But *this*, I stormed on with a chop of my hand coming down, --this, we know no reason for. Except in what our married-up cousins of the Eberu have said---that the god of their cousin Yisryli will have us gone, or dead, or slaves. Their priests, you understand, have marked us for death under what they call the ban, *herem*. Radharani lived what is: they live for what they say will be, when their swords decide it. Who then, WenAmon, will feed your fathers silk, lapis and nutmeg?

--I am afraid I do not know, he answered, shaking his head. --The answer must come from your own kings. The men you call Serens

--Blast! I cried out, hurling my cup past his head into the sea. --How many ages till you hear? The Pulesati brook no kings. At best each one is damokouros, a people's man. And he answers to his people in the circles of sun and moon

--Then what was their answer? said WenAmon, and the calm of his question dropped the belly from my sail. Halted, I had only the urging of the wine to stay true of speech, and I did not like much what it had to say

--Big council. Held in Ekron, well inland near the feet of the mountains: another Pulesati place you only know for olive oil. We always thought it was our strength that our way makes it hard for a man to raise a war. But people came out staggered, or dazed. The judgment still circles in my head. *Had the Danaans not been outcast, Laish would have been an act of war. Can it now be right to burn the highlands, and bleed even more sons who guard the roads?*

WenAmon's head tilted one way, then the other, but he said nothing. It was just like the head-shaking silence that surrounded Radharani after Ekron. But she, I told him, was resolved that we make answer. Now there was another young man, named Woko, to whom she had sworn me as a helper. If Bohan loved the sea, this Woko rose in trades she had forged with Eberu, herdsmen and farmers in the higher pasture country. Sons of a man I had known called Raz, these were people willing already to make marriage of their god with Asherah, and so with their daughters and sons where our peoples broke bread. I had told WenAmon of Radharani's raising of a guard of Annakim for Qadeshah, and now he believed what she did with Woko. She fitted him out like a pride-of-the-islands fighting man, with bronze greaves and leather and a cropped-feather headpiece, the best iron weapons off her forge---and then they traveled the upland country of his trade, hill by house, village by town

The roads, she told anybody listening, had flowed like rivers before any of us had a name. And where now were men of honor, like this one strong and proud beside her---men of honor whatever their bloods and gods of home? Where were the men who, although every one of them had been robbed, could rise to protect their people with the greatness of Keret? For that was a prince no man of war, whose bride had been stolen from him, taken captive to a dark city of the east. And when El Himself, the Beneficent One heard the sorrow of Keret, he told Keret to arise, to win her back

But Keret, his brow to the dust, did not know how. El answered him, *This is the way.* To live with purpose greater than himself. Never to be bought off. And to hold to his honor that his love win out at last. *Are you tired yet,* she demanded, *of life as an insect crawling in the dust?* For years Radharani had heard the highlands crying, *Our bride is in your hands.* The time was come, she said, for men to bring her safely home

In five years, there were joint professional

companies called Kereti, to the number of near five hundred---sons of Eberu and Pulesati fitted out like Woko, bonded by ceremony's vows and marriages, to walk the caravans through in all directions. Gifts, pleasures, honors Radharani lavished on them, as if her life between the worlds were coming true in ways unlooked-for. In rites, she raised people to the highest pitch of being where they were: I could not love her more, to see anyone so turn their spirit inside-out upon her days. That was what she did, and the Serens of our cities had to laugh at themselves keeping up with her

--So you mean, said WenAmon, --she shamed you all into decent behavior

--I said what I mean, I answered. --That men of worth are rising to keep the word of their fathers with your Great House. WenAmon, I said now touching the shoulder of his cloak for the first time, --tomorrow lands you safely home. Till then, stay with me, and fill your masters' hands

--Home, home! Whatever comes, I am ready to die here, WenAmon told the sea; but when he found my hand on his arm, he said, --What? Yes, yes. Go on. I am trying

The young man, Woko, who first stepped forward to that service---Twenty years he trudged and sweated, fought and finally died in battle on those roads. From the middle of the country to the north along the mountains, there was no hill or cliff-hanging pass or deep ravine fit for ambush that he did not know, because his Eberu brothers of that league showed them to him. And in places where, before, a shower of stones and spears and arrows halted caravans till they were turned back, robbed, or taken altogether, Woko and the Eberu's own men beside him paid the passage. I knew him, strong clear eyes, a smirk almost arrogant always at his lips, but it was only his amusement with this world: we met but a handful of times in his life, but he never forgot his Eberu fellows' loss of family and their mortal danger, turning Kereti against their tribes. Out of battle-dress, Woko would not tread upon an ant, but he killed every would-be thief at the front of his fellows. *Because,* he said, *the man using threats of death to steal is asking for it*

  --Brutish, said WenAmon

  --Yes, like the crook and flail to fall on us, if we fail your fathers' promise

  The fall of WenAmon's eyelids confessed it, and the diffident angle of his head said he had seen his masters' failing reach. I told him there were no Pulesati celebrations when we heard, through the Kereti, that highland wars with eastern tribes had been burning the crops and towns of Yisryli families. I asked if he had ever seen Beth Shan's great Hill of the Fortress---and what he thought a captain there like Woko was to do, when Yisryli came down to have their harrow-blades sharpened, and wanted trade for bronze or even iron. *You loathe our women, you will not eat with us, you will not sleep under our roofs. But I see you have no qualm for metals from our hands,* Woko told them---he had already seen the stuff come back on him as weapons in the hills

Their answer? *We came here honest men, to trade. And now that we see how you work this business, to make us need you always like your slaves, you have made a different friend. We promise now, to make your name stink, high and low, up and down this country, which is promised to us by the Holy One of our fathers*

--I beg you! WenAmon suddenly exclaimed. --I see what you people are up against. I hear the threat and I hear no reason for it one can grasp. Believe me, we are a people who know that weapons follow fast behind words. But, friend, do you expect me to remember all this, with my neck under an axe? I beg you---What is it you are trying to tell me? *Make me of service!* You must!

--I am doing my best

--Very well. But tax me not much longer, please

Well, here was a curiosity. A tribesman of the highlands, asked where is the law, pointed to himself. Asked whether he was scarred to the bottom of his bones by kings, he cursed against all kings---and sometimes in the king-cursing phrases of his hated Pulesati. These, I told WenAmon, were the people moving time and again to raise a king, who for them would drive all others with us from the land. If that happened, war would choke the roads of his fathers

--How do you know this?

Things travel. A fellow with a half-Canaani family name who tore down the shrine of his whole town's deities and, surrounded with people's outrage, escaped with his life because he claimed his god was their hope against eastern raiders. When he was gone, his son cut the throats of all his brothers because he thought it would make him *melech*, as some say king, of the middle highlands. Yet, he did fail to murder his one last brother, and that man's words came down the hills with trickling trade

The trees of the world resolved to have a king rule over them. First, they offered kingship to the olive. And why should I give up the fat of my fruit like no other, *said the olive. So, the trees invited the vine.* And why, *said the vine,* should I give up luscious things born of my fruit, that make people happy? *So, the trees turned to the bramble. And the bramble, without flower or fruit people cared for, said:* If this is what you want, come and put your trust in my shadow

--They got a king, my friend. Pricks and shadow were all his fruit. Shall I tell what we heard about the slaughters bestowed on his kinsmen, till he was hacked up by his own in the wreckage of their lives?

--Bramble, prick---Clever, shrugged WenAmon. --Is that not always the way? Do not tell anyone I said that. Taste the air, just breathe it! Home!

It seemed I was speaking too late. Still, I told him that the Yisryli's highland wars had bonded them more in strength and common animus. That their next blow fell at the end of Woko's years as a captain of Kereti, years that had built our northern routes without touching the lands of their passage with a single fortified position. We had strengthened the northern way, and the Yisryli struck a city at the southeast edge of Pulesati farming country, called Lachish. A name that meant nothing on The Nile,

but a town of many peoples' trades, the host of them killed
or scattered and the place a charred tumble of houses,
streets and walls now. Fit only for grazing or penning up
herds from the highlands, by their seasons and their whim

--And even then, your Serens did nothing?

--You go straight to it. Straight to what tormented
Radharani. She, by now at the late end of her years, she
who had mothered the best of the Kereti---what could she
do? There was, yes, a council of the Pulesati, called in
Ekron as before, if ever you heard of it. This was where the
pride of Pulesati walked, and still walks now. A city that
our mothers and fathers off their boats found a tumbling
ruin, a place they built as the hub of many farms, with an
olive press, and a stone-built system of terraces for water,
and good streets and houses of substance---I still do not
know how people climbed off their boats and laid out a
city of stone such a pleasure to walk through

--The Serens talked a week in that place. Half
barking for war, the other half confused or fixed upon
more Kereti forces, and trade as usual. How they grieved
aloud, to know where this put the best strength of every
farm's young men: there was no other way, for those who
had never looked for one. When Radharani arrived, helped
to travel there by her young women, the Serens received
her with honors, and asked her to speak. I will tell you her
words, though they vanished like a dream in the wind

She said, *Sisters and brothers, the stupid, the greedy,
and the violent are going to rule this place. They will rule, no
matter whom they destroy, or how much they ruin---until the*

*smart and the generous and the peaceful do as much the other
way. Sisters and brothers, unless we want to live by war, and
live a lie called peace behind it, there is a way. Make those who
hate us see one thing before their eyes. We are their bride. We are
their bride,* Radharani ended

Futility. The Serens with most of their families
behind them resolved to levy more young men and more
produce of value from the towns. Radharani turned her
back, went home to Qadeshah, and fell into a black silence

--Who would not, said WenAmon. --Having
offered what? Festivals and marriages in answer to acts of
war? You need a nation. Not this---loose confederacy

I got up from WenAmon's side, and walked up
toward the prow. Likely he thought I was angry, but I was
empty and exhausted. The man, except that he knew not
Radharani, was dismally correct. What was I after,
anyway? A few choice divisions of killers off The Nile who
could help us to prove our self-betrayal? We alone had
trapped ourselves, consenting to the service of Great
House. As if there were no other worlds we could have
built in lands of legend far beyond the sunset. And I felt
this mistake from the first day off Karfi, the day when a
chevron of cranes had pointed life to a little girl

--This is Anab, I told WenAmon, coming back and
helping her sit across the cabin from the pair of us. –Anab
was another of the four young ones to whom I was sworn
long ago. Her sister in that was named Yamani

--Sir, I labored on, --Anab put her life into seeds
and plants and medicines, like the one that made you well.

Yamani, I once took to Alashiya, and that place taught her grapes and vines: her trade, Yamani made the grafting of good stocks to the Pulesati hill-farms east of Ekron. Anab here has a tale that might amuse, for the ordeal I gave your ears. A tale of marriage---or at least, the kind of marriage coming straight down the hills, at you and us alike

--How do you do, said WenAmon politely, though he folded his hands in a listener's lap instead of reaching out to touch the bony fingers offered by Anab. She gave a smile that expected as much, and she began

--Can you see the young woman Yamani, trimming the grapes in the high little valleys, where Timnah's birds soar down the plain and up the mountains? There she was in the sun one day. And when she looked up, there was a monster! A giant man too big for the animal hides he wore; a bushy-headed highland-looking man with their wild ways, quite happy out on the land all by himself. A man who glowed, with something more inside him than the usual fire in the crotch

WenAmon still found our laughter inappropriate

--This creature said he liked Yamani, he liked her golden hair. Had Yamani heard that before? She found out why the crazy look. He hailed from Dan. The craziest of all the Pulesati settled there, and then the crazy Eberu moved in. That was some marriage, when the bloods had cooled and mixed: Danaans who fought like animals for Goddess took the god of Yisryli. Why not? It seemed to put behind the curse on them. *Samson*, this huge man introduced himself. She offered him some wine, but he said his power came from touching or taking nothing such. Nothing unclean, Samson said: nothing of the vine, no wine or even raisins, no foods of the uncircumcised. Born to fight for the one true god, he said: a nazirite

--*Go hungry, nazirite*, she told him. He liked that, and he laid on the oil. She did not let him have right away what he wanted. He made Yamani laugh, a mountain-monster going home to ask his parents for their leave to marry her. They scolded him to find a nice girl, worthy of their own. And then, Yamani liked him, because he came back to Timnah even so

--Samson asked her people there for marriage. His heedless ways unsettled them, but he had come to the woman's town, and no small gesture, that, for an Eberu

They liked him that he joined right in the work and feasts and games of contest, wrestling and boxing. Look at him, people said: could it not be a good new thing that two such bloods make a man so wild-alive? If the Yisryli were Eberu with such a daemon, and if she their daughter held him in her hand, why not?

There was always some fishing-for-trouble on Samson' lips; but the benches of communion said this was how it went where peoples met. Yamani they trusted, for her good work on the vines

--He sang the songs of Asherah to have Yamani's flower: the seven summer high days of The Great Year were their feast, and the sun rose up a lion to the full moon in her bed. Yamani came to this world with a fire her own, but his---it shone in her. She told me so. A wild happiness.

And I saw it put peace in her elders' faces; how worried and frightened they had been, until this sign of what our meeting might become

--Then one morning, as they all broke fast together, sure enough, Samson went fishing. He laid out some trick of a riddle that only he could have solved in the first place. The bet was that our fellows could not answer him in three days: the stakes, a suit of festal clothes for every man, or every man owed a suit of clothes for Samson

--Well, they took him on, and tried: the Great Year Pulesati have a flair for games as good as Cretans. When the trick was plain, Yamani's fellows came to her, and asked if she meant to see them robbed? So she went back to Samson, and hung herself around his burly neck, making it sweet for him till he cracked

--No doubt, Wen-Amon interrupted, --they threatened to burn her and kinsmen's house together

--One must think so, Anab rolled on, --if one is brought up where men rob their fathers' graves. Where was I? Ah. Call it Yamani's fault, some do. But that was the first time Samson tore away. Yamani gave the men of Timnah the answer to the riddle, and they gave it to him in the teeth of his own trick

--Samson, beaten, snarled *If you had not plowed with my heifer, you never would have guessed!* And then he tore away from everything. The blood began. The madman roved the roads out of Ascalon, and waylaid Pulesati cousins for the debt. I ask you, what man feels obliged to pay, then kills and steals and throws the dead men's blood-stained robes in our faces? The wisest thing Samson did then was run off. Yamani took up with another man at Timnah: in three years, we paid our cousins' blood-price out of this. And then one day, there was Samson on the hill, with a lamb in his arms, for Yamani again. If Timnah's men would have him

--They would not. Besides, they thought Samson hated her: she was partner to another, and no cow. So, the champion of his god set fires anyplace he could, the criminal clown: in our standing grain, in the olives and Yamani's grapes besides

--How to make him stop? said Anab. --At last, the men of Timnah put it out that they had killed Yamani and her family for his crimes. It made him worse. Samson came right into Timnah spitting rage. Yes, that says it

--You mean, more mayhem? Tell!

--He killed enough, said Anab, --to draw the first real line for Pulesati: to field their swords and spearmen into the hills. To track him down, through the Eberu country east of Ekron, come what might. Now, when the villagers up there saw the weapons coming, they asked what they were for. *For Samson*, said the spearmen, *to do to him what he has done to ours*. This was no war to wipe out all for one, and the Eberu knew it. The tribes mixing up in that good country liked how things had stood these years. You did not, son of Pharaoh, make Samsons of them all. And lo, those people gave Samson over, bound with a murderer's ropes, to the uncircumcised

--So, Yamani almost lived to be one mother of a

kind of law between us. Almost, because the ropes themselves were tricks, and came off Samson's hands. He wanted a fight so badly that he picked up a donkey's jawbone off the sand. He clouted left, he clouted right, he swung to kill every side against spears and swords. Samson fought till a beard of froth hung drooling out his mouth. He raved with joy and swung his bone till the Pulesati backed away. The man was sick in his brain, and plain disgust put by their mission and revenge. Off ran Samson, light as an antelope pole-axed in the head

--What kind of monstrous tale is this?

--I hoped you would know. Well, Samson liked his light-haired houris. He turned up next in the bed of one in Gaza. And still again, he killed his way out when the girls brought in the soldiers. Flirting always with his backward longing that someone overpower him. Running off, the fool tore good wood shutters from somebody's house, and told the shepherds in the hills they were Gaza's gates

--Oh, we never should have looked up from the grapes! But I am almost finished. So was Samson. He thought he had only to come down and take another woman to his taste, and all was well. But she, the next he fell upon, named Delilah---Was she less a daughter of her tribe than the woman who put old Sisera to sleep? A man who struts his power for the world will crave surrender. And, *Oh, my, you big strong man*, Delilah said. *I have never seen a real man before.* Whatever would it take to bind and tame a beast who glowed with fires of the sun?

--Samson got his wish, and played a trick besides.

He asked her to tie him up, as lovers play: the game was, she to bind him tighter every time, and he to break it. When Delilah thought she had him fast, she fell to his own trick: he let her call for soldiers, and then got loose and smashed his way out again. Now he had his proof that she meant betrayal. Yet, as quick as a toad's tongue he came back to her! With another white lamb again his pardon-gift

--*Nothing doing, nazirite*, Delilah told him. The honey-pot was closed until the tricks and games were ended---until she knew, Delilah told him, that he gave himself to her, as she to him. And oh, my, the fox set Samson's crops on fire. She flamed his standing corn, and still no honey. So, Samson told her the secret of his strength: he never let a razor touch his head

--Your *hair*? Delilah laughed. Well then: this time, she was going to bind him fast and shave him, as bald as priests of Isis. By then, Samson was writhing with want of her, and Delilah had a sailor's skill with rope. So, the Pulesati had him. They put the case in Gaza's hands, and he got the death imposed for murder

First they dug his eyes out, and as he suffered like a criminal in any country, people jeered him from the crowd with the insults of the hills coming back to him: *What god will let an unclean people kill his man?*

--Will you hear Samson's last words now? What he said when suffering broke his grip on prayers to kill us all? *Ask in Dan*, he said, *if this is over*

--The Pulesati gave the corpse of Samson to his family. They were looking to see recognitions, perhaps even laws, to come from this. Well, the family took nothing home but a fallen hero. Hear-tell nowadays, Samson's strength was not his hair, but their one true god; who had turned his face from Samson for his loves---his *loves*, among our kind

Anab turned her face to the rolling sea

--And this revolting narrative you tell, what, as my people's fault?

--Forgive me, Anab smiled in both teeth, getting her feet underneath her and rising over him. --I thought you said the world belonged to you and your great god

--I have had---With all respect, I have had enough of this, said WenAmon

On the instant, Anab reached down three fingers and her thumb and seized the man right where he swallowed. He grabbed her wrist and gasped, but he could only hold onto the frightening bony strength of it

--All man, you are, said Anab, with her lips curled back and narrowed eyes. --King of everything, responsible for nothing. You have yet to taste the fruit. This will be medicine, too

--Let go! pleaded WenAmon. --I understand! I hear!

Anab, with a breath that took down the corners of her mouth, retracted her Griffin's claw

--We build north, they hit south. We look south, they---Did my uncle tell you of the place called Qadeshah? Little man, do you see the knives in these two eyes? I took them with me from that day of the end. You see, the pathetic little wall around that sacred hill---it was not even a wall. To anybody civilized, it marked a sanctuary. One place where any comer could be what we truly are---if you vicious, stool-sniffing sacks of lust might let us be. Ah, well. For all Kereti marriages, for all fair friendships with the Eberu, I confess it! We did not know what their Yisryli could mean by *separation*. We did not know how to circumcise our hearts. The crimes of Samson were a matter of law among nations, so nobody looked for Yisryli revenge. We went on living in the House of the Evening Star, and relished the forgetting of his name

--The Yisryli had broken the backs of the mighty Annakim. This we heard from the southern highlands round Hebron, where their guild-house was. So Qadeshah was stretched for even the token swords that made Radharani's people feel safer on her mountain by the sea. They came with morning sun just crowning the mountains behind them, in the summer's last quarter of the moon. Four hundred bearded highland warriors I think, or five--- because they were up the hill and upon us so fast, they jumped like goats and rabbits up the stoniest of places. Organized, too, climbing three sides at once, so that only a few of our kinsmen could run and for the rest it was slaughter with their backs to the sea

--I did not see the deaths of the women in Radharani's house. What, take them for pleasures, for cows to mother more brave men? No. These women with their loose mouths and thighs were befouled---befouled, of course, with the touch of men. I did not see the fires set in every building, in the shrines of our communions, the bakery, even the forge for the metals they wanted! We were in a thicket of sycamores under the hill. It was an endless smashing sound, with screams of many and then screams of a few. You would have said it was the smashing of just everything. Sickening, and all so fast that I never saw Radharani. I know nobody living who saw how she met these new husbands

--When Qadeshah was smashed and burning, and every person in reach was bleeding dead, the highland beards were gone as fast as they had come. Radharani, people found alive, but on her back at the door of her house. As if perhaps she fell down the little stair and struck her head, for she never came out of the sleep. I think she looked back on us from the edge of the other world, and turned away. Her breathing stopped beside a fire of broken doors and tables

--This, Anab ended with a heavy breath, --this is all we ask you to know. Never before have you heard the cries of this country. But you, take this home. Your rivers of gold are under threat. Next time you smash the country open, then, do not blame Pulesati. They die, trying to live and meet the promise

Long after Anab left us, WenAmon stayed silent like a man at a rite of funeral. It broke me down that he scarcely raised his eyes to his land's first sea-way, opening out with the smell of green and fresh water. I asked him if he wanted us to conceal him homeward past the house of Avaris, which had staked him two treasures

--I am not even thinking of that business, he

replied. –No, and thank you. Besides, it is not possible, if I know the river-masters jostling for rank. Still, WenAmon went on. –I would like to give something back, besides your profit for my passage. Will you come to Thebes, then? Can you imagine a construction equal to the name, The Mansion of Millions of Years? I meant my invitation, although your crew would not be allowed

--Ah. Very well. Even so, I can tell you. Within The Mansion, the walls of Medinet Habu are comfort for a man, and a people. Our young men put themselves in the shadow of Great One, and great was the slaughter he made of the forces of chaos. Remember that, my friend. I think you will, because in all you said, I could hear that you know where this world's power lies. Savages will not matter, nor prevail

I gave him sober silence and let him read it as he liked. We landed him at Avaris and rode the next tide out. WenAmon, spared the pleading for our pay, waved till he sank out of sight. From there, as almost ever, I was unsure where to go. There was only the pull of Alashiya, an island strong enough to dream of being left alone

Days later tramping northward, there was the rubble of Qadeshah. I never would have stopped again but for the smokes of campfires off the red hill. Some of them fed Kereti footmen and officers, men with two swords each dispatched from Aphek and Gezer. In their midst, people were rebuilding. And there was Urana sauntering toward me, as gray as Anab but swift and solemn as her mistress. Finches and sparrows were chittering in the hill's surrounding cypress and tamarisks, reminding the world what it is to be happy. And it seemed that sound belonged to Urana as I watched her coming, Radharani's heir

--Do not talk with these Kereti, just now, she quietly told my ear. --We were never afraid of them, before. They say, *Keret's bluff is over*. Well, come, and look! The new doorway to the shrine and the benches of communion will face the rising sun

--We are their bride, Urana declared. --We wait them like treasure on the shore. And you, old friend, Urana smiled, --you can help to make that clear

--Not me, I told her. --I am old, and tired

--Do this! Urana answered, with her eyes two glittering gems between the horns of her joined uplifted hands. --Do this!

9

In three years, Urana and those who lived to remember Radharani raised a larger house of communion on the first stones, and the conches blew as fierce as ever. I could not keep away. In places Qadeshah still looked blackened or broken, but the shells had come as fresh good-luck gifts from the islands, with dancing-masks of Snake and Bull and Lioness and Griffin, and double-axes: the finest gift became their first ceremony, a faience figure of Earth Mother you could hold in your hands, her upraised arms presiding tranquil and strong on the little altar where people shared their meals. Pulesati and islanders, Canaani and Eberu might come just for the feasts and the music and the women, but the red hill was rising again

And if it took that long for Egypt to do something, at least it seemed that WenAmon kept his word. A small host of middling officials arrived in every Pulesati city, decked in the wigs and necklaces of gold and multicolor beads that spoke authority from Thebes. People here called them horse-collars, but there was no mocking their message: secure the roads, or else. I should have expected no better answer to our pleas. Serens drove the resolution forward in every town, to burn the heart out of highland crime. And this had to be with a force that was more than Kereti. It was going to need conscripts. Where comfortable farmers and craftsmen saw, rightly, that forcing young men into weapons opened the way for kings and catastrophes, the fear of Pharaoh's weapons worked. Qadeshah got its visit like every other Pulesati place, and when protection arrived the reply was panic. All its people felt was their being surrounded again, and they ran up the streets spitting backwards at the so-called friendly spears, packing together into the new-laid courtyard

--You two look fit to fight

It was a horse-collar in white and gold with a Pulesati officer, he a muscular thirty with sun-wizened slits of eyes, as dark as his leather cuirass and short slashed kilt, and a scar across his brow below the cropped-feather band. Both looked me up and down, seasoned and severe, and then waited answer from the man by chance with me, called Ittai, an Eberu of twenty-eight

--Deucalion, a trader from Crete long a patron here. This is Ittai, a guest of this sanctuary with his wife and son and daughter: Eberu, of the tribe they call Judah. We are volunteers, spoken for. You can check that yourselves in the house of communion

--We will, the officer replied. --Qadeshah is under the protection of Aphek. Your name is Ittai? How old is your son?

--He is eight, sir, like his twin sister

--Volunteers, the officer mused. --For what?

--Water, and *zuthos* barley-wine, I answered, and after a moment, his eyes relaxed. He knew that every marching mile ran uphill under the sun. And, that killing and burning in the highlands was going to make an unpoisoned well pure luck. When the the pair of them left us, Ittai gave me a sideways look

--We?

--Well, it kept you from a company of spears

--Oh, blast! Ittai exclaimed. --I said I believe in the value of one life. Did I have to say that includes my own?

He stalked away to his family across the courtyard, going with all the heavy tread of his big burly body and his mother-round belly out ahead of him, stretching the seams of his two-piece woolen simlah. Wife and young ones watched him coming with his deep-set rolling eyes cast down, the blue wool cap riding the wild frizz of his hair: there was no smile for them to lighten the line of Ittai's jaw, twice as heavy-looking for the short stiff beard. First thing, though, the four of them kissed, and then they laughed together at something he said

Ittai was not one bone the brute he looked, as all men go by chance, but had made himself a most companionable goon in his stays at Qadeshah. He might have been a blood-son of old Raz, with that wide-open drive to say anything for a smile, and the three moved in under his arms as he explained the trap into which I had helped him. His wife, Bat-Yam or Daughter of the Sea, looked at me and then squinted as Ittai began to listen to each of them: Gil the bony boy they had named for joy, and Nili his little girl, whose name Ittai had worked hard to explain. It spoke what he called the glory of their people, who will not lie

They spoke awhile, shook their heads together, and Ittai came back

--I come here to reach out, he muttered. --If that cutthroat will have a bowman put an arrow in my side for going home, they tell me to stay and take my chances. Bat-Yam's cousins can see them back to the farm. Curse you, Deucalion, we are grateful, again. Alright, so you saved our grapevines. It was a rain-mold, Ittai shrugged with mock of bitterness, but then he put his foot down

–No. I cannot be involved in this. Do you understand that man's intentions? My cousins gather this moon to share unleavened bread in the navel of the land, and to look into their own hearts. Talk about carrying the enemy's water! Come to think of it, Deucalion, have you wondered about your people turning into thugs?

--Yes, I answered. –May I tell you where we seemed to lose our choice? In my grandfather's day, there was a Seren of Gaza named Symoon. This surly bull held his office so long because he was two things: a listener, and a man who always worked ahead of trouble. When robberies on the roads kept getting worse, Symoon stuck his neck out for a council with your highland Yisryli

--He told them plainly that Pulesati had no right in the highlands, wanting only passage on the roads that all men walk. Nor could Yisryli make claim by their fathers on the lands along the sea. If a ship on the ocean paid one in ten measures for safe passage, it was only just that Yisryli receive the same for traffic through their lands. More, Symoon offered them two measures in ten, in exchange for nothing but restraint of their own men. The answer he got, my grandfather heard and told me. *There is no choice.* Their God had commanded them to make no friends uncircumcised, not to mingle, or make kinship, or marriages: to neither teach nor learn, to make no merriment or laws or treaties with our kind. Now, if that was what they wanted, well enough---but this left their men free to make fair game of us and others, robbing the roads? This, Ittai, they explained without explaining. If they disobeyed their god, it would make them our slaves, or they would vanish---but obedience would take the land from Babylon to Gaza

--In fact, the answer said that robbery would serve till they made open war. They leave a hole in the world and dream that we will all jump in. Face it with me, Ittai. No choice? That was a choice. Choice on every side brought thugs upon us

--Sounds about right. We can all die carrying water for Pharaoh's fat priests. Fine, said Ittai, and he swung gaze into mine. --What now, old man of the sea?

Neither one of us got out of it, though we managed our places in the rear working wagon-loads of jars up country: we ate the dust of companies from eight cities' jurisdictions, half bowmen and half swords or spearmen, a column of two thousand weapons climbing the hills eastward from Gezer. Ittai, sick with worry for his family's sake, hid his face with a burnoose before we went out the gates, and he kept it closed day after night. We passed from lowland farms and pastures into woods of oak and pine that slanted off their hills, broken with rocky scrub: the country lay green after spring rain, with snowdrop and cyclamen. Second day, talk came back along the column, and I saw my young friend turn away when we heard it. *The place is called Shiloh. Look for the priests*

--I do not want to be here. I do not want to see this. I will lift up my eyes to the mountains

There was no way out. Third dawn, with all the land seaward spread out below, we turned north, and from there the weapons ahead of us ran at the double beyond our sight. So, by the time we came around a last long low hill and saw the half-hidden plateau, horns and sounds of rally and battle and death were in our ears. It was a double shock, for one quick look around showed a place of fine meadows with a scatter of white houses and herb gardens, flames coming out the windows, and a legion of bright tents rank by row spreading out beyond them, burning

Paths crossed among them so worn that they looked like white stone. Pistachio, fig and olive trees climbed the far long slopes. Most of all, the sight of these ordinary hills punched me harder than a buffet of wind because it looked so like the ordinary valley of Knossos Labyrinth---where a stranger might ask, *Why here?*, and a man born there could put no words to its feel of ancient sanctity. We were now the people laying waste. We had smashed into a place of families and memory. As this horrific stupidity ran wild before our eyes, it felt as if my brain were tearing loose. These hacked-up corpses, that arm, this trail of trickling gore, not one thing needful here, and the long day was still coming

Here and there across the little plateau a melee of pitched groups kept trying to finish or help each other out of the places where slaughter was toe to toe. From one heap of mixed tangled corpses to another, slingers and bowmen of each side kept maneuvering to flank or get behind the flow of enemies into these fights, and pillars of smoke twisted up along the shoulders of the hills, where horns blew and voices shrieked as if coming out of the air. By the first clutches of dead bodies we saw it looked as if the Yisryli had charged full-force down from the heights above their holy place, but that Pulesati spears had then drawn back to let the bowmen drop them by the dozen. There were Pulesati bodies stuck with spears and some few arrows, with brains smashed out by clubs and stones. But the mixed Kereti bowmen in calm and mobile double-ranks were making the difference in who died

By now we were being drawn forward ourselves, and there near the center of the plain we saw the swords and spears and clubs still at it, now in their lines along the wall of one side of an enormous enclosure. It ran east to west, longer than five ships and half as wide, with linens or hides or fabrics stretched between stout posts and guy-lines, as tall as the height of five men: all about it stood lesser tents' encampments in bright groups of colors, burning. If the world has one worst sound it is the chop of weapons cutting flesh and the shrieks and moans of men falling under them, and these the hills around us more than echoed. But the size of this thing shocked me and the blankness of its wall, and I remember words then in my head not like my own: *That outside see not in, That inside see not out.* We could only see the flat roof of a tent rising up inside it near the center, it must have stood ten men tall, as blue as a fair day at sea, densely decorated, burning. My mouth was open to see such a thing and the butchery in front of it, but Ittai cried louder with each flame that took from an arrow, and ran right up more and more enclosure. He writhed as if every weapon stabbed him

--Help me, Deucalion! How did I get here? Pull out my eyes! The center! The end! *Hai-eee!* Mercy! *Mercy!*

And then the wail of a horn like no other sounded off the hills. *Their god!* men said. *Their god is coming out!*

The stretched-cloth sides of the enclosure were turning into flame at the backs of maybe fifty last-stand Yisryli with hardly more than knives. But there at its eastern entranceway, they parted ranks, and shouted their souls into the sky. Something like a great gold-sided chest was coming out, three men to each side gray-bearded and richly robed: it was like a carrying-chair on golden poles, but no one sat upon it. Out it came with appalling courage straight into that slaughter. But the hacking just went on, and Ittai hid his eyes in both arms as the bearers went down under spears and arrows. The great chest fell with them, and the long hills wailed with a scream of hidden hundreds. In the last of it, we watched astonished as a boy with long dark hair no older than Ittai's son came running out under the flaming gate. This boy in what looked like lambskins made it straight through the reach of flailing weapons, through the rain of stones and arrows, and out of sight. When I turned to Ittai again for hearing the rip of his cloak from top to bottom, his head was bloody both sides, because his fists were full of his hair. I tore off a piece of my wrap and tried to help

--Long ago, this happened to my home and family

--And look what you did about it! Curse you to a man, you have cursed my eyes! You smash the world, and now you expect what---order?

--Was that a throne? There was nobody on it

--Oh, Ittai moaned from deep in his chest. --How can---No, he told me trying to recover. –No. The only king is in the sky

--What?

--Deucalion, can you shut up?

I nodded, and hung my head with his. We were there two more days and nights, and Ittai kept his eyes to the ground as we worked our pails and cups and ladles camp by camp. His face had never looked so dark, and made speaking at all an obscenity. Still, the camps kept roistering in the high ways of survival and victory, and when we had our rest Ittai lay face-down with his cloak round his head. We could not avoid sights of plunder, the pulling-down of houses and the sanctuary with them, nor the nights' Pulesati jubilations: there were fights among them and some camps of Kereti, whose mixed men pled mercy for their cousins' lives. If there were no slaves or captives, we saw men at arms loading up for home: they cut themselves huge sheets of curried hides and linens and fine veilings, pulled up every last bronze peg of the sanctuary wall, and talked astonished about the gold if they could not get some. One captain made a parade of his share, as the first to brave their sanctuary's core---a golden holder of candles as broad as his shoulders with what looked like seven points, so heavy that it took both his hands to shake it high. Second day, word spread that the walls inside their central place were sheets of gold. The melee that ripped it to the ground almost brought on a mutiny, as some units stood to lose with their orders to chase down the scattering Yisryli. By the time we began to abandon the place, scouting groups detached along the road north and south, for the setting-up of protected caravanserai. By summer, they had marked each one with a pillar of cedar or stone

The worst for Ittai was the great golden chest. When he saw it had been touched, and opened, and loaded on a cart for the taking back to Aphek, he collapsed to the ground, struck his own face and head with clawed-up dust, then curled up, and shook. If our column left him there it seemed he would never get up. Later, he helped me to understand what had crushed him, that no one fell dead for these doings. There, I told him farm and family needed him. No answer, not even a look. Ittai collected himself, and started walking

We got out of jubilant Aphek as soon as we could. The officers reported extirpation of the core of highland robbery, the Serens and horse-collars pronounced that our promise was secure. But I stood among the cheering with Ittai's one question for tomorrow. I wanted to walk him all the far way home, and asked for a fresh look at his vines

He shrugged, and then it was many miles along the sea before he spoke again

--I said you cursed my eyes. I saw what I saw. But it was a thing a man alive must witness to. And whom can I tell? Family tells family. Then, more family will ask: *And what were you doing there, Ittai? And why are you alive, Ittai?*

--You were trapped, I insisted, stopping and poking his chest on each word. --And you did your best. No one can ask any more of you

--Shows what you know, he answered

News went fast ahead of us, and from Joppa to Gezer and Ekron, we waded through public offerings of thanks, feasts and funerals. East of Ekron, we followed the Sorek's waters up into its valley, and after many turns and narrows the land spread out flat and green between great shoulders of rocky hills, alive with calls of wheat-ears and buntings. Some miles beyond the Pulesati farms of little Timnah, the valley curved away southward toward the city Beth Shemesh. Beyond that, as Ittai said it, the villages of Eberu and Yisryli were sure to be staggering in grief and rage. From the houses of his farm, you could look up the valley and see how close they stood in separation

--Ittai! The lamb told my heart it would be this day!

--Bat-Yam, beloved. Do not talk like that, said Ittai as they kissed both cheeks three times and plenty on the mouth, Ittai running his mitts through Bat-Yam's fine black tresses, kissing her eyes as dark as any on the land. She was a woman just his age and height, but her fine frame and plain comely wraps light blue made her look the young wife he married, now almost jumping at his side as he moved through the family taking cheers and welcome-kisses. There were Bat-Yam's mother and father, an older sister and younger brother, and on Ittai's side two sisters, his wife, and more: they had all been tending a feast of special days that had to be held with or without him. They gripped Ittai both arms to know by touch that he had come home, and the faces that had clearly weathered storms began to laugh and shout thanks up into the blue. *We knew Pharaoh would have to let you go!*

Ittai's house like the other separate ones that faced it was a solid labor in stone and mud-brick. Pale-gray plaster made them all more handsome: you came in through a space between rows of four rough oak pillars, where straw and provender fed their stock, and you saw into all the rooms either side, where Canaani houses kept secrets with turns and doors. Likewise upstairs where they lived: the sun fell all afternoon on their low central table, with Bat-Yam's loom, their beds, neat belongings and plain jars to each side. Weavings warmed the walls and hung bright zagging lines down over their parallel porches. But as soon as Ittai was free to look about, resolve took over his face. Before he asked for his young he was hulking off toward the fields and vines

--Where am I going? To do what we should have done. To do too late what we were told

It was Bat-Yam on his heels, then all the relations after them, then me: we saw Ittai take a wrecker's hold on one of the two wooden posts at the edge of their tillage

--No! Bat-Yam said, pulling his hands away from it. --Asherah brings only blessings here. What is the matter with you? Will you insult Her and cut half my family from the table?

--There is no choice!

--We know better, Bat-Yam answered him, and in the face of his bulk she stood her ground until Ittai turned away. He might have stalked alone into their main house, but his youngsters Gil and Nili came out the door. I saw his knees go as they clutched him from both sides, and everybody moaned: then Gil and Nili ran inside together, and when they came out he was slapping a hand-drum and she was fingering notes from a small one-pipe flute. This was enough to set the place dancing with hands locked all around him, Ittai in their midst dark and dazed

Their custom, already under way, was to roast their best yearling lamb, and at dusk every man smeared its blood on the beams of his door with a sprig of marjoram. When they came to table the farming men were in long shepherds' robes and head-wraps, and they ate with staves in hand or nocked between their knees: I understood nothing of it, nor why they ate their feast so quickly, nor the scolds of their elders that not one bit be left except to burn. Ittai, I saw, was mainly sipping his wood cup of raisin wine: others noticed, and if they had heard things of Shiloh, held back. I would have sat for the family stories starting after, but Ittai got up and walked outside: alone then, feeling the eyes that could not help but look a bit dubious of my presence, I smiled *nature*, and followed. Ittai was back at those posts of Asherah, holding one of them and weeping

--What do they know? They do not even feel it, yet. Do you understand, the total destruction of the meaning in the soul of a whole people? Can you?

And what could Knossos Labyrinth mean to him

--The wise ones promised us fire and death for these things, Ittai said looking up and down the post

--Ittai, what happened was not gods. It was a reckoning out of our failures. Every face of your household says the soul you share will

--Will what? Fail Holy One again? Let me give you the bad news, Ittai said, and when he wiped his eyes he wore a look like stone. --Man is ugliness. The Covenant was to redeem us. The Ark. The memory. Now it is all ashes, and we---I am sorry, Deucalion, but---we are going to lose ourselves among the nations. Among *animals*

He turned his despair away. Standing there I felt like a child with no more than five or six words of understanding. Ittai came about, and asked me to sit with him, there at the edge of his vineyard in starry darkness. Perhaps he felt my ignorance. Ittai began to talk about huge things, one after the other. Once he began, I saw he had tried to be ready, as if he needed me to see something too big to be missed, and certainly too big to grasp

There never was a time when their Holy One was

not. He, alone, divided Earth and sky, and from His hands came all creation, good and perfect. Now, because creation was a garden, the Holy One made man to tend and keep it, and woman to be his helper. But the Tree of Life was also in that garden, and the fruit of this Tree, Holy One forbade to man and woman. It was woman, the being of light that is darkness, who led the man to eat that fruit. And so Holy One drove them from that perfect place into this world, this wilderness, and death. So hard was their new life that their first sons fell to quarreling, the shepherd and the planter. That was the beginning of murder in the world. So lived all men after them, dark and brutal, not understanding Holy One

Such wickedness the world became that He drowned His creation with a flood---all except one man who kept His ways. Noah gave the world many sons. But life was still a thing to be scratched from the world, and the new people found they had to roam to feed their families, from Haran to Egypt and back again. So did some of the sons sojourn in Egypt for a time. But the powers of life and gods there were devouring them. They had become Pharaoh's slaves. Then, wonder on wonder out of the hand of Holy One delivered them, and they poured out into wilderness again. They had nothing, only the covenant promise that Holy One, by their obedience, would give them all the land from Haran to Egypt. How, they could only imagine. And then, in the Sinai, they came to a mountain, thundering, all on fire

Their leader climbed that mountain, and spoke face

to face with El Shaddai, the Mountain One, the Only One, Blessed Be He. If only his people should obey, they would take the land and cover the world with His lawful living in their children: the covenant lived in the stones incised with laws borne down the mountain. But, man was man. Below, their leader found his people reveling, with every kind of man's corruption, around the dead idols of this world's powers and animals. And so began the killing, one his neighbor, one his friend, another his brother, that the people of Holy One come to their inheritance

--Even in the dark you look lost, Ittai joked as he finally took a few breaths

--We were never informed of His promise. This is a new shadow on the sun, I said overwhelmed

--No, Holy One is not the El they tell at Qadeshah. There is no one like Him. I know because I listen to you, Deucalion, with my best mind. Tell me circles of the sun and moon. Tell me the four horns of our altars fit yours, the doubled pairs. I even agree, the lords of nature have limits, and so should men. But the greatest of powers is beyond, outside, separate. You people dream it up that now is forever, the seasons cycling through, divinities in everything

--And you see the hand of Holy One in everything. What is the difference?

--We are going somewhere, Ittai said

--We are somewhere already

To my surprise and pleasure, Ittai laughed. --Come, I said. --Holy One made us all. But He promised everything to just a few, who must take it from others by force, to prove they love Him?

--I can only tell you, Ittai smiled briefly, --that men are bits of dust, and He is a mountain so high that it vanishes in clouds. The merest approach to Him pales the blood, and blanks the mind, and shows how wretched people are. Still, every single man of any family in the world is free to obey, and to live in His eternal light. Was there ever any better way to bring all men together? The world is dead things, plants and animals, and two-legged animals that talk. But, to us, Holy One gave dominion, and a way to live that in righteousness. As we obey and atone, we return to the garden

--Our worst days came of forgetting we are in it. Ittai, do priests of Egypt lie, for their own benefit?

--Of course, he said. --Their crimes begin already to destroy them

--Then is it possible priests in every land deceive that way?

--Possible, Ittai shrugged, --if you include the people around your altars. Using festivals to hide the ragged numbers, Keeper of Days?

Staggering still at what his fathers did with old Canaani memory, I had come again to fail against a wall old as Theseus and Abas. With a shake of his great head Ittai unfolded his legs, stood up, and offered his hand. That was when Bat-Yam came out of the shadows of the trees, with one of their twins under each of her arms. The pair of them smiled my way, but then drew back half-behind her, peeking out like little cats. –Nili and Gil have something to say to you, Bat-Yam told me, but neither could say it

--They wonder can you stay longer, she smiled

I bowed, smiled back and hoped to be no trouble: Ittai walked over and hugged them all together, with a look my way of his deepest pride. And was this liking not the sin that brought destruction from their god? It was not a thing to ask, but there began a kind of living answer in the years of visiting to come. It took half a moon of days to trim his vines and tie them up for thicker stocks and more grapes. If the greater family kept aloof from me as an uncircumcised laborer, Gil they forgave for his questions about seas and ships and islands. Nili worked as hard at Bat-Yam's side, and the sweetness of her flute, played in the evening between stretches of words from memory, was something for players at Qadeshah to envy

Gil was young to think about his life beyond their farm, but Nili saw hers, as a *kedeshot* or singer: more, what they called a *soreret*, a poetess, whose words came from Holy One in her heart. Who would have wanted to help her more than Radharani? But here, that talk might bring trouble. Leaving, I promised to bring Nili a big fine flute from the islands, perhaps a double-reed. And so I found myself coming back many times down the years, going home with Ittai when he made it to Qadeshah

Gil grew fast his father's barrel-strength: he rose to their labors just as goat-kids off Karfi had learned in Alashiya. He whacked olives down off their trees till his hands were swollen red: they sang their songs as soothing hand over hand sorted twigs from fruit, and then shared out the medicine, rubbing each other's hands with the first oil. Gil woke the sun to get to work, he came alive making things and learning---all of that in how he told his first year laying grapes out to make raisins. At the gathering, down came a hundred thousand feasting bees: he had to learn to keep calm in their swarms, shoveling raisins into sacks, but when the last sack closed, the last bee flew. Dear boy, all lit up inside

--Not one sting, Deucalion!

--As if everybody wins, I smiled. --You'd think there's plenty

--Yes, yes!

Yet, age took down the companionable goon in Ittai, dance and revel as he did when he brought new vintage there, in hope that people took home jars and skins of his wine and spread his trade. His vines grew as well as any on the Sorek, but Ittai was cold about it, where a man might walk a little proud having worked so hard. Five years after Shiloh, he asked my presence when his young ones at thirteen came of age. If Gil greatly pleased him wanting the same life as his father, Nili had learned that the double-reed was not welcome where she played. Her brow was her mother's, high and smooth under the strong line of auburn hair, eyes like an antelope's, and not one shadow about them

--I think, Nili said as we were walking once, --the double-reed goes too deep and dark, and the high end makes them nervous. Do they forget that the purest daughters of Shiloh used to leap like lambs, when they danced all in white in the meadows and vineyards there? Surely, Holy One's own wild music lifted them up, and out came joy of living in His hands. Think of the spirit when a woman sung this first:

> *--Then sang Moses*
> *and the children of Yisryli this song*
> *unto Holy One, and spoke,*
> *saying, I will sing to Holy One*
> *for He has triumphed gloriously:*
> *the horse and his rider He has thrown into the sea.*
> *Holy One is my strength and song,*
> *and He is my salvation: He is my Holy One,*
> *and I will prepare Him a living place,*
> *my fathers' Holy One, and I will exalt Him.*
> *The Lord is a man of war: The Lord is His Name*

--Yes, said Bat-Yam later, --no thrush in the valley has Nili's voice. I see her the mother of a tribe. And Ittai growls, *Tribe? What tribe?* I am glad he has you to talk with. There are places in him I never knew. Dry, and cold

So is tinder I answered only to myself. Against my worry, I put all I could to our friendship

--Something else I am fed up with, Ittai tossed my way, many seasons on: we were walking the road from Qadeshah south and east for his home again, this time in the month of ingathering summer fruits

Ittai had grayed and lost many teeth, bringing back the goon, but the rainbow-stripes of his new cotton mantle and the sheen of his meil stole marked him as master of the first country wine to reach the islands

–Look at me, he said. --Two years and I turn forty. What is your black secret? Is it twenty years gone the day I met you? Nobody fools my eye, but you look the same. This is very unjust

I gave him his own grinning shrug. In truth, where in WenAmon's days I began to feel tired, life-weary, gray inside, this had been growing heavier in my bones. For all the dying seen and never suffered, I had begun to feel afraid, as if the blessing sometimes cursed were failing me at last. It was not going to help me after the two of us, during that travel, thought we knew what we should do

We had walked a few miles south beyond Gezer, under eyes of Kereti bowmen on the walls. Ittai said it seemed they watched for trouble only eastward, up the main middle-country road into the highlands. Beyond Gezer, in olive groves halfway to Ekron, we passed a clutch of tents and a two stone-building travelers' house. Men were roasting pig near tables, or lounging half-dressed without the leathers and weapons of their guild

--My, Ittai mused. –Everything safely under the thumb of the right people these days. Wait, how many ewes in that drive just past? You, filching cantaloupe! Halt!

--I know a secret about you, I teased

That Ittai abominated waste. That Bat-Yam had smiled these years at a man so hard who carried the least bits of bread out to feed wild birds. Ittai laughed it off, but it was only part of what Bat-Yam revealed

A year before, with Gil at the age of war, Ittai journeyed east to their holy place Gilgal to answer his elders of the Yisryli. Bat-Yam had felt half-sure they would kill him outright, for he went there to refuse their call. Bat-Yam, waiting and waiting, went out and fed the birds for him, and asked them with her tears to protect and help Ittai, and bring him home. She knew he disapproved of such, but he did come home. --So, she told you I feed birds, Ittai shrugged

--She told me you hate waste. If you do not like or feel any safer with Kereti on the roads, what will you do?

--I can only wish I asked the *hakhamim*. The wise ones did not speak to it

Nor did Ittai offer more about his gamble. It took until nighttime, where by luck we ate and slept under a fruited wild fig a hundred years old, hardly an hour late to make the gates of Ekron. I woke him to listen and help me understand, because from midnight till near sunrise, the wind carried wild voices singing much closer to the city: the sons, no doubt, of the keening voices heard from Radharani's hill

> *--Yes, Gaza is going to be reduced to desert,*
> *Ascalon become a desolation:*
> *Ashdod will be stormed, her people*
> *driven out in broad daylight,*
> *Ekron and Gath torn from their roots alike.*

Woe to the members of the confederacy of the sea!
 Ah, inhabitants of the seacoast, nation of Cretans!
This is the word of The Lord against you:
I mean to bring you down, land of the Pulesati,
I am going to ruin you, empty you of inhabitants,
and you will be reduced to pasture land,
grazing grounds for shepherds, folds for sheep.
Canaan will be the property of Judah,
they will lead flocks there to pasture.
Among houses of Ascalon they will rest at evening,
for The Lord their god will deal kindly with them,
and I will destroy you until no inhabitant is left

--Ugly ululations undo useful understandings

--You and your sea-speech. They talk of nothing we planters want. I was called, Ittai began, --and Gil was called, to make war on Amalekites. Families of sand-farers out of Sinai and Negev, and how they scratch a living no one knows. Deucalion, since Shiloh, it has been every man to his tent. No doubt that fattens your friends on The Nile. But Amalekite is our oldest feud. Every few sons, it joins the hardest of the highlands back into strength, and from there to ambition. Or I mean to say, hope

--So, you and Gil were called

--Yes. And I answered, Ittai said. --I took a terrible chance but it was worth it for Gil's sake. I took along two carts of offerings, grain and wine

--I thought it fair odds you would catch fire

--Well, I have been close. I must tell Bat-Yam to

never talk about the birds. It is dangerous. Well, I came down the road where it falls below the eastern mountains for the Jordan, and I saw the great circle of stones where our first people crossed into this country. I remember thinking how the stones looked only inward at each other

Like the circle of the heroes of Mykenai

--Well, I gave my name and made my offerings. When I came before the wise ones, with so many gray beards looking on, I had been watching, you see, and kept thinking of the stones. I wondered if each stone was trying to be harder than the others, in front of the people. But it is not people who want them to go hard. When they asked my business and where was my son, my heart emptied. I prayed. My tongue said, *War can be needful. But this is only feud. I have just one son to do the work too much for both of us*

--Silence. Rumbles all around me. Alright, I was afraid. And my fool's tongue stammered anyway: *I hear as well that you talk about a king.* But the wise ones' answer asked again where was my son. I said, *He is working for you, under this hot sun, to hold the good land our end of the Sorek. He my only son is soon a father. We are fighting for you---in the only way that has been victory since Shiloh*

--So, the wise ones asked, *And is he your only son because you can only bring the one into the world?* I told them the truth that marks my Bat-Yam's face, that three had died since our twins. But I would try to do better day and night. To a man the gathering laughed. It saved my life, Deucalion, and Gil's

Sons, the wise ones wanted, sons to train against

Amalekites---train for what? And talk afresh about a king?
It would not have helped Ittai to explain his deference to
Bat-Yam, who knew year by year how many could be fed.
But the stones, the beards, knew better

--Are you outcast then, Ittai?

--Even in, he laughed turning over. --The people
who matter are the household. The grief is Nili. We name
the girl one who will not lie. Do you know what she says
these days? *I will not lie. I do not want to marry. Not yet. I will
not lie under just any man chosen for me.* He is not a bad
fellow we have in mind, zealous to keep the rules. Well, I
raised them for spirit. Behold my reward

We lay there awhile

–So, I said. –New rumbles of a king

--The wise ones say, so we can be like other nations

--Seen Egypt?

--No

--Could be worthwhile, I told him: he lay looking
up, breathing sky

–Oh, we hear all our lives about that place. You
start to feel you were there yourself, being devoured,
losing who you are. Look at your Serens, dressed like men
of six nations, what is that?

--Tell of Egypt, Ittai, do they mention that Pharaoh
was first a king?

--Twenty years of visits the man never cleans his
ears, he jabbed rising up on one elbow. –Look. The
gentlemen who accepted my grain and wine kept my
uncle's carts. The asses that pulled them, too---and they

call them unclean animals, Ittai winked. –Bring sheep, get fleeced. They knew it was lucky if I got out of Gilgal with my mouth shut. On the other hand---How can I explain this. You remember the Ark of our Covenant with Holy One. Well, the sun itself is inside it. Not your sun. I mean the sun you feel inside, but always over your head, and at your back. Perfection and power, beating down on you. Making you watch yourself, that He might spare you one corner of cool shade. This is for every man, woman and child---and especially for the *hakhamim*. Who can let not one thing stand between each person and that sun, or comes the end of all of us

 --Deucalion, we think or feel nothing but we rake it over coals, take it apart, question, question. That is our mad touch of the sun. Believe me, the words that talk of kings will face the same

 --We Pulesati do alike, when we make our Serens answer by sun and moon. That is halfway to a marriage that might serve. Ittai, throw warning on your coals. When highland strength meets ours again, people will die. You said it, the land is our dowry

 Ittai only grunted and rolled on his belly. Still, he looked thoughtful, chin on his fist, gazing down, with a sniff of the soil

 --What if we gave back the Ark, he said. –What if we did that? And, as Ittai went on he sat up again and wrapped his arms round his knees. –Do you know where it is these days? Think about it. The gesture we could make. They could see you never meant to break our spirit

--I can find out, I answered. –But, give it to whom?

--I think I know. He is young, which may help us, and already people come to him for wise justice. His name is Samouel, I saw him at Gilgal, and I know he saw me. Deucalion! I have bones that he was the boy we saw running from the Shiloh sanctuary. They say he grew up there among the women, but that day made him what he is. Samouel is now the voice to harden warriors. He lets no one forget how Amalekites cut down helpless stragglers of our people when they ran from Egypt. And, in a battle last year they took an enemy king alive. He was still breathing when Samouel got there. He put the blast of Holy One on their sin of weakness, and chopped the man into pieces

--Very Egyptian, I said

--You people never miss a stab, do you. Still---If Samouel, the Shepherd of the People accepts this gesture, the hard flock will follow. Yes, Ittai declared

The young man's title curled the marrow of my memory. But already I was bracing against a fear that was new to me, fear of death

--Do you know what can happen? I said

--Do you?

That was the man to whom a life meant something. So there in the darkness under a fruited fig, we decided. Ittai went home, and I traveled back toward Qadeshah asking questions. It took very few, because their Ark was in Ekron the first city on my way, like a sign that we should do this. The priestesses and priests said they had been moving it city by city down these years, to stand before Asherah and Dagon in public houses of communion, in memory of Pulesati men from Aphek and Gezer, Ascalon and Ashdod and Gath. It had now been five years in Ekron and there were always fewer people who knew what it was---and more who complained of it, as a mute and ponderous intrusion where even stone pharaohs and island mothers had place along the benches. Likely, said a priestess, a few years would melt it down

I found a place to stay and think things out. No chance that Ekron's leadership would let this go as trivial or miss the message it could send. It needed just the right people of the altar, who could sway them calling it a gesture of Pulesati strength

The Husband of Ekron, these days of the silver Pharaoh, dressed to stand out the imago of Serens in other towns: every detail of his raiment he had fashioned to outdo them. His name was Tokodomo, born of a builder's family and part peacock. His black hair he swept back over his head in Syrian knots, and over this he stuck two Libu falcon-feathers like a pair of horns: there was an island glimmer to his linen under-robe, his mantle was brocade in every color silver-sashed, and from the hawk-painted eyes to his braceleted lower legs and arms, his skin was a splendor of the totem beasts of power in his damos. A moon of work and waiting put me finally in front of him, and he gave it a wave of one hand. *I care not. Let it say some good thing, then. Nothing changes highland hearts that hate us*

--Did it kill anybody? Did they look inside?

--No, Ittai. And, I am sorry but I think they looked

Good thing we were alone on his land, because this hurt Ittai deep in the wound of Shiloh. He said he felt guilty, too, wanting to know what was in it, but no more than I *wonder* came out, and he fixed angry eyes at the sky. I never told him of the two black stones of scratched obsidian, the worn-out sandals, the shepherd's staff, the pot whose moulded contents made them sorry to have looked. Nor, about trying to stop the mockeries crafted in gold with which Tokodomo filled a bronze coffer, for this had been ordered to come with the Ark: he tossed in four or five golden curly-tailed mice, and a few shapeless blobs like something from an irritated backside. The message was, *Your pilfering makes pain where we sit down*

Ittai gathered himself up and told me of his moon: his messages had up-valley answers through Beth Shemesh. Yes, the Ark was wanted back. And there were many more priests' instructions for its return

--I told them our condition, too, that Samouel receive it. Sorry, Deucalion, but the answer to that is No. What do we do?

--I suppose, the one thing we can

Cursed arrogance safe behind Ekron's walls, those jokes in the coffer might prove an insult later, even if this went well. Nothing to be done now among Ittai's household, who were thunderstruck that following spring to see the Ark coming up the Sorek onto their land, and then they embraced each other, crying its deliverance. Nili made bold to bring them all to a circle safely far from the cart and the pair of Ekron cows lashed up to it: she skirled her one-reed flute till they were turning rightwards, clapping, and there was shine in her dark eyes for the gift of unleashing them

Where I looked for some wild-form dance to burst from her, Nili gave their way of hopping leaps and heel-point turns a solemn slowness, that moved them to want her voice and words. She took up their joined hands and sang them her old women's song, that Holy One had triumphed gloriously. This day the stubborn girl sang out the voice of their unfettered joy, and their kicked-up feet paid no mind to their circling a free woman. After, Nili and the land-hardened Gil would not leave their father's side, and he looked twenty years brighter

Every person gave up cloth to make a covering for the Ark. When the barley was in and the wheat's time had come, no less than five Serens of the cities arrived and camped Ittai's land waiting for the going. It seemed that word of this had spread through Tokodomo. Two of the five as young men had seen Shiloh, and came to show memory and strength: the others were Serens likely to worry in the way of Great Year festival, that someone might outdo their generosity. All their greetings grumbled, since none had any say in this event

We all set out into sunrise up the valley, keeping our groups at a dictated distance back of the cart. The land was green and still, the waters rolling past us in morning gold, and Ittai was breathing big in his small talk

--I confess, at Qadeshah, I have felt as I feel here. My hand knows every stone and stalk and twirl of grape.

There, I meet a grandmother I might have avoided, but her hand in the circles came to mine, and now our families visit. The right mind needs a place where you can notice things. Moods of birds. Land and sea talking. Little seeds sail by you on the air. Storms with the smell of mountains. Standing stones that make you feel small and young, you listen and they sing in different winds. Rain. Things, Deucalion---to console our lonely peace. Oh! Ittai broke in on himself. --Remind me to keep the cows and cart

We were walking slowly, near twenty in all behind the hooves and wheels, because the Yisryli had said the cows were to find their own way. But this paid no mind to how green the grazing was either side of Sorek's road. Halfway to Beth Shemesh, where the valley curved a little to the south and villagers hip-deep in wheat stopped and watched, the cows turned, stopping angled at the road's left shoulder: they looked back for trouble, and then dropped their heads to eat

--Now what? –Touch nothing, their eyes are on us! –What blasted difference does it make? --Switch their fat hinds, get on with this!

–Wait, wait! Ittai defended. When the odds turned, he put them all instead to the work removing the patchwork cover from the Ark. From its golden sides and carrying-poles to the two strange figures bending wings toward each other on its crest, it blazed back with the eye of morning sun

The Serens loitered, passed skins, muttered questions---where a people so austere obtained such gold, whence the craftsmen out of villagers who couldn't smelt bronze, who traded for only the plainer pots and garments

But they watched without scorn as Ittai, Gil and their household bowed from the waist, covered their faces, then rolled the cover and laid it in safekeep weeds. As they came back, the cows turned up the road again. Nothing better to do. The Serens' companies grumbled on, as if told they had nothing better either

The lands of The House of the Sun began where the slopes of the valley narrowed and wagon-ruts crossed before us, north, south, and fanning out into the farms. Dense rows of green-silver olives, carob and almond, orange and lime trees---and where an ancient straight line of them ended in more open wheat, the high gray-brown walls of The House of Shapshu looked down on the road. Under noon's blue sky, between the wheat and the rise of bare land up the low hill of the city, one enormous flat-topped rock rose out of a field of barley-stubble

--Shapshu, I said to Ittai. --Compassionate daughter of the Elohim. Have you been inside? They have a big fine public building, field-stone but solid as they come. In front, a big pleasant courtyard and many rooms off that. With an iron-forge no less. The only thing Radharani could not steal, I smiled, --was their cunning underground with rock and water

--We call it Shemesh now. And no pork this whole trip, do you understand? You do not know what you are dealing with

As I chirped him a cheer-up, high cries and a whole

sudden chorus of different songs took the air from the wheat now just ahead of us. The cows felt called, we were seen, it was welcome, and Ittai began to answer the singing as we crossed out into the stubble-field. Never had this big-built man looked lighter on his feet, and Gil, both palms up, backed away from him

The cows kept going till the people at harvest surrounded the whole wagon, half with their backs to us whooping and kicking up their feet. The Ark was home, a hundred steps from the flank of the great bare stone risen out of the ground. My eye had fallen on the stopping wheel when a long, solemn horn from the wall of the city sounded through the air. The Serens and their company halted uncertainly behind me and Ittai, and so did the jubilant noise. The *kohanim* were coming, the priests to receive the Ark home, and the people of the fields in the first circle moved to push the running new arrivals back away from it

--Blast! Ittai said, quietly. --Relieved already of the cows. Now if anyone short of a priest goes near, let me tell you that life is over, in a bad way. You never thought of this either!

--Big stone, little mountain, I said to soothe him

--The Stone of Abel, that. At least some offerings can please, Ittai answered, his features fallen. –Well, here they come, and watch yourself

Who is like Him?
Who can stand against Him?

Who is like Him?
Who can stand against Him?

These, he said, were the words of the soft-spoken chant coming out to us from eight priests, sons of their tribe of Levi, filing slowly from the gate, off the road and over the fields toward the lot of us. Few looked more than forty, but they all had thick beards clean and combed: their heads of manly locks were wound with cone-shaped wraps of different colors, their tunics plain white linen from their necks to wrists and sandaled feet, and a simple sash of white twine clipped in the waist of each fellow, tall and muscular. If they walked with hands calm at their sides, coming closer we saw tears on their cheeks. Meantime, the Serens arrayed themselves a diplomatic hundred steps away. The crowd of people encircling the Ark broke hands and formed a silent causeway for their fellows' entrance, taking up the chant as the priests filed through them. When shouts and laughs and bits of song joined in, one of the priests stepped closer to the Ark, and raised both arms for silence. Obeyed, his face turned skyward in prayer between his palms

--Not Samouel, Ittai whispered when the arms came down. --I suppose he must make careful company. What were we thinking, Deucalion?

--I don't know. Peace? I am tired

A sudden soft talking commotion stirred the priests. It passed when that first fellow gently took the coffer off the wagon, lifted it high and declared: *Penance paid*. Then a choice pair of fellows mounted the wagon as gravely as one could, and looked to the sky for their lives. The crowd let go a moan as each laid hands on the golden carrying-poles, and lifted the Ark back toward four more hands outstretched and trembling

Now they had it, careful, there, down, but the four bearers stood and held it up that it never touch the land. First gesture, their fellows quietly cleared off people who happened to stand between the blazing gold and the view of the Serens, still a hundred paces off

Tokodomo and the Pulesati faces, ignored till now, moved not at all as they watched. Out came four fellows' knives of sacrifice, one produced a little pyx of chrism, too; and while they prepared with more inaudible words, a quiet flurry in the crowd presented wood-axes fetched swiftly in. The priest with chrism purified their blades, and laid one hand between the cows' twitching ears as they were unlashed, prayed over, slain and bled. The Ark hung in air touching nothing on the arms of the bearers as their fellows bathed their hands in the gushing life. And then, while that first man shook his dripping hands gently all over the Ark, the bearers raised a double pair of free fists toward the sky

Who is like Him?
Who can stand against Him?
Who is like Him?
Who can stand against Him?

They turned as one, and took their way with slow matched steps through the Beth Shemesh stubble, heading for the one fit place on top of Abel's Stone. Perhaps one half of the people followed with them. The rest sat down as two priests still with us began to butcher, and the last oversaw dismembering the wagon. The timbers they piled crosswise into an offering-pyre, the wheels to serve as grills: the blood and the portions of Holy One roasted and burned, and the priests sang high and ululating, wavering out of their hearts in the greatness of the day. At last the cows' remains were roasted too, and a solemn meal of it went round, but only to everyone in the circle. I caught not a few outright sneers from the Serens as they turned away and took their company back toward the road. The last three priests were washing each other again as people milled about, well-fed and jovial in their presence. The moment was dissolving

--Do we not have to---try something? said Ittai, and his restless feet took him three steps after a passing priest

–Bless you sir! Pardon me, before you go

My feet had followed at his side, and the priest's eyes raked me up and down. I froze, because it seemed that any movement was a threat

--What? What is your name? Where are you from?

Flustered, Ittai answered. Then: –Are there not some things to say, sir

--We accept your guilt offering. Good day

As the man turned away, Ittai's eyes promised anger if I failed to try as well

--Sir? Would it also please you, I offered, --that after this day, except for road-walkers and people long living in the city, no Pulesati come this far east again?

--What? *Selahhh*, said his right hand sweeping down the air, dripping mockery. --Please me. For you I'll dig the hole. You return, defiled, the pure thing stolen by murder and destruction. Pleased, to see the backs of you. Was it opened, you? What was inside it. Speak!

And all that came out of me was, *Hope*?

The priest looked past me half-startled and then a man's voice spoke from close behind us: deep, calm and cordial, it said that this priest Natan should join the brothers on the Rock. He left us with crooked lips, and we both turned

--You gentlemen have something to say

The man was at arm's length, looking slightly down: his grave brown eyes blinked gently, and waiting he pushed back the falls of his light-blue keffiyeh, a thin leather circlet crossing a forehead straight-up as a wall. His brows, his chest-length beard and the hair we saw were dusky brown, mixing gray: he stood broad and fit as any priest by the stretch of the plain white robe across his chest. His right hand hung relaxed from the tall unpolished shepherd's crook, acacia-wood it looked like

--I am Samouel. Your name is Ittai. You, I know. The fly in the fish-sauce, he almost smiled, with a quick chin-lifting glint of mild interest

A deep quiet walked with him. Now with lowered eyes Samouel hung his free hand at the knot of his white twine sash: his fringed and tasseled mantle was stout people's wool, dusky stone-red from those load-bearing shoulders to his sandals. Out he was among the people of the field before the priests, that they make no procession of his presence

--May I ask something first, Samouel requested

--Honored sir, said Ittai

--You and yours walked with the wagon. Did the animals walk of their own. Did they turn in any way. Did you do anything to keep them on the path

When Ittai told him of their turn to the left, how they grazed awhile untouched and then went on of their own toward the city, neither of us understood the deep descent of Samouel's brows between his eyes, nor why he closed them for a time. When they opened again, he was looking at Ittai

--And what can I do for you gentlemen

--Well sir. Forgive me, this is Deucalion---*pelishtim*, but a good man, twenty years my household's friend. It was his first work arranging this day. I think it falls to him, I mean, he has served here and there as a people's man

Samouel stood and waited

--I wish we could sit and talk, I offered, but people were milling in circles close to earshot, hoping for a word or just to meet his eyes

--I stand between two good men, Ittai comforted with looks both ways. --Say it, like before, he smiled at me

--Is it helpful, sir, I asked this man, --that no Pulesati come again beyond Beth Shemesh?

Samouel held his answer at his lips a moment, and then spoke slowly

--Please Holy One, he said, --no house of Cain will prosper in the valley of this Rock

He gazed straight at me, and I stalled at the pronouncement: if his answer to the question was *Yes*, it seemed that we were no part of why

It was that trivial, and crucial, and for Ittai's sake I stilled an insult's worth of indignation. --Holy One made all of us, I tried to resume---and now as Ittai gave a wince of dread, Samouel held still and solemn

--It can never be right that we demand all this land. No Holy One of ours can make it right to you, no yesterday, no family sufferings. But today we can choose. Today our Serens wonder, can this end what you call our threat. No one west of here wants your life or your land. What is it then, to war against traffic on a road? Those fists raised high---If Holy One is king alone forever in the sky, and one man takes the same kind of power, will he lift more fists into the air?

Samouel listened, clumsy as I was. --Holy One and the people decide all things. I can do nothing

--But! came chirping out of Ittai. --Sir. Who knows better *tzedekah*, our justice by a neighbor. If needless trouble comes---I mean, many lives

--I have told you, Samouel said. --Gentlemen

His eyes no longer with us, he took his way: we were adjourned, hapless side by side in the field as his bearing drew off the last people

There were the wagon's ashes, bones cast off in the meal, and spills of blood in harvest stubble. A pillar of smoke was rising white, turning black, from the top of Abel's Rock. Kindlling of another victory pyre

--Kinsmen, I mumbled, --pull out the nail

--Home, Ittai replied. And the venture was over

I saw him not again at Qadeshah---only once more, two years after. Bat-Yam came out of the house gray and grim, her eyes blank of welcome, cheeks scalded. Ittai lay dying of a stab to his shoulder that smelled like carrion

He said that Samouel, presiding at another gathering in the high hills east of Gezer, had prayed to Holy One for the people. He had named their sin that had crushed them under Pulesati power: the pillars and stones and poles and filthy figures of Asherah. So, these the people broke and burned and buried, each for all to see. And then they were ready to face the small force of Kereti coming up to see about troubling rumors

Lo, for the first time, the men of Yisryli drove them bleeding back down into the plain. And, at the behest of the wise, Samouel anointed some rufous red-head shepherd with crazy eyes, almost seven feet tall, to be their king. Like kings of other nations

--Samouel warned them, too, Ittai said with a wan smile. –That kings will take, and take, and never enough. They came and they took, Deucalion. They took Gil. Put that boy before the Ark and the elders and, bless him, bless him, they will work the best of him their way

--Poor Nili! She tried to interfere. She sang and

played and chanted for Gil's life. It shocked me, tell the truth---as if she thought it had some power. The man still wanting to marry her came with the company for Gil. He knows which way this farm has to grow. Well, old friend, we both tell tales of men stealing brides. But I will not remember kindly how he went about it. The cry of a woman cuts a man. It should. What other god-cursed guide there is, you show me

     --Deucalion, we argued every way for Gil. They warned me, the mercies were done. So, I fought. Huh! I made them stab me down, at least to make the household see them do it. Who talked about being devoured? Argh. Brother, take care of Bat-Yam. I can pay, Ittai said turning his face away, but I saw that his big jaw was gooning

     --Anything to land the last insult, I said

     --No. I mean, a gift of counsel. Terrible, how far you see from here. Listen: *To your ships, O pelishtim.* Deucalion, this is first a war on ourselves. Only the sun that burns us rises from east of the world. Afraid, body and soul, of the bride we so desire. If you know what is good for you---*To your ships, O pelishtim*

     --Rest, Ittai. Heal. Dream. When you awaken, we will be here

     Bat-Yam and I sat together silent a long afternoon in the shade of their yard. As the sun went down in gold, a blue rock thrush piped. Bat-Yam unfolded a cloth from her sash: pale shards of a shattered flute, like bones of a sea-bird scoured by the tide.

--**A** wind of the sea. There is no more to say

A first few Pulesati knew war was upon them. Within two years, Shaoul the rufous shepherd-king cut down the pillar of a travelers' house called Gibeah, and killed every person in reach: he was going to get the war he wanted, not the war he expected. At the far end of Bat-Yam's valley, Beth Shemesh was soon a tumbled pen for grazing animals, any kind but those of Pulesati taste. After that, I must have ferried a tribe of tight-lipped families away to Alashiya, and Crete, the little islands: people with no plain reason for the going, and those were their only words for the end of so much work begun with promise

A household in Ascalon almost missed the tide with their grandmother sweeping every floor once more, as neat as an altar. Some picked up nets or hoes where they landed, and it was enough. Others sailed clear to Delphi just to learn where to go, and the double-axe women taught them western sailing-stars

They were not running from inconsequent routs off the highlanders' gathering-hills. They did not curse the young men of Eberu who turned on their solemn oath of Keret and joined with Samouel's. Nor did they blame their own Serens, since failure to entrap families in bonds of war was the core of their office

They felt the wind like cranes and followed. To one old-time son of lightning who went crazy-wrong on a mountain of his own, they were getting it right the first time. They wanted no part in what was coming over fragrances and metals, for the tyrant priests of distant strangers who despised them

I would have pilgrim-cloaked and gone with them anyway. Near five hundred winter suns, and never a dream of Ariadne. Then, as I slept exhausted at Qadeshah, she burst into vision bright as flame against pure darkness, with a crash and reverberant boom like the striking of a gong with all it took to raise the dead

I might have been looking at a milk-stone carved in the days of her life. All the force of her being rose up sway-back strong out of the great tight-waisted bellskirt of ceremony, whose nine tiers ran the colors of the rainbow: the horns of the ancient mountain flanked and doubled her arms out high, in strength of joy, and green snakes writhed in ecstasy each hand. The proud shoulders lifted her breasts, round and succulent, her crown was Labrys in doubled blades, and beasts of power ramping at her sides kept shimmering and changing, Bull, Lioness, Griffin

All this, and her face was calm, solemn, loving: the light coursing and pulsing through her made me feel her breathing, a woman of my flesh and the core of my soul, immortal, happy, free. As tender and fierce-alive as those faces on my boats

--Lusus is done. Diwonusojo. Come home

I said, --Is this my time? I have done nothing

Another blast split my skull, and she was gone. But the kingdom of the dead had opened on my days. Like one of those first few cranes, letting go felt darkly right

Violence was going to seem to prove the new shadow on the sun. If Radharani worked to make the world a Qadeshah, I was not interested in watching like mistakes unfold in the ways of fathers. My bones walked heavy in weary longing, just to lie down and sleep with my family and be gone, in the soil where after Knossos I had felt this first

We heard from the highlands the first of the rubbish under which they hoped to bury us---that the Ark had come back as our plea for the mercy of their god. Such would serve to purify minds of our intentions, an army of sheep led by lions who, sooner than later, would turn upon their own for less difficult meat

Our like was not to sleep beneath their stars. Marching village by town by conquest nowhere, at last, but away from the sin at the root of their suffering, their idolatry of fathers consigned only them to their covenant's curse. She Wild Alive who mothers and licks up heroes like dust would burst the world laughing in her fangs before she bowed in holy boredom. So would they need to annihilate life, to make a wish seem almost real before it swallowed them

Qadeshah, Paphos, Pttara, Rhodes, Carpathos, Amnisos. The great blunt headland east of the harbor is black in a sky dawning rosy gold. My feet have left the waters, but do not walk still-thriving Knossos Road. The waves are legions of the lives I loved beginning here. And out of the rolling sea's equanimity, the salt and sight and sound of her infinitude, Ariadne *dapuritojo*, Labrys high, a thousand palms and voices lifting up along the shore

Bright sun-orange mantles of snow on the shoulders of Ida and Dikte. Crimson corn-poppies take another brief turn lording over the yellow and white and blue flowers of fallow uplands, loud with bees. There is nothing to want but a place in this place and the turning circles of the sky. Climbing to Lasithi, I manage one night in a farmhouse

Here the stranger might be divinity disguised: their toothless twinkling ya-ya, mother of the Cretan glance, brings goat-cheese in icy water, leeks and barley-bread, honey, a jug of lightning

This burnt offering, I leave in family hands. Hers are as kind and cold as the spring where I met her

--Whatever this bird-scratch is, she shrugs, --maybe give it to damokouros. Or better, wait for the new one. Two moons, the old man falls like summer sun

--Why? I ask about giving this to him, but she answers in her own wise

--Because people are good, unless they get too much power

Their household dances in the evening out under their oak boughs, the githa wails and raki pours and pours. In turn at the center my father dances them the Knossion, with mother's royal abandon. Ya-ya's feet make mine look lazy

Rest, Utnapishtim Flood Rider, take your ease, and savor soothing secrets

What is awakening? Thick white folds of dew enshroud the plateau's miles of trees and fields, cupped as flat as water in the silent circle of the mountains. This place this moment, laid down by the moon, drawn up to the sun, is melting into dream and coming forth

X mark the spot. Seedbed find me in our green water meadow under Dikte, where she is, and night's double-axe coming down like Griffin wings. Mother of All Living, breathe your name. Out of the annihilating fire, the knowing heart.

*

Amnisos 2017

author & other works

Jack Dempsey (b. 1955) grew up north of Boston, Massachusetts USA. He began writing freelance in New York City, and then many stays in Greece led to *Ariadne's Brother: A Novel on the Fall of Bronze Age Crete* (Athens: Kalendis 1996).

Earning his Ph.D. in Native and Early American Studies at Brown University, Jack wrote, edited and produced four books and two films in those fields, including *New English Canaan* by Thomas Morton of Merrymount; *Mystic Fiasco: How the Indians Won The Pequot War*, and *Nani: A Native New England Story*. As a professor for 22 years he also focused on college students' public speaking. With appearances from National Public Radio to Crete-TV, he publishes short works at jackdempseywriter.wordpress.com.

Working on *People of the Sea* through the 1990s, Jack created the collaborative multimedia website Ancientlights.org, and revealed ancient Western astronomy with *Calendar House: Clues to Minoan Time from Knossos Labyrinth*. Residing in Crete since 2015 with Angela his wife, he has published a short biography of the late feminist historian and poet Barbara Mor, and his 2016 book based on public forums is *The Knossos Calendar: Minoan Cycles of the Sun, the Moon, the Soul & Political Power* (Iraklion: Mystis Editions, also in Greek).